QUEST
FOR
KRIYA

Praise for *Quest for Kriya*

"*Quest for Kriya* by Rahul Deokar is an extraordinary work. It is an incredible and inspirational tale that I found absolutely riveting. Deokar's novel touches the soul. I'm humbled because any praise I can give is gilding a literary lily. Bravo!"

- Dwight Jon Zimmerman, award-winning author, radio show host, producer, New York Times #1 Bestseller *LINCOLN'S LAST DAYS*

"*Quest for Kriya* is a beautifully crafted story that resonates deeply with our heart's own wisdom. I could not put this book down once I started reading it; it was that good! I laughed, I cried, I reflected on the spiritual wisdom and I was also at times, in suspense. Read it and see for yourself. It's a true gem!

- Nancy Clark, national award-winning author, *My Beloved* and *Divine Moments: Ordinary People Having Spiritually Transformative Experiences*

"Rahul Deokar explodes on the writing scene with *Quest for Kriya* - truly a modern spiritual classic! It is a delightful reading experience - one that is not only profound and filled with much inspiration, but also very entertaining. It is a gift to all of us from a creative heart! I strongly endorse the book and recommend it for all serious seekers of wisdom, and even for those just seeking some inspiration and moving entertainment."

- Rev. Bill McDonald, author, award winning poet, founder of American Authors Association, international motivational speaker

"The story flows like the life cycle of two salmons as they return to their source to spawn. The streams babble down two diverse, but eerily similar paths, often diverted, sometimes dammed, running rapids, and freefalling jagged waterfalls. But the goodness, spirit and soul of the characters keep hope afloat. Shakti and Shiva are destined to come together only if they prevail over the utter chaotic, tragic and real events of life. This is truly an amazing, thoughtful, spiritual, disturbing, charming and well-written story."

- Navy Chaplain Fr. Ron Moses Camarda, author of *TEAR IN THE DESERT: A Journey into the Heart of the Iraq War*

"This is a beautifully written, spiritually insightful, romantic action adventure that is immediately engaging and suspenseful, laced with humor and strung together with the invisible pearls of love and friendship at its core. Indulge in the private rapture of your imagination, while the characters dance to the rhythm of their hearts as they tango with danger and romance. Behind the veil of its mystical metaphors this enlightening and thrilling excursion is a Zen of Oz philosophy toward the Light, subtly woven into the fabric of an intriguing narrative. I am looking forward to the sequel!"

- Rev. Vera Lauren, author, talk show host, contemporary master, *A channeled sacred teaching: The Measure of Christ's Love, In His Own Words*

"*Quest for Kriya* is a quick, entertaining read for young adults and those on the go. Author Rahul Deokar has put a lot of thought and attention to detail, and those unfamiliar with the Indian culture will enjoy discovering the ideas and lessons, that while ancient are as relevant today as they were then."

- Maria Edwards, president of American Authors Association

"A very engaging book with something for everyone. I could really feel what motivated each character and why they did what they did in the way that they did it. Shiva and Shakti each drew on their beliefs to move through what was thrown at them. I also love the importance this book puts on friendship. Can't wait for the sequel."

- Jo Spring, editor, author consultant, ex-publishing consultant at Hay House

QUEST
FOR
KRIYA

Rahul Deokar

Unleash U
Unlimited

Cover image © 2014 Mohana Pradhan.
Mohana Pradhan Studio (www.mohanapradhan.com)

This book is a work of fiction. Names, characters, and incidents are the product of the author's imagination. Any resemblance to actual people, living or dead, is purely coincidental.

Unleash U Unlimited Publishing
34456 Torrey Pine Lane
Union City, CA 94587

Printed in the United States of America

First Printing, 2014

ISBN: 0990516202
ISBN-13: 978-0990516200
Library of Congress Control Number: 2014943549
Unleash U Unlimited, Union City, CA

DEDICATED TO:

"The lightless light who lights the light that lights the lights of our souls."

Yogiraj SatGurunath Siddhanath

CONTENTS

PROLOGUE

A hushed silence of anticipation descended onto the school grounds. All dutiful students and their parents leaned forward in eagerness. The school principal announced, "And the Student of the Year award goes to…" He paused and looked around. "…none other than Shakti."

The entire school erupted in applause, shattering the suspenseful hush. A bright and colorful rainbow splashed its good spirits across the azure sky.

Shakti's free-spirited heart leapt up in joy. She glanced with love at her family. Her parents glowed in calm appreciation of her success. Her brother gushed with pride.

Shakti began her eager stride amidst a huge ovation. She trotted across the school grounds towards the stage to receive her award. She climbed up the podium steps and marched up to the principal and honorary guests.

Shakti's high school friends encouraged and cheered:

"Congratulations Shakti!"

"Way to go, Shakti!"

"You are the best!"

The principal looked at her in approval and shook her hand. He held out the gleaming trophy – the pride and envy of all students.

Out of the blue sky, dark clouds gathered portent and crammed above, devouring every little ray of light. Sounds of shrieking birds and animals sent out a series of dissonant warnings and a reek of menacing fear spread through the grounds.

The podium shuddered. The principal's hands trembled and the trophy slipped through his palms as he held on to the shaking table.

How could he let the trophy go? Shakti reached out but it fell at her feet. It kept dropping down into a dark and unfathomable chasm. Colossal cracks formed at their feet and everywhere around.

The students were scared. Some cried in agony. Some screamed in panic. Others ran as fast as they could, helter-skelter into each other and towards nowhere.

Shakti plunged into a large, black crevice after the trophy. She extended her hand and her outstretched fingers came agonizingly close. For a split second, she might have even touched it, but then the trophy fell away.

Shakti plummeted alone into an abysmal darkness. Fear stabbed into her chest and crushed her heart. A horrible, blood curdling scream cried through the darkness, somewhere very close. She recognized it as her own, but couldn't stop it.

Shakti descended into a world as soundless as the deepest sea. The chill of death. The choking struggle for breath. She felt the cold hands of mortality reaching for her.

She kept falling and falling and falling. She tried to fight gravity and stop her descent, attempting to hold onto something, anything, but found nothing.

Shakti[1] - the creative and dynamic female principle in the Universe,
often personified as a Goddess

CHAPTER 1

03:55 am. September 30, 1993
Latur, India

It was the stillest of times in Shakti's life. She didn't know this tranquil time was about to be pulled from under her feet. Her life was about to be sent shuddering and screaming into chaos. A far cry from what it was a moment ago.

What...what's happening to me? Where...where am I falling?

Shakti jolted up. She opened her eyes, half awake and disoriented. The agony and disturbing haunt of her own voice had shocked her from tranquility. She pressed her elbows into her sides, making her body as small as possible. She clung to her quilt like a timid kitten holding onto a yarn ball of life that was about to unravel.

Shakti looked around her room in panic. It was merely a bad dream. She sighed with a sense of relief. *All is well.*

And then it happened. Somebody picked up her entire house and shook it back and forth. The floor wobbled. The walls wobbled. The ceiling wobbled. She tried to take a breath but the breath wouldn't come. Her eyes bulged and her jaw slumped. Fear burned through her flesh, tendons, and bones, and electrocuted her nerves. It paralyzed her from head to toe and she lay motionless, frozen in terror.

Shakti's small town Latur, in the western state of Maharashtra, was a quiet, sleepy haven; a place of bedrock values and fertile farmlands. She'd never experienced an earthquake before. She'd learnt about it in school and read stories, but never been in the midst of one. She'd heard from her geography teacher that, depending on the distance from the epicenter,

---

1 Shakti: Sanskrit meaning 'force, power or energy'

1

you could actually hear the earthquake coming. It sounds like a big truck driving down the road, only several times faster and louder. It starts with a slow rumbling and then picks up momentum.

But on that dreadful morning, there was no rumbling to warn Shakti. The trembling didn't start slowly and build up to a crescendo. The violent earthquake began suddenly. It kicked in on high; hard and fast. The stones within the walls twisted. The ground below growled. Plates and utensils screeched in the kitchen.

She didn't make a squeak. It was too much for her to comprehend and handle, but inside she screamed an awful, prolonged, and desperate shriek - the kind you make when you assume you're going to die. She closed her eyes and cried out, in her head, for help. *Make it stop. Make it stop. Please O God. Please make it STOP!*

Instead she heard a great roar, like a thunder of heavy artillery. The earth below and the whole world around her came unglued. The wall in her room moved towards her. The glass of water by her pillow flew across the room. The furniture rattled, her chair turned over and knocked around. Objects began falling down and flying about. Her heart pounded at a thousand beats per minute. Her chin quivered, her lips parted with a shiver. She thought the earsplitting explosion of the earth would leave her deaf.

Shakti squeezed her eyes shut, trying hard to block out what unfolded around her. She thought her room and the whole house was about to cave in. How could the house possibly stand up to what was happening? She felt awful being at the mercy of something so angry and violent but what could she do? She could only hold on and pray.

Shakti stretched out her hand and grabbed onto the leg of the big sturdy desk next to her. She clasped it so tightly that her knuckles hurt and her nails almost peeled off. She tried to stop herself from slipping but the desk leg felt springy and inadequate. Objects fell onto her from the top. She lost her grip and was thrown off her mat towards the door.

The ground began to quiet down. Shakti opened her eyes with hesitation, terrified of what she'd see. Her heart thumped in her throat and her muscles tightened in reflex. She was sure the house had caved in. It was a surprise to see it standing and to discover that she was still alive. She found herself slumped against the door frame.

Her books had fallen off the desk, jammed between the chair and the wall. Her medals and trophies from school were spewed everywhere. Her glass, ceramic and mud treasures lay crushed, without any mercy, on the floor. All her sweet memories lay scattered. All her colorful dreams, the carefree ones that only high schoolers dream, lay shattered in a thousand pieces.

And in those shattered pieces, Shakti gathered the images of a light skinned, petite girl. The twinkle in whose bold, light brown eyes grew brighter when playfulness was in the air. Her voice soft, almost muffled, except when she was in the middle of her favorite things; then she could be heard miles away.

Shakti knew she was a slender girl, but she packed an indiscernible punch. She was a natural athlete with a gymnast's panache. She was so supple she could touch her feet to her head behind her back and contort like a *jalebi*[2]. Her flowing mane of dark brown, curly hair fell to her shoulders and gave her a ruffled, mischievous look. She resisted combing her hair or tying it down and did so only when her mother insisted.

Shakti remembered her friends. They always knocked on her door first, before they set out to play in the evening. They said she was a live wire, full of verve. She was bubbly and loved to chatter like a bumblebee. She was kinetic energy embodied; thinking fast, talking fast, and moving fast. She was unstoppable.

The ground groaned. Shakti stared at her shattered medals, treasures, and dreams. She feared another tremor would start and the house would collapse. It felt like a death trap. She had to get out of her room and out of the house.

Shakti grasped the door latch to unhook it, but it was stuck. The sturdy iron latch looped in a chain and clasped around an eye hook. She tugged and twisted. She tried to yank it off, using her feet as leverage against the door. The latch didn't budge. The earthquake had misaligned it and locked it up. Her numb fingers became useless and she felt the knot in her stomach turn tighter. It was impossible to open the door. It felt like she'd be trapped inside forever.

"Shakti, are you in there? Are you alright?" A voice of hope came through the door, but was she dreaming again? "Are you in there?" asked her brother Sanjay.

"Sanju, SANJU!"

"Don't worry. I'll get you out, little sister."

"Okay, but how? The door's stuck."

---

2 Jalebi: Indian dessert made of flour batter, deep fried in the shape of a coil and served in sugar syrup

"Everything will be fine. Step back. Go all the way to the rear of the room." Sanju kicked the door with all his strength; the room shook with a thump. "Now, check if the latch releases."

Shakti walked through the debris and grasped the latch end to get it off the hook. This time, it slid out with no trouble. She opened the door and felt a relief so colossal that she ran into her brother's arms. "I knew you'd save me." She adored her Sanju; he was always there for her.

Sanju was two years older but he behaved as if he were ten years her senior. Always a mature kid. More responsible and dependable than others his age. He mentored Shakti in her studies. He ensured she did her homework and performed well at in her studies. He cherished his little sister and sheltered her at school and amongst friends.

Sanju was tall and well built. When Shakti was younger, whenever she was tired, he carried her on his shoulders. Her tiny feet gave way all the time when she walked back from school. He loved to gaze at stars and tell her stories. In return, she worshipped her older sibling. It was an amazing bond between them. Sure they argued and had their little spats like any other siblings, but they always patched it up.

The ground began to shudder once again. Objects crashed and crumbled around them. Shakti closed her eyes and hugged Sanju tight.

A scared Shakti remembered the fear of being bullied by a classmate at school.

"What do you have in there? Let me taste it," thundered the bully.

Shakti stared at him, petrified. He was big, dark, and mean. He had flunked his grade a few times and was the only kid in her class with facial hair. She meekly handed over her lunch and he lapped it up, leaving a meager morsel for her.

"*Buurrp.* That was nice. Make sure you get something nicer tomorrow."

This behavior went on for a month. The big bully grew in confidence. He demanded special dishes be cooked for him.

"Bring me potato and *roti* tomorrow."

"I'm bored with plain stuff. Get me some mutton curry. Make it hot and spicy."

"I feel like eating something sweet. Fetch rice pudding for me."

Shakti was too terrified to tell anyone. The bully had warned her, "If you squeal on me to your parents or the teacher, you'll be mincemeat." His behavior would have continued without end to her growing misery.

But one day, she realized the bully hadn't warned her about telling her brother. So she told Sanju, who became hopping mad. But he didn't confront the bully. He said to Shakti, "I have a plan that will teach him a lesson. Are you interested?"

"Yes, anything that gets him off my back."

"You can't tell anybody. It's our little secret."

"I promise."

The next day the school awoke to pictures of the bully all over the walls. He had the body of a hippo, with chunks of food in his mouth and all around him. That morning when the bully made his way across the school corridor to everyone's ridicule, he saw Shakti and knew he had met his match. His bluster melted away in the furious fire of Sanju's intense stare. He showed no fight or retaliation. Sanju said to him as he passed by, "Nobody messes with my little sister."

And that was the last Shakti saw of the bully. He never asked for her lunchbox again. He never asked for anyone else's lunchbox again. He avoided crossing her path, and if he ever did find himself in her vicinity, he hung his face down in shame.

A week later at *Raksha Bandhan*[3], Shakti tied a colorful *rakhi*[4] on Sanju's wrist, her eyes filled to the brim with affection. She soaked in his kind face and prayed for his well-being and long life. She knew he believed in all his earnestness in this *rakhi* thread, this bond of protection. He smiled at her, a picture of Lord Krishna also smiling from the wall behind his head.

One legend traced *Raksha Bandhan* to the epic *Mahabharat*, to Krishna and Draupadi, the warrior queen. Once, Krishna's wrist was bleeding from a battle wound and Draupadi tore a strip of silk off her saree to tie around it. He was touched by her action and declared her to be his sister. He repaid the debt later during her *Cheer-Haran*[5] when she was won in a gambling bet by rival warriors. At that time, he extended her saree perpetually, and through divine intervention saved her honor.

Sanju gazed at her with love. He had that look on his face - the look that said he had taken a brother's lifelong vow to protect her. His eyes brightened. He reached out to the back of his neck and slid off his pendant, his lucky charm. Shakti was reluctant, but he said, "No, little sister. I insist." He

---

3 Raksha Bandhan: Festival to celebrate the relationship between brothers and sisters

4 Rakhi: Sacred thread

5 Cheer-Haran: Literally 'removal of saree'

put it around her neck. It was a ragged, rustic, handmade pendant with a stoneware clay 'Om' at the end.

Shakti fed him sweet candy, which he gobbled up. She hugged him tightly as the sweet aroma of the candy wafted through the air.

And now Shakti hugged him even tighter. But the bitter blend of spewing dust, foodstuffs and spices in the harsh air made her queasy. The ground seemed to stop shaking, but within seconds it would start up again.

"Where is Aai? Did you see her?" asked Shakti, worried about her mother.

"I'll go look for her. You get out of the house. It's too dangerous inside."

"No, I'll come with you and look for her. I don't want to leave you alone."

"Listen to me, little sister. I'll be out there in a minute. Now hurry and get out."

Shakti stepped towards the front door while Sanju walked inside to check on Aai. She barely got to the doorway when a big aftershock rattled the house, making her stumble and fall down the steps. She was propelled across the front yard as the earth shook with more ferocity than before.

Shakti looked back as the ground beneath her home heaved. The walls contorted into strange shapes, cracking and bursting. The windows twisted and shattered. And then the house came crashing down like a house of cards. She stared in shock and disbelief. This couldn't be happening. She convulsed in a sense of despair. "SANJUUUUU!"

She ran towards the house but was thrown off balance. Dark clouds of smoke and deathly dust rose up. Little by little, the worst of the shaking began to die down. The ground swayed more gently, like a mother rocking her baby. The roar calmed down to a groan and she rushed again towards the rubble. She tried to lift the stones, but there were too many and they were too heavy. She tried to push them away but only ended up scraping her hands. She dug through the stones until her fingers felt no sensation.

She rummaged through the rubble in desperation, trying to spot any signs of Sanju, any signs of life at all, any sounds, but there were none. Sorrow trickled down her face as she stood disconsolate on the wreckage surrounded by the insensitive smoke that swirled towards the ground as she descended further into despair. A bone deep anguish spread through her like a shooting pain that spreads through a dismembered limb. She closed her eyes in heartache and nausea.

I shouldn't have listened to him. I shouldn't have left him alone.

When she opened her eyes against the gray of the sky, the whole world around her heaved in mourning. Hundreds of birds flew at full speed, racing like bullets, like shards from the ruins, and headed upwards to some place far away. She gazed heavenwards. She clasped his pendant around her neck and prayed from her heart for his soul.

Sanju loved to hum, "This birth, this life...Love it forever," his favorite song and his theme for living. Unfortunately his life had been cut short, but she hoped his words would continue to strum her heart strings. A star gazer he was, now a Star above; he would brighten up heaven with love and affection, and become her beacon of light, guiding her through the good and the bad.

"Shakuuuu, shakuuuu," called out a whisper.

Shakti looked towards the tamarind tree. She heard a soft voice coming from the distance, but she couldn't see anything through the smoke. Someone was calling out to her from their front yard. The voice was so hard to hear, but it was compelling and it was in pain, pulling her towards itself with a force.

She crawled out of the rubble and crept bit by bit onto the front yard. She heard some rustling to her right and she looked harder, but still couldn't discern anything. The smoke was so dense that it fogged her entire vision and mind.

She scrambled over the big branches of the fallen tamarind tree. She had learned how to climb it long ago. Her Aai often said that Shakti could climb before she could walk. Shakti couldn't remember when she first learned to walk, but she couldn't remember when she started to climb either, so she supposed it must be true.

The tamarind tree was her second home. She hid in it when she didn't want anybody to find her. She sulked on it when she had a spat. It was more than a tree, it was a friend; a trusted, steady, immovable friend. One she had had many long conversations with. She was heartbroken to see the tree uprooted and spread across the ground.

"ShaKUUuu, aye ShaKUUuu." The whisper grew louder.

Shakti knew that voice. The worst fear crossed her mind and a huge lump swelled up in her throat. She made her way through the branches and caught a glimpse of a saree; a familiar saree. She ran hard towards it, oblivious to the scrapes, cuts, and bruises picked up along the way. And there she was. Trapped under the tamarind tree. A giant brute of a branch lay heavy across her Aai's chest.

"AAAAIIIIIIIII!" Shakti tried to yank away the huge bough from her Aai's chest. She grunted and pushed and tugged, but to no avail. The heavy branch was obstinate. She looked around and shouted for Baba, her father. But he was nowhere to be seen.

"Somebody, HELP! Anybody, HELP! My Aai is trapped. Please HELP!" Shakti ran around like a mad girl, screaming in all directions, hoping and praying that someone would come. Nobody did. Some animals screamed, and she heard faint, distant voices, but no one responded to her desperate pleas. Did anyone even hear her cries?

Shakti scurried back. She sat down and held Aai's head on her lap. Aai had weakened further and had begun to cough blood. The branch had caused severe internal injuries and bleeding. Aai was bearing the unrelenting pain with her usual stoicism.

Aai had a traditional strength which saw sacrifice of the self as one's duty in the world. She had relinquished her own needs for the needs of her family. She had surrendered her own meals when there wasn't enough food in the house for everyone. She had given up on sleep when any one of them was sick. She had sacrificed her back during harsh economic times, performing tough farm chores intended for men.

Shakti looked down at Aai's gentle face and her loving eyes. Aai's head rested in peace on her lap. Shakti felt a sense of déjà vu. How ironic? Several years ago, under this very tree, Shakti was injured and her head had rested on Aai's lap. Aai might have recounted that story a hundred times:

"Shaku, you were five years old, playing hide and seek with your brother. While he was looking for you inside the house, you climbed up the tree and hid in there.

He came out looking and you tried to move to another branch, but it broke. You landed on your tiny hands and they couldn't sustain the fall. When I came running out, I saw both your hands were broken, bones jutting out at the elbow. Shaku, I went hysterical. I couldn't bear to see you like that. We got you on the bullock-cart and headed towards the doctor. I was in a panic. My saree was drenched in my tears and your blood as you lay on my lap listless. I prayed and cried and hoped that nothing bad would happen to you.

And then you looked me in the eye and said, all five years of you said, 'Don't cry Aai. It's not hurting me even a tiny bit. I am fine. Please don't cry.'

To this day, I can't forget the strength and resolve that was in your eyes. I thought, 'That's my girl. That's my brave Shakti.'"

Shakti could certainly use some of that strength and courage right now. She had lost Sanju, and Aai was in such a critical condition. Shakti's bravery and resolve had deserted her. Fear had set in; the fear of being left alone.

Aai's voice now trickled out from some distant deep. She moved her feeble hand, touching Shakti's face and neck. Aai mustered her last ounce of strength to pull Shakti closer and kiss her eyes. A hint of a smile broke on Aai's lips, a strange knowing as she breathed out her final words, *"Ring rang raksh raksh Goraksh!"*[6]

Shakti couldn't believe her eyes. She was stunned into a sad stillness. She opened her mouth to let out a cry, but no audible sound could escape her throat. She sat dazed, reliving her memories as rivers of recollections gushed down her cheeks. She closed Aai's eyes and held her hand. A writhing wave of woe swept through her entire body.

She prayed for Aai's and Sanju's souls. They were dead; she couldn't deny it. What a thing to acknowledge in one's heart.

Aai was no more. How could she survive without Aai? Her best friend. Her confidante. Aai wasn't merely the wind beneath her wings, she was the wings themselves. How could Shakti stay afloat in this world without her wings? Shakti dearly held onto Aai's hand; she didn't want to let her go.

And to lose a brother was to lose someone with whom you were supposed to grow old and share life's stories. You were supposed to get a sister-in-law, nieces and nephews, cute little offspring to grow the tree of your life and give it new branches.

And where was Baba? She hoped to find him. To lose your father was to lose the one whose guidance and advice you seek, who's like a tree trunk supporting its branches.

Shakti heard behind her a rumpling of twigs and leaves. She spun around to see their neighbor's dog, Raja. He'd appeared out of nowhere. Raja tugged at her with taut muscles and scared eyes. Thick saliva hung from his mouth like he'd vomited. He was trying to tell her something. He wanted her to follow him somewhere.

Shakti's hand was glued onto Aai's. She looked down at Aai's face on her lap, then to Raja and back again at Aai. Raja began to nudge her with his head and nose. He needed help. Shakti eased Aai's head to the ground. She kissed Aai's forehead in a heartrending, drawn out farewell.

Shakti turned towards Raja. "Alright. So, where do you want me to go?"

Raja sped across the yard towards the neighbor's house and farm. She scrambled onto her legs to follow him. When she got closer, she saw their neighbor's house had collapsed. It had caved in exactly like theirs.

---

6 Ring rang raksh raksh Goraksh: Protect her, my Lord!

She realized why no one had responded to her calls for help. Most town folks were sleeping when the earthquake hit. They didn't even have a chance to react. They were buried under their own houses.

She felt a shudder through her body. She felt miserable. But she still had no idea about the scale of devastation that was inflicted.

The Latur earthquake struck at 3:56am local time on September 30, 1993. It was an intra-plate earthquake that measured 6.4 on the Richter scale.

The earthquake was 12 kilometers deep - rather shallow, but it caused shock waves that resulted in extensive damage to life and property. More than 20,000 people died, whilst another 30,000 were injured. More than 16,000 livestock was killed. All amenities and infrastructure was damaged. 52 villages were razed to the ground. 30,000 houses collapsed. 211,000 houses suffered damages of varying degree.

Most people lived in houses made of stones on soft soil. The roof tiles were made out of stone plates that were readily available and cheap. The liquefaction[7] from the earthquake destroyed the foundations of the houses and caused them to crumble. More than 60% of the deaths were a result of this. People were trapped underneath without food, water, and sometimes even air. Their own houses had become their graveyards.

"Raja, let me catch up. You're going too fast." Shakti labored ahead to find Raja waiting, his jaw undulated from heavy breathing. He began to run again and she ran with him. "Where are we going? Is there anyone out here?"

Raja stopped and gestured towards the poultry farm. A fire had broken out and the unfortunate chickens in their cages were being roasted alive. They had nowhere to go as they squealed in distress. The air reeked of burnt skin, blood, feces, and death, making her sick. She couldn't inhale.

Even as the fire spread fast, Shakti ran in. She covered her face with her left hand to keep the heat and smoke away, and opened up the cages with her right hand one after another. But the chickens stayed inside; they didn't know what to do or where to go.

She helped one chicken out and led it onto a safe path. "Here you go little one. Go towards the tree." The other chickens took cue and clamored towards safety. She opened as many cages as she could to set them free.

Raja watched her intently, his eyes expressing gratitude. He was the guard dog for the poultry farm, and with her help today, he had successfully fulfilled his duty.

---

7 Liquefaction: the phenomenon that causes soft soil to shake loose as a result of seismic activity

Shakti heard voices and saw some folks had gathered up on the road. She ran to them, anxious to meet someone. An older woman put an arm around her and said, "All of a sudden, God's hand comes down and strikes us. But it's not the end of the world."

The earth convulsed once again. It was impossible to stand and the folks threw themselves to the ground, praying in fear. Trees swayed and bent in awkward shapes. Dogs barked in agony. Birds screeched and cattle stampeded.

Shakti looked at the burning poultry farm; the fire had gutted it completely. The place she had stood, only a few moments ago, was now burned to ashes. So much had happened to her family and to her town in such a short time. Her life had changed forever.

She couldn't bear the carnage around her. She looked up towards the sky. *Why, oh why? Almighty God! Why this wrath upon us?* Her eyes fell on the temple atop the hillock, at the highest point in town. For some mysterious reason, the temple seemed unaffected by the earthquake, the fire, the heat, the screams, and the death all around.

Shakti ran. She ran like she'd never run before. She wasn't daunted by the large fissures spreading their tentacles across the ground, several feet wide and hundreds of meters long as they ran amuck all around. Big barns and houses were swallowed up by the fissures. She dodged them and jumped over them. She tripped over the rubble and skinned her palms on the black gravel, but she gathered herself up, and kept running. Barefoot.

She was confronted by bizarre, large clouds of a strange gas seeping from the ground. It belched huge amounts of sand and debris from its gaping fractures. She was nauseated by the sulfurous smell coming up out of the bowels of the earth.

She marched on. She darted up the stone steps on the hillock. She didn't pause for breath. She ran hard until she reached the temple. She stopped and seized her aching sides, bent over until the sweat fell straight from her forehead to the ground, making dark rings on the soil.

She stared up at the *Shiva-linga*[8]. *Why did you leave me behind? Take me to Aai and Sanju.* She rang the temple bell hard - once, twice, three times.

And then Shakti collapsed.

---

8 Shiva-linga: a stone symbol of Lord Shiva

Shiva[9] - the paradoxical male principle of destruction - recreation, eroticism - asceticism and the co-generator of the Universe along with Shakti

CHAPTER 2

03:00 pm. September 29, 1993
San Francisco, CA, U.S.A

Halfway across the world, a different type of earthquake was about to be unleashed. A parallel upheaval that would change a few lives in the heart of Silicon Valley, California.

"Shiva, where are you? It's an emergency. Boss is making a big announcement and he wants everyone in the office right now," exhorted Harry on his phone, giving Shiva the first shock of the day.

Shiva was at a customer site in Milpitas, right in the middle of delivering his product presentation. When Harry called the first time, Shiva's phone was on vibrate mode and he muted it. Harry called a second time and then a third time. Shiva looked at his phone. *I hope he's ok. Hang on, buddy. I'm almost done with the presentation. This is a critical customer account and we have to win it.*

Shiva was an up and coming product engineer at Alltech, a mid-sized firm developing software for semiconductor chip design. A hard working, conscientious young man, he gave his everything for the success of the company. He toiled days, nights, and weekends. To him, work was God.

The Alltech sales team had planned this customer presentation for weeks, setting up the meeting with key decision-makers and influencers. And right now the audience was hooked, listening to Shiva and asking questions.

As he presented, Shiva caught his own reflection on the rear glass wall. He stood at six feet and his skin was a deep, warm olive. In profile, his face was striking; the long forehead descended past a firm, solemn

---

9 Shiva: Sanskrit meaning "pure consciousness"; the auspicious one.

mouth to a confident, angular jaw. He simply wished he didn't have such a straight and sharp nose; it diminished the warmth of his welcoming grin. When he turned to face, his penetrating brown eyes were captivating and at the same time reflected youth, genuine interest, and good humor.

"So this is how our software gives you a unique advantage to win in your market." Shiva concluded his presentation and answered the remaining queries. He could sense the positive effect in the eyes of the customer and the Alltech sales team.

"Harry, are you ok?" Shiva called back as soon as he left the customer office.

"Shiva, where are you? It's an emergency. Boss is making a big announcement and he wants everyone in the office right now."

"Sorry, I was in the middle of a customer presentation in Milpitas. Great meeting. I think we'll win the account. Onwards and upwards, my friend."

"Dude, you should get here fast. Boss has downed five lattes already and he's been pacing his office."

Shiva sped out of the customer site and down the elevator. Akin to an Olympics 100 meters sprinter, he took rapid strides across the parking garage and jumped into his white Honda Accord, breaking all world speed records. With the same urgency, he drove onto 880 North but then everything came to a grinding halt.

He was stuck amidst an unending sea of red taillights. The traffic was a slow, aggravating crawl, a lot of stop and go. He groaned about the number of cars on the road at that time of the day. Bay Area's economy appeared to be picking up again. He turned his face to the right to see an orange streak of light amidst the clouds, and above it the hard black of the sky. Up in the Fremont Mission Hills he could see the sparse sprawl of glittering lights from the wealthy homes.

And then, he was hit by the second shock of the day. All of a sudden, the car ahead of him came to a full stop. Shiva slammed his foot on the brakes, pleading and ordering his Accord to stop. And it did, inches from the car in front; but when he looked into his rearview mirror he saw a red Audi coming in too fast. It couldn't stop in time and rear-ended his Accord. *Screeech. Thud.*

The Audi driver climbed down, all agitated and apologetic. Shiva stepped out, calm and collected. "Don't worry. Such things happen. It's no one's fault." And they exchanged license and insurance information.

At Alltech, Shiva dealt with customers, software developers, quality assurance, and sales. He was in a central position with serious responsibility, but no direct authority. Issues often became quite heated, but he had to stay cool and calm in spite of his own genetic structure. As cool as the city he lived in – San Francisco. A city he loved. A city he loved to live in. A city he loved to fall in love with, again and again.

Shiva swiped his badge and entered the Alltech headquarters in San Mateo. Harry was waiting for him with a flushed face. Harry was about the same age as him, although those years were stuffed in like lumps of flesh and flab that made him look like a big white teddy bear; all soft and podgy and huggable. And an ever-smiling teddy-bear at that. Harry could make anyone laugh with his wisecracks, but right then he held an anxious grimace with furrows on his forehead.

Together Shiva and Harry rushed inside. They passed by Glee, their administrator and the office hottie. In the desert land of Alltech, filled with oodles of testosterone, she was the rare green oasis to soothe their eyes.

"Good afternoon, Shiva," said Glee. She stood up from behind the desk, revealing her slim and sexy figure.

"Good afternoon, Gleeful," answered Shiva. "How goes it?"

"Hey, you forgot me. Good afternoon," Harry said to her, but she merely stared at him. Harry always wore baggy khakis and a rumpled T-shirt with changing slogans. Today it said, "My girlfriend gives sound advice...10% advice and 90% sound". Yesterday it read, "If we're not meant to have midnight snacks, why is there light in the fridge?" His thick, blonde curly hair flopped around in abandon. The soft stubble on his chubby face was never more than seven days from the last shaving.

"Been working out, haven't you, Glee?" said Shiva. "At this rate, you'll qualify for America's next super-model." Suave and sophisticated, like the city of San Francisco.

"Oh, stop it." Glee wiggled in her black-fitted dress that hugged her curves. She showed off a bit of cleavage through a cutout in the dress.

"But we don't want you to leave Alltech. Please stay." Shiva's mom had once said of him that he was two parts nice and one part just plain naughty.

"Haha. Hella funny!" Glee was all smiles.

"Have a great rest of the day, Gleeful."

"Hey, that's a lot of pressure on her, dude." Harry said.

"Have the rest of the day the way it comes." Shiva smiled and rushed off to the break room for a shot of coffee. He grabbed an espresso while Harry got a vanilla latte with cinnamon sprinkles. They rushed into the conference room curious to hear what Boss had to say. Shiva wanted to find out why Boss had been so restless and jittery. Inside, he saw a roomful of people chattering away in nervous anticipation.

Shiva pulled the door behind him and it creaked as it swung and shut. Boss then made his announcement, ushering in the third and biggest shock of the day.

When Shiva got to his San Francisco apartment that evening, he slumped into the sofa, letting out a big groan. He caught his reflection in the living room mirror. Though his mind was still grappling with Boss's words, none of his inner anxiety could be outwardly seen. He had trained himself to be poker-faced; his expression gave nothing away, ever.

Shiva had inherited mostly his Pa's facial features. He did have his Ma's clear skin and eyes, but none of her emotional transparency. He knew that all of Ma's anger and impulsiveness were innate to him, but he had learned to restrain himself. He had discovered early on – in the adolescent lanes of tumult – how to wield the shield of impassivity. It gave him the strength to withstand any challenge that life threw at him.

But today he was worried. Alltech had filed with the SEC earlier in the year and was expected to IPO. He held considerable stock options and had indeed put his blood, sweat, and equity into his first job, but Boss's announcement changed everything.

Shiva stepped to the window. It was bright outside. One of those September evenings when loitering light suggested summer, but the air held the cool of November. And a chilly breeze gushed in, whistling in December earlier than expected. He turned back in. His living room was tidy, comfortable and basic; a large circular carpet, slip-covered easy chairs, a spotless sofa, and a long wall of paperbacks. There was a big-screen TV at the center, and a modern library table stacked with periodicals.

Poise. Plainness. Privacy. Purity. Propriety. All Shiva's individuality and persona captured in the décor and meant to handle his demanding, hectic, professional calling. While Shiva wasn't a social butterfly, he was quick to make new friends. He was gregarious, especially when he hung out with his close buddies. But social personality apart, at his core, he was a quiet man of powerful presence and an intense latent energy.

Shiva tried hard but couldn't get his mind off Boss's announcement. He needed to distract himself, to think of something else. He turned on the TV news. The new US President, Bill Clinton, was going through one of the shakiest starts in history. He had swept into the White House on a wave of high expectations. He was the candidate of "change", a word he used often during his campaign against the incumbent, George Bush.

However, within weeks of Clinton's inauguration, the new administration wobbled. Among his first acts was to seek an end to the military's long-standing ban on homosexuals in the ranks. Though the move was popular among gays and many others, few had thought that he'd move on such an explosive issue so fast.

Shiva looked out of the window again. He gazed past the cushioned window seats and colorless cotton curtains and saw the Bay Bridge lit up against the night sky. He remembered the numerous support rallies for Clinton on both Embarcadero Road and Castro Street, organized by the thriving gay and lesbian community in the city.

The newscaster on TV reported, "And finally, the President has something to celebrate. After a heated debate, President Clinton has managed to reach a compromise. All homosexual servicemen and servicewomen can now remain in the military if they don't openly declare their sexual preference; a policy of 'Don't ask, Don't tell.'"

Shiva looked away from the window. The TV news wasn't helping. He needed something lighter. He switched the channel to MTV to play some foot-tapping music. Instead, MTV was playing the new *Alice in Chains* song *Down in a hole, feelin' so small*. Shiva shook his head. He couldn't help but wince.

Shiva switched off the TV. It wasn't alleviating his worry. There was only one way to get it out of his system, his favorite way. He changed into his work-out gear, put on his wrist wraps and boxing gloves, and headed to his gym corner to beat the stuffing out of his heavy bag. The stereo he'd turned on churned out some loud and fast music.

With hands up, Shiva shuffled forward and struck the bag head high with his lead right hand – a straight jab. He circled right and then left and delivered a series of jabs. He shifted to the jab-cross for a two-punch combination. The gloves now were part of his arms and he felt it in his bones.

Circling the bag, he went high-low and low-high. The stereo blared out the *Prince* song *Cream*.

Shiva imagined himself in the boxing ring. A big, rotten opponent with a nasty face teased and taunted him. Shiva moved to his right and struck blows at a 90-degree angle - a hook, jab-hook, low-high-low, high-high-high, and high-high-low. He knew he had to get on top. He built up a good momentum. His feet moved all the time, raising heat and sweat. He knew it would go to the wire, and that he couldn't stop.

Shiva lowered his shoulder. Corkscrewing his right hand, he threw a solid punch into his opponent's ribs making him grimace and crouch. Then the big sledgehammer came out. A mighty upper cut to the slumped chin, snapping the head back and causing a whiplash-like action. Opponent on the floor. *Creamed*. Game over.

Shiva felt better. The flurry of concern in his head slowed down and he didn't fret about Boss's announcement. After a shower and a quick dinner, he lay down with his favorite book. A little re-read of *The Fountainhead*[10] for some inspiration from Howard Roark, the individualistic young protagonist who chose to struggle in obscurity rather than compromise his artistic and personal vision. Succumbing to no one, Roark rose from being an unknown architect who was kicked out of school for drawing outside of the lines to designing many landmark buildings, all architected against convention.

Shiva felt goose-bumps every time he read about Roark's battles. He had first read the book in his teens and it was a constant source of motivation ever since. His eyes narrowed. The book never failed to stimulate new ideas in his mind. He wondered how Roark would deal with his current situation. How would he react? What would he do?

Roark's trials revealed a powerful coalescence of romantic drama and profound philosophy. Shiva felt a warm current rush all over his body. The courage. The conviction. He wished he could roar through life like Roark.

The phone rang. It was Pa calling from India. He had an uncanny intuition for such situations. "How are you, son?" asked Pa.

"I'm doing fine. So good to hear your voice. How's everyone in Bombay?"

"We're fine, but did you hear about the Latur earthquake?"

"Yes. I'm so sorry for the people out there. You remind me that I need to send in my check to the Red Cross tomorrow."

---

10 The Fountainhead: a 1943 novel by Ayn Rand. The protagonist Howard Roark is Rand's embodiment of the human spirit and his struggle represents the triumph of individualism over collectivism.

Within a few minutes of conversation, Pa asked, "What's wrong, son? Is something weighing on your mind?" He'd realized something was amiss.

"Well, it's nothing, simply something at work." It never ceased to surprise Shiva how Pa had a knack for reading into his mind and words.

"Is it serious?"

"Our CEO made this crazy announcement today that's sure to hurt Alltech."

"If you feel so strongly about it, why don't you talk to the CEO?"

"I could. But once he's made up his mind, he becomes bull-headed."

"I'm sure there's someone in your company that he'll listen to."

"I wish but he doesn't listen to anybody except some lackeys around him." Shiva paused to catch his breath. "And they only know how to flatter his ego."

"Now I'm curious. What did your CEO announce?"

"Please keep this to yourself, Pa," Shiva confided in the most somber tone. "Our CEO has filed a lawsuit against our largest competitor over IP[11]."

"Really? I'm surprised. Typically the big companies go after the small fish like Alltech - suing them and sucking them dry."

"Yeah, I'm shocked too. I don't mind battling on the technology front, but we don't stand a chance in the court of law."

"So, why is he doing it?" Pa was at a loss to understand the CEO's motivation.

"Pa, there's a thin line between courage and fool-hardiness; a thin line between ambition and greed."

"So then, what do you plan to do, son? I know you've been toying with the idea of your own start-up, right?"

"The market is still risky, Pa. And I'm not sure if I've the energy and drive to do a start-up in these conditions."

"Now listen up. Do you know why we named you Shiva?" Pa continued. "You were born during *Maha Shivaratri*[12] – the most auspicious time in the entire year."

Shiva pressed the phone into his ear, sorely in need of a pep talk. He wondered, though, where Pa was going with this.

"Son, during that new moon, the gravitational pull of the moon over the earth is the highest, causing the highest tides of the year. In a subtler

---

11 IP: Intellectual Property

12 Maha Shivaratri: The Great Night of Lord Shiva. Celebrated on the 13th night/14th day of the Maagha or Phalguna month of the Hindu calendar. Typically occurs in February or March.

way this pull also affects the energies of a human body, kindling the energy and raising its levels."

Shiva listened with patience. When Pa was in such a spiritual mood, there was no stopping him.

"My boy, you were born under this new moon. Power and energy should be at your beck and call. You are a born leader. Go do the right thing."

"Thanks Pa. You've raised my spirit for sure."

"Don't listen to your Pa. Think twice before you leave your company." Shiva's mother interjected.

"How are you, Ma? I miss you so much."

"Starting your own small company? I say no, don't do it. No decent family will want to marry their daughter to you."

"Ma, I'm not starting any company." Shiva knew that Ma had one and only one thing on her mind - his marriage. And in India, being in a start-up was like being a struggling artist, without the glamour. Marriage prospects would be bleak to nonexistent.

"Good. Are you eating properly or only Big Mac and pizza? How about fresh vegetables and fruits?"

"Yes Ma. I'm eating all the major food groups, and drinking milk, too."

"Are you being careful? You were so accident-prone when you were growing up. My heart stopped every time you fell or got hurt." Ma couldn't hide her nerves.

"Ma, I'll stay safe." Shiva remembered his earlier car accident on 880N. She knew him too well.

"You better be. I don't want to see any cuts or fractures on you. If you truly love me, promise me to be extra careful. And control your temper."

"Come on Ma, I don't get angry. But I promise to be careful." Shiva couldn't help but smile. From Pa, he'd learned the glories of reaching out for the stars. Ma taught him the ground realities, the ABC's, and laundry.

"Good. Now Pa wants to talk to you. But don't listen to him."

"Son, mark my words. You are destined for big things." Pa's words came strong and clear. He hadn't lost his conviction.

"Thanks Pa. Right now though, I'm worried about Alltech's destiny."

"Why?"

"It's sad. But I see a slow death for Alltech. Pa, we are in big trouble."

"Give of your hands – to Serve and of your hearts – to Love"
- Mother Teresa

CHAPTER 3

The morning brought a melancholic silence over Latur. The sun, in mourning, refused to show his head. A few renegade yellow sunrays sneaked through the clouds of smoke and gave Shakti a warm nudge to open her eyes. She lay curled up in a fetal position in the womb of the Shiva temple.

It was a bad dream. Shakti insisted with her eyes closed. Aai had told her that God didn't listen when you prayed with your eyes open. *I'll make a pact with you, God. When I open my eyes, everything will be alright. Aai, Sanju, and Baba will all be safe.*

But the scrapes and bruises on her feet, arms, and legs reminded her of the reality of the previous night. No Aai anymore. No Sanju. No Baba. A desolate frostiness crept over her. A cold shiver ran down her spine.

"SNAKE!" Shakti screamed. A slithering reptile slid aside and smiled at her as if it knew something. Was that really a smile? It then sashayed away into the shrubs.

She stood up in a rush and looked down the hill, appalled by the devastation. Her entire town was razed. Death and destruction surrounded her. Yet, she'd survived. She wondered if the snake was in the temple for a reason. It was almost as if it was there to protect her; as if to ensure her survival.

Shakti witnessed rippling waves of people deserting Latur, bundled together with what remained of their families and belongings. Folks trundled out of the town with the heaviness of leaving their losses behind. Shakti ran down the hill. She spotted a neighbor's family - ragged and bruised but alive. Their meager possessions were on a bullock cart as they hobbled out of town.

The grandmother of the family took Shakti in her arms and they both wept. "I'm so sorry for your loss. I'm sure you're going through a lot."

Shakti said through her sobs. "I miss Aai and Sanju. They…"

"Shakti, they're fine and in a much better place. God loved them and wanted to be with them. Don't worry. They'll look after you from the skies and protect you."

Shakti gazed at her through the tears, wanting to believe her words.

"Why don't you come with us? We'll find a new place, a new beginning. There's nothing left in this forsaken town." Grandmother's eyes kindled a hope for a better future.

"No, I can't. I can't come with you."

"Why? You've lost everything. Think of us as your family now."

"I can't leave the town. I know Baba will come back. I have to wait for him."

"But Shakti…"

"Thanks, but you carry on."

"May God give you strength. Take care. Stay safe and at peace."

Shakti knew she had to stay strong to get through these challenging times. Without any second thoughts, she walked towards the center of the town.

After a night of terror, the sun finally came up but brought no relief from the tremors. Another big aftershock hit Latur, at least as hard; maybe worse. Many homes and barns that had endured the night quake now clattered to the ground from the massive shock. Reverberations continued through the day, and the already disheartened people could now see in broad daylight the unrelenting havoc run deeper all around them.

Amidst the wreckage, the reflection of the sun on shards of shattered glass was intense. Shakti found it difficult to hold her eyes open as she teetered. The odor of death was now part of the air, reminding her constantly of the night before. The tile-covered heaps of collapsed houses reeked of decease, blanketed with vast swarms of flies.

Shakti noticed a motherly woman in despair, sitting by some rubble. Her little toddler wailed next to her - hungry and frightened. But the woman seemed oblivious to his cries. Her eyes were swollen as if she had held a long vigil. Streams of tears had dried on her cheeks. Her hands were dirty and cracked. It seemed she'd battled against the stones in the rubble but the battle was too massive for her.

"Can I help in some way?" Shakti asked.

The woman woke up from a stupor. She pointed towards the rubble and said in a hoarse voice, "My baby, in there, my baby."

Shakti shouted out to a rescue worker for help and he put a blanket around the mother. He tugged on her to come with him so he could provide first aid and food for her and the toddler, but she resisted and pointed at the rubble again, "My baby in there."

The rescue worker looked at Shakti and shrugged. They peered through the rubble. Glimpses of body parts peeked through the pile of stones. No one could have survived that twisted mess. Judging by the stench all around, the rescue worker was convinced that the woman had gone mad.

And then, Shakti heard something. It was a faint cry from beneath. She began to claw at the rubble. Her energy surged at the prospect of re-uniting the mother with her baby. Shakti and the rescue worker struggled to lift huge chunks of the broken walls. With each layer of debris removed, the cry became clearer. The voice was still faint, but it was a baby's frantic cry for its mother. Little by little they cleared a small tunnel.

After an hour of hefting large pieces, Shakti finally saw the baby. What a miracle! She climbed down into the tunnel. The baby stopped crying and gaped at her in wonder. She cradled him, wiped his tears, and lifted him to the rescue worker above.

When Shakti climbed out of the tunnel, her heart filled with joy. The mother held the baby in her lap and leaned over him, touching his face and his arms. The baby lifted a small, pudgy palm towards his mom and she kissed the baby's fingers and his face. She raised her hands to the sky, shaking her head back and forth. "Thank you, God, for sheltering my baby. Thank you from the bottom of my heart."

Shakti was always a girl of nature, always one with nature. She loved everything that Latur's soil had to offer. She loved the pitter-patter of the first monsoon raindrops as they loosened up the dry, hard summer earth to release a heavenly, reassuring aroma from the ground. She loved to till the soil on her Baba's farm, sow saplings, and fertilize them. She loved to climb up trees, walk on the branches and pluck her favorite *kesar* mangoes.

When she looked around now, Shakti felt heart-broken. She couldn't comprehend the fury that was let loose on the very mother earth that nur-tured and nourished its people. The helpless soil lay split open, crying in agony.

Shakti tried to forget what Latur had lost and what she had lost person-ally by helping other unfortunate souls. It was her way to cope with what had happened.

She stayed on her feet the entire day. She ministered to the injured, the sick, the orphaned, and the dying. She picked up little crying kids and showed them affection. She gave them a plate of rice and a piece of bread, but she didn't have a bite to eat. She didn't take a break to rest. She helped the townsfolk until the sun went down.

"Little girl, how are you?" asked Kaka. Everyone in town called him Kaka. "I can't begin to tell you how deeply sorry I am to hear the sad news."

"I'm trying to stay strong. It's hard. How is Kaku?" Shakti asked about his wife.

"She's safe. She's fixing up the house. How about Baba?"

"He's out of town on work, but he'll come back soon." Her voice was full of hope. She missed her Baba. *I wish he was here with me now to comfort and console me.*

Her father was an industrious farmer who looked after his ancestral land. Baba took to agriculture with gusto, like a bull takes to farm-work. He began his day early before sunrise, even before the rooster cock-a-doodled the arrival of morning. He was the first one on the farm, feeding the animals and nurturing the crops.

Baba was a strong man with a gentle heart. He was ready to help anyone in need. He was the first one that the town's poor and unprivileged turned to in difficult times. He always helped them out in any way he could – money, food, or work.

"Where will you stay?" asked Kaka.

"I don't know. I'll find a place." Shakti ran into her Baba's arms every time he walked into the house after a hard day's work. He loved to spend time and play with his kids and to tell them stories. Even though they didn't make much money, they were a happy family. And Shakti was the darling of the household. Oh, how she missed them.

"Come over and stay with us. It'll be so much safer."

"Kaka, I don't want to be a burden."

"Oh, no... Not at all! You won't be a burden. In fact, we could use your help."

Rescue, Relief and Rehabilitation:
On October 2, 1993, the first convoy of 120 trucks departed Bombay with relief material like tents, blankets, food and clothing, medical supplies and shelters. Many people were rescued alive by the Armed Forces. First aid and medical aid was provided on a vast scale. Foreign and local donors reacted at once to the tragedy and law enforcement agencies rushed their personnel to help with the large number of casualties.

Dead bodies trapped under the debris were disposed of on war footing, to prevent the spread of epidemics. The method of community burial was adopted in the villages.

Life stayed paralyzed for a long time. The Government and social organizations contributed their best to bring life back to normal. They undertook an ambitious program for the rehabilitation with the help of institutions like World Bank, Asian Development Bank, and The Red Cross. Relief in the form of money was also announced for the next of kin of affected families.

Shakti was saddened to see Latur remain a war-zone. Aftershocks rumbled in the area for the entire month, ringing temple bells as far as Pune and rattling utensils in Bombay. Frightened residents believed they were suffering the wrath of God. They took the earthquake as a sign that they needed to clean up. After people calmed down, they began to rebuild. A massive revamping began in the town. Residents abandoned their splintered houses and set up make-shift shelters. Many of them lived in tents.

Shakti saw people grow weak right before her eyes. She heard the grumbling noises of emaciated stomachs and the wailing cries of famished children. Times were hard. The town all around seemed ailing and lifeless. People barely got by on a dwindling supply of the rationed provisions from the relief squads. She wondered how she would have survived without Kaka and Kaku. They had given her a great shelter and because of them she could help the other people in town.

Now the relief squads were joined by reinforcements. Shakti saw some new relief workers whose clothes, though faded with frequent washing, were not sullied as yet with sweat and soot. She continued to help with the relief and rebuilding work.

One day, Shakti was tired and took a break earlier than usual. When she reached Kaka's house, she heard animated voices from the adjacent barn. She stepped closer. Two male voices were engaged in a dispute. One of the voices was Kaka's but she wasn't sure about the other. Why was Kaka in the barn? He seldom went there.

She peeked through the tiny crack and saw an elderly man with a hump and a walking stick. She'd never seen him before. Perhaps he was from a neighboring town.

"Take these five thousand rupees. That's what I've got." The elderly man screamed at Kaka with authority.

"I won't settle for anything under ten thousand. That's final."

Shakti wondered what they were negotiating.

"Kaka, you're being unreasonable. Last year when I paid you for the bullock, you asked for only one thousand rupees. I'm telling you. Ten thousand is ridiculous."

"Have you looked at her? She's the most exquisite beauty you can imagine, and a pure virgin at that."

The tiny little hair on Shakti's arm stood straight up.

"But I know she's trouble. What if someone comes looking for her? I won't pay any higher with all that risk." The elderly man pointed his walking stick at Kaka.

"No one will come looking. Her mother died under a tree and her brother inside a collapsed house. Her father is missing. She's got no one."

Shakti's mouth parched up as she tried to gulp that big lump in her throat. Why didn't the earth simply swallow her up? Why didn't the raging forest fire just wrap her in its flaming arms? Why didn't God just take her back to her kind, loving, Aai and Sanju? She staggered back from the window, her eyes swelling up with sadness. Her knees gave way and she fell, her cacophony of thoughts brought down to the ground, silenced.

Kaka heard the falling thump. "Who's there?"

Shakti gathered herself and her thoughts. She bolted to the house and managed to scamper inside. Kaku wasn't in the house. Shakti sneaked to her little assigned corner and held her breath as she stood against the wall in a scared stillness. She heard Kaka outside. "No one here. Maybe a stray dog. So, where were we?"

She brushed away unfallen tears with the back of her hand. She spread out a piece of cloth in a hurry and tied the few things she had into a roll. She opened up the knot on her handkerchief to check how much money she had. Twenty-five rupees. That wasn't going to be enough. She knew where Kaku kept Kaka's money. She darted to the kitchen nook and opened the orange cooking jar with the big roll of cash. She yanked the money out and replaced it with a heaving load of chili powder. *I trusted you, Kaka. How could you think of selling me away? Now take that.*

Shakti held the cloth bundle to her chest. She couldn't go through the front yard. Unlatching the back door, she peeked out anxiously. She wanted to run and hide, but she made herself walk across the rocky field slowly, putting one foot in front of other as if she had all the time in the world and no reason to be afraid of anyone.

She thought she could feel Kaka's eyes like insects crawling on her skin under her clothes. If she turned to look behind her, she knew her courage would desert her. She kept her gaze to the ground until she reached the main path on the far side. Then, she ran. She ran past kids hitting a piece of wood, past women squatted in doorways separating wheat from chaff, past bubbling pots on makeshift brick ovens, past everything.

She ran under the sky churning with clouds of change. Folks paused to watch her go by. Some even called out to her, but there was no stopping her. No slowing her down. Tears streamed down her cheeks. Her hair swayed in the angry breeze. Her feet spewed out fire and dust. She ran until she reached the central bus-station.

"One ticket to Bombay." Shakti peeped through the tiny ticket window.

"Single or return?" the ticketing clerk asked.

"Single." Shakti wasn't coming back to Latur. She glanced back at her beloved hometown and its charming memories. Latur was singing to her the sweetest song, urging her to stay. The town was clinging to her, tugging at her heart. Should she simply stay here? No, she couldn't. What if Kaka got hold of her again?

Her eyes tried to soak in all they could, from the distant rolling brown hills, to the lush, green swaying trees, to the simple folks in simple whites. Her ears tried to draw in every little sound and store it in the recesses of her brain, from the lazy mooing of the cows, to the busy chirping of the birds, to the resounding bells of the temple. Her nose tried to inhale every faint odor around, from the earthy fragrance of the soil, to the smell of the cows and buffaloes, to the aromas of all kinds of delicious brick oven foods.

With a heavy heart and moist eyes, Shakti grabbed some soil with her hand. She watched in sadness as it slipped through her fingers, like slipping sands of time. She turned around and got onto her bus to Bombay. It was packed, but she found a seat by the window next to an old lady and she hoped the bus would leave soon.

Shakti was fidgety and kept looking at the door. She peered outside the window, straining her eyes. She was paranoid that Kaka might appear out of nowhere. She was afraid he would yank her back and sell her off. She felt fear constrict her breathing. The old lady, meanwhile, was chattering away. Shakti answered her in monosyllables.

At last, the bus took off and began to pick up speed. Shakti felt relief. Kaka couldn't get to her anymore. She relaxed a little and yawned.

"You look tired. Why don't you take a nap?" said the old lady.

"No, I can't."

"Don't worry. I'll keep watch."

"No really. I can't fall asleep." Shakti closed her eyes. *I shouldn't fall asleep.* She was knocked out in minutes. She slept like a baby through the journey. Only when the bus stopped several hours later at Vile Parle, Bombay did she open her eyes again.

Shakti had seen maps and aerial photos of Bombay and had learned about it in her geography class. From the sky and space above, the city looked like a helping hand. As if the Hindu goddess Mumba-devi, from whom the city got its name, was extending her arm, welcoming all to her sanctuary. Her top thumb was full and flexible, with the tips of her bottom fingers curved out as if to say, *Welcome, poor dreary soul. Come to me.*

All along the surface of her forearm, Bombay seemed supple from the sandy soil cover near the Arabian Sea. In the suburbs and interiors, the soil cover became loamy. Both outside and inside, Bombay remained warm, offering her solace and shelter to the aspirations of hundreds of thousands of migrants from all over India.

The underlying strong bone in Bombay's helping hand was a sturdy volcanic rock. The bottom of her hand, straining to contain the millions of its inhabitants, was the jutting outgrowth of land near Trombay. She received an intravenous boost from the tube that went across the sea connecting her to the up and coming New Bombay.

Shakti got off the bus, tugging her bundle close to her chest. She was besieged by the cacophony of sights, sounds, and smells. People and cars hurried past her in every direction. She saw a few shops on the other side of the road but was terrified to go across. Like a deer frozen in headlights, she was too stunned to move.

She waited for the cars and crowds to subside. Every time she made an attempt and took one step forward, she had to scurry back five steps.

"First time in Bombay?" a lady asked, seeing her dilemma. "Don't worry. Simply stand next to me and walk with me."

When the right moment came, they shot across through the maze of cars, bicycles, auto-rickshaws, and incoming pedestrians, like water that makes its way through tiny crevices, in any which direction it finds.

Shakti was captivated. Bombay was unlike any place she'd seen. It was raw; teeming with life. She heard laughter, shouting, and a multitude of tongues spoken.

She felt the influence of Bollywood[13] everywhere. Movie posters were plastered on walls and shops. Banners hung overhead. Music blared on every street. Superstar Madhuri Dixit smiled at Shakti from the many post-

---

13 Bollywood: informal for the Hindi film industry in Mumbai. Derived from Bombay and Hollywood

ers and banners of her recent super-hit movie, *Khalnayak*[14]. The songs from the movie filled up the muggy air. They were an instant hit, both for their choreography, and for the notoriety of the suggestive lyrics.

Shakti saw a friendly chai-wallah. "Brother, where to make a phone call from?"

He was humming Madhuri's *Cholee ke Peeche*[15] song, doing a bit of the jig himself. He held two glasses, one in each hand. He poured the tea from one glass to the other and back again in one continuous sweep. No single drop was spilled. He didn't look at her. He didn't pause from his busy activity. "Go straight. Then right by the lamp-post."

At the phone booth, Shakti pulled out a little piece of paper with Kriya's number. Kriya was the daughter of a family friend. Shakti hadn't talked to her in two years.

As she dialed Kriya's number, her mind teemed with thoughts; the worst possibilities. What if the number had changed? Would Kriya even recognize her? Shakti didn't know anyone else in Bombay. Where would she go? What would she do?

"Hello?" queried a female voice.

"Hello, Kriya *didi*[16]?" Shakti asked with hesitation.

"Yes. Who is it?"

"Kriya *didi*, this is Shakti, from Latur. I arrived in Bombay a few minutes ago."

"Oh my God! Shakti! It's been such a long time. I watched the earthquake on TV a few months ago. How are you, dear? Your family has been in my thoughts. I was sending prayers and peace your way. Is everyone alright? Aai, Baba, Sanju?"

Shakti broke into tears when she heard the names. "I lost them. I lost them all."

"Oh no! I can't find words to express my feelings!" she said, overpowered with emotion. "But don't fear my little sister. Tell me where you are? I'll come and get you."

Shakti didn't have to wait long. A tall, angelic lady stepped out of a taxi-cab. *Kriya didi!* She wore an off-white *salwar-kameez*[17] with a yellow *dupatta*[18] around her neck. Her face glowed with piety and concern. She came rush-

---

14 Khalnayak: Villain

15 Cholee ke peeche: Behind the blouse

16 Didi: Sister

17 Salwar-kameez: Pants and the top of an Indian dress worn by women

18 Dupatta: Piece of cloth worn by women around the neck

ing up and held Shakti in a warm, affectionate hug. Tears streamed down their cheeks. Not a single word was spoken.

Shakti knew it right away - with Kriya *didi* to protect her, she was safe. Kriya *didi's* soft black eyes were compassionate. Her kind-hearted smile was endearing, and her caring touch was healing.

"Come, let's go to my apartment." Kriya *didi* hailed a taxi-cab.

Shakti watched and absorbed the new world around her. Elaborate British Raj buildings juxtaposed with modern, mirrored towers. She saw housing buildings and office structures, tall ones and short ones, different styles, shapes, and colors. A diverse mix adorned and embellished the welcoming hand of Bombay.

Shakti didn't know what to make of her new surroundings. She'd never seen a skyscraper before. And here, every other building looked like a skyscraper. She felt she was in some enchanted wonderland. To her sad eyes, the city seemed like a beautiful savior, offering her new hope and a new beginning.

Kriya summoned the doctor to her apartment. She was worried about Shakti. *Poor girl.* She looked so pale and malnourished. She didn't speak or smile. Numb inside, her body seemed to slowly shut down as if she had died in the Latur earthquake too. She couldn't function from one day to another; she didn't know how to live without her family. Nothing seemed to matter to Shakti anymore.

"Doctor, please tell me she'll be fine," Kriya urged.

"The girl's in a state of shock. Her whole world as she knew it was devastated."

"Yes, she's been through a lot."

"You have to be careful. Very watchful."

"Yes, I understand." Kriya had seen Shakti's feelings and emotions take her to the depths of despair where she no longer wanted to live.

"She's fragile right now, both emotionally and physically. She's got a sense of fear and distrust for everything around her."

"What can I do to help her?"

"There's no silver bullet. Be patient and persevere. It could take her a while to get back to her natural self."

Kriya took time off from her work. She knew it wasn't the most practical thing to do; she barely knew the girl - a daughter of a family friend, with whom she'd last spoken two years ago. Kriya didn't know how long the girl would stay or how long she would need her help. But if she didn't care for her, where would Shakti go? Who'd support her?

Kriya had come to Bombay with no support, staying in a girls' hostel and doing part-time jobs to sustain her college years. Her dad was old and sick; he couldn't move about or travel and her mom had devoted herself to caring for him. After her studies, Kriya began her job, helping uphold her parents and finance her dad's treatment.

From the outside, the City of Dreams appeared all glitzy and welcoming but as a single, poor girl, living all alone, Kriya had seen and been through the shadowy alleys of Bombay. It was so easy to fall prey to the razorblade tentacles lurking in the dark labyrinth of the city. The thought sent a shudder through her spine.

And the March 1993 Bombay bombings, a series of 13 explosions, had made the city an even more unsafe place. It was the most destructive terrorist act in Indian history, with the single-day attacks resulting in over 350 fatalities and 1200 injuries.

Kriya held a simple philosophy in life: *Extending one hand to help somebody was a thousand times more valuable than folding two hands in prayer*. She was a giver. She nurtured Shakti, giving her all the love and affection she needed, and more. For weeks and months, Kriya was her mom, her dad, and her brother. She worked to pull Shakti out and bring her back to the living.

Shakti began to gain her lost strength and resolve, her shine and her vigor, little by little. But every so often, she regressed and fell back into a blue mood.

Kriya couldn't bear to watch her in the doldrums. She knew how Shakti felt, as if she was part of a broken dream and she had no one to turn to. *Don't worry little sis. I'll always be there for you. I'll always stand by you.* She would comfort Shakti and play the song *Good Heart* from the *Greatest Hits of Starship*. It was Kriya's favorite and she played the audio cassette over and over again while Shakti's head rested on her shoulder.

One day, Kriya spotted Shakti with an overcast July demeanor exactly like the monsoon skies outside. Her eyes were swollen up like the clouds, and ready to pour at any moment. Kriya went closer. Shakti's head was burning up. Kriya checked her temperature with the thermometer. 101 degrees Fahrenheit.

"Shakti, drink this up. Now!"

"What is it?"

"My mom's concoction of clove, ginger, and basil; it'll drive away your fever."

Shakti took a sip. "Terrible. Please. Don't make me. It's worse than the fever."

"Trust me, it's good for you."

Shakti shut her nose, closed her eyes, and gulped it down. She coughed and made a face as if it was poison.

Kriya tucked her under the blanket and placed wet strips of cloth on her forehead to bring the fever down.

"Why? Why do such terrible things happen in life?" Shakti sniffled.

"Close your eyes, little sister. I'll tell you a story. You've heard of King Akbar[19] and his minister Birbal[20], haven't you?"

"Yes. We read their stories at school." Shakti wiped the moisture from her eyes.

"One day they went hunting and Akbar cut his finger, sharpening an arrow."

"Ouch," Shakti said in a feeble voice.

"It sure hurt. But when Akbar griped to Birbal, he said, "My lord, whatever happens, happens for the best. Don't worry."" Kriya paused. "This irked Akbar and he was enraged at the unsympathetic Birbal. Akbar wanted to even the score with him."

Shakti gazed at her with puzzled anticipation.

"At the end of the day they were tired. Akbar asked Birbal to go down into an abandoned well and fetch water. It was a deep, dark, and desolate well."

Shakti narrowed her eyes.

"After Birbal went down, Akbar pulled the rope up. He said, "Birbal, stay there now. Whatever happens, happens for the best!""

"Oh no! I'd be scared down there all alone." Shakti flinched.

"Akbar wandered into the jungle, lost his way, and was captured by a forest tribe."

"Serves him right."

"On that day, per tribal customs, they had to sacrifice a man to the Gods."

"Oh my. He didn't deserve that."

"They were about to chop off Akbar's head when the tribal chief noticed his cut finger. He alleged that Akbar wasn't perfect and hence, not fit

---

19 Akbar: a popular emperor who ruled India in the 16th century

20 Birbal: Akbar's favorite minister. A very wise and witty man

for the offering. Akbar repented and returned to rescue Birbal. He apologized and explained what had happened. Birbal replied, 'That's okay, my Lord. Whatever happens, happens for the best.'"

Shakti seemed bemused.

Kriya continued, "Akbar exclaimed, 'How can you say that? You spent an eternity in utter misery inside that creepy well, through no fault of your own!'"

Shakti perked up in attention.

"Birbal smiled. "My lord, if you hadn't left me in the well, we would've gone into the jungle. We would've gotten lost and captured by the tribe. They would've left you because of your cut finger, but without a doubt, they would've chopped my head off."

Shakti looked at Kriya, tears in her burning eyes.

"My little sister, wipe off your tears and put on that lovely smile. Whatever happens, happens for the best!" Kriya felt a small rattling at her knees, coming from the bed. Shakti's body arced and came towards her like a blind, snuggling animal, and held her around the waist with both hands, warm in emotion and fever.

"Kriya *didi*, promise me you won't leave me, ever. Promise me you'll always be with me, just like my breath." The sound of her sobbing was infant-like.

"Yes, Shakti, I promise." Kriya comforted her, patting her softly on the shoulder and the back of her head.

Soon the medication took its effect and Shakti dozed off. Her fever, however, refused to back down. Kriya stayed by her side throughout the night. She changed the wet strips on Shakti's forehead and gave her medication every few hours.

Kriya didn't catch a single wink of sleep. But Shakti's temperature kept rising: 102, 103, 104…

"Float like a butterfly, sting like a bee."
- Muhammad Ali, Heavyweight boxing champion

CHAPTER 4

"You know why Muhammad Ali was the greatest boxer of all time?" asked Shiva as he sipped his Starbucks coffee at the steering wheel of his Honda Accord. The afternoon San Francisco traffic on Van Ness Avenue seemed heavier than usual.

"No. You tell me, Mr. Einstein," Harry said from the passenger seat.

"Because he floated like a butterfly and stung like a bee." Shiva loved that line.

"Whoa, that's a steep incline," Harry said as they turned right and drove up Lombard Street on Russian Hill. Today his T-shirt said, "I tried to catch some fog. I mist."

"See, Ali was a smart strategist. Smarter than people give him credit for."

"Yeah, right. Ali was a great strategist, my foot. I cringed when he trash-talked opponents with crazy rhymes. *It will be a killer and a chiller and a thriller when I get the Gorilla in Manila.* Yikes."

"All part of a plan, my friend. Remember the *Rumble in the Jungle* against George Foreman?"

"Yeah, I saw it on ESPN Classic. It was a few years after Ali was stripped of his title. Your Ali was a washout by then."

"Foreman was the undisputed favorite with a much superior punching power. In a head-on, blow-for-a-blow fight, Ali was dead-meat. So he used the *rope-a-dope.*"

"*Rope-a-dope?*"

"Sort of like a losing dope on the ropes. Ali let Foreman swing away but he hit nothing except air. Soon, the bigger and heavier Foreman tired himself out."

"Oh, I get it." Harry set down his Starbucks Venti cup and leaned towards Shiva, warming up to the conversation. "Ali put himself in what seemed to be a losing position, only to turn around and emerge as the eventual victor."

"Exactly. Harry, I wish Boss would learn something from this. Ali didn't start out all crazy, trying to box out the superior puncher Foreman."

"I see what you're trying to say."

"Did *you* see that match, Hong?" asked Shiva. He looked in the rear view mirror to the third passenger in his car. They had forgotten about him.

Hong Lee was their class-mate from Cornell University. He was finishing up his PhD in computer science and wanted to check out the San Francisco Bay Area before he finalized a job location. And Shiva and Harry, the consummate friends they were, had planned out a great weekend for him.

But right then, Hong's skinny frame had turned rigid as stone. His bespectacled face was frozen in fright. His throat locked and his lips went pale. Shiva realized what was happening. The drive up Lombard Street was at a steep vertical incline and the stop and go, trapped between cars, could get edgy. *Hang in there, Hong.*

"Are you okay? You don't look that great," Harry said. All of a sudden, Hong shook involuntarily, with anxiety surging though his entire body. "Shiva, I think he's hyper-ventilating. How long to the top of this incline?"

"We're almost there, Hong. You'll be fine." Shiva pulled to the curb and stepped out to check on him. There was still no word from him and he looked pale and dizzy. "Breathe, Hong, breathe."

A few eternal seconds passed by. At last, color returned to Hong's face. "Weird. This has never happened to me before, but I feel much better now."

"Here, drink this. It will cool you down." Shiva handed him a water bottle. "Should we take a break?"

"No, no. Let's simply nip my brush with death in the bud and move on. I'm perfectly fine. Where the heck is Crooked Street?"

Shiva smiled. Hong was mixing his metaphors again; that meant he was getting back to normal. Soon they headed down onto the one-way section of Lombard Street, the 400 meters red-brick road between Hyde and Leavenworth Streets. Eight sharp turns that had earned it the distinction of being the most crooked street in the world. Born out of necessity, it reduced the hill's natural 27% grade, which was too steep for most cars.

"This is so cool," Hong said. "Did you guys know that Alfred Hitchcock's *Vertigo* was set on Crooked Street?"

Shiva was glad Hong was now in his true element. *Attaboy!* Hong had to know every little fact that was to be known. He was the topper from Fudan

University in Shanghai, having skipped high-school and been directly admitted to college.

"No, I didn't know," Harry said. "I do know that I've a fear of heights. The funniest comment I heard was from Bill Cosby."

"Bill Cosby?" Hong asked. USA shows weren't put on air behind the Red Curtain.

"An American comedian, actor, and author. He once said, 'They built a street called Lombard Street that goes straight down. And they're not satisfied with you killing yourself that way—they put grooves and curves and everything in it. They put flowers there where they've buried the people that have killed themselves. Wonderful Street.'"

All three broke out in boisterous laughter.

After a brief stop at Coit Tower for a 360 degree city view, the three musketeers headed towards the Golden Gate Bridge - the most photographed bridge in the world.

"When's your birthday?" Harry asked Shiva.

Shiva was taken by surprise, but he didn't show it. "18th…February 18th. Why?"

"18. 1+8 equals 9. Number 9. Your personality is a 'Rebel with a cause'[21]."

"You can tell that from my birth date?" Shiva winced.

"Yes sir," said Harry with the confidence of a numerology guru. "All 9 people, I mean people born on 9, 18, or 27, are ruled by fiery Mars."

"Fiery Mars, eh?" Shiva hid a smile; his poker-face came in handy at such times.

"Yes. You're destined to be aggressive and noble. You've oodles of energy and speed and you love to fight for the weaker guy – the underdog."

"Don't tell me every such 9 person is like that."

"It's a statistical science. Check out the birthdays of the fastest pitchers in baseball, or the fastest bowlers in your cricket."

"Now, come on…"

"Okay then, check out the birthdays of action movie stars, or successful military leaders, or fearless CEO's of companies. You'll find they are by and large 9 people."

"Oh, look at that," said Hong as they passed the Exploratorium and he caught a glimpse of the Golden Gate Bridge over his glasses. "Beautiful. Aren't we stopping?"

"Yes, on the other side. The view's much better from there," said Shiva as Hong clicked pictures with his camera.

---

21 Refer to Appendix for your 'Personality' map in "Harry's Numerology for Birthdates"

"You know, the good thing about all 9 people is that you're very straight-forward," Harry continued. "There's no politics – in fact, you hate politics."

"Now you're clearly making that up, since you already know me."

"No really. When you're committed to a cause - something you believe in, you will give your life to it. You will do anything for folks you consider your friends."

"Hmmm...You've done some serious research on this subject, haven't you?"

"But here's the downside. You tend to be politically-incorrect. You show lesser diplomacy when dealing with authorities."

"Hey, you can't say that. I'm showing some serious tact, right now."

"Also, you need to find a way to get your anger out. The gym is a MUST or else this energy will come out in all the wrong directions."

"Enough about me. Time to enjoy the view." Shiva pulled into a parking spot.

"Whoa, it's windy out here," Hong shivered. "Let me grab my jacket."

"I still haven't figured out why it's called the Golden Gate Bridge," Harry pointed out. "I've seen it so many times, but the bridge still looks orange to me."

"International orange to be precise," said Hong. "It complements the natural surroundings and enhances the bridge's visibility, even in a dense fog."

Shiva looked at him in awe. Hong was well-informed. Not a surprise though. He was so inquisitive. He always got to the root of things, on all kinds of topics.

"It's such a clear day," Hong said. "I can see Coit Tower, Fort Mason, the Trans-America building. And what's that? Yes the Twin Peaks."

Shiva took pictures of Hong with the backdrop of the bridge and the skyline. The air was nice and moist. It had a comforting marine aroma to it. Seals and sea-gulls celebrated the good weather with their joyous sounds. "See, isn't San Francisco so beautiful? It's the best city in the U.S. You should come here and work in Silicon Valley."

Hong nodded. "This is such a unique design." His glasses, all fogged up, were fixated on the bridge. "It introduced deflection theory for the first time."

Shiva and Harry gave him a blank look.

"A thin roadway flexing in the wind to transmit forces via suspension cables to the bridge towers," Hong continued. "That's why it has withstood so many earthquakes and remained intact even when other neighboring modern bridges fell. Isn't it amazing?"

"You know what? More people die by suicide at the Golden Gate Bridge than at any other site in the world." Harry had to burst Hong's bubble.

"Really?"

"Yes, really. After a fall of 5 seconds, the jumpers hit the water at around 75 mph. Most die from impact trauma on contact with the water." Harry ignored Shiva's angry stare. "The few that survive the initial impact die of hypothermia in the cold water."

Hong seemed petrified. His eyes oscillated like a pendulum, from the bridge down to the water and back to the bridge, to size up the deadly fall. It was a long way down.

The trio then drove around Sausalito, the Marina, and back onto Lombard Street for a quick dinner at Harry's favorite restaurant, Mel's Drive-in. Shiva was fond of it as well; he loved the ambience, the setting, and the history of Mel's.

"Mel's reminds me of the diner that Sally and I hung out in Cornell. Life was good then," Harry said with a dreamy expression.

Shiva had read about Mel Weiss and Harold Dobbs, who started Mel's Drive-in back in 1947 when they built their first San Francisco carhop eatery. With a staff of fourteen covering a huge parking lot, they lured in the hungry with local radio personality broadcasting. As music reverberated through car radios in the drive-ups, the curb-stepping gals became a new paradigm for service. At any hour of the day and night, crowds of patrons that fancied dining-in-your-car came early and often.

"How Sally and I played jokes on friends by unscrewing the tops of salt shakers and ketchup caps," Harry reminisced. "How the haunting sound of an electric guitar banged out the *chunka-chunka* rhythm of *Green Onions* on the juke-box."

Mel's Drive-in reigned for twenty years, until a parade of fast food outlets outpaced their service. As the new philosophy of *serve yourself* began to reprogram attitudes, Mel's began its gradual decline. A New York conglomerate purchased most of the faltering units, and it appeared that Mel's success story was about to end.

"I haven't talked to Sally for two days. They keep her too busy in Australia." Harry ordered a half-pounder with grilled onions, french-fries, and a milkshake.

In the 1970's, filmmaker George Lucas was scouting out locations for *American Graffiti,* his rock-n-roll fable. He leased the Mel's burger spot prior to its demolition. Crews descended on the site and soon it was lights, camera, and action. Mel's was back in business, immortalized in 35mm.

Out in the parking lot, Ron Howard, Richard Dreyfuss, Harrison Ford, and Suzanne Somers took their first steps into future stardom.

"This burger needs salt, which tells me the butter is fresh," Harry mumbled through the big bite of his juicy burger. "And the milkshake is superb. Yum." The waiter interrupted to lay down Harry's favorite homemade hot apple pie with cinnamon sauce.

Shiva and Hong enjoyed their clam chowder in silence. Shiva visualized the bulldozers that razed the last remnants of Mel's while trucks carted off the debris. *American Graffiti* opened in theatres and memories of the fifties dominated people's imagination like a jukebox replaying the same old record. They remembered their early years of romance - how they first met at Mel's, dated, and in the end, got married. With the surge in public demand, Mel's was resurrected in 1985.

"I miss Sally. I'm gonna ask her to hop on a plane and come on over." Harry finished his pie and slurped down his milk-shake.

"Yes, you should. We haven't seen her in ages," Shiva said as he paid the check. "So, what are we doing next?"

"Freshen up, change into something dapper, and meet up at Cat Club," Harry said.

"I'm kind of tired today," muttered Hong. "I'm thinking of crashing early tonight. You guys go ahead with the plan."

"Come on, Hong," said Harry. "Glee and her friend will be joining us. Cat Club's got two dance floors – one playing the 80's, and the other playing hip-hop tonight."

"I'm sorry guys, but I'll take a rain-check," Hong insisted.

"Hey Harry, can I skip too? I've got to resolve a customer issue," Shiva said.

"No can do, Shiva. Not tonight. It's Glee's birthday. You can't miss it."

When Shiva reached Cat Club, Harry, Glee, and her friend Cindy were waiting in line. Glee sported a stunning slinky black dress with a rhinestone buckle and a neckline that skimmed her navel. Cindy wore a gunmetal shimmer mini with draped bodice.

"A very happy birthday, Gleeful. You girls look great," said Shiva.

"Thanks. But is that like…the best you can do?" said Glee.

"Oh, how about this? You girls look like a million bucks, freshly minted and with a devilishly sexy feel." Shiva smiled, "Two parts nice and one part plain naughty."

"And you look hella suave." Glee blushed and returned the compliment. "What did you do to your friend? Did you like…lose him or something?"

"He was exhausted from the sight-seeing. He's called it a night," said Harry.

"Where's your ID? That doesn't look like you," boomed the big bouncer, walking down the line. A young couple – teenagers really – got into a scuffle with him, shouting obscenities. They were lifted away by the muscled man. "No tennis shoes. Now, scoot."

Shiva stared at the bouncer as he kicked out some more people.

"You better keep it locked, *Hulk*," said Harry.

"Why do you call him *Hulk?*" Glee asked. "I've heard you say that like… so many times. But I've never seen him angry; he's always smiling."

"Ignorance is bliss." Harry looked at her and winked. They went by the bouncer without any incident, paid the cover charge and stepped into the club. The place was throbbing with people, strobe-lights, and music.

"Pink drinks." Glee beamed as they passed a smoking alley and a go-go cage.

Shiva was impressed by the state-of-the-art lights, sound, and video. No wonder Cat Club was the number 1 San Francisco nightlife destination. It had the coolest music and the best crowd in town.

"I wanna go to the hip-hop floor." Glee held a pink drink with a tiny umbrella. DJ Dangerous Dan was spinning *You Got It (The Right Stuff)* from the *New Kids on the Block*. "Hey, that's a hella cool song…my favorite." Glee dragged Shiva onto the floor.

Harry and Cindy joined them. DJ Dangerous Dan was in his element that night, bringing down the club with songs by Dr. Dre, Prince, Mariah Carey, Selena, and Boyz II Men. The foursome shook their legs and gyrated to the beats.

"Look, some PDA." Glee pointed to the far corner of the dance floor where a few freak-dancing females were engaged in girl-on-girl public display of affection.

Shiva looked around. A few roving grinders lurked at the periphery, like hyenas eyeing their prey for a kill. Without a doubt, everyone's least desired club attendees. The roving grinders strayed all over, trying to blend in. Moving their heads up and down in a cool swagger, but mostly zeroing in to grind on absolutely random women.

Shiva wondered if the grinder's goal was to simply set an individual grinding record. Maybe he was merely an ill-advised dreamer. Maybe he hoped that someday one of his meat-buns would turn around, look into his empty eyes, and say, "I love it when bizarre men grind their penises into my booty. Let's begin a relationship."

The foursome was having a good time until a couple of drunken guys started an altercation with them. One guy got behind Glee for some grinding action. She turned away in disgust, but he persisted. He yanked her and squeezed her butt.

"Stay away from her, man. She's with us," Shiva stepped in.

"Who's gonna stop me? You?" He was a huge black man, well over six and a half feet and much bigger and heavier than Shiva, and twice as broad across the chest.

"Let's get out of the club. No point getting into a tiff," Harry said. He hated fights, but it was too late. The air now held the impending inevitability of trouble.

Shiva felt blood rush away from his face and hands. The veins in his arms, neck, and forehead bulged out like cables, turning a furious blue and green. His angular jaw clenched. His knuckles were taut.

The big guy planted his thick legs apart in a defiant stance, like a burly bear. His arms, the size of normal people's legs, were primed by his side, itching to release anger. "Fuck you, asshole." He charged towards Shiva and swung a huge blow with his giant right hand; a blow that had the power to rattle prison rails and bank vaults.

Shiva feigned, moving his face aside faster than the guy could see. With the new angle, he created an opening in the guy's defense. Shiva threw a hard punch at his solar plexus. He tightened his fist, and shifted his weight from the back to his front leg as the punch landed. Shiva twisted his whole body to put maximum impact into the punch. And then he pulled his fist back fast – the entire action over in one second.

That single punch knocked the wind out of the hooligan, physically and mentally. He was incapacitated. He couldn't breathe. A minute ago he was full of bravado, like a bear with a swagger. Now he retreated like a dog with his tail between the legs.

Harry looked up from behind the bar counter, only his mop of thick, blonde curly hair and his beady eyes showing. He climbed over and jumped into the fray with all the grace of a tightrope walker having suddenly discovered courage. "Come on. Which asshole wants to deal with us? Anyone? Huh…I thought so."

A sting of pain swept up Shiva's shoulder, but the pleasure of it throbbed in his head. He went up to the hooligan's face, staring him in the eye. The hooligan backed down, but Shiva was seething. No mercy. "Say sorry to the lady."

"Sorry ma'am."

"What? I didn't hear that. Louder." Shiva could feel angry heat erupt from the volcano of his eyes.

"Sorry. I'm sorry. This won't happen again."

Glee accepted the apology. Shiva jostled his way out through the crowd and onto the road, his chest and heart heaving. He wanted somebody else to hit, something, anything, but the cars raced by out of reach. He knew he had to restrain his anger. He clenched the cold, rusty pole of the street sign and cursed and cursed.

"Now you know why I call him the *Hulk*," Harry said to Glee. "He doesn't get angry very often, and seems all calm and collected. But be forewarned, all enemies; anger our friend Shiva and you shall face the wrath of the *Hulk*."

"Your hand is so soft and your fingers so thin and artistic," said Harry, holding Glee's hand. They were at Boss's pool party in his Los Gatos home. "Wow. You've got such a well-developed Mount of Venus."

"What does that mean? Is it like…good or bad?" Glee asked. She'd taken a dip in the pool and was now enjoying the warm sun as it caressed her bikini body.

Harry was happy simply lounging on the pool-side chairs, sipping freshly made cocktails. His swim-trunks were still dry, and he preferred them that way. He was jazzed up about his new T-shirt; it simply said, "A dyslexic man walks into a bra."

Boss's backyard was lavishly designed. Shrubs and trees trimmed neatly. A dozen Adirondack chairs set out in precise alignment. The lawn perfectly manicured and raked, the birdfeeders topped off, and fresh flowers on each of the three patio tables.

"It's good. It means that you love art, music, and a good life."

"Well, that I do."

"You've an attractive personality and you could very well be an actress."

Two exquisite birds began their own conversation in their ornate cage. Painted buntings – the most beautiful, painted birds in the USA. A male and a female. The male had an amazing display of colors - a key ingredient in mating rituals. The birds were excited with all the people around; they became loud and melodious at the same time.

"Wait. Are you like…teasing me or something?"

"No, no, I'm serious. The good news is that you don't have an excessive mount."

"Why? What would an excessive mount mean?"

"An abuse of worldly pleasures. Over-indulgence in drugs and alcohol. It could result in kidney issues. You don't want that, do you?" Harry's phone on the side table buzzed out loud. He glanced at it and picked it up at once. It was Sally.

"Hi honey, how're you doing?" Harry asked.

Pause.

"Me? What am I doing? I'm merely reading someone's palm."

Pause.

"Who? It's just Glee from our office. She says hi to you."

Long pause.

"No, no....yeah, yeah, I'm looking forward to it. What time are you landing?"

Pause and a smile.

"Yes, we'll be at San Francisco airport on time. Shiva and I. Don't worry."

Pause.

"Miss you too. See you soon. Bye."

Harry gave an embarrassed, teddy-bearish look to Glee. He felt flushed.

Shiva was in the pool with his colleagues and their discussion soon veered to Clinton. "Man, that was a tough year for our President," Shiva said.

"But he's finishing it with an impressive record, moving more legislation through Congress in his first year than any other President since Eisenhower," said a colleague.

"But the economy still seems to be in a slump," another colleague cut in.

"It's getting better. The gloom that has hung over us for years is finally lifting. Every economic indicator is better." The first colleague was confident.

"Like what? Mass layoffs? And is the beer cheaper? That's what I want to know."

"150,000 new jobs created every month. Signs of renewed vigor are all over."

"Alright, alright, but how about them 49ers?" The second colleague shifted to his favorite topic. "Without Montana this year, we're gonna get our ass whooped."

"I'm glad that the biggest quarterback controversy in football history is finally over," Shiva said. "If Montana had stayed and started, there would've been problems. If he'd stayed and Steve Young had started, there would've been problems."

Three other colleagues suddenly darted past the pool with urgency. Shiva sensed mischief in their grins. Where were they going? They ran towards the lounge chairs, and Harry didn't see them coming; he didn't have a chance to think or react. They caught him by his hands and feet and picked him up off the chair.

"No guys, I can't swim," Harry protested as he tried to hold onto the chair, then the table, then anything that his fingers could grasp. But the guys didn't listen. They carried him towards the end of the pool and flung him in.

Harry fell in, splayed flat across the water with a splash so big it almost emptied the pool. "Help me! Somebody, help me!" Harry yelled at the top of his lungs. He was panic-stricken, as if his whole life was passing him by. "Mom, Dad, save me!"

Shiva swam fast and tugged at Harry, helping him to the edge. Harry looked at him with an immense sense of gratitude; he was relieved to be alive. But before Harry could begin to thank him, Shiva said, "Hey bud, simply stand up straight."

Harry's face turned sheepish as his feet touched the bottom. It was only five and a half feet deep. The guys were laughing out loud. He screamed out at them, "You idiots!"

Shiva ordered him a drink and within a few gulps, Harry forgot the episode.

"What's the full birth date of someone you admire?" Harry asked.

"Not now Harry."

"Just tell me... the full birth date, with the year."

"Oh, well. Pa's birthday is the 3rd of September, 1942."

Harry began calculating on a napkin. He had such seriousness on his face: Eyes squinted in concentration; Lips pursed; Frown on the forehead; Ears flushed red. He seemed so involved as if he was solving the world energy crisis.

Shiva tried to sneak a quick glimpse at Harry's scribbling.

"I'm merely adding up all the numbers. Here's the analysis. Look. Pa's life-purpose is number 1." Harry beamed with a big sense of achievement.[22]

03	September	1942
3	9	1+9+4+2
3	9	16 = (1+6) = 7
3	+ 9	+ 7
= 19 = (1+9)		
= 10 = (1+0) = 1		

Pa's Life-Purpose = 1

"What does that mean?" Shiva asked. "I did a quick mental math and my full birth-date sum comes out to be the same as Pa's; Number 1."

"Well," Harry began, "your life-purpose is ruled by the Sun, for both of you. It symbolizes the soul, ego. A pioneer. An inspiration. Also stands for being aloof, a loner."

"Yabbadabbadoo. All gobbledygook to me."

"You have entrepreneurial abilities. The sun originates light by burning itself."

"Look out at the horizon. The sun is going down... look," Shiva added in jest.

"Shiva, this is a real science. The sun starts something new. I'm telling you. Your life-purpose is to start something new, something original."

At that moment Boss walked out to the pool area; a slow, dreadful walk, with worry in his eyes. The color had run off his face as if someone had died a moment ago. "Guys, huddle up. I've some good news and bad news. Which one do you want first?"

"Good news," some guys in the pool shouted.

"Here's the good news. Alltech is now officially in the big league as a company."

"And the bad news?"

"The bad news is that our competitor has decided to counter-sue our IP claims."

Shiva gave Harry an I-told-you-so look. A murmur buzzed all around as everyone grappled with the news. Boss continued his speech, full of corporate jargon and legal mumbo-jumbo. He finished and walked back in, a number of questions left unanswered.

---

22 Refer to Appendix for your 'Life Purpose' map in "Harry's Numerology for Birthdates"

"Okay, bud. I've got to go talk to Boss. I need to," Shiva said.

"Mr. *Hulk*, take a chill pill. Now's not a good time. He looked pissed to me."

"Hey, I don't have a temper. I simply have a quick reaction to bullshit."

"I know, I know. That's why I worry."

"Well, now is as good as any other time." Shiva dried himself, put on his clothes, and walked in after Boss as Harry looked away in the other direction.

"Sir, I understand we're down this path," said Shiva, "but it's not too late. Can't we come to an agreement outside the court?"

"Don't be so timid," said Boss. "We've got to show some balls. Clearly, we have the advantage and we will prevail."

"That's what I'm worried about. We might have a technology advantage, but now we're fighting on their turf, in the court of law. They have the financial advantage, a bigger patent portfolio, and a bigger team of sharks."

"We've got great lawyers on our side too." Boss seemed convinced.

"Sir, with due respect, they have decades of litigation experience. Plus our founders came over to Alltech from there. We're at a huge risk."

"You're overthinking it. Leave that to the exec team."

"Sir, this lawsuit can drag on forever and our competition will spread FUD[23], creating doubts in customer minds about our survival. No one will buy from us."

"Now you're dramatizing it." Boss simmered; he couldn't hide his displeasure at being challenged. "I've thought about everything."

Shiva knew he had to restrain himself, but he couldn't. "No sir, I don't think you have. What about our IPO? The lawsuit can complicate things and push out the IPO indefinitely. Sir, Alltech can't afford to be stubborn on this."

There are moments in life which occur right after an unfortunate comment trips from your tongue. One wishes to simply recall those last few words – but since, once spoken, speech can never be recalled, that reckless comment may eclipse everything else one ever does for the rest of one's life. This was precisely such a moment for Shiva.

"Who are you calling stubborn?" Boss boiled in annoyance.

"Sir, I didn't mean to anger you. I apologize. I know you want to do the right thing for the company and for the employees." Shiva's heart rose to

---

23 FUD: Fear, uncertainty, doubt

his mouth and fell down to his toes, leaving behind the taste of ashes on his tongue.

Boss jerked to his feet, sending his chair flying. It hit the wall with a bang. "Now *you* will teach me the right thing?"

Shiva put on a brave face, aware as he did so that his fate was already sealed. "Sir, I'm sorry, but I can't watch the company go down. I might have to quit."

At the back of his mind, he knew he was leaving so much on the table. It wasn't only the stock options and financial gains that he would be giving up. It wasn't only the rung of the professional ladder that he would be losing out on. It wasn't only his green card that would need to start again from scratch. This could be a big setback; he could lose on every front. But he had to do the right thing, and he didn't believe in the lawsuit.

"Quit? No. You are FIRED!"

Shiva had sacrificed his time and efforts to several late nighters and weekends to solve customer problems and help Alltech succeed. He'd missed out on important family events and weddings of friends in India even when he'd wanted to participate. He'd given up vacations and fun times with his friends, who had pranced on a Cancun beach during spring break without him. All the things that he'd given up for Alltech; all was lost.

"I know every single person of any importance in the industry. I'll make sure no one gives you a freaking job. You think you've got a spine? You know what? I'll break you. I'll bring you down and leave you wallowing in misery. That's my freaking promise."

Shiva wondered what would become of him. Alltech was his first company, his first job. And the news of his firing would spread around the valley fast. He was a greenhorn in the industry. He had accomplished nothing so far. What would he tell his parents? Pa had such great expectations of him. And here he was...fired from his first job. Shiva felt bleak. He rubbed his face with his palm.

Shiva thought of Roark, who was expelled from his institute for not adhering to the conventions of architecture. Despite a later offer from the Dean, Roark chose to leave. *If Alltech doesn't value me, I can choose to leave.* Roark had roared into New York City to work for a disgraced architect whose work served as an inspiration. Shiva grew strong in his belief. *I have to find my own Roark roar. I have to find my own inspiration.*

"We'll see." Shiva's eyes blazed. It made Boss stop; he was taken aback. Shiva looked at him with disdain. The short-sightedness and pettiness of the man. Shiva turned his back and stormed out of the patio door, shutting it with a thunderous thump.

He gave a parting glance to his friends. He felt sorry for Harry, Glee, and the rest of his colleagues. Boss's super-sized ego would drive Alltech into the ground. He paused for a moment, opened up the bird cage door and walked out to the driveway.

Shiva was filled with restless energy. He started his car and pulled away. He looked back up. He saw the two painted buntings soar up to the sky - colorful, noisy, and happy. The thrill of adventure ran through him. *FREE.*

Ten Years Later...

"I lost everything I had, but in the process I found myself."
- Rumi, 13th-century Persian poet and mystic.

CHAPTER 5

A loud, urgent knock on her apartment door yanked Shakti awake. Who could it be so early in the morning? She was tired, sleepy with jet-lag. By the time she pulled herself off the bed, a series of impatient thumps shook the apartment.

"Open up, it's the police."

"I'm coming." Shakti hurried to the door and opened it.

Two strangers stood there, an Inspector and a constable. The squat, overweight Inspector wore a tight khaki uniform and a big police belt around his waist. Like many of his peers, he'd squeezed himself into a uniform that was at least two sizes too small. His belt couldn't make up its mind whether to be above or below the girth in the center. The constable's blue attire was worn out, and it hung loosely on his malnourished frame.

"Is this Ms. Kriya's home?" asked the Inspector in a thunderous, stern tone.

"Sorry, I just woke up. And yes, it is. But she's not at home right now."

A silence followed for a few seconds. A silence of discomfort and menace. Shakti wanted to say something but she didn't know what.

"I'm sub-Inspector Gore and this is constable Mane, from the Bandra police station. Who are you? And what are you doing here?"

"Sir, I'm Shakti. I live with Kriya-di. What's the matter?"

The Inspector studied her and blurted out, "Girls today are too thin. They must start eating more."

"Pardon me? What?" Shakti looked away to the full-size mirror in the living room. She saw an attractive young woman in her early twenties, with a slim figure, patrician features, and bright sandy-brown eyes. Dark brown curls fell to her shoulders. She wished she didn't have such a round face; a long one would've made her look taller.

"Can we come in?" The Inspector barged through the door. "We got a call at the police station that Kriya has gone missing from Bandra. Have you seen her?" A gust of sweaty, earthy air rushed in along with a grimy, residual trace of crime and punishment.

"What? Oh my God! No, I haven't seen her. I only flew into Bombay last night." Shakti felt blood gush to her face. She didn't know how to react.

"It's now called *Mumbai*, not Bombay."

"Sorry. I flew into *Mumbai* last night." She knew about the name change, but Bombay was still ingrained in her mind. In the 16th century when the Portuguese came, they couldn't pronounce Mumbai so they called it Bombaim. After the British gained possession in the 17th century, it was anglicized to Bombay. In 1996, it was changed back to its original Mumbai – a big source and symbol of pride for the locals.

Kriya-di told her that Bombay's name might have reverted to what it was a few centuries ago, but globalization and outsourcing were propelling it fast-forward. A city and a whole country that stood at the crossroads of time, reveling in the promising uncertainty of the future, while still rooted in tradition.

"When was the last time you saw Ms. Kriya?" the Inspector's voice bellowed.

"About seven days ago. My flight was heading out of Mumbai and I saw Kriya-di at the airport. Her flight had barely arrived."

"Did you talk to her on phone after that?"

"No, but hold on. Let me call her cell phone." Shakti speed-dialed Kriya-di's number. The phone kept ringing. There was no response.

"What do you ladies do?"

"We're flight attendants on Trans Pacific. We have crazy schedules and don't run into each other for several days, even though we live in the same apartment." The look on the Inspector's face changed. Shakti knew that look. She had seen it before in other men's faces, in their eyes. They thought that since she was an air hostess, she must be "hostessing" the pilots on their stopovers. Shakti was annoyed; she turned her face away.

"When was she supposed to be back?"

"Let me check her schedule...God! She should have returned three days ago!"

"That's what the caller said. Three days. Something happened in Bandra."

"Inspector, may I ask who this caller is?"

"We don't know. Did you and Kriya have a little disagreement of late?"

"No."

"Are you sure? Try to remember. Or maybe you got into a major fight about a boyfriend or expenses?" He had taken his gloves off, ready to get tougher.

"No sir. We didn't have any big fight over any boyfriend or expenses. A little disagreement about my flight schedule maybe."

"Ah, so you did have a disagreement about something."

Shakti had seen this line of interrogation in Hollywood movies. What was it called? Yes... *Overshooting.* The cops used it to cajole confessions from criminals they believed were lying. The technique was simple: Affirm the information you want confessed. Then contend something far worse. It gave the criminal a chance to choose the lesser of the two evils - in most cases, the truth.

"It was nothing. Kriya-di didn't like my flight schedule, which forced me to come home at unearthly hours. She was merely being a caring sister."

"Is that right?"

Shakti could sense no compassion or kindness in the Inspector. Perhaps it was the uneasiness of his tight uniform that gave him his meanness.

"Isn't that top too large for you?" he asked, and then stared at her slippers.

"I'm wearing Kriya-di's top and her slippers. They're just nice and comfortable."

"Isn't it true that you have a reason to lie?"

"I'm sorry? What?" Shakti felt her stomach get rock hard. That query appeared out of nowhere, like a cramp. She crossed her arms across the pain in her stomach.

"A reason to lie, Ms. Shakti?" The Inspector took a stiff stride towards her.

"No sir. I don't lie." She felt like a cornered kitten.

"Never, ever?"

"No sir. I always speak the truth."

"Oh, don't deny. Everyone lies, particularly if they have something to hide."

Besides his cruising altitude gaze, the Inspector had two other expressions: *takeoff* and *landing.* His *takeoff* expression was fixed, like the progress of a Boeing 747. His eyes never veered to the left or right. One would really need a giant obstacle to swerve him off his flight-path, but he made everyone else in their tiny planes turn sharp, change directions, and reduce altitude. As for the *landing* expression, he hardly ever used it. He didn't need to brake and slow down, or withdraw an assertion very often.

"I really don't have anything to hide." Shakti's heart beat faster, confronted with his trial by ambush. She had to get a hold of herself. She had to calm down her nerves.

"How about checking at the Trans Pacific office?" The Inspector softened his tone. "Maybe someone there knows."

"Let me try," whispered Shakti as she dialed her phone. "Hello, Monica? It's Shakti. Have you seen Kriya-di? When did you last see her? A week ago? Oh, nothing. I'm sure we'll find her." Her eyes welled up with tears; she wiped them away. "Inspector, if you don't mind, can I use the bathroom?"

Shakti shuffled to the bathroom and locked the door. She felt alone. The fear and loss from ten years ago came shuddering in. She felt weak in the knees and her legs wobbled. She felt her emotions settling into the middle of her chest as if a cement balloon was expanding, making it hard to breathe.

When she left Latur, how she had missed her Aai and Sanju. How she had searched for Baba for so many years but still couldn't find him. She had fought off sleep every night because it only meant she would have to relearn the ruthless reality in the morning. She had resolved to never go outside again. She had wanted to kill herself.

It had been ten long and painful years. Every day passed, when they weren't in her life, but not a single moment passed when they weren't in her thoughts. If all of her tears from those years could only flood and float a life raft up to heaven, she would've oared her way there and brought them right back down.

Kriya-di had rescued her from the dead, helped her stand on her feet. She said, "I can never fully understand your pain. I can only imagine what you're going through. But now this is your new home and I'm your family. A new world waits ahead for you." Kriya-di supported her and gave her courage. She nursed her when she had high fever. And now Kriya-di was gone. Where was she? How could Shakti live without her?

Shakti noticed on the bathroom mantle the bronze statuette of *Jhansi ki Rani*[24], a huge inspiration to Kriya-di, who referred to her as *JR*. Kriya-di had told her so many stories of *JR*'s defiance against the British and her exemplary gallantry. *JR* roused a fervor that gave birth to leaders and revolutionaries who would free India from the British.

Although Shakti went through the motions of moving on, her loss remained permanently imprinted in her nerves, sending tremors that rendered her confidence fragile. It mutated her from a fearless, vivacious girl into a frightened, anxious wreck. When it thundered loudly during the monsoons,

---

24 Jhansi ki Rani was the queen of the princely state of Jhansi. She was a leading figure of the Indian Rebellion of 1857 and for Indian nationalists a symbol of resistance to the British rule.

she scurried scared from her room and crawled into Kriya-di's bed. When Kriya-di had asked her, "Why are you so scared? You are a survivor. Like *JR*." Shakti had replied, "I'm a survivor, but I'm not a fighter like her."

Now, in the bathroom, Shakti couldn't control herself and sobbed disconsolately. She opened up the tap and washed her face with cold water. Her tears flowed with the water as she reminisced.

"You can do it," Kriya-di said.

"But our college has never won that intercollegiate science competition." Shakti shrugged her shoulders.

"There's always a first time. You won't find out until you try. Go have a little fun with your friends. Stop worrying."

Shakti got together five of her college mates and architected a well thought out, elaborate project on ecological conservation. The team worked days and evenings and pieced together a working model of a "green" town, self-sustained by renewable energy. Their friendships grew stronger as they bonded over the course of the project and gelled into one strong, cohesive unit.

One such evening, Kriya-di joined them at the Prithvi Theater café in Juhu while they chatted away over coffee, cheese-balls, and brownies to celebrate the project's completion. Shakti and her friends had a great time with Kriya-di.

"You know why frogs are so happy?" Kriya-di asked. No one replied. "Because they can eat whatever bugs them!"

Raj, a college mate, laughed out loud. "Good one! Now, tell me, what did the volcano say to his wife?"

"I'm hot?" Shakti guessed, with narrow, unsure eyes.

"No, silly. The volcano said, "I lava you so much!" Raj burst out with laughter.

"Okay, okay, here's another; why is electricity so dangerous?" Shakti asked.

"Because it gives you a shock?" Raj made a valiant effort.

"Nice try. Because it doesn't know how to conduct itself properly."

"Very funny," giggled Kriya-di. "Tell me, what did the sea say to the shore?"

"What?"

"Nothing, it simply waved." Kriya-di grinned ear-to-ear.

The day prior to the intercollegiate competition, Shakti, Raj, and the rest were handed the rules and regulations for the event.

"Remember to take our college banner," Raj said.

"And don't forget the canister to transfer the water," a college mate said.

"Oh my, look at the next page. Only five participants are allowed."

"What? They changed that rule from last year."

"What do we do now?"

Shakti remained silent. All of them had worked hard on the project. It would be cruel to drop any one of her friends.

"Let's draw straws and decide," Raj suggested.

"I don't want to draw a straw. I can't back out now."

"Perhaps I should back out," Shakti said.

"No, you can't. You are our leader."

"You brought everything and everyone together." Raj had a determined look on his face. "Don't even think about it."

"Maybe she *should* back out," another member of the group chimed in. "She has won so many awards. She doesn't need another one. I could use the first award in my life."

"But if we don't have her on the team, we might not win." Raj stood up tall.

"The project's already done, and she can still help us. What do you say, Shakti?"

"Yes and yes," Shakti replied. "It's our dream to win the intercollegiate science competition. I'll make sure you have the best talking script for the project."

Kriya-di had once told Shakti that *JR* was highly admired because she cared for her people and carried them with her. *JR*'s was a tale of an ordinary girl who went on to become an extraordinary ruler and a courageous fighter for her people. She always put their welfare before her own personal glory.

"What about you?" Raj looked her in the eye as he sat back down.

"Don't worry about me. You five can go and do it for our college. I know it."

Later when her mates walked up on the stage to accept the first prize, Shakti's eyes welled up with tears of pride for her teammates. Tears of joy to see their principal's beaming face. Tears of love for Kriya-di for teaching her the best lessons in life.

And now, her tears flowed along with the cold tap water. Shakti shut the tap, dried her face, and stepped out of the bathroom.

The Inspector was peering around her apartment. Shakti liked to keep the drapes drawn and windows closed, to shut out the smoke, heat, and traffic noise, but the Inspector had opened up all the drapes and windows.

"Nice apartment. You make good money?" he asked.

"The pay is good with international airlines and they sign long term contracts." It was a well adorned, third floor apartment in the Sea Princess building in Versova with a living room, a study, two bedrooms, and a bathroom. It was furnished in good taste, with high grade furniture. Plush red leather sofa, two comfortable chairs with matching cushions, a full-size mirror, a coffee-table, and exclusive, framed wall art.

"How much do you get?"

"Well, it depends on how many hours we fly and the layover allowances. We have a base salary and a variable part. It's not bad at all."

"Do you mind if I look around?"

"No problem. It might be a little messy though." Shakti walked the Inspector inside while the constable stayed out. "This is my small room. And this here is Kriya-di's bedroom. It's bigger and has windows."

"How come her bed is all ruffled up?"

"She wasn't at home last night and I simply plopped in her bed. It's more comfortable than mine."

The Inspector looked around. The room's highlight was the big queen-sized bed and headboard. The nightstand held an exotic lamp, a clock-radio, and the telephone. There was a big dresser with a full-size mirror and cupboards along the wall. "Hmm...How about the neighbors? Do you think they might know anything?"

"I'll check with the aunties. Hold on a minute. I'll be right back."

The Inspector ignored her and followed her out.

Shakti rang the first doorbell. "Sita-kaku, have you seen Kriya-di?"

Sita-kaku scrutinized the Inspector and the constable. "The last I saw her was two weeks ago. She borrowed a cup of milk. Is she ok?"

"Let me check with Nisha-aunty." *Triing, tring.* "Have you seen Kriya-di?"

"I saw her only yesterday," said Nisha-aunty.

"Really, when?" asked Shakti all excited. Kriya-di wasn't missing. She was fine.

"Yesterday, was it? No. Today? No. Maybe two weeks ago."

"Why are you even asking Nisha?" said Sita-kaku. "She has no sense of time. She has ten clocks in her house, but doesn't know if it's yesterday or tomorrow."

Shakti dropped her shoulders. Nisha-aunty gave Sita-kaku a stern glare.

Sita-kaku continued, "I see this Nisha outside her apartment door all confused. She doesn't even remember if she was going out or coming back in."

"Well, if you remember anything, anything at all, let me know," Shakti said.

Shakti and the police walked back into her apartment. "Sir, if you don't mind, I have a severe headache and I need tea. Will you have some?"

The Inspector and the constable nodded and Shakti went into the kitchen.

"How did you become an air hostess?"

"Kriya-di was already a flight attendant. So, when I finished my college and -"

"You like to copy her?"

"I was fascinated by planes and flying. It was always a dream of mine."

"So Ms. Kriya used her connections to get you a job?"

"No, it's not her nature to ask for favors. She let me go through the rigors."

"What rigors?" The Inspector yawned.

"You know at that time, we didn't have FrankFinn, the training institute. Kriya-di taught me everything she knew. How to articulate and speak effectively. How to pronounce correctly and build my vocabulary. Proper manners and gestures."

"Well, she's done a good job. She seems like a good teacher."

"Yeah, she's the best. I always wanted to be like Kriya-di." Shakti brought out the tea along with some toast and Parle-G biscuits.

"Good chai. It's got a nice punch of ginger to it."

"Kriya-di loves it this way." The herbal aroma of ginger awakened memory of Kriya-di; she was so grumpy in the morning. You couldn't talk to her until the first sip of her ginger-infused tea. She dipped in her toast and ate it soggy. Then she got all chatty.

"Shakti, was there anything out of the ordinary in the last few months? Anything you can remember?" asked the Inspector, with a furrowed brow.

"Well, now that you mention it, there was this weird guy. This stalker. Initially, we didn't know who he was. Every week he left a long-stemmed red rose outside our door, cut nine inches precisely and with all thorns removed."

"Hmmm…"

"One hot and sweltering day, the courier delivery boy rang our bell. He wiped his forehead and asked Kriya-di for a glass of water. The kind soul that Kriya-di is, she went into the kitchen to fetch it. When she came out, Vicky was gone and on the –"

"Vicky?"

"His actual name is Vikram. He was gone. And on the coffee table, right at this spot, was a long-stemmed red rose, cut to nine inches and with all the thorns removed."

"How does Vicky look?"

"Average height, say five feet, six inches. Skinny like a pencil and with a slight slouch. Very young, maybe in his high teens. He looks innocent, like a kid."

"Like a kid?"

"Yeah. Like a kid. His face is clear and his eyes are round, child eyes. Wavy hair. Sunken cheeks. He was such a shy and reserved boy. We were surprised when he acted like that. And yes. He stuttered. Mostly on any 'K' or 'C' words. He would go 'C...C...C...Courier' or 'K...K...K...Kriya'. It was terrible. We felt sad for him."

"Did he do anything after that incident?"

"Once when I came from work, I found a large envelope by our door with the rose. It said "My Dearest Kriya" on the top and it smelled of a cheap street perfume. Kriya-di was furious when she opened it later that night. A letter."

"Do you have the letter with you? Can I take a look?"

"Certainly Inspector." Shakti brought it out and the Inspector read it:

My Dearest Kriya

It hit me...hit me hardly. I come your house...you not inside. I walk around like fool. I do nothing. I hear nothing but your voice...I see nothing but your face. I want to hear you call me 'Dear'...and give glass of water.

I stop street beggars from singing...I want to hear your voice. When I with you...I forget all. I sit on sofa...I wish I feel your head on my shoulder.

I think I go to bed. I write half-hour...will you write to me I hope you will. How I sign this to you I no sign at all...not know what to call myself. Boyfriend Lover?

"This Vicky sounds crazy. A complete mental case," said the Inspector.

"Yes, we were distressed. We bolted all doors and windows and kept the lights on at night. I was afraid so I slept in Kriya-di's room."

"Did you two tell anyone?"

"No, we didn't want to alarm people. We complained to the courier agency and asked them to remove Vicky from our delivery route and to put him someplace far away. All went quiet for a few weeks. No long-stemmed roses at our doorstep. We were relieved, until one Friday evening when Kriya-di found a second envelope at our door."

"Where were you?"

"She had sent me to the bank to get cash from our joint account."

"What did it say this time?"

"When Kriya-di read it, she dropped it to the floor in disgust. Here, you can read. It's written in blood."

My Dearest Kriya

You suffer...I know you suffer. How much I love you...I know you love me more. But you afraid of people...you hide your love.

People no let me come to your house...I laugh. If no you, no food for me. Our love holy...our love secret. No tell anybody. People no understand.

You and I same person...where you be I be. If we no live together... we die together. You and I be together in heaven... after we die.

Love you with my blood.
Vicky

"Did you to go to the police?"

"We were scared Vicky would harm us. He had warned not to tell anybody."

The Inspector scowled and shook his head in disapproval.

"We gave the building watchman some money to keep Vicky out."

"Did that help?"

"Oh yes. Our watchman is dedicated. And he has his guard-dog, *Tiger*; this large, intimidating Doberman."

"So then, your Vicky troubles were over? Chapter closed?"

"No sir, then the blank phone calls began. We could hear breathing on the other side, only deep rhythmic breathing, but no one spoke."

"That could've been anybody."

"I know it was Vicky. Maybe he got our number from the courier agency. So, we got our phone number changed. That stopped his calls at last."

"That must have pissed him off. If you don't mind, can I take a smoke?"

"Uh, ok, yeah, that's fine. Umm…Can you please do it on the balcony?"

The Inspector stepped out onto the terrace. He took out his cigarette and a small, red lighter from his left pocket. He lit it in one shot. As he blew out smoke puffs, Shakti could sense his mind churning away. He seemed absorbed in inhaling and breaking down all the information he'd received. What was he thinking?

The balcony door opened and the Inspector stepped back in. His cigarette stench walked in with him. Oh, how she hated that disgusting odor. Smoke always brought back to her the unsettling memories of that fatal night in Latur. When he opened his mouth to speak, the nausea slapped Shakti across her face.

"So, was that the last of Vicky?" The Inspector waved his hands to drive the cigarette smell away, realizing that she wasn't comfortable around it.

"No. About three months ago, Vicky followed Kriya-di to work and stopped her outside the office. Rocky-da rescued her and they -"

"Who's Rocky?"

"He's Kriya-di's boyfriend. After he rescued her, they started seeing each other," Shakti said with shyness. She scrutinized the Inspector's face for any reaction. Dating wasn't an accepted social behavior in India.

"No, that's alright. Nothing wrong with it," said the Inspector. But she could see he didn't mean it. He continued, "So tell me what this Rocky does."

"Sir, he's a pilot with Trans Pacific. That's where Kriya-di met him. They hit it off from the first moment. He's one of their best. I like Rocky-da. He's a good guy."

"Okay, go on. What happened when Kriya ran into Vicky?"

"She got down from the auto rickshaw outside her office. Out of nowhere, Vicky appeared with a rose. He went down on one knee and said,

'Will you marry me?' Kriya-di was taken aback. She stood there, pale and frozen; she couldn't move a muscle."

The Inspector and the constable didn't make the slightest noise.

"By chance, Rocky-da was parking his motorcycle at the same time. He sensed something wasn't right and he edged towards them."

The Inspector crouched up at the edge of the sofa.

"Vicky shouted at Rocky-da to mind his own business. Kriya-di managed to unfreeze herself; she said Vicky was stalking and tormenting her."

Constable Mane scratched his arm in anticipation.

"Rocky-da gave Vicky a tight slap that sent him flat to the ground. He warned Vicky that if he ever troubled her again, he'd be behind bars."

The Inspector eased up on the sofa.

"At last, the message entered his insane, stubborn mind. Vicky got up with great effort and walked away. That was the last we saw of him."

"So, you haven't seen or heard from Vicky in the last three months... You think he has a hand in Kriya's disappearance?"

"Yes, he might have something to do with it. He has a motive and a prior history."

"Thank you so much for your help. Can I keep the letters? I'll make copies."

"Yes, Inspector. No problem."

"Can I also get Kriya's photo? We'll publish her description in a police notice and flash a wireless message to all Mumbai police stations."

Shakti darted into the bedroom and came out with a picture. "Here it is. Let me know if you have any more questions. I'll be glad to help."

The Inspector stepped out and pressed the elevator button.

Shakti shut the apartment door and stepped out onto the balcony for some fresh air. From the hanging flower pots that she'd watered came a steady, volatile patter of water dripping onto the floor. She rubbed her eyes with her palms. Her breath slowed.

I pray from the bottom of my heart that Kriya-di is safe. I wish she would simply ring the doorbell and appear before me, teasing me, "Scared you, didn't I? Where would I go, dear? I was tricking you. I wanted to see how you'd be without me."

"Don't ever do that to me again. I can't live without you," Shakti said aloud, and pointed with her index finger. It brushed against something - a small red object. She picked it up; the Inspector's lighter. He'd forgotten it, but he couldn't have gone too far. She could still catch him.

Shakti rushed out of the apartment and down the stairs. She didn't want to wait for the elevator. She stepped into the parking garage and saw the

Inspector walk towards his motorcycle. His phone rang and he answered it as he stood next to his bike.

"Hello. Yes, this is Gore. Yes, I finished talking to her."

Shakti slowed down in her stride. She could clearly see and hear him from behind the garage wall. He now held his *takeoff* expression. It was fixed, like the progress of a Boeing 747. His eyes never veered left or right.

"She was predictable, exactly like the caller said. She even suggested Vicky as the potential suspect."

Shakti stopped dead in her tracks.

"She gave me all kinds of involuntary clues. Either she is super-smart or she thinks we're stupid. But without a doubt, she has the motive."

Shakti's head reeled. She felt light and dizzy.

"She wore the victim's top and slippers. She was sleeping in her bed as if she knew the victim wasn't coming back."

Shakti's knees shook. She held onto the wall for support.

"Yes, I was careful. But she revealed a lot: 'Kriya-di taught me everything I knew...I always wanted to be like her...We have a joint bank account.'"

Shakti now squatted on the floor. The harsh wall pricked her back.

"She went on and on. She liked Rocky, the victim's boyfriend."

Shakti couldn't breathe. She couldn't think.

"Yes, order a *masala dosa*[25]. I'll talk to you when I get to the station."

Shakti sank to the ground, her eyes in a daze. Her ears involuntarily tuned out, missing the deafening roar of the motorbike starting. Her nose oblivious to the sickening smoke from the bike's exhaust. Her tongue unaware of the salt in the tears that trickled down. And the skin of her back immune to the scratches from the rough concrete wall.

Shakti looked at the Om pendant around her neck. Through the lenses of her tears, it flickered with a rainbow glimmer. She kissed it, looked heavenwards, and whispered: *"Ring, Rang Raksha Raksha Goraksha.[26]"*

---

25 Masala dosa: Fermented crepe with spicy stuffing
26 Ring, Rang Raksha Raksha Goraksha: Protect me, my Lord!

"The question isn't who is going to let me; it's who is going to stop me."
- Howard Roark, The Fountainhead

CHAPTER 6

"It's turbulent today," said the Canadian with an evil grin. "Gonna be a fun ride."

As the plane rose to 13,000 feet, Shiva looked ahead at Hong. His pal from China was silent, with pale skin stretched taut over his high cheekbones. Hong's eyes squinted through his glasses, almost closed in denial, while his face puckered in tension.

Right across the aisle, Harry's eyes stared wide open. He was busy muttering. Shiva tried to tune in. Harry was praying to the Lord with all his life.

"I was a techie like you guys." The Canadian behind Shiva chattered away. "I worked my ass off at Intel, doing the boring 9-to-5 thing. I was fed up. One day I said, 'Hell with it,' and I went looking for life and adventure."

At that moment, an instructor opened the exit door on the little Cessna, a rolling shutter door that rattled as it withdrew. Cold wind rushed in and smacked Shiva in the face. Why the heck were they doing this? It was crazy. It was insane.

First up was Hong. He was the closest to the exit door. Hong's face froze, his jaw clenched, and his lips sealed shut. His tandem instructor dragged him along and made him suspend his legs off the edge of the plane. Hong's arms shook against his will. Anxiety surged though his entire body.

Shiva thought of the advertisement they had read earlier: *You've watched others do it, seen the videos and photos, and thought to yourself, "I've really gotta try that one day." Well, don't put it off any longer; let Bay Area Skydiving make that dream a reality today. Imagine the thrill of 60 seconds of freefall. A tandem skydive is the easiest way to make your first skydive. It's a fun, low stress introduction to sport parachuting.*

Hong dangled half-way out. His face didn't reflect fun or low stress at all.

Ten years ago, right after he was fired, Shiva had approached Harry and Hong to start a company together. But they had expressed doubts and reflected on the past failures of other co-workers. They asserted that doing a start-up was a huge risk. A big plunge. It was a world where the rules of survival were vastly different. Challenges were more dangerous and the price of a mistake was much higher.

"My father won't be happy," Hong said. "He won't support me."

"It's a no-brainer. Do you want to be a creator or a parasite?" Shiva asked.

"My father would rather have me work for a large company first," Hong replied. "Get some experience before I jump into a start-up."

"The creator stands on his own judgment. The parasite follows the opinions of others. The creator thinks. The parasite copies. The creator produces. The parasite loots." Shiva transformed into his passionate, convincing best - his Howard Roark best.

"My father will question me. My first job. Why am I not opting for stability?"

"The 'stability' of a large company? That's clearly an attempt to force men into a herd of brainless, soulless robots. It's only bureaucracy and politics there."

"If I wanted risk and uncertainty, I should've stayed back in China, he'd say."

"Think of the reward. If we're successful, you'll have ten times the money."

Hong fell silent as his mind churned.

Harry had his concern. "I have a good position at Alltech. People are reporting to me, and Boss has hinted at a promotion. He's promised more people on my team."

Shiva remembered Roark. His truth was his only motive. His work his only goal. He held his truth above all things. He went ahead whether others agreed or not, with his integrity as his only banner. "My dear Harry, throughout centuries there were men who took first steps down new roads, armed with nothing but their vision. The great creators, thinkers, artists, scientists, and inventors stood alone against the men of their time."

"I understand. But I'm comfortable in my job." Harry crossed his arms as he worried about the insecurity of their future. "The start-up path is invariably doomed, like walking on a landmine. Three out of four start-ups fail."

"I agree that the path is full of risk and that the challenges can drive people insane. But what's the fun without some challenge? Every new thought was opposed. Every new invention was denounced. But the men of unborrowed vision went ahead. They fought, they suffered, and they paid - but they won." The passion in Shiva's eyes could have lit a real fire. Howard Roark would've been proud in his imaginary grave. Ayn Rand would've smiled in acknowledgement.

Harry and Hong exchanged quizzical glances.

Shiva continued, "In life, you can choose to roar like a lion, like Roark, or moo like cattle in a herd. Innovation, hard work, and triumph. The thrill of a lifetime. I can't do it without you two. Let's roar, guys!"

Harry and Hong were inspired, hypnotized by Shiva's passion and his clarion call to entrepreneurship and achievement. They joined him on the journey and plunged into the start-up adventure with their heart, mind, and soul.

"Ready?" asked Hong's tandem instructor. Before Hong reacted, they plunged.

Next up was Harry. His prayer to the Lord had only increased in volume, from muttering to fervent pleas. Harry held onto the railing at the side of the exit door. His arms tense and fists clenched. Every part of his body screamed out a big NO.

"Ready, set, go!" Harry's instructor yelled, and they zoomed away from the Cessna. Harry screamed out his prayers.

Shiva was the last one to jump. A smile broke across his face.

"Remember. First tug - freefall position. Second tug - spread eagle. Got it?" said his Canadian instructor

"Got it." Shiva's heart hammered against his chest.

"Ready, set..."

Go was to be the next word. Shiva didn't hear it as they flung out. All he heard was the wind. The sound of earth rushing towards him at 120 miles per hour.

Shiva remembered the waiver. *Sign here. Initial there. Yes, I agree to sign my life away. I've no rights. Initial there. Yes, I acknowledge that Bay Area Skydiving isn't responsible for anything (initial), anytime (initial), anywhere. Sign there. No, I will not attempt to sue. Initial here. How can I sue if I'm dead? Print name. Sign below.*

One tug and they took the free-fall inverted V position with head and feet arched back and hips forward. They sped like a dart away from the propellers. The first few seconds were unreal. Shiva's lungs throbbed. His stomach roiled. His heart popped into his mouth and so did some other unrecognizable internal organs.

"Don't open your mouth," his instructor had warned Shiva.

Shiva let out a loud primal scream, a liberating roar. He let the rushing wind play with his face and hair. His mouth and lips were aflutter, flapping in freedom.

Second tug. Shiva stretched out his arms and legs in a spread eagle, slowing him down into a cruise-control mode. He felt like a bird, like an eagle floating in the skies. The view was stunning. The landscape a patch-work quilt. Tiny green pastures. Serene crystal-blue lake. Quaint red-roofed houses. The curving life-line of roads. Beautiful. The colorful canvas would be forever etched in his memory.

To top off the experience, it was the sunset load – the last skydive for that day. The evening sun blazed a brave fire from behind the distant mountains. Shiva's eyes shone with the bright spectacle of bold colors. He was ecstatic. Heaven.

He spotted Hong and Harry further away in the sky, waving in elation and having the time of their lives. All of them came closer, moving with the wind and then dispersing.

"Time to pull," his Canadian instructor said. "There it is. Grab it and pull."

Swooosh...yank. The parachute opened up and floated in the air. It went from a loud, rushing noise, like being on a motorcycle, to calm and peaceful, like being suspended in a luxury car. Peace and serenity of the canopy flight.

Shiva played with the direction of his parachute. Left. Right. A little up. Slow descent. He looked across to Harry, who was guiding his parachute down. At last, the trio glided into a soft, safe landing, back to earth.

"We came, we fell, we saw, we conquered. And we lived to tell about it. Amazing, isn't it?" proclaimed Harry.

All three of them held the biggest grins on their faces all day and all week. Shiva felt incredible. Charged up and energized. Adrenaline pumped through his body like never before. It was an awesome high. It was as if he was on a hundred cups of coffee.

It was a life-affirming event. Truth be told, Shiva, Harry, and Hong had risked their lives together and had come out stronger. Their bond grew tighter that day.

Ten years ago Shiva was fired. It was a life-changing event. He took it on the chin and didn't break. He started his own company out of his apartment. Harry threw away his cushy job. Hong moved to the Bay Area to work with them.

Shiva wondered many a time if he'd do it again. Had it been easy? Of course not. It had been a roller-coaster ride. Many ups and many downs. Several gut-wrenching moments. But they were lucky; the ups were more than the downs. They had stuck together through thick and thin.

All men dream, but not all in the same way. Those who dream by night, in the retreats of their minds, wake up in the sun to find that it was merely a fantasy. But the dreamers of the day are death-defying, for they act on their dreams with open eyes and make them happen. Experience warned Shiva and team that it was unachievable, and reason said that it was reckless, yet they decided to dream anyway. In their greatest challenge, they found opportunity. They dared to march to a different beat.

Hong was the innovation engine. He was the brains of the company. His mind was a fertile farmland that sprouted thousands of brilliant seeds. The number of genius ideas that he spawned was incredible. He kept their start-up paranoid and hungry for radical leaps. He ensured a technology lead over the competition.

Hong believed in the power of the idea. He had the killer idea for their company in the middle of Dumbarton Bridge as he drove across from Palo Alto to his apartment in Union City. The idea was so powerful that when Shiva heard it, he said, "Hong, hang up the phone. Don't say another word on your cell. I'm coming over."

Shiva drove like a maniac to Union City and they went for a hike up the Seven Hills Peak. Ideas blended as they brainstormed in synchronous lockstep. They hurdled over the obstacles together, like two battle knights striding side by side. The sun had let loose brilliant streaks of red, orange, pink, and yellow across the skies. The resulting vivid medley over the bay was unique and audacious.

It was such a powerful idea, that sleep was out of the question for Shiva that night. The seed now germinated in his head, absorbing water and nutrients from his brain's soil. The idea drew in his mind's light for photo-synthesis and grew into a wondrous sapling. Shiva stayed up all night staring at the Bay Bridge, jotting down key elements of their business plan. That's how their journey began, on the flying seed of a powerful idea.

Hong's favorite spot was in front of his computer screen, his mind churning out the next best thing. He'd say, "The real work of Silicon Valley occurs in the mind; in the minds of geniuses sitting still in their cubicles, staring at small screens, and meditating on challenges. That's where innovation occurs. That's where paradigm shifts happen. That's where the action goes frenetic without moving a single external muscle."

Hong embodied Franz Kafka's[27] unique Kafkaesque style. Hong didn't need to leave his working space. He remained seated at his desk, listening. He didn't even listen; he simply waited. He didn't even wait; he simply stayed tranquil. The world of ideas gifted itself to him, to be unveiled; it had no choice as it rolled in bliss at his feet.

Harry was the arms and legs of the company, the efficient implementer. Any idea, no matter how brilliant, is a waste if not executed in the right manner. Harry had the ability to not merely execute and deliver, but to exceed all expectations. He traveled anywhere, anytime, if the customer demanded. His straightforward style went well with them; they connected with him and opened up with their needs. Customer success was his passion. He lived it and breathed it, and made everyone else live and breathe it too.

Beyond work, Harry loved only two things that could match up to his love for Sally: laughter and cooking. Harry's humor had in it more spice than his chicken *vindaloo*. After a few alcohol shots, his humor took an unprecedented zing. People were found rolling on the floor, laughing in hysteria.

Shiva was the fearless leader, the heart and soul of the company. He brought passion and optimism. When things got tough, people turned to him and he helped them in their internal and external struggles. He was the Noah of their Ark, captaining the company as it sailed through turbulent waters. And he was no distant, ivory tower figurehead; he preferred to roll up his sleeves and be amidst the guys with the oars.

Shiva got everyone harmonized. That's the essence of what a leader does because when harmony breaks down into cacophony, all minds grind to a halt. Nobody is productive. Mental energy is diverted to infighting. That can drown a start-up in the raging waters of competition. Getting everyone synchronized can make all the difference. Shiva harmonized the company, moving it like a well-oiled ship towards a destination.

"Every morning Shiva came to work," joked Harry, "straight from a breakfast meeting. Then lunch with someone and after work he put on a

---

27 Franz Kafka: German author regarded by critics as one of the most influential authors of the 20th century. He heavily influenced genres like existentialism.

suit to have dinner with a third person. He's a networking maniac and he's good at it."

Shiva knew that in Silicon Valley, the only kinds of people the network discriminated against were those who turned their noses up at networking. It was a meritocracy but a perverted one, based more on the merit of how well you knocked on doors than the merit of your C++ or Java code.

Shiva was fearless, but sometimes his back would be right up against the wall. On one occasion, their cunning Alltech ex-Boss spread poison and misinformation to three key beta customers. If they lost those customers, it was end of story. Chapter 11 bankruptcy. Boss's words echoed in Shiva's mind: *I know every single person of any importance in this industry. You think you've got a spine. You know what? I'll break you. I'll bring you down wallowing in misery. That's my freaking promise to you.*

Shiva worried about the personal responsibilities of his team. Hong was now married. Harry had put in a significant down payment towards his first house. Two other colleagues had their first babies. Shiva was determined not to let Boss have the final laugh. No way would Shiva lose the three beta customers; no way would he let down Hong, Harry, and his team. It was time to call up Pa for inspiration. Shiva always looked for strength from Pa, and why wouldn't he?

Pa was born as Jagannath in a small, remote town in rural Maharashtra. His friends later called him Juggernaut. He lost his parents at an early age, even before he turned six. He had a rough childhood, raised by his stepmother. Everything was a struggle. Struggle for food. Struggle for clothes. Struggle for affection. He was always at the bottom of the totem-pole. Nothing was given to him easily.

When milk was served in the morning, Pa would get the last glass, filled more with water than milk. When chicken was cooked in the house, he would get the bowl with only the bones, no meat. He was not entitled to new clothes, only hand me downs. His clothes were always muddied, always torn in some place.

Pa's struggles had only made him more resilient. He walked eight miles every day to school. Come sun, cold, or the thunderous monsoon, he sprinted through them all. He excelled in studies and was a star in the sports arena, winning his school trophies at district and state level competitions. His teachers were proud of him. His spirit and courage grew with age. He kept dreaming, kept striving, and kept achieving.

Pa's mental strength and ambition took him to college, then engineering in Pune and a job in Mumbai, which lasted for only a short while. He was bold enough to venture into his own business, into a domain that was not the forte of his clan. But like everything else he touched, he turned it into gold.

Shiva picked up the phone and dialed Mumbai. "Pa, need your advice."

"What is it son? What's bugging you?"

"My ex-Boss is up to his mischief again." Shiva explained the customer situation.

"You remember Raktim, the big bully in your high school? You remember your boxing match with him?" Pa asked.

"I remember that fight." Raktim was this tough kid and the school boxing champ, but that boy really was the Leonardo da Vinci of cuss words. He created masterpieces that starred your mom, your sister, a minimum of six body parts, five vegetables, one historical relic, and three types of farm animals. And that was only to say hello.

"Shiva, I can still see it in dramatic colors. The anxious excitement in the noisy arena. The red color of your defiant gloves. And the worried look on your mother's face."

"Pa, we're hanging by our finger-nails. I've put on a bold façade of strength to motivate my team, but I'm a worried man deep inside." Shiva couldn't hold back his thoughts. He could feel Boss's breath creeping down the back of his neck.

"My dear son, I bring up that fight because you can apply it to your current situation. Raktim was shouting taunts and striking poses, but you weren't intimidated. You went to the middle and gave him a strong intense stare. You meant serious business. The first learning was to send out a clear, powerful message."

Shiva listened with intent.

"The second learning was to fight to your strengths – not to his. You changed the game. He was taller and bigger, had more power, but he lacked your speed and agility. And you didn't go for his face which was out-of-reach. You went inside, into his body. Short spurts of body-blows. You resorted to guerilla warfare."

Pa's words made sense.

"And the third learning was to remember that it's all in the mind. You believed and fought like a winner. The crowd began to believe in you. That played on Raktim's mind; he couldn't focus. His mind weakened and he lost the fight."

The wheels of Shiva's mind shifted gears. He comprehended Pa's message.

"Remember what your boxing coach always said. The old man was wise. His truism for boxing, and for life as a whole, was: *Jo dar gaya so mar gaya*[28]."

"Thank you. Thank you. Thank you." Shiva couldn't help but smile in gratitude.

"One more thing, son…"

"Yes, what is it?"

"Once you've resolved your issues, can you make a quick trip to Mumbai? Your Ma's health isn't keeping too well."

"Certainly. Is everything ok? Should I come over right now?"

"No, no. It's not that serious. Come when you've things under control. She'd be happy to see you. And so would I."

"Sure Pa."

In less than a month, Shiva did three things. First, he partnered with a strong customer advocate who announced the successful launch of their flagship product, all enabled by Shiva's software. It was timed at the most prestigious industry conference, sending out a clear, powerful message to all.

Second, he engaged each of the three customers at an engineer-to-engineer level. Harry identified the biggest problems with their competitor's tools – their Achilles' heels. Hong then attacked these problems and conjured up an industry-best solution, producing results that were far superior. Guerilla warfare.

Third, Shiva behaved like a winning leader from a winning company. Everyone else in the company began to behave like winners too. The three customers believed in them, seeing clear value in their product, and doubled down, buying more software seats. Shiva and his company climbed out of danger zone. It was onwards and upwards again.

Now in Mumbai, Shiva wondered how he had let Ma trick him into coming. She was all hale and hearty. After he had landed, she let him rest for a day and then took him to a family friend's house the very next day. Pa, her loyal accomplice, was in tacit tow.

Within minutes of small talk, everyone in the living room went silent. Out walked a pretty girl in a modern *salwar-kameez* with gold *dupatta*, serving tea from a silver pot while the rest watched in eagerness. Shiva realized he'd been set up.

---

28 Jo dar gaya so mar gaya: One who is scared, is as good as dead

Ma spoke about how the girl was educated and cultured; knew cooking, singing, embroidery, and even wrote poetry. Questions were asked and answers given with sweet smiles, but afterwards Shiva couldn't recall much of what had been said. He watched the hot steam disappear from his cup and a thin layer form on top as the tea went cold.

When they stepped out of the family friend's house, Shiva was quiet.

Ma said, "I don't understand why you don't want to get married."

"Ma, it isn't the right time. I'm extremely busy. I've no time even for myself."

"If you wait too long, all the good girls will be gone."

Shiva didn't answer. Pa jumped in to his rescue, trying to change the topic. "I'm sorry your friend Harry couldn't make it to Mumbai this time."

"Yeah, it's a shame."

"And what's with your President George W. Bush sending in troops to end Saddam Hussein's threat and the Iraq insurgency?"

"I know. Now, after Saddam's capture, the CIA is admitting there was no imminent threat from weapons of mass destruction."

Shiva closed his eyes as he lay in the back of the car, pretending to sleep.

Ma complained to Pa, "I'm sure he has some secret, manipulative white girlfriend. She's got him wrapped in the blanket of her peach skin and trapped in the dreams of her blue eyes. She's stealing my poor little boy away from us."

After coming home, Shiva escaped to his room and sunk into the bed. Ma stormed into the kitchen, tearing around the cabinets and cutlery. She liked to keep busy when she was upset, and let everyone else know.

Suddenly, she appeared in his doorway with a bowl in her hand. "What type of girl are you looking for? Who's this celestial princess you're waiting for? Who, who, who?" She started to whisk the eggs in the bowl.

Shiva was unable to shed light on her question. He was unable to condense the girl he was waiting for into a list of ten qualities. He was unable to summon up the words for the amorphous rebuttal that rose from his gut.

Ma realized he wasn't going to answer. "Shiva, I want to go to Badrinath temple."

Shiva rose up from his bed. "What?"

"I want to visit Badrinath temple in the Himalayas."

"Now?" Shiva rubbed his eyes and swung his feet to the floor. "Well, I'll take a longer vacation next time I come to India and we can go."

"I'll go only when you get me a daughter-in-law. That's a sick woman's dying wish." Ma was beating the eggs at about a hundred angry miles a minute.

"Ma, please don't talk like that. There's nothing wrong with your health." Shiva walked to her and hugged her firmly.

Ma sobbed at his chest. "I want to see you married. Then I can die peacefully."

"Pa, it looks like I'll miss the flight to San Francisco." Shiva called from the taxi on his way to Mumbai airport. "Sally reached the airport on time and her flight to Australia has already left. But my cab has been in the same spot. Nothing's moving."

"You left the house way before your boarding time. Traffic can be a mess on Juhu Lane though. I hope it clears up soon," Pa said.

Little by little, the cars began to move. There was some hope. A tiny sliver. Shiva exhorted the taxi-driver to go faster, but he continued to be lethargic. What was wrong with the guy? Why wasn't he listening? Maybe he couldn't understand the accent.

As soon as they got to the airport, Shiva rushed through the doors, hoping the check-in lines would be short. But it wasn't his lucky day. He found dozens of passengers in the long queue ahead and it was moving at a snail's pace. He urged them to let him bypass the line. No such good fortune.

Shiva's phone rang; it was Pa. "I contacted a friend who works at the airport and explained your plight. He's sending someone to help you; a flight attendant named Shakti. She's at the airport right now. She'll make sure you get onto your flight."

Shiva waited. The check-in line crawled. He was worried. He couldn't miss his flight. He had to get back to San Francisco. He scanned around for Shakti. He didn't even know what she looked like.

Then he saw her.

A slender woman with lustrous skin and dark-brown hair that seemed to sway in a gentle heavenly drift. A rainbow colored halo shone all around her. Time paused as he absorbed her radiance. Her lips arched in a sweet angelic smile.

"Are you Mr. Shiva?"

Her voice tickled his ears. It made the bristles on his arms tingle. He'd heard people say that voice was more than half of love. His heart nodded in pulsating agreement. Her voice triggered a symphony in his head.

"Yes, I'm Shiva."

"My name is Shakti. Jeet Sir asked me to help you." Shakti took his passport and ticket, bypassed the queue, and walked straight to the counter.

Shiva followed her in a trance. He studied her. She wasn't that tall but her upright shoulders, perfect posture, and a head held up straight gave her a quiet, resolute charisma. Her Trans Pacific flight attendant dress accentuated her infatuating shape. There was a certain innocence in her smile and a friendliness in her round face.

"Mr. Shiva, would you prefer a window or an aisle seat?"

"Shakti, please call me Shiva. And yes, an aisle seat would be great."

She was the most beautiful woman he'd ever seen, and those light brown eyes... Shiva was lost in her eyes, plunging in and suspending himself without restraint in the iridescent lake of her gaze. She had the most amazing sandy brown eyes. It was the brown of the sands that surround blue oceans in vibrant dreams. It was the brown that a heavenly beach would be, if the beach was perfect.

"Shiva, here's your boarding pass. Now let's head for immigration."

Aha, the sound of his name on her lips, without the distancing, divisive *Mr.* It resonated in his head. It lingered on inside, even amidst the airport clamor outside.

Then, Shakti transformed into a woman on a mission. She sliced through the crowds. She skipped arduous immigration queues and pleaded urgency to the security officers. She was like Joan of Arc leading the battle for him and paving a victorious way.

It was the fastest he'd ever navigated through an airport. They reached the gate with time to spare. "Shakti, thank you so much. Allow me to treat you with a coffee."

"You're welcome. Sure," she said, and their eyes locked in anticipation.

"Great." Shiva couldn't hold back his joy. He rushed across to Barista Lavazza, the Espresso chain that claimed to capture a true Italian coffee experience in a cup.

Shakti watched Shiva as he walked towards Barista Lavazza. She couldn't help but marvel at him. She stood back, trying to suppress her propriety and decorum. How handsome he looked. She gazed as if in a dream.

He wore jeans and an easy white T-shirt that accentuated his V-shaped torso, barely covering his toned biceps. His face was striking, with a confident angular jaw, captivating brown eyes, and a sharp nose. He had tanned in the Mumbai summer to a dark olive, while his smile and teeth were radiant and blinding, almost like an eclipse and hazardous to gaze at - as if one would succumb to the brilliance.

Shakti tried hard to rein back her senses. It was futile. With one look into her eyes, he had the power to render her weak in the knees. It was unimaginable not to appreciate him. It was tough not to want to do something to enclose that handsomeness. Snuggle into his shirt and rest there for the remainder of her life.

Shiva walked back, focused and careful so as not to spill any coffee. He handed her the hot cup. The touch of his fingers sent a tickle up her arm. She saw that the coffee was too dark, not enough milk. But she knew it would taste delicious to her anyway.

He looked at her sides, first to the right and then to the left. Then he paused.

"What is it?" she asked.

"I'm searching for your wings. The wings that make you fly. You're an angel helping me fly back to San Francisco, aren't you?"

The words came out of his mouth and strummed her deep inside. Not the words themselves, but the sound of the words. He had a rich, soft voice. Not a deep bass like a radio announcer, but husky, like raw-edged velvet. There was a unique quality to it that reached out and drew her closer. Inviting and reassuring, it felt like a warm embrace. She said, "Haha. I'm no angel from heaven. Jeet Sir sent me."

He flashed an impish smile and blinked his eyes.

She loved the shape of his jaw and the bright grin as his lips parted. She pointed to the pin on her uniform. "The only wings I have are these. And I'm proud of them."

"Those are beautiful."

"Yes, aren't they? I still get goose-bumps when I remember our graduation ceremony when they pinned these wings onto our uniforms." *And I owe it all to my Kriya-di; she gave me the strength and confidence to fly on my own wings.*

"Nice. Like the Air Force and Army personnel getting their honor badges. Was it a tough journey to it?"

"The ceremony was all song and dance, but that was the finale of a long selection and training program. Guess how long I had to wait on my first round of interviews?"

"Umm...I've no idea. Maybe two hours?"

"Think again. Hundreds of kids in a long serpentine queue. I had to wait in the hot and humid sun for five hours. No food or water."

"Five hours! Holy cow!"

"That was merely the beginning. They made us speak one sentence in front of the judges and then moved us into the waiting room."

"One sentence? After waiting five hours in the sun?"

"It was Round 1. The organizer came into the room. He announced a list of names and took them with him. I was so disappointed that my name wasn't announced."

"Really, how's that even possible? I wouldn't reject you." Shiva had that mischievous smile again. Mostly goodness. A little naughtiness.

"It turned out the ones left behind were selected for Round 2. It was such a relief."

"That must've been nerve-racking," Shiva said as he bent towards her. A waft of his refreshing cologne enveloped her. He had no American airs about him. No attitude. Purely a simple but exciting charm with a splash of humor thrown in.

"Then came the written exam and the results. I had my fingers crossed, hoping and praying that my name wasn't announced, but it was, so I had to leave the room."

"What? You were rejected after the written exam?"

"Well, this time, the ones left in the room were the ones rejected. The organizers switched their method on us. Funny twist."

"Haha. That was very devious of them. Was that it then?"

"No. We had group discussions, emotional IQ testing, and then the final interview with the top management in a structured panel."

"Whoa. Even the U.S. President doesn't go through such rigor."

"They wanted to ensure that we didn't just talk the talk but could walk the walk."

"So, when did you start flying?"

"After a three-month training program on flight services, security, safety, and first-aid. First, they put us on two familiarization flights."

"Familiarization flights?"

"I didn't have any real work on those flights. I had to observe and learn. It was the first time I was in a real airplane."

"What? You hadn't flown before?"

"No."

"I'm glad you went on those flights. I wouldn't want my life in the hands of someone who hadn't flown before." Shiva flashed his impish smile again.

"I love to travel. In fact, if anyone wanted to win me over, all one would have to say is, 'I want to hike the Great Wall of China,' or 'I want to scale Machu-Picchu.' He could be a pencil-thin chap wearing thick soda-bottle glasses and I'd be like, "Let's do it."

Shiva rubbed his chin and asked in a casual tone, "So, you must meet interesting people when you travel from one place to another. Are you seeing someone?"

Shakti moved her hand towards her chest and crossed it across her front as if she'd been caught touching something that she wasn't supposed to. She knew her top priority was to find Kriya-di. "I…I'm not really looking right now. And it's tough to maintain a long-distance relationship anyway, what with all my travel."

"Oh no, me neither," Shiva added fast. "Work, you know, keeps me super busy."

"Well, you got my story," Shakti said, "but you haven't told me much."

Shiva grinned as wide as he could, exuding warmth. She was right. He scratched his brow, trying to mask his sharp nose. He hadn't told her much. But she was so adorable to listen to. She had such an aura of naiveté, mystique, and affection.

He took a deep breath. "I was born and brought up in Mumbai. I went to the U.S. to study and I've been working there for a decade. I have a simple philosophy: In life, you can choose to roar like a lion or meow like a cat with its tail between its legs. Roar…"

"Meow…" Shakti laughed and he felt a soft feather tickle his ears and heart. "Do you come to Mumbai often?"

"I come to see my parents, but I'd like to make more trips."

"What do you do?"

"I work in the semiconductor industry. I once told that to a relative of mine and he said, 'What? You aren't good enough to be a full conductor?'"

"That's funny," Shakti smiled, "though Mumbai's changed a lot since you left."

"But in my heart, I'm still a Mumbai boy. I love so many things about it. Tell me what your favorite part of the city is."

"I love Bandra. Fashion Street with its sidewalk shops. Bandstand with its big rocks and even bigger waves crashing against them."

"I had fallen on those big rocks when I was a kid and fractured both hands."

"Awww...I'm sorry..."

"No, don't worry. It was such a long time ago." Shiva pulled his sleeves back and stretched out both his hands in front, palms held up. "See, my right hand curves at the elbow like most people's hands, but the left hand is absolutely straight. Let me see yours."

Shakti stretched out both her hands in front, palms up, as he had done. They bent slightly at the elbow. She had slender, lustrous arms and he felt the urge to feel their warmth and softness. He refrained.

"See, I told you. I've got a uniquely straight left hand thanks to Bandra bandstand. But I have a bent index finger to make up for it. Here, see? It's bent to one side."

"Goodness! What happened?"

"At my friend's house in California, the automatic garage door was stuck. I tried to pull it down manually from outside. My right index finger got stuck in the panel folds and it dragged me all the way down to the ground. If I hadn't yanked it out by sheer will, the bone would've been crushed into a hundred pieces."

"It must have hurt badly." Shakti touched his fingers in distress, sending a current through him. "Broken hands, bent finger; you seem very accident-prone."

"Exactly what my Ma says." The words slipped out before he could stop them. Something in the sincerity of her look made him forget his inner censor. Who brings his Ma into a first conversation and also admits a flaw, when trying to impress a woman?

Shakti's brows remained arched in concern. She couldn't hide her nerves.

"But a bent finger has advantages. As they say in India, if butter doesn't come out with a straight finger, then you bend the finger to get it. Ha ha! I'm better prepared to tackle the world now." Shiva flashed his playful smile, making her smile too. "Shakti, there was a lovely church next to the bandstand, right? I forget the name."

"Father Angel church," Shakti said. "I love how the walls of the church rise up from the rocks. Bright green moss and climbing vines spill over the wall and wander out to the sea." In her excitement, she raised her arms and her long slender fingers made a little journey along the back of his hand as a climbing vine might have.

"Love that imagery." Shiva basked in her light, fleeting caress. His skin tingled in the memory of its magic. He couldn't believe how intoxicating it felt to be close to someone he had only just met. "What else do you like?"

"I love Marine Drive with its sparkling lights at night."

"Come here with me," Shiva said, as he stepped to the glass window and held his hand out to her. "Look at the sparkling planes land against the night sky."

Shakti left behind her coffee cup and took a tentative step towards him. She tripped over a small bag, falling against him. He turned to hold and steady her. He slipped his hand into hers as he led her to the window.

He felt the nervous pressure of her hand in his. It was a soft hand, and yet in its softness there was certain strength. A coy, rosy pink tiptoed to her cheeks. Her gentle fingers relaxed along his fingertips. Her touch was precisely what the touch of a soulmate's hand should be - familiar yet exciting. It was the pluck of a chord that stirred so many things inside him. A whispered warm melody of a promise. He felt an overwhelming urge to take her fingers and place them to his lips. Maybe he should've done that...

The loudspeaker interjected. Shiva's plane was ready to board. The announcement sent a chill between them and they stood frozen. He had been the prince of smoothness, but the announcement immobilized him. He didn't want to board. His heart urged him to stay back. He wanted to know her better. What were her passions? What did she hate? Who were her friends? But his rational mind reminded him he had a company to run and goaded him about all the work to be done and expectations to be fulfilled.

Shakti seemed to feel the contagion of his paralysis and stood with downcast lids. He reached forward and gave her a warm hug. Her aroma engulfed him, enticing him to stay. A few seconds seemed like an eternity, but still not enough. Strangers that they were, they stood lost in each other anyway, holding their longing gaze for some timeless moments. All the responsibilities that held them back, and all the possibilities they could let loose, whirled around them in turmoil.

At last, after searching about for a good opening, he cleared his throat. "The sky is overcast. There could be a chance of rain."

She broke out of her thaw. "Rain? Do you think the flight might get canceled?" She blushed red as the query escaped her.

Shiva drew closer. Her cheeks brushed against his, a light caress. He snuck in a peck on her cheek, as silent as the morning dew. He walked towards the gate. He paused in the doorway and glanced back, just in case she called out to him. He saw her face move in a shy, slow motion.

Shakti had edged closer to the railing. She leaned out for a parting glimpse. The Mumbai moisture settled on her long eyelashes and a speck of the Mumbai dust made its way into her eyes, making them wet and forcing her to blink.

"In a cat and mouse chase, the cat runs for its food and mouse for its life."
                                                    - Tom and Jerry (unconfirmed)

CHAPTER 7

Shakti stepped into the shower and stood under a throbbing stream of hot water. She knew someone was following her. Someone was stalking her. She had watched Hollywood movies and had read about stalkers in suspense thrillers, but they had always belonged in a different, distant world.

The water torrent was powerful, so she hovered below it with her face held up to it. She let it pound against her skin, moving the sting from the front to the back, and all the way down her body. She pondered the disappearance of Kriya-di, trying to pierce through the maze of the mist and the whirr of the water. She wished Kriya-di was safe. She couldn't figure out who would want to hurt her.

Shakti finished her shower and was stepping out when she heard a noise outside, a crash. She wrapped herself in a towel and tiptoed out of the bathroom. The water from her wet hair and body dripped onto the floor as she inched into the quiet living room. She saw no one, but the window was open, and the curtains flew aflutter. Her flower vase lay on the floor broken into pieces. It must have been the wind. She fastened the window shut.

Since the Inspector's visit, she had woken up in the middle of every night, gasping for breath and soaked in perspiration. She had a feeling of impending disaster. She tried hard not to lose her calm. She tried hard not to panic. She had to get out of the apartment. It was getting claustrophobic in there.

Shakti got dressed and went down the elevator. The parking garage seemed deserted and the watchman wasn't in his cabin. Something was amiss. She raced across the gate to the main street and onto the bus stand. Her heart pulsated under a sky the color of gloom, foreboding, and malevolence.

Rain was forecast, but Shakti insisted, with her eyes shut. *It's not going to rain. The sun will come out. I'll make a pact with you, God. If it doesn't rain, it means everything is alright. Kriya-di is okay and no one is following me.*

At the bus stand she still had an overpowering feeling that *he* was shadowing her. But who? And why? She scanned wide with her peripheral vision. Everything looked normal, but every intuition told her otherwise.

Bus #222 arrived and she got in with several other people. She felt safe. *Then it began to rain.* It wasn't a weak drizzle. The skies opened up. Drops the size of table tennis balls burst against the windows. The windshield wipers ran full blast, but visibility stayed low. The drumming on top of the bus sounded as if they were caught in the middle of gunfire. When the rain gods became angry in Mumbai, they unleashed hell.

The bus made its regular stops and wet faced passengers stumbled in. People with soaked umbrellas and raincoats, drenched clothes and hair climbed in, stamping their feet and wiping their faces. They brought the deluge from outside into the bus. Soon everything and everyone inside was wet.

Shakti was forced to stand, since all the seats were all taken. She glanced behind her. A gaunt man in a cotton blue shirt was staring at her. Could this be the stalker? But then the fat bloke next to him gazed at her too. Shakti veered her neck to look straight ahead. When she glanced back again, she noticed most of the men were ogling.

Indian men loved to stare, particularly in public places like buses and trains. Shakti and the other Indian girls were accustomed to it, but when her Trans Pacific colleagues from other countries came over, they found the staring uncomfortable. Even when a girl caught the men staring, they didn't show any shame; they continued staring.

Shakti remembered Kriya-di's explanation. First of all, India is a conservative country. Girls with western outfits will invite attention. Secondly, the men stare because that's how they show they're attracted to you. In the western world you're taught not to stare; it's bad manners. On the contrary, in India, some men not only stare but point fingers and smile too, as if they really want you to know that they're talking about you.

Some girls liked the attention, if it came from a nice, sweet guy. But as Tara, her colleague at work said, "The saddest part is that it's never the hot, good-looking guys who stare. I'd love to have them lock eyes, and maybe other body parts too, with me. But I only get stares from the ugly looking ones that scratch their balls in public."

Kriya-di had a solution. She'd say, "If they stare at me, I stare back. I show them that I'm not afraid to raise some tension. Whoever breaks

eye contact first is scared and stops. I never look away until they back off.
Believe me. You succeed doing this, because you catch them off guard.
They don't see it coming."

A school boy got up to dismount at his stop. Shakti sat down, at ease and
away from all the gawking eyes.

Shakti peeped out of the window. Roads had begun to become water logged. Mumbai always faced the brunt of heavy rains. Last year, the
monsoons were especially brutal. Clogged up drains. Submerged roads.
Toppled trees. And the unrelenting thrashing of the Arabian Sea. Walls
and bits of buildings had collapsed in some areas, killing people. The sub-
urban railway, the backbone of Mumbai's transportation system that ferries
millions of people every day, was jostled and shut down.

Shakti chided herself. She should have stayed at home. This happened
every year in Mumbai; its century old drains were unprepared to handle
even a meager rainfall. Poor drainage combined with high-tides flooded
the entire city and created havoc. After days of incessant rain, garbage and
waste lay scattered, causing further water logging. She didn't want to wade
through dirty chest high water and all the floating debris.

Then the rains stopped as suddenly as they had begun. The sun came
out from behind the clouds. Traffic picked up some speed. Everything glistened. The green trees. The washed up black roads. The polished multicolored apartment buildings.

Her eyelids now felt heavy, and the swaying bus didn't help. She hadn't
slept well the whole of last week. The bus rocked like a cradle, lulling her
towards slumber. She recollected events from the previous night.

It was the middle of night. Pitch dark. Shakti's dream had started
again. She woke up every night gasping for breath and soaked in perspiration. Fear stabbed into her chest and crushed her heart. It was always the
same dream.

Shakti stood on her school grounds, with her parents and brother
watching her. The stage and podium trembled. The principal's hands
shuddered and he let the trophy slip through his palms. Colossal crevices
formed and grew at their feet. She plummeted through a large, black fis-
sure. Her fingers came excruciatingly close to the gleaming trophy. For a
split second, she even touched it, but then the trophy separated away and
she plunged alone into an abysmal darkness. She kept falling. She tried
to fight gravity and stop her descent, attempting to hold onto something,
anything. She found nothing.

Shakti sat up on her bed. Eyes wide awake. What was that noise? Was it her cellphone? She kept it next to her pillow, hoping for a call that might come any minute to tell her that Kriya-di was fine. But no, it wasn't her phone. She held her breath and listened. Click-click-clicket-click-clickety-click-click. Not one cadence, but several uncoordinated clicks. She brought the clock on her nightstand to her ear. But the sound wasn't coming from her timepiece.

The faint, hurrying, ratcheting, dry clicking went on. She swept aside her blanket and crept out onto the balcony. The night outside was brighter than her room. She felt the low backdrop of the wind on her face and neck. The clicking sound grew much louder and faster. Its tempo was mixed – someone was running rods at different speeds along an iron railing. And it came from less than a block away.

Shakti stepped to the edge of the banister. She stretched and leaned over to peer down into the street. She couldn't detect anything. Then all of a sudden, it stopped. She stared into the eerie night. The chill of the wind started to bite her. As she turned around to go back into her room, it began again. Click-click-clicket-click-clickety-click-click. What could it be?

The sound was much closer and more earsplitting than before. It sounded like a hysterical woman's desperate laughter, but it was now ac-companied by footsteps. Slow, heavy steps. Possibly rain-boots.

No one else in the apartment building seemed affected. Was she the only one hearing the sounds? Was she imagining things? Then someone shouted out, "Stop that noise! We're trying to sleep in here!" It was Mr. Desai from the 2nd floor.

Smash. A bottle crashed to the earth, shattering into a thousand pieces. The ringing of each one of those thousand pieces of glass reverberated in the quiet night air. Shakti ran inside and bolted the balcony door.

A dog wailed a sad cry – a prolonged, high-pitched howl of pain and suffering.

The bus swayed like a boat but then suddenly stopped. "Bandra. Linking Road. Fashion Street," announced the bus conductor. Her destination.

For days after Kriya-di's disappearance, Shakti felt wrong to seek the company of anyone else. Loneliness offered its own form of company; the steadfast stillness of her rooms, the unwavering tranquility of the evenings; the reassurance that she would find things where she put them; that there would be no disturbances, no shocks.

But then, the objects and memories in her confined walls began to spook her. Every little thing reminded her of Kriya-di, from the toaster to the tea-cup; even the salt shaker. The recurring dreams of falling into an abyss made it that much worse.

Shakti felt she'd soon go certifiably crazy if she didn't step out of the house. She needed to get her mind off the recent events. She knew that Kriya-di's return was the only permanent remedy for her anxiety but until then, as Tara suggested, she had to rely on retail therapy - something to keep her brain cells distracted and occupied.

Shakti walked away from the bus stop. She heard a clanking jangle. She turned around, alarmed. She saw a beggar traveling on a small wooden platform with metal ball-bearing wheels. He spun off the footpath on the other side of the street. He pressed himself ahead with his hands until he was in the center of the empty road, sweeping to a stop with a theatrical whirl.

His bony, scrawny legs were folded beneath him on a piece of timber no bigger than an airplane food tray. He wore a cleaning-boy's uniform of khaki shorts and a khaki shirt. Although he was a man in his thirties, the clothes were still too large for him.

His hands, though, were massive for his body, his arm muscles sinewy like thick twine. Those were his primary tools for everything. His fingers and palms were wrapped thickly with cloth, like the inner wraps of a boxer's gloves.

"Abdul!"

"Shakti *memsaab*[29], how are you?"

As he came closer, she saw ugly bruises and scrapes on his right elbow and arm. "What happened, Abdul? How did you get hurt?"

"It's nothing. Dogs chased me down and I fell off my platform. By chance, some kids saw me and saved my life. But my bruises don't hurt."

"That's terrible. Dogs are attacking people now?"

"They're a big danger. Calm in the daytime, but hunting in fierce packs at night."

"Really?"

"*Memsaab*, a drunken man was attacked by a violent pack of dogs on the border of our slum last week. He's still in the hospital."

"What do they want? Can't they be stopped?" Shakti was saddened. Life in the slums was hard.

---

29 Memsaab: a variation of Memsahib, an Arabic term and a title for a woman in a position of authority

"I don't know what they want. But look at me; I'm such an easy mark. They go after anything small. A young child was killed in Dharavi on the spot, only a month ago."

"Oh my God."

"The child's body was shred to pieces. And the remains were spread across such a wide area. It took the whole day to locate and recover all the pieces."

"Poor child and poor mother; I can only imagine her plight. Why don't you arm yourself with a weapon or something?"

"Exactly!" Abdul dug into his back pocket and pulled out a sling-shot; a crude wooden fork with tubular bands and a leather pouch.

"Would that really help? It doesn't look very strong."

He reached into a small crack in his platform, took out a box and opened it. It held three small blue darts. He whispered, "Poison darts. When I launch these into the dog, it will die in a few seconds. Guaranteed."

The darts looked minuscule to her. How could they possibly kill a dog?

"Very good. You take care of yourself, Abdul." She searched in her purse and handed him a hundred rupees note.

"*Shukriya*[30]." He raised his right hand, then held his palm to his heart and made a fist of strength in a signal of fighting courage. With a spin, he boosted himself ahead along the road, gaining momentum as he rotated down the moderate slant, and singing, "*Naam Abdul hain mera…sab pe nazar rakhta hoon.*"[31]

The Fashion Street mall on Linking Road was a fusion of modern and traditional. Here, the East met the West. Street stalls contrasted with brand name shops. An Indian roadside food vendor on one side and a Kentucky Fried Chicken outlet on the other.

"It's so crowded today," said Shakti as she walked into her regular shop. "Don't all these college students have their classes to attend?" The street thronged with youngsters in t-shirts and hot pants. The vendor's trendy clothes, jewelry, and colorful footwear attracted them, with ample choice and economy.

---

30 Shukriya: Thank you

31 "Naam Abdul hain mera…sab pe nazar rakhta hoon" = "My name is Abdul…I keep an eye on everyone"

"You should come and see at festival time, madam." The shopkeeper had been in the trade for over a decade. "It gets crazy. No time for us to eat lunch."

Shakti spotted a tall guy with broad shoulders in the crowd. Was that Shiva? No. But they looked so much alike. She wondered if she'd ever see Shiva again. Her thoughts were interrupted by a couple of teenagers rummaging through a rack of clothes.

"I come here to upgrade my wardrobe," said the first teenager.

"I hate this place. It's too cheesy for my taste," replied the second one.

"Oh yeah, Miss Princess from Delhi. I love it here. It's like a one-stop-shop. I come to see what the latest fashion trends are."

"Really? Fashion trends here? I don't get it girl."

"You bet. And there's something new every week."

Shakti smiled. The Mumbai girl was right. The mile-long Fashion Street was a gathering of Delhi's popular Janpath, Sarojini Nagar, and Lajpat Nagar, but all in one single place. Mumbai had such an intentional casualness in dressing up. In Delhi, people were fixated with proclaiming status; they overlooked that a short dress could be picked up from Linking Road and worn with a Louis Vuitton bag.

The street brimmed with youth, color, and energy. But in the midst of the chirpy teenagers and the ripples of bobbing heads, Shakti noticed an anomaly. A short, bald, pudgy middle-aged man stood out like a wolf in a flock of sheep. He was very dark. A large black scar ran across from the top of his right eye, over his crooked nose and rough cheeks, and all the way down left to his stubbly chin. What was he doing there?

Shakti turned towards him. The man avoided her stare and pretended to check out some leather belts. While he was turned, she bolted away, past a chain of clothing stores to a footwear shop, and snuck inside.

The shop had a large collection of fancy footwear in different shapes and colors. Designer bags and clutches were at throwaway prices to add to one's temptation. She tried out a few slippers but didn't find anything she liked. She stuck her neck out to check on the street. Maybe her mind was playing games.

The short, bald, pudgy man was in the middle of the street, looking up and down, trying to find someone. He turned towards her. She had no time. She hid behind a group of people. A worm of fear squirmed in her stomach.

"If you want to buy stuff here, remember bargaining is the keyword," a Mumbai girl explained to a visitor. "If you can't bargain, forget about coming here. And as a rule of thumb, don't pay more than half the quoted price."

The worm of fear inside Shakti's stomach began to wiggle its way up.

"Look at these slippers," continued the Mumbai girl. "I love them. The jewels on top, aren't they lovely?"

"Umm. They're ok. Too shiny for my taste," said the visitor.

"The mall charges 400 rupees. Here they are at 100. And I can bring them down to 50 or even 30, with no trouble."

"Oh, come on. Really?"

"The trick is to show indifference. Even walk away if necessary. They'll call you back and drop the price to what you want."

The worm of fear climbed up to Shakti's throat; it was hard to gulp it back down. *When I look out, he won't be there*, she insisted with her eyes shut. *I'll make a pact with you, God. This girl loves the slippers; if she buys them, it means all's well. My eyes were playing tricks on me, and the short, pudgy man was a figment of my imagination.*

The big group of people finished their shopping and moved to the next shop. The two girls walked out without buying the slippers. Shakti remained frozen. The worm of fear made her sinus sting. She felt an uncontrollable urge to sneeze. "Aaachooo!" She hoped that the pudgy man didn't hear or see her. She peered out. He was a few shops to the left, still searching. She waited until she couldn't see his shiny head.

She lunged forward, her heart pounding, and fled to the right. She was hit by strong whiffs of tangy *pani-puri, bhel-puri,* and *sev-puri*[32], mixed with the aroma of tea. She ran away from the food stalls, the shops and stores. She crossed SV Road, the rail-tracks, and several small streets. She ran until her feet ached.

Shakti paused to catch her breath. She had come a long way. She turned and glanced back. The pudgy man was behind her. *Oh my God.* Her chin quivered. Her heart raced faster. She forced her tired feet to press on the pedal again. But she didn't spot the pothole in her path. She tripped over and fell.

She looked over her shoulder. The man was gaining on her. Somehow, she pulled herself up. Her leg hurt; it was badly bruised. Her right knee was all scraped up. She hobbled ahead, dragging her leg. He was catching up, getting closer with each step.

---

32 Pani-puri, bhel-puri and sev-puri: Savory snacks, typically served at road-side tracks from stalls or carts

And then out of nowhere, she saw the Bandra police station to her right. She staggered up the steps and limped by the constables.

Shakti asked for sub-Inspector Gore. The policemen gazed at her, that vacant and lascivious stare which routinely undresses a single woman in Mumbai.

Kriya-di would've looked back at them and asked, "What're you looking at?" She had confronted drunken passengers, pilots, customs officials, rickshaw drivers, and policemen. Policemen were the worst, sheltered by their power and high on a dose of the belligerence and sexual depravity that they dealt with every day.

Shakti found herself too timid for confrontation, as if she were some steely metal spring that had lost its early tenacity and resilience. She waited in patience. Finally, she was shown to the Inspector's cabin and she scampered in. "Inspector! Inspector Gore!"

"Shakti, what's the matter?" Gore jumped up from his seat.

"I think someone is following me. Can you please take a look outside?"

"Are you sure?"

"Yes. A short, bald, pudgy middle-aged man with a girth that equals his height. Very dark. He has a large scar that runs across his face." Shakti visualized him and shuddered as she felt the blood run from her face. God had made him as sinister and ugly as he could, and then hit him in the face with a shovel to leave behind that creepy scar.

"Have you seen him before?"

"No. But I think he might have been at our apartment building last night." She looked around. His cabin looked like an ordinary office, with white plastic chairs, files, and stationery. Except for a police cap next to him, nothing about the place suggested that matters of crime were discussed here. Pictures of several Gods peeked at her from under the glass on his desk. "Is it possible that Kriya-di's kidnapper wants me dead?"

"Thousands of people walk our streets. Not everyone is following everyone else. You are being paranoid."

"But Inspector, I really–"

"I've seen people imagine such things when they're under huge pressure. Usually, it turns out to be nothing."

"But Inspector –"

"Listen Shakti, the police station is the last place a young woman like you should be in. Do you know how many dangerous criminals are brought here every day?"

"But –"

"Let me show you what sort of scum ends up here." He walked her through the door and into a narrow room with a big glass wall. She could see and hear what happened on the other side while they remained oblivious to her presence.

Culprits were lined up, all squatting down on the floor. Constable Mane, who had come to Shakti's apartment, sat at an end table. He stared at a scrawny youth of twenty, who held his head down as he scraped the side of one torn slipper against the other.

"Come here," Mane growled.

The boy hobbled. He brushed aside his superstar Shahrukh Khan styled hairdo and looked up with his sunken, black eyes.

Mane brought his mean fist down onto the table. It was thunderous. The boy was startled. He tottered back. Mane seized him by the scruff of his neck and bent him over the desk. "Where do you get the drugs?"

Shakti couldn't imagine this was the same under-nourished, silent constable Mane from her apartment. He was capable of such fury.

"*Hawaldar-saheb*[33], I run a simple video rental shop. I'm an innocent boy. I don't know anything."

"*Bhikar-chot*[34], don't put on an act. You sold that shit to our decoy. We nabbed 1 kilogram of cocaine from your video shop. That's no innocence."

"*Saheb*, I'm a small pawn caught in the middle of all this."

"But a very smart one, *bhikar-chot*. You've been peddling drugs for the last five years. How come we can't trace any cellphone to you?" Mane whacked the side of his head with an open palm. As the boy crouched, Mane inflicted two more tight slaps behind his ear. The side of the boy's face and his ear turned crimson red.

"They told me not to buy a cellphone in my own name. They told me to change my phone numbers every month, in case my calls are monitored."

"Who did?"

"You know who. They have bigger drug peddlers than me working for them and many high-profile people on their client list."

"No, *Raandichya*[35], I don't know. Tell me. Who? Who gets you all the drugs?"

"The Mumbai drug mafia, *saheb*. They've got politicians and police on their payrolls and deep links to Bollywood."

---

33 Hawaldar-saheb: Constable-sir

34 Bhikar-chot: (Marathi term) Beggar's dick

35 Raandichya: (Marathi term) Son of a whore

"I need a name. A name to the face of the *bhikar-chot.*"

"Qasim Jardari and *Bhai*[36] are the big fish. But nobody can touch them. They are powerful and pay a lot of money. Even your police force is scared of them."

"*Raandichya,* don't tell us who we're scared of. You little piece of shit." Smoke bellowed out of Mane's ears and he was about to smack the boy again but stopped.

"Remember the ten kilos of hashish that vanished? It disappeared from the anti-narcotics police warehouse, right under their noses. You know what really happened?"

"No."

The boy smirked. His face smacked of an arrogance that defied his age. "*Hawaldar,* the police sold it back to the mafia. They explained to the press and public that the hashish was eaten by white ants."

Mane couldn't control his anger. He smacked him again behind his ears, making an awful explosive sound. Blood trickled from the side of the boy's head.

"Why are you picking on me? I'm a nobody. If you've got balls, go after Qasim Jardari and *Bhai.* Go after the big fish."

"*Aai-zavadya*[37], you think you're tough? Not scared of anyone? Let me show you what we do with a *tapori*[38] like you." Mane dragged him across the room, raising him off the floor with every step.

Shakti cringed. Mane looked malnourished, but he had surprising strength.

Mane locked him behind bars. Kicks and punches followed until the boy coiled himself into a corner, all bloodied and sullied and left with a faint trickle of life. "Next time I'll break your legs. *Aai-zavadya,* you'll have to move around in a wheel-chair."

Inspector Gore walked Shakti back to his cabin. "You see what sort of scum ends up in the station?"

Shakti nodded and sunk into the white plastic chair, too shaken to respond.

"Listen, we've sent out field enquiries to all guest houses, hospitals, railway stations, airports, bus stands, cinema theaters, and parks."

"Thank you, Inspector."

"We've also made inquiries at the missing person's bureau."

---

36 Bhai: Mumbai underworld Don

37 Aai-zavadya: (Marathi term) Mother-fucker

38 Tapori: (Marathi term) Vagabond, rowdy

"Any news, Inspector?"

"No, we haven't heard back from any of them yet."

"So then, what next, sir?"

"With your consent, we can publish Kriya's photo in the newspapers and local TV channels. Are you okay with that?"

"Yes. Please go ahead. Anything it takes to get her back."

"Shakti, one more thing. We checked on that Vicky guy. He's a mute. You said he could talk. How's that possible?"

"He's no mute, sir. He had a stammer, but he could most certainly speak."

"We got his home address from the courier company and grilled his neighbors. None of them had ever heard a single word from his mouth. They said he was aloof, but he helped them. We brought Vicky into the police station for questioning two days ago."

"Where is he? I want to meet him. I want to ask him a few questions myself."

"We let him go. The guy had nothing to do with Kriya's disappearance."

"You let that Vicky go?"

"We interrogated him for a few hours and he responded with a pen and paper. He was out of Mumbai the whole month, for his sister's wedding in Nagpur."

"Inspector, he's making up stories." Shakti was puzzled at how the Inspector could believe Vicky's lies.

"He showed us his train tickets and the dates checked out fine. He was away when Kriya disappeared."

"But he could've come back to Mumbai any time in the middle of the month."

"Of course, we thought of that. So, we called up the Nagpur police station and talked to the head constable. He confirmed that Vicky was there all that time."

"With all due respect sir, how would they know for sure?"

"The head constable's son was married to Vicky's sister. So, they know for sure. He was in Nagpur all that time, busy with the wedding preparations."

Shakti was at a loss for words. She sat in silence. Muted.

The Inspector excused himself for a phone call. Shakti stood up and looked at the bulletin board on the wall. She was surprised to see so many missing people pictures ranging from little kids to senior citizens, from teenage girls to married women, from boys to adult men. Tall and short. Thin and fat. Fair to wheatish complexion to dark.

I can't believe some of these people have been missing for more than five years. Some even ten. God, please get back my Kriya-di soon.

"Who else might be a suspect?" the Inspector interrupted. He had finished his phone call. "You saw Kriya last at the airport. Who was she with?"

"Well, there was this American guy. A big, white guy. What did Kriya-di say his name was? Hmmm…"

The Inspector waited while Shakti ransacked her memory.

"Hmmm…Harold…Harold something. Yeah, Harold Walker."

"Who's this American guy? Did she know him well?"

"No, he was a passenger. He was screaming at the immigration officer."

"About what?"

"Some issues with his passport and visa. His arms flailed. His face was all red, all agitated. He was sweating profusely in the unfamiliar heat."

"So, why was Kriya talking to him?"

"The Good Samaritan that she is, Kriya-di had to help him out. She took him to the head of immigration."

"So did they let him in?"

"I don't know. It was getting late and I had to go for my flight."

"Give me the contact number for immigration. I'll check out this Harold Walker."

Shakti walked out of the police station, hoping that the bald, pudgy man wasn't waiting for her. She looked around when she heard a voice over the din of the traffic.

Four times out of five she wouldn't have paid attention, but there was something about Rocky's voice that captivated her. It was electrically charged with a thousand volts, and it commanded significance. It filled the air, the sound catapulting from his mouth and careening off the building walls. She spotted him at the corner of the street talking with vigor to someone, partially blocked in view by the building.

"Rocky!" Shakti shouted from across the street.

Rocky turned towards her in surprise and waved to her. He stood towering and noticeably erect. His dark black hair was short, almost military style, and spiked. He had a bit of gray at his temples. His face was bronzed except for two circles around his unruffled eyes where his skin had been protected by sunglasses. His eyes were furrowed at the corners and squinted somewhat from being out in the sun on his motorbike.

"Who were you talking to? I thought I saw someone with you," Shakti asked.

"It was an old friend that I bumped into. He's gone. What are you doing here?" Rocky was clean-shaven. His was a tough face, with no trace of tenderness. Perhaps he couldn't hide his grief from the loss of Kriya-di. From a distance, his face appeared deceivingly youthful, but up close, he looked much older than even his real age.

"I was in the police station talking to the Inspector. I don't understand what's taking them so long to find Kriya-di."

"It's probably not their only case."

"I told them about Vicky but they let him go. They think he's innocent. I hope they make some progress soon."

"I know. It takes them forever for even a simple step. *Chai?*"

"Sure, thanks. How are you holding up?" Shakti knew it had been tough on him as well. They headed to the local *Irani* cafe that was more than a hundred years old, originally opened by Persian immigrants in the 19th century.

"Not too good. I wish I could do more. Do the police suspect anyone?" Rocky pulled back the black, bent wooden chair for her to sit. The café had a subtle colonial touch; high ceilings and wooden tables with marble tops and glass jars that allowed a peek into the mysteries they held.

"No. They don't know who's responsible, or where she is. I'm sure it's Vicky. He's such a creepy guy." As Shakti sat down, she smelled his cologne in the air, manly and sturdy, like a rock.

"I'm surprised Vicky had the guts to come back. I thought he'd never show his face again after that office incident."

"Inspector Gore shouldn't have let him go. I said it openly to him. But he's so intimidating and stubborn."

"Shakti, you shouldn't get mad at the police, especially in a police station."

"Why are you taking their side?" Shakti lamented, sipping her hot *chai*.

"I'm not taking their side. Inviting the Inspector's anger isn't good. Remember this is his area of authority. You shouldn't make enemies with him."

"My sister, my life, has disappeared. And the police don't seem too interested in finding out where she is. You're willing to let it rest at that?"

"Kriya's disappearance is dreadful and disturbing. Believe me, I miss her too. I'm miserable without her. But you and I can't do much." Rocky looked to the floor, defeated.

"She's vanished right under our noses. We're involved in this whether you admit it or not. I don't like the fact that the kidnapper is walking around free in the city."

"Please don't do anything risky. Promise me you won't. The Inspector might be slow but he deals with this every day."

Shakti had never spoken to Rocky at length. She had always met him with Kriya-di. He was so easy to talk to. She realized that he was right. She had to rely on Inspector Gore and his team to work the case. She didn't like it but she had no choice.

The topic soon veered to Rocky's life and career. He was self-effacing. "My life? It's very easy to explain. It hasn't been the exciting air show I dreamed it to be. But neither have I dug with the rats and mice."

"Oh, come on. You've done well. You're a captain for an international airline."

"Well, I suppose my life has most resembled a jumbo-jet; rather safe and sturdy. Steady takeoffs, smooth landings, and racking up a lot of positive miles over time."

"That's good, isn't it?"

"Maybe. But it's not a space-shuttle with a high-octane thrust. Dream high, fly to the moon and beyond. That type of a flight comes with high risk, but it's more fun."

"That's an interesting view."

"Not everyone has a pilot's career and money, this I know. But I'm nothing special; of this I'm sure."

Shakti couldn't help but be impressed. He was such a good man. A humble man and an honest man. His eyes welled up when they talked about Kriya-di; he insisted it was the steam from the *chai*. Kriya-di was lucky to have met him.

She looked behind him at the huge glass mirror on the wall designed to create a feeling of space. She saw the reflection of his broad shoulders, and sensed a whiff of baking reminiscent of her special Barista Lavazza moment with Shiva at the airport. *When will I see him again? I wish Kriya-di could meet Shiva. When will I find her?*

Rocky ran his palms over his face, up across his eyes and the grey at his temples. The gesture mopped away his sadness. "Which would you rather have from other people?" he asked in a somber tone. "Would you want love, respect, or fear?"

"Respect, I think," said Shakti. "No, love. Yes, I'd beyond a doubt want love. I want someone who'll adore and love me for who I am." Shakti finished up her *chai*. The crowds in the *Irani* restaurant had dwindled and the noise level had subsided.

Rocky rolled his neck, head held up straight, moving his chin to the left shoulder, stopping with a jerk and then moving it to the right shoulder, stopping with another jerk. His bones creaked. "Not me. I'd choose fear." The bitterness in his voice was disturbing. His jaw was set in a grim expression as he stared at his joined hands.

She frowned. Her friend Tara had a similar neck habit. It was irritating. "Why?"

"It works better. Look at Mumbai's *Bhai*. Nobody loves him or even respects him, but entire Mumbai is afraid of him. As a matter of fact, it's the only thing that works. Fear goes deepest to the core and it stays longer than anything else."

Shakti couldn't challenge his assertion. Her Latur loss had indeed left a fear inside her; a deep-rooted fear that refused to leave. Right then her phone rang, making her jump. Nisha-aunty? Turning, she said, "I've to go. It was good running into you, Rocky."

"Stay in touch, Shakti. I know how hard it is for you without Kriya. Call me if you need anything."

"Where are you, Shakti? I rang your doorbell all morning," Nisha-aunty said.

"I'm in Bandra. Is everything okay?" Shakti began to walk back to the bus stop.

"Oh, you haven't heard the news yet? He was killed this morning."

"What? Who was killed?"

"They found his dead body in a big pool of blood. He was drugged and then his throat was slit. Poor guy."

"Nisha-aunty, that's so tragic, but *whose* throat was -"

"It happened in the middle of the night when everyone was sleeping. Even the watchman had dozed off. Or maybe he was drugged too."

Was it Mr. Desai from the 2nd floor? He was vocal and opinionated; he might have had enemies. Or was it Mr. Gupta from the 5th floor? He had a secretive import-export business and he always had weird folks visiting his place. Or was it the lone, retired grandpa from the 1st floor. He was such an easy target.

"Shakti. Shakti, are you listening?"

"Yes, Nisha-aunty."

"He was young. It was so early for him to die. God can be cruel sometimes. All the kids in the building are sad. They're crying since morning."

Shakti was at a loss. How could this be happening? First Kriya-di went missing. Now a kid was murdered in cold-blood in their apartment building.

"That is so sad. Who –"

"I used to watch him from the balcony playing ball with my Pinky. He was always cheerful and so well-mannered."

Shakti played cards and board games with all the kids on the weekends. Who would commit such a gruesome act? And why?

"Nisha-aunty, please. Can you please, please tell me who was murdered?"

"Oh, I thought I told you. Our Tiger was murdered. His throat was found slit."

"Oh no, poor Tiger! Who did this to him?"

"I don't know. Oh, someone is at my door. I've to go. Let's talk in the evening."

Shakti was stunned. The click-click-clicket-click-clickety-click-click sound. The bottle crashing. The prolonged, high-pitched howl of pain and suffering that she'd heard last night; that was Tiger's. Someone had killed him! That big, ferocious beast of an animal who could tackle five men at a time! Now, with Tiger gone, their building and the residents were so vulnerable.

Shakti had difficulty swallowing. Something sinister was brewing.

CHAPTER 8

"Hey bud, you're in love," Harry said.

"But I hardly know her," Shiva replied, as they lounged on the green lawns of San Francisco Marina. "I haven't even gone out on a date with her; I didn't get her number." The only thing he knew about Shakti was that she was a flight attendant and she liked Bandra, Marine Drive, and to travel.

Shiva watched the paper kites flying in the sky and the dogs chasing Frisbees. He gazed at the young and old men and women jog their way into fitness.

"That doesn't matter." Harry looked straight at him. "Dating and courtship are overrated. You might date a person for years and not quite know her."

Shiva realized there was an element of truth in that. He had dated girls he thought he knew well, but not really. He remembered the French exchange student from New Year's Eve - she could do things with her tongue that were beyond imagination. The Jewish girl from college, who tossed her hair and flirted with him during class - she loved to party wild. The Mexican chiquita and the hot salsa number she enacted - on the dinner table, the dance floor, and the trembling bed. All of them had fizzled without a whimper.

Then there was Glee; they went out for a while, but it was too sad to see her get into drugs. It was easy to access marijuana in the city. She started out with pot at parties, then every weekend, then every day. She graduated to cocaine. She became stupefied. Shiva couldn't stop her. He couldn't get back the chirpy old Glee, so they simply called it off. Weeks later one night, he saw her with an Italian restaurateur and a regular junkie from Nob Hill. Shiva smiled at her, but she couldn't make him out in the crowd.

Shiva felt no longing for any of those girls; none of them seemed right. Maybe it was his prudish Indian mentality. Maybe it was something else.

He couldn't get Shakti out of his mind. He thought of her all the time and it sent an electric current through him every time. He thought of her when he awoke in the morning and when he rode the Caltrain to work. He thought of her all day long as he went about his business, during meetings and customer visits. He thought of her at lunchtime, during his coffee breaks, and when he rode the Caltrain back home again.

"Then you meet someone special and it seems like it is meant to be," Harry said.

"She's had an impact on me for sure. I can't stop thinking about her." Shiva even thought about her when he went for evening jogs near Fisherman's Wharf, and when he dreamt of diving into the banana-split ice cream at Ghirardelli's. He thought, during his dinner of naan and curry from the corner Indo-Pak restaurant, of how beautiful she was as she stood at the airport gate. He thought of her as he shut his sleepy eyes each night.

"My dear Shiva, the universe is much larger than you and I. Much larger than we can comprehend or even imagine."

"What?"

"Don't you feel it on a dark, winter night when you stare at the stars in the Milky Way? How tiny we are? How little we know?"

"What are you talking about, Harry?"

"The surprises that God has in store for us. The unforgettable moments of magic. Tell me, why were you stuck in traffic on your way to Mumbai airport?"

"Because my driver was pathetic?"

"Tell me why of all people, Shakti materialized as the angel to help you navigate through your flight woes? Tell me."

"I don't know."

"It happened because you and Shakti were fated to connect. It was a mere unfolding of your destinies." Harry gesticulated with heart-felt conviction.

"I'm from the East and you're this big, white American guy who loves his beer and burgers. I always wanted to ask you; how did you get into all this Oriental stuff?"

"Long story short: when I was a teen, my mom took me to India on her spiritual quest. We stayed at Sri Yukteshwar's[39] Ashram in Puri[40]."

---

39   Sri Yukteshwar was an educator, astronomer, a Vedic astrologer, a yogi and a believer in the Bhagavad Gita and the Bible. He was the Guru of Paramahansa Yogananda (author of *Autobiography of a Yogi*) and was considered as Jnanavatar, or "Incarnation of Wisdom".

40   Puri is a city in the eastern Indian state of Orissa. It is situated on the Bay of Bengal.

"I didn't know that. Wow!"

"I read books; Listened to talks; Picked up palmistry, numerology, and astrology. I had a natural knack and affinity for it. Tell me, why don't you believe in destiny?"

"Well. I don't like the idea that I'm not in control of my life."

"Ok. Hmmm...but we digress. Let's talk about Shakti."

"No, no. Your India experience sounds more interesting."

"I'm telling you, bud. A karmic connection exists between the souls that are destined to meet and be mesmerized and mate with each other."

"But how would one know?"

"She's recognized right away. She's loved in every gesture, expression, and subtle movement, every pulse of lilting sound, and every mood that springs from her eyes."

Shiva saw Shakti's face appear in the sky amidst the clouds and the paper kites in the wind. Her sandy brown eyes sparkled and she beamed the most angelic smile.

Harry continued, "You know her by her wings that only you can see. Wings that fly her to you. You've got to do something about it."

"What? I can't go to India right now."

"Why can't you?"

"Oh come on. We've got to get funding. Our company can't survive without it."

"What does your heart say?"

"My rational mind tells me to do my duty. Funding is my top-most priority." His heart silently whispered *India* but his mind knew how he'd always given up on pursuing romance. Since he couldn't give his partner sufficient time and attention, he didn't want to be unfair and keep them hanging, so he set them free. Work was his God then and now.

"Never put your head before your heart, my friend."

"Who said that?"

"A very wise and spiritual man who walks on this planet. He's a little hairy though. The name's Walker. Harold Walker."

"Very funny, Harry. But I do like your quote."

"Don't merely like it. Act on it."

"Not now. My work is here in the Bay Area right now."

"If it's meant to be, your work will take you to Mumbai."

"I'll wait then."

"Here's another quote to remember. It comes from Rumi. Such beautiful poetry. 'I once had a thousand desires, but in my one desire to know you, all else melted away.'"

Harry reminisced about his romantic time with Sally in Australia. When he was with her, he felt as grand as the canyon. He didn't give a hoot about the world.

They had taken a trip to Yarra Valley, Victoria - a magical escape, similar to California's Napa Valley. Forty wineries from small, family-owned establishments to sprawling big-name estates, and the finest pinot noir and sparkling wines. They checked into a lovely inn. The lobby was filled with tourists from a dozen countries.

Harry said to the reception clerk, "A reservation for Mr. and Mrs. Walker." Sally looked away as if the entire lobby was staring at her, knowing what she was doing.

The next day, they lingered over a long lunch of fresh local produce, close to the waterfalls. She had a *sammie* – Aussie for sandwich, and they drank Devonshire tea high in the Dandenong Ranges. That night, he'd planned their first Valentine's dinner together at the beautiful Chateau Yering Hotel. She tried on dresses for their romantic rendezvous.

"Harry, can you zip me?" she called out. He put down his pinot noir and helped her get into her striking burgundy red wrapping.

"Yes," they both said as soon as she looked in the mirror.

He knew she had his mind wrapped for sure. "Beautiful," he said. He meant it. It was a dress that used her proportions to advantage, making her look slim rather than emaciated. Looking at her reflection, he realized how much she meant to him. They were meant to be together. He was rooting for them.

A Clydesdale-drawn carriage drove them around and through a sweeping rose bordered driveway leading to the fine restaurant at the Chateau Yering Hotel.

"I'm sorry for the fracas with your co-worker in Melbourne," Harry said.

"Don't apologize for that *dingaling*[41]. I wouldn't *piss on him if he was on fire.*"

"Still, I shouldn't have lost my temper."

"Harry, as we say here, no *wucking furries*. Everything's fine."

---

41 Dingaling(Aussie slang): Dick, prick, penis, stupid/silly person

He reached out to hold her hand.

Sally seized the chance to look at his palm. "Hmmm…interesting."

"What? My line of life, right? I know it's short," he said.

"Short? You should look at mine. You can barely see it."

Under the shining dining lights, her eyes were radiant jewels of desire. Her lips widened into a luminous half-smile that was his – a moment that was his alone. His heart, the beggar, began to hope and pray. She saw the look on his face and kissed his cheek.

Harry obeyed his impulse to kiss her on the mouth. The taut bow of her lips dissolved into his. There was such sad tenderness in it. He floated free and adrift in its inexpressible kindness. He had thought of Sally as streetwise, tough, and almost cold, but that kiss was pure, undisguised vulnerability. The gentle loveliness of it shocked him and he was the first to pull away.

They rushed back to their lovely inn, walking through the lobby hand in warm hand as Mr. and Mrs. Walker. Once in the room, he looked at her eyes again; they were moist. He kissed her and she curled into him. She kept her lips on his; her tongue was warm and lissome. She moved up over him as they edged onto the bed. They chuckled together as he grimaced and shifted his thigh from under her knee.

Sally kissed him again, on his lower lip, tugging and suckling on it. For a silent instant they were motionless and he felt the warmth of her breath. The flecks in her eyes danced in the light of the night-lamp; behind them was a gentle, enigmatic darkness. She smiled and reached down to grab his nervous hand, and brought it to her breast.

He began to unzip her burgundy red dress, but he had difficulty midway. She sniggered and curved her back to help him as he went lower. He mimicked her giggling and she came back to him, her cheek against his as they laughed together. She slid the dress off her shoulder exposing a glistening spread of peach skin and slithered down beside him. He tilted over her as he took his shirt off. She ran her warm, moist palm all over his soft, tender flesh. She stopped at the back of his neck and drew him into her.

Lying with Sally under the sheet, skin against damp skin, Harry wore a satiated smile. A pleasant ache permeated his body.

Harry had been awkward and self-doubting, but somehow none of that made a difference. It had been good to be held by her and to feel the living rhythm inside her. It was good to lie next to her now and move her hair away from her pretty face. He faltered. "I'm sorry. I didn't plan for this to happen…"

"It's okay," she smiled, leaning away from him with her hand still on his chest. "You're going to forget me once you go back to America, anyways."

"No, I'm not."

"You'll be a free bird. Single and ready to mingle."

"No. Of course not." He frowned, looking at the rotating blades of the ceiling fan.

"Why? You're a good looking, kind hearted man."

"Because I'm in love with you." There, he said it.

"No you're not," she snapped. It felt like a slap.

"I can't help it. For a long time now I –"

"Stop it," she interrupted him, "You're not. You're not. Oh, how I hate love."

"You can't hate love, Sally."

"Maybe not, but you sure as hell can be afraid of it. There's too much love in this world and there's too much pain."

"What are you afraid of, Sally?"

"I'm afraid of what love does to people. I'm afraid of how one loses their identity for the sake of another." The fan breeze lashed her hair into his face and it stung. "I'm afraid of the aftermath of love. Boredom. Cheating. Fights. Break-ups. Humans can't be chained. They're born to be free."

He stared at her sharp canines; they made her face look cold and piercing.

"Look, I don't want to be in love," she said, in a softer tone. She raised her eyes to gape into his. "I really, really like you, Harry. Can we leave it at that?"

But Harry couldn't leave it at that. He didn't want to settle for "I really, really like you." He wanted it all. "That's alright, Sally. That's good enough for me," he lied.

"Holy cow, you guys. We've only got one hour to look decent and reach the VC[42] office." Shiva stared at his wristwatch in disbelief.

It was a special morning. Shiva had set up a meeting with Creative Venture Partners. He was with Harry and Hong, double-checking the pre-

---

42 VC: Venture Capital

sentation slides and the software demo intended for the partners at the venture firm. It was a big meeting.

Look decent? All of them had been so focused on the software and the look of the presentation that they'd failed to remember their own grooming. Shiva stared at his reflection on the computer screen. Whoa, he hadn't shaven in four days. He was in a pair of khaki, baggy shorts and a T-shirt, with a GAP logo gaping out in bold letters.

The previous week, Hong had added a new graphical user interface and a visual debug module to demonstrate the beauty of their software. But a last minute snag made the software crash. Hong managed to fix the issue in the morning. Harry did the testing and Shiva made sure all the t's were crossed and the i's dotted.

"Can we drive by Hong's house?" Harry asked. "It's on our way. We could find something more appropriate to change into." His T-shirt revealed his hairy chest and said "PMS jokes aren't funny. Period." Hong wore his usual jaded track pants with a coffee stain in the most indecent of places.

"There's no time," Shiva said. Here he was, one hour from the most significant meeting in his life, and one would think they were all homeless guys.

"Harry, I for sure don't own a pair of pants to fit your forty-eight inch waist," Hong said. "And Shiva's right. We don't have time."

At eight-thirty a.m. on a Wednesday morning, no clothing store would be open. There was nothing they could do. They carried the laptops and supporting material down to his car. The VC firm was located in Palo Alto on Sand Hill Road, seven miles away.

At about the third mile, Shiva swerved across the road and took a rapid U-turn.

"What the hell are you doing?" Harry was yanked across his seat.

"We might find something to wear at the Indian clothing store." Shiva parked the car in a tiny slot. He was surprised the store had an *Open* sign that early in the morning. Harry managed to squeeze out from the passenger side and they ran into the store.

"We're closing down the store," said the owner. "All on clearance."

"You've anything for us?" asked Shiva. There wasn't much to choose from.

"I have a few men's *kurta-pajamas*[43] in the back, if you like to see."

---

43 Kurta-pajamas: Indian traditional-wear, with a loose shirt (kurta) up to the knees of the wearer and the loose-fitting pajama pants.

"Yeah sure. Why not?"

The owner disappeared. When he got back, he held bright red *kurtas* in his hands. Fancy gold embroidery and ornate, large buttons ran down the chest. The *pajamas* were in a vanilla cream color, the saving grace being they were big and had strings attached to adjust the waist size, so even Harry could fit into one.

"Do you have a *kurta* in navy blue?" Harry asked the owner. "Perhaps a cobalt or indigo shade of blue? I'm not too fond of red."

"No time, Harry," Shiva interjected. "We'll take these."

Shiva drove while Harry and Hong changed into their new clothes in the back seat. Then Harry took the wheel as Shiva slipped into his new attire.

Creative Venture Partners was located in a traditional office complex off Sand Hill Road - the equivalent of Wall Street for private equity. During the dotcom boom of the 1990s, commercial real estate on Sand Hill Road was more expensive than almost anywhere else in the world. Traditional brick buildings sprawled with straight-laced facades. Several signs declared that Sand Hill was a bike-friendly community.

Shiva was amazed at the prim and proper of the place. Not a single speck of dirt on the ground. He wondered what would happen if he threw a small piece of paper. A spotlight would shine on him from the skies. A janitor-police would come running in to whisk him away to the trash-prison. And all that before the paper even hit the ground.

"The VC's seem to be fitness and hygiene freaks," Hong observed.

"I'm sure they burn more calories counting all the clean money they invest and multiply," Harry said. Out of nowhere, a bike appeared and Harry was taken by surprise. He jammed on the brakes. The car went into a skid and they were all yanked forward.

The biker stopped in his tracks and took off his red helmet. It was an older guy. He held a somewhat constipated look on his face. He stared at them with anger and condescension as he pointed to the bike sign on the side of the pavement. He put his helmet back on and rode off down the bike-trail.

"Close call. Where did he come from?" Harry brushed the hair off his forehead.

"You've got to focus on the road," Hong said, adjusting his spectacles.

Harry tried to find parking amongst the bright, shiny Mercedes, Jaguars, and Porsches. The few empty parking spots were marked *Reserved*; some even had the initials of the occupant. After a slow crawl around the main lot, they parked in a smaller lot at the back for visitors. They began the long walk back to their future.

They ambled through a lacquered, glass front door and into an elegant reception area. Shiva was aghast when he saw their reflections. They were so out of place in their bright red *kurtas* and vanilla-cream *pajamas*, the fancy gold embroidery and ornate buttons running down their chests. They looked like ushers at an Indian restaurant.

Creative Venture's seven full partners and three associate partners each held an area of expertise. Shiva's key contact, Gary Blalack, was a semiconductor man. Gary could quote the foundry manufacturing costs in Taiwan. He could churn out performance metrics on the ARM design cores. He was on top of all quarterly earnings numbers.

Although Gary also held his own strong views on the various legal issues in the industry, he wasn't the final authority. When it came to Creative Venture's business, Gary had to yield to the opinion of their legal expert, Dave Nunn.

Gary had tried to reach Dave for the past week to get him to read the IP[44] waiver that Shiva had faxed over. The trouble was, Dave Nunn was on vacation in Yosemite Valley with his family, quarantined from civilization amidst mountains and wilderness.

While Shiva set up his presentation and demo in the conference room next to Gary's office, Gary read the contract on his speakerphone to Dave line by line.

"Gary, can we do this when I get back to the office?" pleaded Dave. You could hear his wife in the background. She was complaining that he never left his work behind. "We're in the middle of a hike going up Half Dome[45]. It's a treacherous climb."

"I'm sorry but this can't wait. We need to move fast." Gary didn't want to risk the delay. Creative Ventures hadn't hit a single home run in the last few years. They had missed out on Sabeer Bhatia's Hotmail. They had missed out on Jerry Yang's Yahoo.

"Ok. I'll pause here. We just finished the hundred feet of granite stairs."

"Thanks Dave. I appreciate it."

---

44 IP: Intellectual Property

45 Half Dome is Yosemite's most familiar rock formation, 4,737 ft above the floor. The impression that this is a round dome which has lost its northwest half is an illusion. Half Dome is nearly as whole as it ever was.

"But we've got to be careful. We can't get burnt like some of the other venture firms in the dot-com bubble."

"Come on. This is not a dot-com company; it's semiconductors. Hard, tangible stuff. Not vaporware like some of the internet companies."

"I'm simply saying we don't want another Pets.com on our bloody hands."

"I know, we won't. That's why we're doing our due diligence."

With the dot-com bubble and bust behind them, VC money was once again venturing into investments and Creative had to get on this train. But it was hard to find the right company. Last year, a network switching start-up had approached Creative looking for three million dollars. Creative engaged in the standard VC protocol, verifying for competition, and bargaining more percentage ownership. Meanwhile, the network switching market exploded and the start-up financed its own expansion through earnings.

The start-up executives stopped responding to Gary's voicemails and emails. Now it was set to go public. If Creative had skipped all the posturing and funded them, the value of the three million would've been thirty million. Gary didn't want to commit the same blunder again. So, when he was introduced to Shiva with a chance to invest, he wasn't going to be slow to take decisive action.

"Gary, I don't have a pen or paper here to make notes. I can't legally be critical."

"You're being unreasonable. This is a standard IP waiver."

"There's never a standard one. There's always some gotcha."

"Come on, Dave. You can finish this fast and go back to your vacation. You can get on with your cable ascent up the summit. Do you see anything that's dubious?"

"The short list of patents worries me. How do I know for sure that they don't infringe on any of their competitors' patents?"

"Let's suppose that they don't. Are all the other things okay?"

"Gary, this is hard. Can they get us a list of all their competitors' patents?"

"Dave, be logical. That's not practical. I know that and you know that."

"Okay. Presuming – and I stress presuming - their technology doesn't infringe on any of their competitors' patents, then everything else seems satisfactory."

Gary ran out of his office and into the conference room. Three nerds in absurd clothes stood around, exchanging awkward pleasantries with the partners. He held a quizzical look on his face, fighting off the urge to judge them on their appearance.

Shiva introduced his team. He glanced at Gary, who still held a puzzled look and seemed occupied with making some mental notes. Perhaps Gary was thinking that these *kurta-pajamas* are the in thing. Perhaps he'd go home and remind his wife to find him decent Indian attire. Perhaps he'd wear it the next time he went to Vinod Khosla's house.

"Let's begin," Gary said.

"The consumer market is moving towards mobile, connected devices." Shiva showed them charts validating the growth and market size projections for the wireless sector. The partners stared with blank expressions. It wasn't clear if they were interested.

"Is it a greenfield opportunity? Any competition?" asked a young partner.

"Granted, there are existing companies, like Alltech, that provide software for this market. But their architecture has run out of steam."

"Is that right?" the young partner said, with a smug glance to his neighbor.

"A revolutionary solution is needed, built from scratch and equipped to address the new challenges of today. Our software enables designers to create products with the best power and performance."

"But how does it impact the end consumer?"

"Consumers won't need to plug their devices into power outlets every two hours."

"Really? That's valuable," one partner said, annoyed and animated. "I'm forced to plug in my phone every half hour. That damn thing doesn't have any juice. Ridiculous."

"You need a new phone," another partner joked. "Stop hoarding up those dollars in your bank account." Everyone broke out into a chuckle.

"Sir, our software will make your phone last longer. And the good news is that you won't have to purchase a new phone every year."

The partners chuckled again.

"In fact, the possibilities are endless. I can clearly envision a single device that combines phone, navigation, and internet, and with a touch screen interface."

"Hmmm... But how fast does your software run?"

"Perfect segue." Harry walked over and launched the software on the laptop. "It runs blazing fast. Let me show you on this example design." Harry entered a few inputs into the graphical user interface as he explained what he was doing.

Hong was biting his nails. His forehead wrinkled as nervous thoughts seemed to dance inside. Will the bug show up again? Will the demo run without crashing? But there were no glitches. No hiccups. The results looked great in his new visual debugger.

The partners began with a barrage of questions: "How long has your team been in software development? How many customers are engaged? Why did the team wait so long to get venture money? What's your exit strategy? What returns can we expect for any investment we put in your company?"

When they started asking about exit strategy, Shiva knew he was on the right track. He saw light at the end of the tunnel. "I confess that we don't have much financial acumen. But we have five paying customers and they've used us on real designs."

"Then why now? Why do you need the money now?"

"We need to reach out to a broader customer base. We need the additional capital to expand into different geographies and to hire sales and support staff."

"How much money are you looking for?"

"I expect we need about five million dollars." Shiva gauged their reaction. The partners didn't balk. "That would support and grow the company for at least three years."

"We like to do a two-phase investment," Gary said. "With the first phase, we get you through early expansion. If that goes well, we have an option and right of denial to fund your next phase."

Shiva could see the light get brighter. He could visualize the dollars. His palms opened up as if to accept the first installment. Onwards and upwards.

An older guy in the back coughed out aloud. The room went silent. He had a rather smug look on his face. He turned straight towards Shiva. "It's nice to see your hallucinogenic sense of optimism. It amuses me."

Shiva knew the face. Where had he seen it? Darn. It was the biker with the red helmet. They had almost hit him in the parking lot.

"What if your enthusiasm is only a self-induced, late night fancy that could downgrade from a quest to a dull cocktail party conversation in a flash?"

Shiva was dumbfounded. He didn't know how to respond.

"So how much of your work comes from Alltech?" the old guy asked.

"Sir, all of it was invented after Alltech. It's clearly spelled out in the legal waiver I mailed to Gary. We have the patents to prove it." Shiva balanced his words as deftly and with as much nervous energy, as a knife juggler with a case of the hiccups.

The old guy frowned. He looked unconvinced.

Shiva looked for help. Hong's leg was trembling like a leaf, with worry. Harry was fidgeting with a pen, mumbling under his breath. The light at the end of the tunnel was turning out to be the high beams of an oncoming train about to crash into them.

"Dave Nunn gave us his legal approval," Gary interjected.

"Did you check with Alltech?" the old man persisted.

"Well, I thought…" Audacity and skepticism warred in Gary's eyes.

"We have to call Alltech and verify." The old guy turned to Shiva. "Don't take it personally, but we are just getting to know you. We'd like to understand your history."

Shiva looked down at his shoes and wiggled his toes inside. He withdrew and disappeared into his childhood home where he polished his black leather shoes with fretful focus. He showed them to Pa who was a stickler for perfection, much more than any other teacher in school. Pa had impressed upon him the urgent lesson that the best outfit could be ruined in its effect by a sloppy pair of shoes. If Pa were to see Shiva today, he'd be disappointed. Both his shoes and outfit were less than ordinary.

"I'll call Alltech right after this meeting," said Gary, trying to get over the prickly situation. "I'm certain this will get sorted out soon. The CEO is my ex-colleague." Gary turned to Shiva. "He knows you, right?"

"Umm…we know him. But…he was high up in the hierarchy. He may not remember us." Their Alltech CEO was a Machiavellian politician. All he knew was deceit and manipulation. Weren't these folks aware of his financial irregularities?

"The quintessential semiconductor man," continued Gary. "He was around the industry even before it officially started. I'm sure he'll have good things to say about you."

"We're screwed," said Harry, as they got into the car. "Screwed, screwed."

"I can't believe it," Hong said, "They had almost transferred the money."

"It was almost in our bank. *Poof.* All vanished in a jiffy," Harry added.

Shiva groaned, fast-forwarding in his mind to the next phone call with Pa. He didn't want to fail Pa or not live up to his expectations, hopes and dreams for his son. But Shiva had always been the perennial underachiever. In school he was in the top ten, but never *número uno*. In sports he ran great races and would medal, but never the gold. He could never live up to Pa's exemplary achievements and standards. Pa never said anything but Shiva could see the disappointment on his face.

"Our cunning ex-Boss will rip us apart." Harry spelled it out, "He doesn't share any love for you, Shiva. And he was hopping mad when I left. We're royally screwed."

"Can't we simply go to another VC firm?" Hong suggested. "We can spread our wings and knock on multiple doors."

Shiva couldn't even break a smile at Hong's metaphor mix-up. He started the car and pulled it out of the parking spot in a jerky fashion. "Every VC will ask the same natural question, 'Who the heck are these guys?'"

"And no VC will invest without verifying references, and that means they'll talk to our favorite ex-Boss. And we all know what that beast will say," Harry said.

Shiva drove on in silence. He remembered the day when he had scored an admission to Cornell University. Pa was so proud he went around distributing sweets. Shiva worked his way through graduate school by taking teaching assistant jobs and waiting tables. Pa was thrilled when he landed his first job at Alltech. Shiva thought he was on the right path to pursue the American Dream until he was fired.

Shiva started his own company. Many of his colleagues jumped on the dot-com bandwagon, became successful, and made millions before the dot-com bust. Folks like Sabeer Bhatia and Jerry Yang succeeded beyond anyone's wildest dreams. The dot-com cycle had passed Shiva by, and his little company was still stuck in limbo land, in an uncertain state between success and failure. He was struggling to get capital, wondering if they'd survive; a question he shied away from because he was afraid of the answer.

Shiva drove onto University Avenue and they stopped at *Pizza My Heart* for a slice of consolation. They settled into the outdoor seating, but their minds were far away. Shiva searched for a reset button for his brain as it wallowed in defeat.

He peered at the newspaper on the table. The 2003 season had been one of turmoil for the 49ers. The relationship between quarterback Garcia and wide receiver Terrell Owens had turned sour. When Owens' publicly praised the backup quarterback Rattay, Garcia responded with a cryptic, "we can't let the sickness spread." That prompted Owens to wear a surgeon's mask at the following practice. The 49ers finished 7–9, missed the playoffs, and finally traded off Owens, tired of his on and off field antics.

"We're screwed. Screwed. Screwed," Harry blurted out. He took a bite of his Big Sur slice, loaded with roasted garlic, pepperoni, sausage, and green onions.

"Let's not freak out yet," Shiva responded. "Gary's gonna make a call to Alltech. Big deal. Boss was glad to get rid of us. What does he care what we're up to now?" The linguisa in his *Maverick*'s slice was both seasoned and smoked a bit too much.

Harry and Hong made no sound.

"Boss has got plenty of other issues," Shiva continued. Fear nagged at him, but he wouldn't give in. "We're too small to appear on his radar, absolute nobodies. I doubt if he even remembers our names."

"You really believe that?" Hong said, before biting into his *Maui Wowie* bacon.

"I'll tell you what I believe. I believe in you and Harry. I believe in our software; it will attract money, one way or another. And I believe that one who's scared is as good as dead. We can't fear our ex-Boss and let him bring our aspirations down, can we?"

"That old VC guy was so adamant. Did you look at his thumb?" Harry asked.

"His thumb?" Shiva was perplexed.

"Yes. A thumb is the single most important aspect in the art of reading hands. It gives you the quickest insight into a person, revealing even more than the face."

"How so, Mr. Palmist?"

"The old guy's thumb was absolutely straight. It didn't bend even a little. That says he's a person unwilling to compromise his thoughts or principles, bordering on obstinacy. No adjustment. No flexibility."

"You're simply saying that in hindsight."

Hong's phone rang. It was his dad from China. He stepped inside the restaurant.

"Have you ever looked at Hong's hands?" Harry asked.

"No Harry. That never occurred to me."

"You should. Palmistry can be very effective for people like us in sales and marketing. Many times when people are carefully controlling their facial and verbal expressions, their hands are telling quite a different story."

"Hmmm...Corporate palmistry." Shiva smiled. Harry never ceased to surprise him.

"Hong's thumb bends outwards. He's a flexible, team player who wants to take the middle ground and find a mutually acceptable solution."

His friend Harry was either a nutcase or pure genius. Shiva wasn't sure which one. "But what about Hong's issues with his strict, authoritarian dad?"

"Sometimes, if the thumb is too flexible, one tends to become a push-over. It shows a lack of ability to stand up for what one believes in."

A convertible stopped at the traffic light on University Avenue. Two mops of hair in the car bounced to blaring Bollywood music.

"This music reminds me of Sally," Harry said as his face turned sad. "She's such a big Bollywood fan. She played that foot-tapping music all the time in Australia, and we watched a couple of Bollywood movies together."

"Well, here's a funny story," Shiva added. "I was driving her to the ho-tel in Mumbai and we stopped at a traffic light. A Japanese sports bike zigzagged through the traffic and paused next to us. It was all jazzed up, purring such a beautiful mellow whirr."

Hong finished his long debate with his dad and walked back out.

"Sally got all excited; shouting, screaming, and jumping up and down."

"Where's this? Sorry, I missed the beginning," Hong asked.

"This was in Mumbai when Sally visited. So, as I was saying, this Japanese sports bike stopped next to our car. Sally got all excited."

Harry and Hong drew in closer, listening in attention.

"The light turned green. The bike let out a wildcat growl and raced ahead faster than a speeding bullet. Sally yelled, 'Did you see? Did you see?'"

Harry and Hong drew in their breath.

"I was like, 'Of course I did. The bike was super cool.' Sally looked at me bewildered. 'Not the bike, silly. That was Salman.'"

Harry laughed out loud. His body jerked so hard that he almost broke his back.

"Salman Rushdie?" Hong asked, "The famous writer?"

"No. Salman Khan."

"Who is Salman Khan?"

Shiva and Harry rolled in laughter.

Shiva's cellphone rang. It was Gary Blalack. Shiva thanked him for call-ing so soon. Harry and Hong huddled around him.

"Listen Shiva, it's not our operating style to give counsel or make remarks when we refuse funding to entrepreneurs," Gary said. "Your technology has merit. Frankly, our reasons for denying funding are due to internal obstacles and guiding principles."

"Gary, are you saying that you won't finance us?"

"Well, yes, but like I said, it may not be in any way a disapproval of your business. We have stringent criteria and an appetite for certain risk profiles."

"And we don't meet those?"

"If you ask me, our criteria can often be quite unyielding. Many first-class ideas are still first-class ideas, even if they don't meet our criteria."

"Alright. Well, thanks. I appreciate you calling us and letting us know." Shiva waited for him to hang up, but Gary had something else on his mind.

"But what I'd like to do, if it's okay with you, is refer you to a friend of mine."

"A friend?"

"He's not affiliated with Creative Ventures, but he can help you if he finds your company interesting. Is it okay if I tell him about you?"

"Well, of course. Please, go ahead and tell him."

"Great. I'll check with him and get back to you."

A few days later Shiva got a call from Mr. Sunny Singh, a successful lawyer and friend of Gary Blalack. Mr. Singh scheduled a breakfast meeting at the elegant Ritz Carlton on Half Moon Bay, renowned for combining the beauty of the Northern California coast with the history of old Scotland, only a few miles south of San Francisco.

This time, Shiva and team put on their best formal attire. No *kurta-pajama* fiasco. When they walked into the lobby, he couldn't help but admire the changed look of Harry and Hong. "I barely recognize you guys. You should dress like this more often. It suits you." They gave him a long, hard stare that said, *Get lost. Not in our worst dreams.*

The hostess took them to the corner table by the windows with arguably the best view of the coast and the golf course. Mr. Sunny Singh was in his mid-sixties. He was a tall man with a bulbous nose, large black eyes, and fair skin. He had a Sikh red turban adorning his head and a rich, grey moustache which he loved to twirl.

Singh wore a lawyer's jacket. Underneath he had a golfer's polo shirt, well pressed and open at the collar. A gold Cartier watch shone on his right wrist. He held a little gizmo in his left hand. It looked like a palm-sized robotic dog. "So tell me. Why do you want to go through this tough start-up journey?"

That was simply the spark Shiva needed. "Sir, thousands of years ago the first man discovered how to make fire. He was probably burned at the stake he had taught his brothers to light. But he left them a gift and he lifted darkness from the earth."

"So, your technology is like fire. You see, I don't understand technology. Never did in the past and never will in the future."

Stunned silence. Nobody spoke. Hong downed his entire glass of water in nervous gulps. Harry stared at the tiny robotic canine in Singh's left hand.

"Sir, what is that?" Harry couldn't resist the urge. His curiosity burst out.

"Meet Mr. Snoop Dogg." Singh pressed a button on the canine's nose and placed him on the breakfast table. The robotic dog started to play music. He grooved to the beat of Snoop Dogg's *Beautiful.* Bright multicolored lights flashed on the dog's face.

"That's cool," Harry shouted out. Folks at other tables cast glances towards them.

"Who's a good wittle Doggie?" Singh continued. "You are. Does my wittle Doggie want its bewwy scwatched? I bet you do."

Harry's eyes were wide like saucers. He couldn't hide his grin. He was enamored.

"I'm not a techie, but I love to play with it. I trust Gary's opinion and he said you also have some truly cool technology; as cool as LL Cool J, my other favorite rapper."

"Sir, we have designed a unique software that excels when you are designing mobile, connected devices," Shiva tried to explain.

"Oh, yes. Like my Snoop Dogg here. I know that all dogs like to be off the leash; my Snoop Doggie can go wireless too. Take him anywhere music is playing. He learns, he sings, and he dances. Isn't that amazing?" Singh belted out a sonorous laugh.

"So are you interested, Mr. Singh?" Shiva asked.

"Yes, I am. I like you three. You're good kids. How much money do you need?"

"We're looking for five million dollars."

"Five million dollars? That's why I like my Snoop. All he needs is music. Good wittle Doggie. My wittle Doggie wuvs his bewwy scwatched. Wait a second...is this piss on my table? What the fuck. Down, down."

Shiva tilted his head with narrowed eyes. Harry looked around seeking answers.

"Who let you on the table, anyway? And turn off that damn music." Singh flicked Snoop Dogg's tail. The dog tilted his head, lifted his ears, and made a purring sound.

Shiva said, "Sir, we need to expand into different geographies and hire sales and support staff. Anything less than five million wouldn't help."

"I've made tens of millions of dollars. Every penny hard-earned." Singh tapped Snoop's ear and the pup fell down to take a nap. "No risks. No splurging."

An awkward silence followed. Only the wheels in their heads churned.

"I'd love to be twenty-five again. I'd do it differently, though. I never took chances when I was young. I've no kids now. No family. I could take a little risk." The words came as a lightning bolt from some unseen place in the sky.

"Right."

"But I'm paranoid. My money should go the distance. I recently invested in another start-up. I had them sign a legal agreement to open an India office."

"You want us to open an office in India?"

"Yes; the costs will be kept down. My money will go a couple of years further." Singh's phone rang. "Excuse me." He stepped out to the edge of the golf course.

"Let me get this straight," Harry said. "The guy doesn't know a thing about our technology but he's ready to give us five million dollars if we have an India presence?"

"That's right," Hong rocked up and down in his seat.

"One thing I know is that we need the money fast," Shiva said. Their company had made slow progress over the years, like a sluggish elephant compared to the swift dot-com cheetahs. This was their chance to speed things up or risk becoming extinct like the mammoth. "He's not forcing it on us. He's helping out."

"Helping out?" Harry echoed like a trained pet.

"I'm sure he can help incorporate the India office and other legal stuff."

"Wait a minute. Slow down. I've never even been to India," Hong complained.

Shiva smiled and looked at Harry. "Harry has been to Mumbai. Well, to be precise, he's been to Mumbai airport. Haven't you, Harry?"

Harry growled. He fidgeted with Snoop Dogg who lay napping on the table.

"I need to hear this story," Hong stated with curiosity.

"Some other time." Harry picked Snoop up and tried to twist his tail. Snoop slipped through his fingers and landed into the ice-filled glass of water. Panic. Harry looked out to the golf course. Singh was busy on his phone. Harry reached into the glass and rescued Snoop from the water. Who said Harry couldn't swim?

Hong stared on in nervousness. Harry wiped Snoop clean with his towel. He got the last little drop off Snoop's ears and put him down on the table.

"So, where were we?" Singh walked back and picked up Snoop. "Ah, yes. I was saying the only way I'll fund you is if you set up an office and hire in India."

"Five million dollars?"

"Yes. Sign an agreement to open an India office and I'll write you a check tomorrow. My offer stands. Take it or leave it."

Shiva looked at Harry and Hong. They looked at Singh, then at Snoop. And then they looked at each other again.

What are we gonna do now?

"Straight trees are cut first and honest people are screwed first."
- Chanakya, 4th century strategist, political theorist

CHAPTER 9

*O**h my goodness! What are those two doing together?***
Shakti had followed Vicky after spotting him at Natural's Ice-cream in Juhu. She was stunned to see him. She hopped into a rickshaw and pulled her *dupatta* tightly over her head and nose to shield against slimy exhaust fumes. She crouched into the seat corner and trailed him all the way to J49, the disco bar at Juhu Residency Hotel.

The night scene in Mumbai was hot and happening. Plenty of nightclubs and discotheques. And even more plentiful, party hungry men and women. She saw Vicky walk into the club with no trouble, while all the other guys jostled for their places in a long queue. It looked like he was a regular here. It was *ladies night*, free entry, so she walked in after him.

The entire place reeked of cigarette smoke. When she inhaled, the nausea slapped Shakti across her face. Oh, how she hated that disgusting stench. There were cleverly placed mirrors all over, Egyptian statues in discreet corners, and fancy strobe-lights flashing a young and hip image. Unlike some other cramped discos of Mumbai, J49 had decent floor space. Trance and techno music blared out loud.

She tried to stay out of the limelight. She snuck to a nook from where she could scan the bar and the floor. Her eyes searched for Vicky.

Oh my goodness! What are those two doing together?
Vicky and Rocky!

Rocky looked much different. She hadn't seen him in a while. He was still towering and erect, but his short, military style hair had morphed into much longer black tresses, rolling down over his ears to his jaw and neck. His clean-shaven face had given way to rough stubble and a bristly goatee.

Rocky gave Vicky a man hug. It seemed they knew each other well; too well for her comfort. A tingling sensation began in the bottom of her heels. It didn't forebode well.

Rocky turned around to the bartender and ordered drinks. Vicky reached down and handed him a book-sized packet. Rocky grabbed it with impatience and slit open a corner of the bag inside. He wet the tip of his little finger, dabbed inside the bag, and tasted the white stuff. He flashed a wide, white grin.

Shakti was shocked. *Is that what I think it is?*

The two remained engaged in an intense tête-à-tête; their eyes didn't even veer to the scorching dance floor. The bartender brought out their drinks – a tall, blue drink for Vicky and a whiskey shot for Rocky. They tapped their glasses together in celebration and Rocky patted Vicky's shoulder as if in appreciation for a task done well.

Rocky downed his shot in a single gulp. He rolled his neck, moving his chin to the left shoulder and stopping with a jerk, then moving it to the right shoulder and stopping with another jerk. Shakti could imagine his bones creaking, making a menacing sound.

Rocky lit up a cigarette and blew out the toxic, white smoke. It meandered and discoed its way onto the dance floor. He blew out a circular ring in the air and then shot out an arrow of smoke through the center of the ring, like an arrow piercing a target.

Rocky squashed his cigarette and advanced towards a young, sexy girl in a tight, curve squeezing micro-mini. The girl smiled. Her face was familiar, maybe a Trans Pacific flight attendant. She was in her early twenties with a provocative figure and an exotic look; high cheekbones and honey-colored hair that she had let loose, free, and wild.

Shakti's friend Tara had once said, "If you're beautiful and have a brain and a vagina, you can own the world." This girl in the club seemed to share that notion. Shakti, on the other hand, found her own looks a disadvantage. Men were always propositioning, but few took the trouble to get to know her. The tingling sensation that started in her heels was now a shooting pain, running up her nerves.

The girl blazed across the dance floor. She writhed to a rhythm that no one else could match. Rocky joined her and they cleared up a space amidst the hot and sweaty bodies. Everyone stopped and watched them sway their hips. They practically owned the floor, mimicking a scene out of *Dirty Dancing*. They merged into one smooth, sequined organism that gyrated to the techno-beat towards an orgasmic union.

Shakti couldn't bear to watch. She tried not to look but it was like driving past an accident. She couldn't help it. Her gaze ended up back on them. She felt sick and queasy to the core. The shooting pain was now an explosion in her brain with agonizing flashes.

She realized how Rocky had masterminded everything. Vicky was merely a tool to stalk Kriya-di and to set Rocky up as the gallant rescuer. All the red roses and the letters were a hoax. A façade for Rocky's evil intentions. Even the episode where Vicky went down on his knee was orchestrated to get Rocky closer to Kriya-di.

She felt certain that Rocky was behind the missing person call to Inspector Gore, setting her up as the prime suspect. It all became clear in her mind.

Kriya-di, Inspector Gore and me, all of us were fooled and suckered by Rocky. Hook, line, and sinker. How could I be so stupid? How could I not see through him? What are his intentions? Where is Kriya-di now?

Shakti felt claustrophobic in the cloud of smoke. She couldn't breathe. She coughed in disgust and walked out of J49, fuming, fallen, and fretful. Tears welled up in her eyes. *Rocky is the key to the door leading to Kriya-di.*

Rocky and the girl took a break from their virtual sex on the floor. He watched her leave to powder her face as he wet his lips and gulped down the saliva dancing in his mouth. He stepped to the bar and ordered drinks.

"Your *lauda*[46] was sticking in her *gaand*[47], her nice and juicy *gaand*. I had the biggest fucking erection." Vicky's eyes glowed in adoration.

Rocky smirked. This kid had a lot to learn.

"Look, he's still erect. *Lauda*, say hi to my hero Rocky."

The bartender set the three cocktails on the table.

"O *Chutiye*[48], this was the trailer. I'm gonna tear that *gaand* up tonight," said Rocky, as he slipped a little something into the girl's cocktail.

The girl came back and downed her cocktail in thirsty gulps. Soon she was in one of the hotel rooms cozying up with Rocky.

He waited on the bed. He didn't like the lighting in the room; it was too bright. The girl stepped out of the bathroom. She wore nothing. Why did

---

46　Lauda: Dick, Prick

47　Gaand: Ass, Butt

48　Chutiya, Chutiye: Idiot, Fucker

Indian women have such huge hips and big asses? It didn't really matter as long as he got a piece of it.

She slid into the bed beside him, put her arms around him, and whispered, "I'm so glad you chose me, dear. I wanted you from the first moment I saw you."

"Sure. I feel the same way, baby." Rocky controlled his laughter. The bitch had seen too many movies; or was it the drug talking? Either way, he didn't care.

"Do you like me?" she asked in a bashful tone.

"Yeah. I'm crazy about you." Rocky began to stroke her breasts and felt her nipples get hard. He squeezed.

"Ouch."

"Move your head down, baby."

"I don't do that." She shook her head.

"Really?" He stared at her. The next instant, he grabbed her hair and pulled.

"Please, no!" she screamed.

He slapped her hard across the face. "Oye *randi*[49], make one more noise and I'll crack your neck." He pushed her down between his legs. "There he is. Make him happy."

"Let me go," she whimpered, "You're hurting me."

"Hey, *you* wanted me. Remember, *randi*?" Rocky tightened his grip on her hair.

She glared up at him, her eyes filled with terror.

"You can go." He let go of her hair.

She didn't. The look on his face must've stopped her. She realized there was something terribly wrong with him. But it was too late.

"There's no reason for us to fight," she said, placating. "You and me…"

"Enough of the talk. Now shut up and go to work." His fingers dug into her neck.

"Of course, sweetheart," she whimpered, "Of course…"

"Rocky is the mastermind. He played all of us." Shakti seethed in Gore's office.

"Calm down, Shakti." The Inspector sat all the way back in his chair, spine straight like a police baton.

---

49 Randi = Whore

I don't need to calm down. "Rocky and Vicky are into drugs. I saw them. And I know they've got Kriya-di. She's in trouble."

"Why don't you sit down first?"

Shakti supposed that she could sit down. Her throat kept filling with unpleasantness. Her tongue held it back. As she pushed it back down, her stomach roiled. The putrid feeling she had last night never diminished. It got more rancid.

If she sat down, it would be like abandoning Kriya-di. *Did the Inspector think Kriya-di was sitting down? If Shakti ate, would Kriya-di eat? She shouldn't do anything Kriya-di couldn't do or was being prohibited from doing. Was she weeping? Had Rocky locked her up in a stifling place?*

"We followed up on that Harold Walker guy. He's an American software professional who was trying to visit India for vacation."

If she sat down, if she took it easy, wouldn't Kriya-di feel her resting? If she relaxed, wouldn't Kriya-di think she had decided to call off her quest? Wouldn't that deflate any hope Kriya-di had for a life-preserver? Wouldn't Kriya-di feel disappointed that her best friend, her sister, had failed her?

"Shakti, are you listening? That Harold Walker was an absolute dead end..."

"What? Oh... Inspector, forget Harold Walker. I followed Vicky to J49 and ..."

"That's the police's job. You can't take matters into your own hands. It's risky."

"I'm telling you, Rocky is the real mastermind."

"First you tell me Rocky is a great guy. Now you tell me he's the mastermind. Can you make up your mind?" The Inspector held his *take-off* expression, fixed, like the progress of a Boeing 747. His eyes never veered left or right.

"But Inspector..."

"You gave Vicky and Harold as leads. Both turned out innocent, with solid alibis. I can't be wasting my time on wild goose chases. I have other cases, you know. Three arsons, two murdered girls, five cases of domestic abuse, and two gang related deaths." Gore crushed the end of his cigarette with such force that sparks and ash flew into the air.

"I'm sure they broke into my apartment. All the things in Kriya-di's bedroom were scattered in a mess. They searched for something."

"Maybe Kriya knew about the drugs. Maybe she helped Rocky." The Inspector was forcing her tiny plane to turn sharply, change directions, and reduce altitude.

"What?"

The Inspector took a big gulp of his tea with a fluttering sound. He wiped his lips with his wrist, made a loud throaty noise and spit into the trash can. He held a scowl on his slanted mouth and looked straight into her eyes. "You are a liar."

She was taken aback. She looked down at him with unabashed brown eyes. "Why should I lie? I've nothing to lie about. I've nothing to hide. My best friend, my sister, has disappeared, and you're sitting here twiddling your thumbs."

She walked towards the door, red in the face. Her heart thumped against the walls of her chest. Her entire body trembled in rebellion. She stopped and turned around. "Don't *ever* call me a liar."

"Put some extra spicy sauce on mine." Rocky ordered the roadside sandwich outside of Mithibai College. His *lauda* still ached from the night before as he ogled at the taut, nubile girls on the college campus.

"Rocky-da, what's so great about this small roadside stall?" asked Vicky.

"Take one bite and you'll know. It's a gastro ticket to orgasm."

People alighted from cars, ranging from Mercedes to Marutis, all waiting for their slice of the tasty bite. Was it the special butter, the fillings, or the magic in the hands? Rocky thought the secret was in the special, spicy sauce.

"Rocky-da, you're such a stud." Vicky couldn't conceal his admiration as they sat down on the library steps. "I adore the way you live your life - King-sized."

"I love to live life in 5-D."

"I've heard of 3-D but what's 5-D?"

"I love Drinking, Dancing, Damsels, Drugs…"

"And what's the fifth D?"

"Death to my fucking enemies." Rocky swiveled his head as some college girls walked by in their tight hip-hugging jeans and tiny tops. He enjoyed his bite. "Vicky, it's all about the gratification of that big, overarching D. *Desire.* Each and every *desire* that originates in me, I have to indulge and satisfy."

"Every desire?" Vicky gazed doe-eyed. "I wish I was half the man you are."

"Yeah. Self-control and moderation are for sissies." Rocky looked up. The sun was scorching, but worth the burn. The girls were a cooling balm for his eyes. "I'm a simple man with a reasonable brain."

"But when you get into the zone, like you did last night with that chick…"

"*Chutiye*, that's only a blood supply problem. As long as it flows up, I'm ok. But once it flows down to my dick, my brain goes to sleep. I have no control over myself."

Vicky lapped up every bit of information. Golden nuggets for him.

"My *lauda* becomes the king and I become a hostage who follows his whims. He's gotten me into trouble so many times. Nothing I can do about it. I'm mere putty in his hands. And he's a massive, throbbing, royal scepter in my hands."

"When did the king have his first victory? Whose fertile ground did he conquer and thrust his flagpole in?"

"That's a long story. But I'll tell you where it all started."

Vicky was eager to learn. His eyes focused, his ears in attention, and his brain waiting with a memory pen to make indelible notes.

"I had this smoking hot high school teacher. Mid-thirties, full figure. She wore tight, sleeveless, low-cut blouses that exposed a whole lot of cleavage."

Vicky rolled back the saliva that pitter-pattered in his mouth.

"I could tell the weather from her bosom. On cold days, her fucking nipples would be all perked up, pointing straight out to me."

Vicky opened up his sleeve buttons, releasing his wiry arms. He folded the sleeves back in agitated anticipation.

"I loved to get into trouble in her class. I made noises. I skipped homework. I talked to my neighbors. You know why?"

"No," said Vicky, his voice a little smaller than before.

"She made us kneel by the board. I could be right next to her. Feel the breeze from her hair. Smell her sweet fragrance. Almost touch her undulating booty. She had a rear like two ripe, juicy watermelons. I wanted to bite into them and suck them dry."

Vicky opened up his top shirt button to placate the heat.

"When the duster slipped from her hand, she bent to pick it up. I could glimpse the smooth white flesh of her boobs and the dark, treasured valley in the middle."

Vicky took out a ballpoint pen from his pocket and began to fidget with it.

"And *bhenchod*[50], one rainy day, she came to class all drenched in a transparent chiffon red saree that clung to her. It was a fucking wild day with crazy winds."

---

50 Bhenchod: Sister-fucker

"Then what happened?" asked Vicky, sitting perfectly still, his voice little more than a hoarse whisper.

Rocky smirked. No hope for this fucker. "It was raining cats and dogs outside. My doggy mind was hypnotized by the curve of her waist, her belly button, and the small fold of flesh above the knot of her saree. I didn't even have to undress her. I was smitten."

Vicky ejected the ballpoint pen from his hand in premature excitement. He picked it back up and gripped it tightly, his eyes fixated on Rocky.

"The big fucker that I am, I had to get into trouble. I wanted it so bad. Soon, I was kneeling by her. The duster fell, she bent down. I seized the fucking chance."

Vicky shifted on the steps, his pants getting uncomfortable.

"I said, 'Let me pick that up for you, Ma'm,' then I lunged for it with my right hand. I grazed her right boob with my elbow."

Vicky scratched his toolbox, unable to control the itch in his pants.

"*Bhenchod*, I'm telling you. That sent the craziest of fucking sensations all through my body and above all to king *lauda*. Oh, the softness of the white flesh. Oh, the perkiness of the nipple. It was the best fucking moment."

Without warning, Rocky's cellphone rang and interrupted the dance of the little sperm inside his scrotum. "Hello *Bhai* ...yes *Bhai*...very good *Bhai*...okay *Bhai*."

He switched his phone off and turned to Vicky. "*Bhai* said we have the photos. I've to go to Thailand on the next available flight."

"You are in love with Shiva," Tara teased Shakti.

Shakti stood with a coffee cup at the airport terminal window, watching planes land and take off. It was the same spot that she'd stood with Shiva. "No I'm not." She averted Tara's gaze. If she didn't know before, that she had fallen for him, she did now. She knew what a charade felt like. It showed in her quivering chin and cracking voice.

"Oh, don't even try to deny it. The miserable thing is that you're too scared to do anything about it but sulk."

Shakti took a long sip. She drew in her elbows and tucked them into her sides. As usual, Tara had summed up her intricate, tormented thoughts into one simple verdict.

Shakti hadn't seen anyone since Raj from her college days. Raj and she were two opposite sides of a coin. She was active, she loved to see new places, and she needed to be busy, doing something. Raj, on the other hand, was chilled and laid back. He loved to slouch on his couch and watch endless hours of cricket. They had always known that they were different, but it seemed that they nicely balanced each other so they got engaged in a small, private ceremony.

But then Shakti started her flight attendant job, began traveling, and their relationship went sour. During the courting, Raj had found her travel bug cute and charming, but later he grew tired of her long absences and her jet lag when she was in town. He preferred to hang out with his friends and drink rum and coke while discussing what stocks to buy. He wanted her to quit her job and be by his side, like the other businessmen's wives at socialite parties. After a marathon bout of quarrels, they decided to break off the engagement and go their different ways.

"Own up to it," Tara insisted, and gave her a deep, penetrating gaze.

Shakti crossed her left arm over her right elbow. She couldn't. She wouldn't. Shiva had come into her life, however brief, like a whiff of fresh air. She knew that he was different from Raj and any other guy she'd known. She dreamt about him. But he was so far away. She remembered his straight left arm and bent index finger. She hoped that he wasn't getting into any new accidents.

"Okay, be tight-lipped about it. But you can't hide what's obvious."

"Well, you've no idea about the truth," Shakti snapped, but without a shred of certainty in her voice. She pawed through her hair and touched her neck. It felt cold.

Tara sat on the chair next to the terminal window. "Shakti, pay attention to me. You're in love. I've known you for a long time now. You've never been like this before."

"What are you talking about? I'm perfectly fine."

"You have to be brave, okay? You have to find Shiva's number and call him. You have to tell him how you feel."

"What?" Shakti sat down next to her.

"Promise to God, if you don't, you'll be sorry for the rest of your timid life."

Shakti knew Tara was spot on and she didn't attempt to counter her. She stared down at her feet, her palms damp with sweat. "What if Shiva doesn't love me?" Shakti held her breath, expecting and hoping for encouragement as Tara mulled over it. She wanted Tara to say that of course he loved her. She wanted Tara to say that it was obvious from the look in his eyes. How could he not? But Tara didn't say that.

Instead, Tara leaned in and moved closer. She lightly touched Shakti's forearm and took her hands in hers. "You won't find that out until you show some daring."

"I was once a daring girl, free-spirited." Shakti's eyes welled up. "I had the best family and a carefree life, but that was all taken away. It's been a while, but I'm still recovering. That daring Shakti is hidden somewhere inside, deep inside and cowering."

Tara's eyebrows curved down and her eyes narrowed in sympathy.

"Kriya-di got me back on my feet. Now she's missing and I'm a lost soul." She felt drained, physically and emotionally. "What can I do about it? Nothing. I have to rely on the incompetent police who think I'm responsible for her disappearance."

Tara pressed her shoulder in understanding. "Shakti, I didn't mean to …"

"Fear is etched in my mind. Fear of losing loved ones." She had lost Sanju, Aai, Baba, and Kriya-di. "I trusted Rocky, but I was wrong. I can't trust my judgment. I can't figure out a friend from a foe. I feel I'm falling into some dark, unknown place."

Tara came closer and hugged to comfort her.

"No Tara, I can't be brave. I don't feel brave. I'm not ready to reach out to Shiva. That will have to wait."

Shiva lay on a workout bench in his gym in San Francisco. He pushed the 50 pound dumbbells he held into a chest press. He felt the twinge in his pectoral muscles, triceps, and deltoids. He changed the bench position to an incline to target the upper region of his pectorals. He looked out through the windows of the gym. The only thing he could see was Shakti's face. Her lustrous smile. Her big brown eyes.

He shifted to the biceps curl and triceps kickback, exhaling to raise the dumbbells and inhaling to lower them down. He peered into the gym mirror to see Shakti at the Mumbai terminal window, watching planes land and take off. She held a coffee mug in her hand. It seemed like a portal, allowing him to escape from reality into a dream, like a memory that transfers the past and transforms the present. Nothing short of magic.

He closed his eyes. He could feel the reverberation of the exercise machines within his core. The loud clang of the free weights filled the air with a mass almost as heavy as the remembrance in his heart. He recalled the clamor of Mumbai airport and how Shakti had transformed into a woman on a mission. She had sliced through the crowds and skipped through the immigration queues. A Joan of Arc in battle, tangoing her way towards victory.

His earphones played *Pasional (Passionate)*, the famous tango from *Mario Soto*. He felt the nervous pressure of her soft hand in his. He recalled her touch, a soulmate's touch - familiar yet exciting. It sent a current through him as it ignited his chest with passion. He felt ablaze inside with a thirst, a fear of losing her and of never seeing her again. She'd never know how it felt like to die a million times of longing. He imagined her in his arms as they strode together through throngs of people at Mumbai airport.

The *Pasional* now throbbed in his ears. He danced with Shakti in his embrace, transmitting the pulsations of music to her. They twirled in lockstep, adjusting to the emotion and speed of the tango. Their embrace varied from open to closed, connecting chest to chest and face to face. Her lips smoldered and her eyes set him on fire, swathing him and tormenting him. Their feet began to float in the air, their ankles and knees brushing as one leg passed the other. He felt inside him an inferno of insatiable yearning.

Rocky stepped out into the Phuket International airport terminal. Even though it ranked second in Thailand in passenger volume, to him it was a dreadful affair. The terminal was swamped with people and chaos. He felt it was more like a bus station; dirty, small, and extremely overused. He wanted them to tear it down and start again, or at least separate out the domestic and international flights and passengers and add some space.

But there were some distinct advantages. For one, the security was lax. Rocky valued that in his line of business. His luggage was already waiting for him at the baggage claim. Within minutes of his landing, he was through immigration and customs, had picked up his luggage, and was out the front door. Thailand, let's rock-n-roll, baby.

A short, bald, pudgy middle-aged man waited for him outside the terminal. A large black scar ran across his face. "Welcome to Phuket, Boss."

"Hey Ganjoo! *Bhai* told me the photos are awesome," Rocky said as he got into the car.

Ganjoo handed him a pack of pictures while he focused on the busy road, cutting ahead of the *tuk-tuks*. His real name was Ganesan Yeddyurappa but everyone called him Ganjoo. The poor sucker had lost all his fucking hair thanks to his three marriages. He could keep none of his wives happy, and they left with his money. No one knew the true story about his scar. Rocky had heard many versions; the only fucking believable one was that it was his third wife's departing gift from a sickle blow!

"Excellent! Great job, Ganjoo! Our mission will be successful. That *madarchod*[51] will be forced to surrender."

"Thanks, Boss." Now at one hundred and some kilos and no money in the bank, Ganjoo was as marketable as a used condom and they both knew it. But he remained a useful tool for all of Rocky's dirty work.

"How's the pigeon holding up?"

"Boss, your girl is safe. We're taking good care."

"*Sa wat dee khrap*, Chanarong," Rocky greeted the guard outside the apartment, asking him how he was doing.

"*Sa baai dee.*" Chanarong replied with a wry face that he was fine.

"*Khaawp khoon maak khrap.*" Rocky gave him cash, thanking him for his work. He entered the apartment and gave a hug to Zeenat. "Great photos on the beach, Zee."

"Thanks. Ganjoo did Patang and Kata beaches. I covered Karon and Surin."

"Is the wild one still throwing things?"

"No. She's stopped hurling. And she's eating now. At last."

Rocky unlocked the room latch and walked in. Kriya lay on a dirty mattress with stains and discolorations. She looked shriveled. Her eyes, a fearful, pale yellow, sunk deep into their sockets. Her cheeks clung on to the jaw, making her cheek-bones and chin protrude. Her arms and legs resembled sticks. She looked frail and weak.

"Kriya, I'm glad you've started to eat. It'll bring you some strength and color."

"Why Rocky? Why are you doing this?"

"You remember why, don't you?"

"No, that's the problem. I don't. I had carried a package for you on my flight. I gave it to you and was headed home. But I forgot to tell you about the Harold Walker incident, so I stepped back into the room ..."

---

51 Madarchod: Mother-fucker

"You shouldn't have come back."

"I saw Ganjoo, Zeenat and you. The package lay open with some white stuff. I felt terrible. You made me carry drugs. You dog."

"You weren't supposed to see that," Rocky scoffed. She had been so gullible.

"I was mad. I was about to rush out...I don't remember anything after that."

"After your unexpected feat, we knocked you out with chloroform. We had to."

Kriya stared at him in anger.

"We knew you'd come back to your senses soon. If we left you there, you'd go to the police. We couldn't take that risk. Ganjoo suggested we kill you and dispose of your body. I like you, Kriya. I wouldn't let that happen."

"How very considerate of you." Sarcasm dripped from her voice. She had so believed in the power of their love. She held a probing stare, questioning how in the world she could have trusted him. How could she have loved this chameleon?

"Ganjoo and Zee were all set to fly as Mr. and Mrs. Shoaib Akhtar. I looked at Zee. She's about the same height as you. Same face structure."

She folded her hands, her hair drooping over her face, and looked with moist eyes.

"I asked Zee to transfer her ornaments onto you and add some make-up. Once inside the *burkha* you were as good of a Mrs. Shoaib Akhtar as Zee."

"Rocky, you should've left me in Mumbai. I would've kept quiet," she sobbed.

"I couldn't take that chance. We drugged you and put you in a wheel-chair. I knew a crew member so getting you onto the plane wasn't a problem."

"Didn't anyone suspect during the flight?" Her sobs grew louder.

"You were a sleeping beauty on the flight and we used the wheelchair to get you here. Zee joined us on the next flight." Rocky closed in to hold her feeble body.

Kriya flushed red with contempt - a sharp pang of pain in the deepest chamber of her heart. Her eyes screamed betrayer! Traitor! Her words were blurred by her weeping and his chest against her mouth. "Please, let me go, Rocky."

"I can't do that. When you had an asthma attack, I was terrified I'd lose you. I killed the Doberman and broke into your room for the inhaler. I love you. I really do."

Rocky remembered the only other time he had said those words - to his high school teacher. He had been truly, madly, deeply in love with her. One day, he had found her alone in the science lab after school hours.

She was angry when he confessed his longing for her. "Go away," she whispered, suffocating with anticipation. "Go away or I'll scream."

He stood there rejected, dejected.

She locked the door. "I'm your teacher," she murmured. "It's almost as if I were your mother." She moved aside the test tube stand from the desk. She propped herself up and opened the front buttons on her blouse, pulling him to her soft, white mounds. He suckled on them like a voracious animal, tugging at her nipples until she moaned with soreness. She fondled the front of his bulging pants and unzipped to release his manhood. She stepped down, pulled up her saree, and bent over the desk. "Take me from behind."

They fucked in the lab, the library, the teachers' lounge, the janitor's closet, and on classroom benches. He would've done anything for her; he would've killed anyone or even himself for her. Everything went great for a year. One evening Rocky realized he'd forgotten his science workbook in the lab. The front door was shut but not locked. He pushed it open and heard sounds from inside. He stepped in quietly. And there they were. She was bent over the desk exactly like their first time and this broad-shouldered, fair-skinned, *madarchod* cricket coach was thumping her from behind.

Rocky walked out of the science lab, never to see her again. That two-timing bitch! At first the feeling inside him was nausea, then it morphed into anger, and then finally into revenge. That's what kick-started his sexcapades. Every bitch was no more than a fucking hole. Age, no bar. Color, no bar. He fucked them all. Bar dancers, college girls, red light district whores, and housewives.

Until he met Kriya. She was different. She was kind. She was a giver. It was more than how he felt about her. It was about how she made him feel about himself. He felt different around her. He felt changed. He stopped messing around with other women. Maybe he had strayed and succumbed once or twice, but he stopped his irresponsible ways when he was with Kriya. She was his savior, rescuing him from the swamp of his recklessness and debauchery.

"I love you, Kriya. You don't have to suffer here, my love. Join me and we will rule the world, you and me."

Kriya's face dripped with abandonment. She seethed with disappoint-ment. It was a crisis of her faith in love. The idea of love seemed dead to her. She reached out under the mattress, pumped the inhaler twice into her mouth and took a deep breath. "But why? Why do you need all this drug stuff? You're doing well as a pilot."

Rocky bent his head for a peek at his wristwatch. His arm was around her. His cuff was pulled back far enough to leave the watch uncovered. It was fucking late. He had to go. "That isn't good enough. I don't want to shuttle stupid people for the rest of my life. No thanks. I want *more*. The pilot's job isn't going to give me that *more*."

"What *more*?"

"I want fucking more money and more power. I want people to fear me. I want to live my life in 5-D. I want my every little desire gratified."

"But Rocky, people trusted you, they loved you."

"Kriya darling, there are two types of people in this world: fuckers and suckers. I want to be the biggest fucker of them all."

Kriya looked at him as if she couldn't believe her ears.

"I want the whole fucking world at my feet. All the people who ever cheated me, ridiculed me, put me down...I want them groveling, scared, and pleading at my feet."

Tidarat Thongchai was a worried man. The Thai government was tar-geting drug dealing kingpins like him. The Thai police had launched a se-ries of raids and Thongchai's ground level drug dealers were being rounded up right, left, and center.

It had all started with the December 2002 speech when the King of Thailand, on the eve of his birthday, noted the rise in drug use in the coun-try. The Thai government was called on to establish a special court to deal with drug dealers. The belief was, "If we execute 60,000 the land will rise and our descendants will escape bad *karma*".

The Thai Prime Minister launched the controversial *War on Drugs* cam-paign to rid "every square inch of the country" of drugs. The government increased the penalties on dealing. It went out of its way to publicize the campaign through daily statements of arrest, seizure, and death statistics. More than 2,000 known drug dealers were killed.

Tidarat Thongchai's secretary buzzed. "Mr. Thongchai, there's an Indian gentleman, Mr. Rocky, here to see you. He doesn't have an appointment but…"

"Then why are you bothering me?" Thongchai snapped down the intercom.

The new policy had reduced drug consumption, particularly in schools, by increasing the market price. Thongchai's customer base was threatened. He'd built up a lavish lifestyle: houses, cars, wives, mistresses, and children. If he couldn't sell his drugs, his income would come to a grinding halt. What was he going to do with the three manufacturing facilities he'd set up? The stagnant drugs in his facilities, if not sold for exorbitant prices, were simply like any other white powder – *worthless.*

His secretary buzzed again. "I'm sorry to disturb you. Mr. Rocky says he has a message from the *Bhai* in Mumbai. He says it's very important."

A message? Strange. Thongchai was a member of the Thai underworld. He knew of the *Bhai* from Mumbai. It was an inter-connected underworld family; not always on friendly terms, though. Why would *Bhai* send him a message?

"Send him in."

"Yes, sir."

Rocky barged into his office and looked around in approval. "*Sa wat dee khrap*, Mr. Thongchai. Nice of you to see me on such short notice. I'm Rocky."

"You have two minutes."

"*Bhai* sent me. He thought you and I should have a talk."

"Really? And what exactly do we have to talk about?"

"Do you mind if I sit down?"

"I don't think you'll be staying that long."

Rocky settled himself in a chair. "I've a fleet of aircrafts, pilots, and crew at my disposal, Mr. Thongchai. I fly things to different parts of the world."

"I see. And you want to do this import and export in Thailand?"

"Exactly."

"Why did *Bhai* send you to me? There are so many other people he can go to."

"We have a problem in Mumbai. There's such a big untapped market for drugs, you can't even imagine."

"And?"

"But there's a limited supply. That fucker Qasim Jardari has his own sources, but our *Bhai* is running short."

"You want me to supply to *Bhai*?"

"No. I want one of your manufacturing plants. You can keep the other two."

Thongchai glared at his audacity. "And you expect me to...? Get out of here, before I call the police." Thongchai reached for the phone. He detected a newbie gamble when he saw one. Rocky's overconfidence was his giveaway. Thongchai knew you caught a con not only by their contradiction, but also if they sounded rehearsed. He had reduced hardened men to tears in a matter of minutes.

"I'd like to speak to them too. I'd like to tell them all about the two French tourists who overdosed on Patong beach last month."

"What are you talking about?"

"I'm talking about the two people who bought drugs from you and are now dead. Penalties are severe these days, I hear."

Thongchai's eyes narrowed.

"I've heard five other stories of death in the last nine months: two on Kata beach, one on Karon, and two on Surin. You want to look at some pictures?"

Rocky threw a pack of photos towards him. Thongchai went through them. He felt blood rush to his face as a shockwave charged through him. The pictures showed tourists buying drugs from his men, inhaling and injecting the drugs. They showed him and his men disposing of the dead bodies of tourists.

"Do you think, maybe, the police would be interested in that story, or the other ones, Mr. Thongchai? If they aren't, maybe the press would be, huh?"

Thongchai rearranged the photos and looked at them again, eyes wide open. He had carefully stayed away from police scrutiny by putting up insignificant goons as his front men, instilling them with an unflinching sense of fear and loyalty. The investigators had suspicions, but they never got their hands on anything that would incriminate him.

"I can see the headlines now, can't you? 'Mr. Thongchai sentenced to death for murder.' Can I call you Tidarat? *Bhai* told me all your friends call you Tidarat."

Thongchai drew back sharply. He gave Rocky a blank stare.

"You and I will be good friends. Do you know why? Because good friends don't *rat* on each other, Tida*rat*. We'll keep that little stunt you pulled our secret, shall we?"

When Thongchai spoke, his voice was hoarse. "What do you want?"

"I told you. I want one of your manufacturing plants. And you and I being such good friends, I don't think you'd want to charge me for the plant, would you? Let's say it's a favor traded for a favor."

"I can't let you do this. How do I know you won't go public with the photos? If they ever got out, I'd lose my whole business." Thongchai took a deep breath.

"But they aren't going to get out, are they? In my business, I don't advertise. We're going to do this in silence. And think about it...this is your chance to play with the big sharks...be part of the big Mumbai crime syndicate. Big business, Tidarat."

"You're making a big mistake. You can't blackmail me. Do you know who I am?"

"Yeah. You're my new partner. You and I are going to do business together and have some fun, Tidarat baby."

"What if I say no?"

"If you say no, I go right to the police and the newspapers. And there goes your reputation and your fucking empire, right down the drain."

A long, painful silence. "How...how did *Bhai* find out?"

Rocky grinned. "That's not important. What's important is that I've got you by the balls. If I squeeze hard you'll become a eunuch. You'll be singing soprano for the rest of your life. And you'll be singing loudly in a prison cell with horny inmates."

Thongchai opened his mouth to reply, but no voice came out from his throat.

Rocky looked at his watch. "My goodness, my two minutes are up." He rose to his feet. "I'm giving you sixty seconds to decide whether I walk out of here as your partner – or simply walk out."

Thongchai stared at the mirror behind Rocky. His face was drained of color. He felt and looked ten years older. He held no illusions about what would happen if the true story of the tourist's deaths came out. The press, public, and government would eat him alive. He would be portrayed and punished as a monster, a murderer.

"Your sixty seconds are up."

Thongchai nodded in reluctance. "Alright," he whispered, "alright."

Rocky beamed down at him. "You're smart."

Thongchai rose to his feet in slow motion as if weighed down by something heavy. "I'll let you get away with this for a year. I don't know how you do the export, or when. I'll put one of your men inside my manufacturing plant. That's as far as I'll go."

"It's a deal," Rocky said. He thought, *Maybe you aren't so smart. You export heroin for one year and you're hooked, Tidarat baby. There's no way I'll ever let you go.* Aloud, he repeated, "Sure, it's a deal."

There are two types of people in this world: fuckers and suckers.

"Who is Salman Khan?"
- Hong Lee, Silicon Valley entrepreneur

CHAPTER 10

"Whoa, that's a hot chick next to your seat." Harry was bursting at the seams.

Shiva smiled. He stretched his arms across his chest and then behind his shoulders. He knew how excited Harry could get. They stood by the restrooms, taking a break from all that sitting in one place on the long plane ride from San Francisco to Mumbai. After days of debate they had accepted Mr. Singh's offer to set up an India office.

"That's a Russian chick and she's got some very cute stories." Shiva waved to the girl who smiled from her seat and waved back.

"You're always the lucky one. How come I never have a cute girl beside me? Look at that guy next to me in 54B."

Shiva looked towards the rear of the plane. That was one scary looking dude.

"You won't believe it. He had the flight attendant mix him red wine and coke."

"That's sacrilege. Did he add cream and sugar too?" Shiva asked.

"Hey, you never know." Hong joined in the discussion. "Next you'll hear he's raking in millions on a product called cocovino. He might do better than our start-up."

"Crazy," Harry said. "Reminds me of the incident several years ago when someone told me 'make me a light peg of beer; add more water.'"

Shiva and Hong laughed.

"So, why is the Russian chick headed to India?" Harry asked. "She wants to act in a Bollywood movie? A dance item number, maybe?"

"She's not going to Mumbai. She's changing planes in Frankfurt for Moscow."

"Darn."

"But she does know about Bollywood. She's a big fan. I'm telling you. That's how India is conquering the world…through these song and dance movies."

"Bad luck. We could've shown her around Mumbai," whined Harry.

"Yeah right. Even you two haven't seen Mumbai yet. At least nothing more than the airport, right Harry?" Shiva winked.

"Hey, curiosity is killing the cat in me," Hong insisted. "What happened when Harry was in Mumbai? You've got to let the cat out of the bag."

"It was nothing exciting," Harry interrupted with a catty caution.

"Ok, here's the short version," said Shiva. "We had planned a grand reunion. Harry came from the U.S., Sally from Australia, and I was in India to check on my Ma."

"Cool. Sounds fun."

"Sally arrived earlier and we waited outside the airport. And we kept waiting. Three hours went by. Passengers from all the incoming flights came out and went their merry way, but there was no sign of Harry."

"Where the heck was he?"

"At last he called. His passport was about to expire and the Indian immigration wouldn't let him into Mumbai. He had to head back to the U.S. on the next flight."

"That was a bummer. I was so looking forward to meeting you guys, but the officials wouldn't listen. This friendly flight attendant, what was her name…Krissie, no…Kriya, yeah, Kriya. She tried to help me but no luck. I was forced to go back."

"So Shiva, what did Sally and you do?" asked Hong.

"Well, she was in Mumbai for a week, so I showed her around. We went to South Mumbai, the Gateway of India, the Taj, and Marine Drive."

"You traitors," Harry blurted out.

"Sally had a fancy for Indian food, so we went to a whole bunch of restaurants and she willingly tortured herself with all kinds of spicy food."

"I wish I was there."

"We missed you. We had a good time except for that one incident."

"What happened?" both Harry and Hong asked at the same time.

"It was her last day in Mumbai, so we decided to splurge. We headed out to Aurus in Juhu – a fine dining, sea-facing restaurant that serves up modern European cuisine."

"Aurus, huh?"

"We loved the ad: *Looking to delight your senses? Aurus is the place to be. Yield to the opulence of the decor, the sensual lights and sea breeze. Transport to a time when fine dining was an extravaganza, an experience much more than merely the food you eat.*"

"It turned out to be a disaster instead, didn't it?" Harry said.

"The place was great. An ambience to die for. An open air beach lounge with a nice breeze. An array of cocktails like our Tangerine Capiroshka."

"Capi what shka?"

"Capiroshka. We could listen to the waves and watch the moon. Moroccan lamps on the tables. No wonder famous celebrities visited that place."

"So the food must've been terrible then?"

"The food was an affair in itself. New world cuisine with a twist. King prawns with wasabi and oven roasted baby lobster with red pepper jelly." He peeked at Harry.

Harry's mouth was watering with visions of king prawns and lobster. He caught Shiva observing and took a gulp. "Okay. So, what was the incident? Are you gonna tell us or what?" He was out of patience and the savory food description didn't help at all.

"Sally said, 'Don't look now, but that man has been staring at us for the last fifteen minutes.' I told her all men in India stare, more so if you're a white woman."

Harry's ears perked up.

"We were cracking jokes and laughing aloud. Sally froze up all of a sudden. 'That guy took my picture. I saw him. His face was a mask of hatred.'"

"Really? Someone took Sally's picture?"

"She said it was the guy at the bar with the navy blue blazer. So I moved across the tables to the bar area. I saw three guys in navy blue blazers."

Harry and Hong leaned forward.

"I said hi to the first one. He had a quizzical look on his gentle face. Not our guy. I rushed to the second one. He said hi back with a smile. Not our guy either."

"Two down, one to go."

"I moved across the crowd as fast as I could, but the third guy in the navy blue blazer was nowhere to be seen."

"What? Where was he? Was he the guy who took Sally's picture?"

"I don't know. I ran through the lounge to the entrance. A man in a navy blue blazer got into a taxi and I ran after it but the taxi zoomed away on the clear night road."

"So you never found out who it was?" asked Harry.

"Nope. It was a dampener for the evening. But we decided to put that episode behind us and forget about it."

"Well, no harm done. You had a good time overall," Harry said.

"Let's do some of those things this time, the three of us. Harry and I have two weeks in Mumbai," Hong said.

"It'll be hard. We have to finalize our office and interview all the candidates," Harry added.

"No worries, guys. We'll find time to taste a bit of Mumbai," Shiva said.

At the transit stopover in Frankfurt airport, all of them gave hugs to the Russian chick. They wished her well on her journey to Moscow. Harry and Hong insisted that she visit India next time, so they could show her around.

Hong couldn't resist. "I have a question for you." He peered through his glasses.

"Yes?"

"I heard you're a big Bollywood movie buff?"

"Yes. That I am."

"So tell me. Who is Salman Khan?"

Shiva smiled. Hong was incorrigible; he had to get to the root of things on all kinds of topics.

"Ooooh! Salman Khan! I love him!" The Russian chick went bonkers. "I love him so much I've no words to describe him!"

"But he's an okay looking guy, isn't he?" Harry said.

"You must be kidding me. He's the best-looking man in the whole world. First guy whose poster I put in my room. I got into trouble for that with my dad."

"You did?"

"But it was worth it. He's such a handsome, romantic charmer."

"Really? Which Salman movie is worth watching?"

"I must've seen his *Hum Aapke Hain Koun*[52] a hundred times. And of late, I loved his *Hum Tumhare Hain Sanam*[53]."

"One hundred times?"

"I get goosebumps when I hear his name. I want to touch him. If I see him I'll be ready to elope with him. Anytime, anywhere..."

The trio cleared the Frankfurt airport transit security to get to the connecting gate for their flight to Mumbai. They stepped onto the escalator

---

52 Hum Aapke Hain Koun: Who am I to you

53 Hum Tumhare Hain Sanam: I am yours, dear

going down. Shiva looked ahead. What a freaking happenstance. Or was it a twist of fate? Their ex-Boss from Alltech was on the escalator; he had got on at the same time and stood right in front. Shiva hadn't seen him in the ten years since his firing at the Los Gatos house.

All the poison that their cunning ex-Boss had spread came back to haunt him in the last few years. He reaped what he'd sown. Alltech lost the IP lawsuit against the big competitor and was forced to pay through the nose. The long, drawn out legal battle and distraction made their products lag in technology. No great innovations were made and customers stopped using their products.

Boss tried to wheedle a deal where the big competitor would buy Alltech at the price of peanuts. He'd get a sweet settlement himself, but the rank and file employees would get nothing. All those years of long hours and blood and sweat from the employees would go down the drain. But the deal didn't go through. Employees deserted in droves and he was forced to shut Alltech down.

Shiva's Boss reminded him of Ellsworth Toohey[54] from *The Fountainhead*. Like Toohey, he had no true genius. Toohey's mission was to destroy Roark's excellence through a smear campaign. Boss's mission was to raze Shiva and his company. Toohey said: "Enshrine mediocrity and the shrines are razed." Boss epitomized mediocrity.

Boss turned around on the escalator. He looked up with a sheepish expression. His shoulders sagged. All his bravado had disappeared. Oh, how the mighty had fallen.

Shiva looked down at Boss. Gloating was natural. "It's a temporary setback. You'll find another opportunity. My best wishes to you," said Shiva instead.

Boss was stunned. He wasn't expecting such a response. "I fought you and tried to bring you down every day and in every way I could. You must hate me."

"You were free to do what you pleased," Shiva said, like Howard Roark.

"Shiva, we're alone here. No customers. No press. No media. Only you and me. Why don't you tell me what you really think of me? In any words you wish."

"But I *don't* think of you," Shiva answered in a calm tone. It was the same line Roark had said to Toohey.

---

54 Ellsworth Toohey from *The Fountainhead* was an outspoken socialist and architecture column author. He covertly rose to power by shaping public opinion through his column and circle of influential associates.

The trio walked down and away to their departure gate for the flight to Mumbai.

Boss's head stayed slumped down as if Shiva's words still echoed in his ears: "But I *don't* think of you."

Shiva watched Hong and Harry closely to capture their first impressions when they landed in Mumbai. Both twitched their noses to the strange smell of the air. It was the smell of the movements and outputs of millions of humans and animals, wild and domesticated. It was virtually the smell of the immortals, the mortals, and the ones in limbo. It was actually the smell of dreams and ambitions, setbacks and victories.

As soon as they stepped out of the airport, heat waves surfed towards them and their clothes broke into a sweat. Harry and Hong both found it tough to breathe. In that Mumbai heat each breath was a well fought, tiny triumph. They complained that the city seemed to be covered in an invisible hot and wet blanket.

But today was different as Shiva showed them around Colaba in downtown Mumbai on a horse and buggy ride. It had been a week since their arrival, an arduous week filled with hundreds of candidate interviews. Finally they'd decided to take a break.

"Why are these buggy rides called *Victorias*?" asked Hong.

"I don't know…maybe something to do with Queen Victoria when she visited from England," said Shiva.

"This place is awesome compared to the dump we were in," screamed out Harry.

"Hey, it wasn't that bad in the suburbs." But Shiva knew what Harry meant. Colaba was a time-machine travel where you went back a hundred years; the old world charm, the eclectic architecture, the Arabian Sea; the entire atmosphere. It was ethereal.

"I love the architecture," Hong said. "It reminds me of Old Shanghai. It takes you back in time and you want to stay there."

"Mumbai had a variety of European influences similar to Shanghai," said Shiva. "You can spot the German gables. Dutch roofs. Swiss timbering. Roman arches. Tudor casements. And then the traditional Indian features – all combined together." In Colaba, Portugal met England with glimpses of old English and Portuguese mansions and the quaint charm of narrow lanes and colonial style buildings. All so picturesque.

"Last week was exhausting. I'm glad we've some recreation time today."

"Thanks to both of you, we now have fifteen employees selected, all set to work in our Mumbai office," Shiva replied. Their *Victoria* passed a series of shops and restaurants, with long lines outside of Café Leopolds and Mondegar, and the Art Deco Regal Cinema. They came to a stop outside the Gateway of India[55]. "Here's where the last of the defeated English troops were sent packing out of post-independence India."

"It's bigger and more impressive than the pictures," Harry said. A swarm of peddlers besieged them, trying to sell postcards, trinkets, and books.

"Not interested," Shiva told them in a stern voice

Most peddlers went away, but one was relentless. After five minutes of constant badgering, he resorted to aggressive behavior. He even tried to tie a 'blessed' bracelet onto Harry and then hassle him for money. At last he gave up.

"It's a shame to see all the litter and potholes," Hong complained. "But then I've gotten used to it after spending a week in Mumbai. It's so different from Shanghai."

"As Indians, we don't believe in half-measures," Shiva said. "When we build potholes we make sure they're big enough to house all of Pakistan." He joked, but at the back of his mind was the August 2003 twin car bombing in Mumbai that killed over 50 people and injured over 200. One of the explosions was right here at the Gateway of India, but he didn't want to scare Hong and Harry. "On a serious note, this is civic irresponsibility at its worst, and points to the lethargy of the municipal authorities."

"Still, I wish our office was here instead of SEEPZ[56]," Harry said, "though I know it would be far too expensive."

"We were lucky to get help from the MLA[57]." Shiva knew how hard it was to get things done on time in Mumbai. Pa had connected them to the MLA who expedited the process to get them an office in SEEPZ - a special economic zone, subject to liberal economic and taxation incentives to attract foreign investment and technology. The MLA had confidently told them, "Welcome to India where rules are made up as you go."

"You're right. We should thank the MLA profusely when we meet him for dinner tonight," Harry added.

---

55 Gateway of India was built in 1911 by the citizens of Bombay as a grand memorial to the English King George V when he had landed in India.

56 SEEPZ: Santacruz Electronics Export Processing Zone

57 MLA: Member of Legislative Assembly

Shiva watched the waves emerge from the sea and crash against the rocks. His favorite thing about the Gateway of India wasn't the arch at all – it was the sea beyond and its raging beauty. The seawater splashed over the boundaries, sending rain showers on the people and sending flocks of pigeons flying in frenzy.

Shiva led them next into Jehangir Art Gallery - the uncrowned Mecca of art in Mumbai, with a direct historical link to the renaissance of Indian art. It was the most sought after venue for artists to exhibit their oeuvres, but the wait list for a showcase was more than five years. However, visitors to the public art gallery had neither waiting times to contend with nor the queues one witnesses in Mumbai.

"I've never interviewed so many interesting guys before," said Hong.

"You mean crazy guys?" asked Harry with a smile as he stepped into the Gallery.

"Most guys were smart, some even brilliant. But the work culture here is so different. There's an element of lethargy," Hong whispered.

"So true. An attitude of *Ho Jayega*[58] prevails. There's no sense of urgency," Shiva said. "Everything gets procrastinated. That's hurting the country. I hope it changes and India propels itself to the full glory it's capable of."

The Gallery was filled with well-dressed folks engrossed in studying the nuances of color and concept. An intelligent silence pervaded the air.

Harry whispered, "Funny story. An interviewee's folder said 'Laziness is the mother of all habits. But in the end she's a Mother and we should respect her.'"

Hong and Shiva burst out in laughter, turning heads towards them amidst disapproving nods. They tiptoed downstairs, away from the rebuking stares and into the popular Samovar café at the Gallery.

"I'm hungry!" Harry's stomach growled for fuel.

The Samovar café had a long, narrow setting and a unique charm reminiscent of the 70s socialist culture. Shiva had been surprised here many a times by a casual world-famous painter sitting next to him, sipping tea.

"You know, I had a little fun at the interviews," Hong said. "I asked a few of them at the end, 'Who is Salman Khan?' and I got some interesting responses."

"No. You didn't."

"Yes, I did. One guy said Salman Khan is such a self-centered idiot, always strutting and swaggering. He's all about me, myself, and I."

---

58 Ho Jayega: It will get done some time

"Oh wow. The guy didn't hold back, did he?" Harry said.

"Wait, there's more. He said that Salman was the perfect proof of being a destiny's child. Short, dwarfish guy. No acting skills. Simply a big-headed bison."

"What?"

"The guy went on and on. Salman can't dance. He's got ugly bulging eyes and muscles. And still he's one of Bollywood's biggest super-stars. Go figure."

After lunch at Samovar café, the trio took a taxi up Malabar Hill to the highest point in Mumbai. Malabar Hill housed the high and mighty - the Governor, Chief Justice, and Chief Minister of the state, and many more powerful and rich. It was the calm haven of the city and it had a soothing effect. The Kamala Nehru Park and the Hanging Gardens on the Hill were manicured prim and proper, designed like an English Park.

Shiva felt a cool breeze ruffle through his hair. A sweet bouquet seeped into his heart, reminding him of Shakti. Her sweet fragrance. The swaying trees and branches reminded him of her dark brown, shoulder length hair blowing in the wind. The chirping birds reminded him of her voice and it tickled his ears. It made the bristles on his arms tingle. Time seemed to pause in that moment.

"What is it, Shiva? Are you lost?" Harry woke him from his daydream.

"No. Nothing. I'm right here." *I wish I would run into Shakti once more. I can then tell her how my heart feels.*

"Who were you thinking about?"

"Nobody." Shiva gave him a stare. Stop it, Mr. Walker.

"Oh, come on buddy. I know who."

"Pa had brought me here once when I was a kid," Shiva said. "I enjoyed going up and down the old lady's shoe, that big slide out there. And the animals molded from the shrubs. Hmmm…they looked much bigger then."

"It's wonderful you two share such a great relationship," Hong said. "My dad never took me anywhere. We argue all the time. I dread going to China to meet him."

"I'm sure things will get better with your dad," Shiva said. He knew his own visit with Pa to the park was actually a rarity. He remembered maybe twice in his entire childhood that Pa had brought him to a park. Though Pa had found tremendous success in his work, he couldn't find time for his family. He was always busy working, traveling, and attending to business clients.

Pa promised to attend school functions, sports meets, and to take him on long trips. But then some work came up and he would back out. Ma got hopping mad at him that he couldn't free himself for his son. Shiva would be disappointed, but he always sensed that Pa was doing the best he could. He understood that Pa ran hard, living his life on the treadmill of work existence.

Maybe that's why Shiva was the way he was. Maybe a bit of Pa had passed into his own DNA. Like Pa, work was his God. Maybe that's why he let his romantic pursuits fizzle; he couldn't commit. That's why he didn't make more effort to seek out Shakti.

Ma had now stopped bugging him about marriage. She saw that he was married to his work exactly like Pa had been. She had resigned herself to her fate; there was no hope for the two men in her life.

"What's your birth date, Hong?" Harry interrupted Shiva's thoughts.

"It's the 4th of September."

"Well, does your dad's birthday fall on the 8th?"

"Oh wow! How did you know?" Hong was flabbergasted.

"An educated guess, the dates 4 and 8 are the polar opposites of each other,"[59] Harry continued. "See, the 4s are change agents like you – unorthodox. Dominated by the absent-minded genius planet Uranus, which acts and thinks like lightning."

Hong clasped and unclasped his hands as he listened.

"You live fifty years ahead of your time. Forward thinking. Excel at advanced sciences. You don't want to be bogged down by societal rules and rituals."

"And what about my dad?"

"The 8s love status quo. They're dominated by the conservative planet Saturn. They go by the rules of society. They depend on past data. Tried and tested approach. Step by step progress. They don't like flashy behavior."

"Spot on. I challenge the status quo. My dad loves the status quo."

"Guys, enjoy the skyline view. You can challenge the status quo when you fly back to the U.S.," said Shiva, pointing to the splendid sight that spanned from Nariman Point to Walkeshwar, the Chowpatty beach and the vast expanse of the Arabian Sea.

"Indeed, a view to die for," exclaimed Harry.

"Speaking of death, see that vulture high in the sky? You know why it's hovering up there?" asked Shiva.

---

59 Refer to Appendix for your 'Personality' map in "Harry's Numerology for Birthdates"

"The bird of death is an omen of unwelcome news," Hong said with a serious face. His voice was unusually high, almost like a shrill teenager.

"Vultures are attracted to Malabar Hill because the Parsis have their Towers of Silence out here," Shiva said.

"Parsis who? And what the heck are these Towers of Silence?" Hong asked.

"Parsis, my friend, are descendants from Persia. And the Towers of Silence are seven huge cairns where the Parsis lay out their naked cadavers to be picked clean by vultures who can smell the ripening remains from as far as thirty miles outside Mumbai."

"Yikes. That sounds so gruesome."

"If you ask me, they have found a green, eco-friendly solution for disposing of their dead." Shiva's phone rang. Eerie. It was their lead engineer from the SEEPZ office.

"Sir, the power was disrupted again. AC and fans aren't working and the laptops will soon lose their battery. Third time in two days. And again, it's only our office."

"Mumbai is so unpredictable," said a visibly irked Harry.

"Infrastructure is woefully inadequate," Hong added. "Unpaved roads. Poor energy supply. Ineffective airports. The government isn't doing enough."

"Guys, hold it, this isn't an infrastructure problem," Shiva said. "Someone is vandalizing our property and playing with the power line."

"That may be the case here, but there are other issues. Take corruption and bureaucracy. It's such a pain doing business in India," Harry continued.

"Add to that the political and regulatory risks which keep changing constantly. The delays and inefficiencies are mind-boggling," Hong persisted.

"Guys, come on. It isn't that bad. The new India is being built by its people."

"What will happen if someone steals our IP and starts selling it at half the price?" Harry gesticulated. "We'll be out on the streets with begging bowls in our hands."

"Now, now, Harry. It's time to reign in your wild imagination." Shiva tried to be the voice of reason, but his voice fell on deaf ears.

"I'm telling you Shiva. We should have held our ground against Sunny Singh and told him NO. It's too difficult out here."

After that unwelcome news, the overall mood remained somber even as they sped along Marine Drive. Art Deco landmarks and some of the most expensive real estate in Asia adorned the entire stretch. Shiva had read that Mumbai had the second largest number of Art Deco buildings in the world after Miami, Florida. Famous as the Queen's Necklace, Marine Drive dazzled with night lamps gilding its huge crescent along the sea.

But Shiva's mind was on the lights in their SEEPZ office. Who was sabotaging them? And why?

They reached Khyber restaurant well before the MLA. Entering through a wooden door decorated with Urdu couplets, Khyber welcomed them with its rugged frontier charm, old oil lanterns, and frost-weathered woodwork. It was a gateway to India's rich Islamic heritage, infused with modern day comforts.

The mood at their table, however, wasn't very comfortable. Shiva tried to lighten things up. "We landed here once, a group of friends. The menu was inviting but we were taken aback by the prices. We were mere college students…we didn't earn any money. We checked our pockets and realized we were short – way short."

"So, what did you guys do?" asked Harry.

"Well, the challenge was how to get out of the place and still save face. We couldn't admit we were paupers, could we?"

"Hmmm, that's tough."

"I came up with this brilliant, hare-brained scheme. When the waiter came to take our order, I asked if they had any Chinese food."

"You didn't."

"Yes I did. He looked surprised, and said no. I said I wanted to eat Chinese and huffed and puffed out of the restaurant. The rest of the gang followed."

"That's so freaking hilarious," Harry burst out laughing. The mood had changed.

"You know what another guy replied to, 'Who is Salman Khan?'" Hong asked.

Shiva and Harry were all ears. This was becoming an interesting study on socio-psychological perception and behavior. It reminded Shiva of the often-repeated question "Who is John Galt?" from Ayn Rand's other novel *Atlas Shrugged.*

"He said Salman Khan is a Greek God. He's got the best male body in both Bollywood and Hollywood, a body to die for."

"Greek God, huh?"

"Salman's chest measures 42 inches, his biceps 17, and his waist only 30."

"The guy knew his physical measurements. Unbelievable." Harry shook his head.

"Salman breathes fire. He's a guy's guy. Women love him and guys idolize him."

"That guy should start a fan-club or build a temple to Salman Khan."

"Believe me, he was an encyclopedia. He listed all Salman's girlfriends: Sangeeda, Sawmee, Ashverya, Katreena... a few more names I forget."

At last, the MLA arrived. He was an hour late, but Shiva was glad he could make it. They all stood up as he entered. The waiters recognized him and saluted.

"You don't have to stand up, boys," the MLA said in an unconvincing manner.

"Sir, we're really thankful for the SEEPZ office. It was impossible without you. Let us know if there's anything at all that we can do."

"Don't mention it, boys. I don't like to receive gifts."

"No sir, we insist. Let us know and we'll do it with pleasure," Shiva said.

"You're different from your Pa. He refused to give gifts to a public official. You know; his discipline, ethics, and all. He's such a tough, regimented guy, your Pa - a self-made man. You've got some big shoes to fill, kid."

"Yes, I know."

"I told him, if you don't dole out gifts, how will you get ahead? And he always said, 'I've soared as high as I can. My son will go higher.'"

"He said that?"

"Yes, he still speaks about you all the time. I remember when you took your first flight to America; he distributed sweets, *barfi* and *rasa-malai*."

Shiva remembered the *rasa-malai*; the sugary, creamy taste that contained the promise of a saccharine future. "I'm a lot like Pa about some things, and on other things I aspire to be like him. But I insist on the gift. Tell us."

"Okay, okay, why don't you boys send a carton of Lagavulin to my house? I'm a big fan of single malt Scotch."

"With pleasure, Sir," replied all three in unison.

"You know at one time I lived on Indian Scotch, if there's a term like that."

"Indian and Scotch - such a contradiction," Harry was perplexed.

"It's all the bootlegged stuff. You know there's more Johnnie Walker Black Label sold in India than was ever manufactured in Scotland."

"Really?"

"Now I only care for the originals. Get me Lagavulin and I'll be happy."

Hindustani classical songs played in the background, rousing an appetite for exotic delicacies. Classic Mughlai cuisine - gourmet food of the Mughal era with its intricate masalas and elaborate preparations. The restaurant claimed it was ambrosia, the food of Gods. The huge urns and realistic wall art added a touch of support to that claim.

The MLA ordered a feast. It began with tender *seekh kebabs*[60], *kali mirch rawas*[61], and *chicken badami*[62]. That was followed with Khyber lamb, mutton chop Mughlai, and piping hot naan bread. Harry smiled; he was in heaven.

The MLA loved the sport of cricket and he loved to talk about it. He was all gaga about India's star batman, Sachin Tendulkar, who hailed from Mumbai. The MLA knew everything about Sachin, every detail of his playing style and his statistics. His face lit up when he spoke of him.

"Good to learn about Tendulkar, but sir, who is Salman Khan?" Hong asked.

The MLA's face changed color. Joy and verve were replaced with contempt. "Salman Khan is a burden to humanity. He's a stigma to Mumbai. He drove over, injured, and killed homeless people sleeping on the pavement."

"I didn't know that."

"Those charges were dropped later. But he was sentenced to one year in prison for hunting an endangered black buck deer. Again, he got out light."

"I never knew this dark side of him..."

"You know he's a menace to society. He couldn't handle his break-up with Aishwarya. He stalked her. One night, all drunk, he stormed into her house and broke the furniture, threatening her family. They filed a police complaint. Nothing came of it."

Long silence. They were full, but the MLA insisted on ordering goat *biryani*. Harry aligned with him. And once again, the overstuffing of their stomachs continued. Since Mughlai cuisine is rich, the MLA was firm about having the decadent *rasa-malai* to cleanse their palates. Harry was bursting in a blissful rapture; enjoying the party on his palate. The MLA belched out his satiation. "Anything else I can do for you, boys?"

Shiva paused and then broached the topic on their minds. "Sir, someone is sabotaging the power line in our office."

---

60 Seekh kebab: Minced meat with spices and grilled on skewers

61 Kali mirch rawas: Fish seasoned in black pepper

62 Chicken badami: Chicken in rich almond sauce

"Are you sure?" The MLA gave him a concerned look. "Mumbai has these power issues on and off. Did you check with the electrician?"

"Yes sir, we checked. Everyone else was fine. It seems that vandals are targeting our office on purpose. It's the third time in two days that some-one blew the fuse."

"I'll send someone. But what's going on? Is someone playing a prank on you?"

"We don't know, sir." Shiva shook his head in disbelief. Someone want-ed them out of SEEPZ. Who could it be?

Shiva sat in the MLA's office, waiting. His lead engineer sat next to him, with a bruised and swollen arm. The MLA's office was expansive. Ornate wood-paneled walls, oil paintings, Persian carpets, leather rivet chairs, and a mahogany desk. The room was abuzz with an incessant drone from the computer on his desk.

The MLA walked in, rather, powered in, through the doors. "Hello boys, nice surprise. What brings you here?" His handshake grip was strong.

"Hello sir." Shiva felt weighed down, and a bit like a burden.

On the desk stood two framed pictures; one, a portrait of the entire family with his wife and two daughters; the other one, his teenage daugh-ters. They looked similar, and of the same age; most likely twins.

"Sir, looks like you're very busy," Shiva said, in a feeble attempt at small talk.

"You know, if that new mall development project goes through, it will surely get more hectic." The MLA sat down at his desk, jostled the mouse and logged onto his computer. Shiva saw him type three short keystrokes in rapid succession.

"Sorry sir, but that's a password?" Shiva was baffled.

"What?" The MLA glanced up. He was a rarity in the political cast at the time. He had embraced the digital office to maniacal proportions, avoiding the overflow of file cabinets for the compact, searchable simplic-ity of his personal computer. He was internet savvy and his computer was his secret ground. He was the Al Gore of Indian politics.

"Your password is only three keys? I thought the tech guys tell everyone to use at least six characters."

"The tech guys are teenagers. They should try remembering six ran-dom letters when they're over forty. And they ask you to inject numbers and special characters. I'm not going to do that. Besides, the door has an alarm. Nobody can get in."

"What if someone slipped in while you were in the restroom?"

"And tried every combination of passwords?" The MLA gave a skeptical laugh. "I'm slow in the toilet, but not that slow."

Shiva and his lead engineer laughed with him.

"So, what's on your mind? Did the power issue in your office get resolved?"

"Yes sir. Thanks for your help. No power issue anymore. But a different problem has come up. And it's even worse."

"What is it?" The MLA's face clouded.

"This is our lead engineer. You see his arm? A goon beat him up and threatened to kill him and throw his dead body in the gutter if he didn't quit our company."

"Looks terrible. Do you know who he was? Had you seen him before?"

"No sir. I don't know. He came out of nowhere," the lead engineer said.

"The same goon has beaten up five of our employees," Shiva added. "Three of them have already quit and the rest are scared to come to work."

The MLA asked the engineer a bunch of questions and then concluded. "Thanks for your info, I'll tackle this goon. You may go. I need to talk to Shiva alone." After the engineer left he turned to Shiva, "Your Pa ate such goons for breakfast."

Shiva said, "Pa's a tough guy." Was the MLA telling him not to come running with every little problem? But Shiva couldn't help it; he had been out India for so long, and with every passing year it had only gotten harder. He felt like an outsider. He was clueless as to how to work the system now. His increasingly structured American sensibilities were becoming less and less equipped to tackle the chaotic workings of India.

"Do you have any enemies? First the power sabotages. Now the beatings."

"No sir. I haven't lived in Mumbai for more than a decade. How could I have any enemies here? I don't know who's doing this."

"Here's what I'll do. I'll send out a couple of local policemen to guard around your office. Let's try that for a week and see if it makes a difference."

"That would be a great help, sir. Otherwise, they'll all quit."

"Don't worry. I'll take care of it. There are hundreds of these small time crooks all over Mumbai. This petty goon doesn't know who he's dealing with."

"Thank you, sir."

The MLA smiled. He moved his mouse again and made a few clicks. His face turned white as snow. He froze, and his eyes widened into hailstones.

"What happened, sir? Is everything alright?"

The MLA didn't speak. He was engrossed in reading something on his computer screen. His eyes stared in cold disbelief. At last, he turned to Shiva. "I'm sorry, I can't help you. You're on your own on this one."

Shiva couldn't believe his ears. Here was one of the most powerful men in Mumbai and something or someone had made him shake in his big boots. "Sir, you can't back down now. I have no one else to go to. You promised."

For the first time, the MLA raised his voice. "You're here as a personal courtesy. I'm not obliged to do anything. You got that?"

The MLA's secretary rushed in. "Sir, it's an emergency. I need you right now."

"I'll be back. Wait here, Shiva," he said, still shaken up as he followed her out.

Shiva wondered what just happened. What did the MLA read?

A thought crossed his mind. He knew he shouldn't; the penalty would be severe. But he couldn't control himself. He moved across the desk and slipped into the MLA's chair on the other side. He cast a furtive glance at the door, holding his breath. The screensaver was a slideshow of the Indian cricket team. Dozens of photos of Sachin Tendulkar rolled across. He jostled the mouse and a security dialogue box came up.

ENTER PASSWORD:

Shiva expected this. It shouldn't be a problem...or so he thought.

From across the desk, he'd seen the MLA enter his three-key password. The MLA's hand was positioned over the top left rows as he typed in rapid succession using only his index finger. All three characters were close to each other on the key board and Shiva knew the MLA didn't use any numbers or special characters. That cut down the possible alphabet pool for his search. He needed to look at about nine letters in the top left section and their combinations.

Shiva, with his trained ear, had also heard the MLA mouth a soft hiss as he typed the first letter. The first keystroke had to be S. The MLA's index finger then moved to the top row for the next two characters.

Shiva typed *SQW* and waited.

INVALID PASSWORD - ACCESS DENIED.

Shiva gave a despondent scowl. He tried a few other passwords that seemed possible: *SWE, SWQ, SER,* but none worked. It wasn't as easy as he'd thought.

His phone rang all of a sudden and it startled him. His lead engineer. He shut the cell power off. He didn't have much time. The MLA would be back any second.

Shiva was unsure of his next move. He paused a moment. The computer's screensaver set in and all the cricketers' images rolled across once again.

He stood up in excitement. Could it be that?

He jiggled the mouse and typed a three letter password: *SRT*

The screensaver evaporated right away.

He stared, incredulous.

SRT for Sachin Ramesh Tendulkar. The MLA was the star cricketer's biggest fan.

In the middle of the screen was an open email from bloody007@ hotmail.com. The one that caused the MLA to quiver in his pants:

Dear MLA Sir,

I respectfully write to you with a little bit of advice.

I have one simple request. You can't help this Shiva and his friends. If you do, the consequences will be unpleasant. I don't like to do this. You know how gentle I am, but you leave me no choice.

The picture on your desk is beautiful. Your daughters have a lovely smile. May they live and smile forever.

Regards,

Your well-wisher.

Shiva stepped out of the MLA's office like a zombie. He didn't hear the secretary shout out goodbye. He walked out of the building, past the people and through the iron-gate. He staggered amidst purposeful pedestrians and lunging cars. His head was pounding. Wheels within wheels within wheels. He wanted very much to park himself down and rest his unsteady knees, but he kept walking,

He paused at the bend, blinking. He didn't know where he was. He turned up to gaze at the store name and the street sign. He recognized he'd somehow crossed a busy street that was as extensive as a wild, spiraling cyclone, and the interminable vortex winds of vehicles swept everything around it.

He didn't know how he'd gotten across, with such peril to his life, but here he was. He didn't hear the loud din of the cars and their honks. The noise inside his head was louder than any noise outside. He felt physically ill. It was the most gut-wrenching moment in their company's life and future.

Someone, devious and influential, seemed hell-bent on destroying their company. Why? Who was it? Even the MLA, with all his political clout, was afraid of this powerful enemy. How could three regular software guys stand up against this unknown force?

Maybe if they shut the SEEPZ office and moved to a different location the problem might go away. But what was the guarantee? If they moved to another suburb or another city what was the guarantee that this powerful enemy wouldn't show up? Rearranging the deck chairs on the Titanic wasn't going to solve the problem.

Perhaps Hong and Harry were right. They shouldn't have opened an office in India. There were too many unknowns. Too many things could and had gone wrong. But if they retreated, Sunny Singh wouldn't put in the rest of his money. He would back out. Without his money they couldn't scale or survive. Promises had been made to customers who'd be left in the lurch, holding onto empty words.

Did I do the right thing by coming to India? Will I let my team down if we retreat from Mumbai? Am I putting my friends' careers, families, and lives at risk?

No. I have to make this work. This is my one final chance, seemingly hopeless, but I have to make it right.

*"The flute that soothes your spirit is carved from the very wood
that is hollowed with knives."*
- *Khalil Gibran, Lebanese American artist, poet, writer.*

CHAPTER 11

Something told Qasim Jardari that he wasn't alone. It was an instinct born of decades in the Mumbai underworld drug mafia where you're always looking over your shoulder. He hadn't felt that in a long time, but he felt it now.

"Begum?" Qasim called out for his wife. He patted his bald head and scratched his grey beard in annoyance. No answer. It was probably nothing.

His wife and kids were away at a party. These days all parties were so over the top. He was glad that there was quietude in his Byculla house. Nothing against his wife; he loved her a lot. She took care of all the things related to his house and kids. Best of all, she never asked any questions about his enterprise. They were a perfect match.

Qasim relaxed on a cane emperor chair in the courtyard of his palatial house and rubbed his rotund belly. His favorite old *ghazals*[63] played out of his prized gramophone. The *chillum*[64] in his hand and the whiskey by his side made him forget all his worries.

The courtyard was a large, round space open to the sky, right in the center of the house, as if a great hole had been cut in the ceiling. Cactus pots adorned the periphery. A normal individual would prefer a garden with colorful flowering plants, but he favored the forsaken, resilient, and prickly cactus. A harsh reminder of where he came from.

The gramophone went quiet between two *ghazals*. Qasim thought he heard a sound from the corridor. It was a thump of some kind, as if someone had dropped a heavy bag. Maybe his wife and kids were home? No, it was too early.

---

63 A ghazal is a poetic form consisting of rhyming couplets expressing both the pain of loss or separation and the beauty of love in spite of that pain.

64 A chillum is a straight conical pipe used to smoke cannabis, tobacco, or opiates.

He had his most trusted bodyguards Salim and Javed guarding the house. They were the best that money could buy. He needed them. They would let no one but his own family in, without his permission. The business he was in involved cutthroat competition – literally. He had personally slit many throats and so had Salim and Javed.

He decided to sweep through the house once and put his fears to rest. He got up from his emperor chair and grabbed the old pistol from the antique desk in his study. He turned to the narrow corridor that passed a number of closed rooms.

"Salim…Javed," he called out. There was no response. Only darkness and shadow. As he walked through the corridor he flicked on the lights. No sudden image of an intruder. Nothing but emptiness. Feeling more confidence than fear, he strode forward.

A hand covered his face and pulled his head back. A searing pain shot through his neck. Another hand grabbed his pistol and twisted his wrists until he thought they might break. He was pulled off his feet and dragged across the corridor, back to the courtyard.

Qasim pumped his arms and tried to hit the assailant with an elbow. He made contact with the body, but with hardly any force. He tried to twist out of the grasp but his head was snapped back again, causing incredible pain. In the next instant he felt himself being shoved into a chair and a rope being wound around him.

The hand on his face released him. But before he could turn his head, a thick blindfold was wrapped tightly over his eyes. He tried to move his arms, but the rope restrained him. He was completely incapacitated and blind to the world.

There were two men. One of them turned a chair around. Qasim could hear activity in the background. Perhaps they were ready to talk and negotiate. Perhaps they weren't unreasonable men after all. "What do you want?" he asked.

Qasim felt the blindfold lift. He blinked, his eyes burning from the pressure. He could make out a blurred image. But he didn't see the powerful punch that struck him on his left jaw. His neck snapped back. Before it swung back to the front, another punch hit him on his right cheek. He heard ringing in his ears. He could taste blood in his mouth. He tried to focus, but he couldn't see his assailant.

"Tell me what you want," Qasim persisted through the pain.

"*Bhonsadi ke*[65], we can take it ourselves," said the man across from him.

---

65 Bhonsadi ke: Born from a slut

"Rocky? Is that you? What have you done to Salim and Javed?"

Rocky pointed to his partner, a skinny kid who was pulling two dead bodies into the courtyard. "We wrote the closing script for Salim-Javed. It's your turn next."

"My gang will be here any minute." Qasim knew he had to get to his cellphone.

"Don't count on it," Rocky said, as he smashed Qasim's phone in the courtyard.

"Can I talk to *Bhai*? It must be some misunderstanding."

"No you can't. I've got clear instructions."

"Tell him he can have it all. I don't want a single rupee. It's all his."

"It's too late to negotiate, *Madarchod*."

"I'll leave. I'll take my wife and kids and go to Delhi. I won't come back."

"Now you want to run away. You should've done that much earlier. *Bhonsadi ke,* your mom's legs should've stayed shut on your parents' honeymoon."

"I've known you for so long, Rocky. Forgive me."

"*Madarchod*, you fucked *Bhai*'s business for ten years. Forgive you?"

"Please spare me. I'll pay you many times more than *Bhai*. You'll be rich beyond your wildest imagination. Give me a number. Any number."

Rocky shrugged. He rolled his neck. Bones creaked and made a menacing sound. "Qasim Jardari, there are two types of people in this world; fuckers and suckers. Now SUCK on this…" Rocky thrust his Smith & Wesson model 10 revolver in Qasim's mouth.

Bang! On the gramophone, a *ghazal by Ustad Ghulam Ali* played out *Hungama Hai Kyon Barpa, Thodi Si Jo Pii Lii Hai*[66].

"*Bhai*, your work is done. Qasim is no more," Rocky said as they walked up the stairs together of the dilapidated green building in Dongri. They entered into a large, rectangular, carpeted room, hung with green silk and filled with people and hookah smoke. Loud middle-eastern music blared through the speakers.

A curvaceous belly dancer gyrated, her belly, midriff, and hips moving to the rhythm of the beat. She slithered through the tables in the room.

66 Why is there so much hue and cry if I have had some alcohol?
I haven't robbed someone nor have I committed any theft

Hookah pipes filled the air with blue smoke and the perfume of *charras*[67]. Waiters moved around, serving beer and whiskey. Rocky was hypnotized by the body movements of the dancer. *Look at that randi's bellybutton. I want to drink whiskey through that well of pleasure.*

"*Inshallah*[68], I knew you could do it. Good job." *Bhai* patted him on the back.

Rocky was glad that Qasim Jardari's extermination had transpired smoothly, like a well-oiled *lauda* into a wet cunt. His chest swelled with pride. In this line of business it was good to keep *Bhai* happy.

Bhai's family had emigrated from Pakistan during India's partition in 1947, losing kith and kin, losing their property and belongings. His father came to Mumbai with nothing in his hands; he worked hard, toiled on the Mazagaon docks, and died, still with nothing in his hands. *Bhai* wanted better things in life and he wanted them faster.

His rise in the crime world was phenomenal. By the age of thirty, he was lord of the Mumbai mafia – the council system that divided the city into fiefdoms ruled by the local dons. He was the Don of the dons. The city's underworld moved through phases of rain and shine, war and peace, compromises and bloody power struggles. *Bhai* knew how to play the game. He was the best. He had survived and thrived through every change.

Rocky had so much to learn from him. *Bhai* was a master strategist and a ruthless player of the mafia chess game. He evaluated every move in his mind's checkered game board, arranged in an eight-by-eight grid. He waited, toyed with his prey, and took his sweet time with the kill. Most of his victories came from the voluntary surrender of his scared enemy. *Bhai* seldom went for the jugular, but when he did, it was a checkmate. There was no hope for escape. Qasim Jardari had found this out the hard way.

Bhai settled down at his special reserved table. The belly dancing came to an abrupt stop. The look and feel of the place changed in an instant. At the end of the room was a small, raised stage. Four musicians walked in, bowed to *Bhai* and then sat down on silk cushions. Waiters moved from group to group, now serving tea in long glasses.

Low tables with cushions bordered along the wall. Pale green, bell shaped lanterns were suspended from the wooden ceiling and cast trembling hoops of yellow-gold light. *Bhai*'s face shone with a messiah like radiance in the soft light.

---

67   Charras: A form of cannabis
68   Inshallah: God willing

"Rocky, that girl Shakti has become a thorn in our neck. She went to the police and informed them about the drugs. Can you knock some sense into her?"

"She's a naïve kid. Don't worry, I'll scare her. She won't bother us again."

"And what about the other girl, Kriya? Don't let emotions get in your way. I can't have anything go wrong."

"Yes, I understand. I won't hesitate to kill her." *Oh my poor darling, Kriya.*

The waiter poured hot black tea from a narrow-spouted kettle through a meter of air. He placed the tea before each of them and offered sugar cubes. Rocky picked one up. He was about to drop it into the tea, but *Bhai* stopped him.

"Come on, Rocky," he smiled, "Show some culture."

Rocky felt clueless. Did he do anything wrong?

"This is a Persian place, isn't it? In Persia, do as the Persians do."

Bhai took a sugar cube and placed it in his mouth, holding it firmly between his front teeth. He lifted the teacup and sipped the tea through the cube. Rocky followed suit, imitating the steps. The sugar cube crumbled bit by bit and melted away.

"*Inshallah* it must look like an accident. Make that Kriya disappear like a sugar cube. Can you arrange that?"

It was an insult. Rocky could feel the anger rising in him. That was a question you asked some amateur you picked on the streets.

Rocky was tempted to reply with sarcasm; *Oh yes, I think I can manage that. Would you prefer indoors? I can arrange to break her neck falling down a flight of stairs.* Like the bar dancer in Delhi. *Or she could get drunk and drown in her bath.* Like the flight attendant from Bangalore. *She could take an overdose of heroin.* He'd gotten rid of three women that way. *Or perhaps you prefer something outdoors? I can arrange a traffic accident, a disappearance at sea, a car bomb explosion, or even a plane crash.*

Rocky said none of those things. In reality, he was afraid of the man seated across from him. He had heard too many chilling stories about him, and he had reason to believe every one of them. "Yes, *Bhai*. I can arrange an accident. No one will ever know."

Bhai studied him with cold, black eyes. At last, he spoke. "Very well. I will leave the method to you."

Three blind singers joined the four musicians on stage and sat in front. A gradual silence settled in. All of a sudden, the three men began to sing

Qawwali[69] in powerful, thrilling voices. A luscious sound. A layered and gorgeous chorus of passionate intensity.

The three blind men didn't merely sing; they cried and wailed in song. Their voices beckoned God, reaching out to him in such heartfelt fervor. Real tears ran from their closed eyes and dripped onto their chests. Their voices reached out to each and every soul at every table in that room.

Bhai stopped all conversation and immersed himself in the experience with all his senses. His eyes were moist with emotion.

Shakti was in her kitchen, doing dishes. She watched the white foamy lather build up and then the soothing warm water wash away all the sticky muck. It worked like magic to calm her nerves, almost like watching Mumbai's warm sea waves rolling onto the sands and then receding back out to deeper regions.

The CD player lulled her with her favorite song from the recently released movie *Kal Ho Na Ho*[70]. She loved it; the words had such deep resonance. She hummed along...*Har ghadi badal raha hai roop zindagi, Chaav hai kahhi hai dhoop zindagi...*[71]

Suddenly, the music stopped and the lights went out. She toggled the switches, but it had no effect. She leaned out from her balcony. Strange. Her apartment was the only one in darkness. She called the watchman from her cellphone but he didn't respond, so she went down the elevator. It was very quiet outside and he wasn't in his cabin.

He soon returned from helping Mr. Desai with his grocery bags, and they walked to the power room to check. "That should fix it. The fuse switch had come loose."

Shakti went up the elevator and unlocked her apartment door. The lights were on now. She was hit by a wave of air from the balcony. That was weird. She had latched the balcony door before stepping out. She rushed to close it and bolt it tight.

"You need some oxygen, Shakti."

She turned around, surprised to see Rocky slouched on the sofa. His electrically charged voice sent a zapping shock through her body.

---

69 Qawwali is a form of Sufi devotional music, originally performed mainly at Sufi shrines

70 Tomorrow May Never Come

71 Every moment, life is changing its form, Sometime there's shade, at times sun

"Look at your pale face. Oxygen will do you some good." He had grabbed an apple from her kitchen, and was peeling the hard skin with the blade of his knife with an element of precision. The skin gave way easily.

"How did you get inside?" Shakti felt she was seeing some scary ghost.

"A duplicate key isn't too hard to make, and it isn't the first time I've broken in."

Shakti remembered the incident. All the things in their rooms had been scattered.

Rocky took a bite of the apple. "Mmmm…let me get to the point. If you go to the police again, if you squeal, believe me, you'll disappear…poof… exactly like Kriya."

"Where is Kriya-di? What have you done to her?"

"Kriya is long dead. Forget about her or else you'll end up like her."

Shakti couldn't believe her ears.

"You better stay silent or I'll dump you in the Towers of Silence where you can squeal to your heart's content. In an hour's time the vultures would shut you up for good."

Shakti's skin tightened as it withdrew from the attack of a thousand stinging claws. "We trusted you, Rocky. Kriya-di loved you. What have we done to deserve this?"

Rocky walked over to her, his face very close to hers. "It's not about you, it's about me. I want to become the kingpin of Mumbai. I want to flood drugs into every suburb, every street, every household, and every kid."

Shakti whimpered. Her fear, cold and distant a moment ago, became more urgent. The irregular pounding sound grew nearer and noisier.

Rocky held the knife at her throat. "Last warning, *kutiya*[72]. If you get in my way, I'll feed you alive to the vultures. I'm sure they'll love your beautiful body."

Shakti couldn't sleep that night. She tossed and turned. She put a pillow over her head. But sleep never came. She arched her neck and contorted to find the clock. It was almost dawn. She could feel anger gather in her stomach like a dead weight. She couldn't stem the increasing gravity of her accumulated, unexpressed rage. Against Rocky. Against Vicky. Against Inspector Gore.

She needed help, but she didn't want to go to Inspector Gore. She hated his guts. How dare he call her a liar! Solely because he was a policeman he thought he could say anything. She hated his ineptitude. She was frustrated

---

72 Kutiya: Bitch

that he was still flying blind; he was nowhere near finding Kriya-di. But Shakti had nowhere else to go to. She knew of no one else who had the power and the network to help her.

"You've got to arrest them!" Shakti screamed at Inspector Gore as they stood in his office. The folks outside could hear her, but she was incensed. She was determined to be stern with him and to get across to him that she knew her rights quite well.

"Take it easy, we're trying our best." Gore sneezed, clearly not in the mood but nevertheless resigned to a conversation. "Constable, get a cold drink for the girl."

"Somehow your best isn't enough. And I don't need that cold drink! I'm not a girl and I'm not naive. I don't like being talked down to." She didn't feel scared of him anymore, of his authority or intentions.

Gore was stunned. For the first time ever he was at a loss for words. He snorted and blew another sneeze into a big kerchief, his eyes visibly watery, nose nearly crimson.

"Last night, I got a death threat from Rocky."

"Ok. Maybe we should have taken you seriously sooner."

"Yes, you should have. Now Rocky and Vicky rove around the city at will." She flailed her arms. "They killed Kriya-di, killed Tiger, and now they plan to kill me."

"Shakti, calm down. Please. There's no point getting agitated."

"I'm a mad woman? You are so darn correct. I am mad. They have a master plan to make Mumbai and its innocent pay a terrible price. You bet I am mad."

"What plan?"

"A plan to spread drugs all over Mumbai, like a disease working its way through a body. Every suburb, household, and to every school kid. Which suburb do you think they will start with? Your kids go to school in Bandra, right? How old are they, Inspector?"

"But we don't have any evidence, Shakti." Gore wore his *take-off* expression; fixed like the progress of a Boeing 747.

She leaned forward and swiped her hand emphatically, knocking a table lamp onto the floor. "I have evidence. Not the sort of evidence you'd like. No weapon. No incriminating photo. No legal proof. But I've seen them and heard them. I know."

"Not enough. Even if I detain them, the lawyers will get them out in no time. My bosses will ask for more. My hands are tied." Battling his cold, he blew into the formerly white kerchief and bound it tightly around his knuckles as if preparing for a fight.

"I received a death threat warning me not to come to you. I took the risk and came anyway, and this is what you tell me? That your bosses will ask for more?" She wondered if Gore's actual boss was a piece of paper with Gandhi-ji's photo on it; she was sure he was getting paid under the table by Rocky. Perhaps it was this dirty money that was tying down his hands.

"We can't take any action yet." He absently bit into his kerchief, thinking hard, tugging it with his teeth as if insight could be sucked out of cotton.

"What sort of a man are you?

These people are a hazard to Mumbai, to your family and kids. Are you going to wait for all planets and stars to align to arrest them?"

"You don't know how…"

"What I don't know is who can help me. My mind is going crazy. I can't think straight anymore…" *When will you come to your senses, Gore? I can't wait forever for you to do something useful. Rocky is clearly the key to the door leading to Kriya-di. I guess I have to take matters into my own hands.*

"Well, do you need a doctor?"

"No. A competent police Inspector would do."

Rocky climbed into the bus and a traditional Rajashthani-saree clad lady got in after him. She was covered head to toe. The loose end of the saree went around her head and veiled her face, eyes, and ears as she held it in her mouth. He shook his head in disgust. Why were these village bumpkins infesting and polluting Mumbai?

It was afternoon and yet the bus was jam-packed. There was no room for even sunlight to pass between the bodies. People hung out of the rear door. Many fell every day and bruised themselves, but that didn't stop these idiots.

Rocky leered. Busses were a goldmine for his lecherous itch. His king *lauda* was acting up again. He loved it when nubile college girls in their tight jeans climbed aboard. He had a foolproof modus operandi - target the girl with the most curvaceous booty coupled with a demure demeanor; one who wouldn't object to his shenanigans.

He spotted his prey and worked his way through the crowd to get behind her. As the bus stopped, he used the opening to brush against her rump, testing the waters to gauge if she had the cheek to resist. Sometimes, the girl would shuffle and move away, but that was rare. He had a knack for picking the right girl with the right rear, and today was no exception.

The saree clad lady sat in silence on her seat and peeked ahead through her veil.

He tasted his first booty touch. Step by step he increased the time of contact, starting with his leg and then with his *lauda*. As he grew in confidence, he thrust his erect *lauda* into her tight, warm butt crack and left it there. Hot waves spread from her asshole like a bitch in heat. Oooh. That felt good. The *kutiya* was enjoying it. Or maybe, there wasn't a single inch for her to move ahead. Either way, he didn't care.

Rocky held his throbbing, bulging *lauda* in her pulsating ass heat, dry-humping her. As the bus moved, her butt swayed and rubbed up and down his rod giving him a sadistic pleasure. Soon he worked himself up into a frenzy and jerked off. Who needed the privacy of homes? These mass transit vehicles were his private masturbation rides.

The saree clad lady alighted at the same bus stop as Rocky, but he didn't notice. She looked around at Dharavi - Asia's largest slum, home to nearly a million people. A smell hit her; the most appalling and overpowering smell. It was as if human excrement physically permeated the air. She felt it might settle on her skin in a slimy, thickening ooze. She gagged and swallowed back the impulse to vomit.

Dharavi held sprawling acres of wretched poverty. Thousands of tiny huts housed the city's poorest people. Their miserable shelters were patched together from rags, scraps of plastic and cardboard, reed mats and bamboo sticks. The shelters slumped together, one attached to another and barely holding each other up. Narrow lanes ran between them in all directions in a confusing maze.

In this place the stench reigned. It would be inconceivable anywhere else in the world. Thousands upon thousands of odors formed an invisible layer that filled the narrow gullies. The stench was a mixture of human and animal smells, of water, stone, ashes and leather, of aromatic incense and soap, of kitchen waste and bodily waste, of fresh-made rotis and curries, of ginger, garlic, and onions, of the diseased and the dead, of grease, soggy soups and dry, cooked rice, of sweat, alcohol, and tears.

Rocky walked right into the nucleus of Dharavi. He seemed to know the place like the back of his hand. The saree clad lady followed him, staying about fifteen steps behind. In the lanes she saw people and houses so densely packed she felt sorry for the inhabitants, her heart clutched by painful talons of shame and guilt.

But Dharavi was a wonderland in its own unique way. It was a city within a city. Hospitals, hotels, schools, movie theatres, mobile galleries; everything was in there. The saree clad lady spotted bakeries, dyeing houses, plastic recycling centers, soap factories, block printing, and other enterprises. She had read somewhere that the Dharavi economy was estimated to be worth more than half a billion U.S. dollars.

It was hustling and bustling with sounds and activities. She walked by the Muslim tanners working in the leather factories; by the workers from the state of Tamil Nadu making sweets and savories; by the people from Uttar Pradesh sewing, stitching, and tailoring. It was drizzling and the skies were overcast, but the industrious people kept working. They created an impression on her heart.

Some referred to Dharavi as the dirty under-belly of Mumbai, but she realized that it was really the hidden heart of Mumbai.

Rocky stopped all of a sudden and looked back. The saree clad lady halted her stride and turned towards the pottery making unit run by the people of Gujarat. She held her breath. He lit a cigarette and exhaled smoke rings. He looked around once again to make sure no one was following, and then entered a thatched hut.

The saree clad lady snuck into an alley and stood with caution by the window of the hut. She could hear voices inside. She peered through a crack. Rocky was talking to two guys – a thin, young boy and a short, bald, pudgy man.

"That *bhenchod* Qasim's chapter is closed. It's our time now." Rocky opened up a bottle of liquor to celebrate and poured it into three glasses. "Vicky, do you even know why killing Qasim was such a big deal?"

"Rocky-da, he sold drugs in our areas," Vicky said with a sheepish grin.

"*Chutiye.* He sold at rock bottom prices. Now we decide the prices; we dictate the profits. What do you say to that, Ganjoo?"

The short, bald, pudgy man with a scar down his face had his head down in a bowl, devouring peanuts like crazy. "Boss, we are now the undisputed kings of Mumbai," Ganjoo mumbled through the peanuts in his mouth without looking up.

"Yes. We're the fucking kings of all the suckers in Mumbai. Vicky, *chillum*."

Vicky dug out a funnel shaped pipe from his jacket, placed it on the table, and set about combining some stuff. Tobacco smell filled the air. He pressed a ball onto the end of a matchstick and burned it with another match. The *chillum* was ready. He offered the first puff to Rocky who took a deep, long inhale and passed it to Ganjoo, and then it came full circle back to Vicky. No one spoke. Stoned silence.

"But Rocky-da, where will the drugs come from?" Vicky took another *chillum* puff. "The government has shut down our drugs from Afghanistan and Africa. Last month those *madarchods* seized 18 kilos of our drugs in 4 incidents at Mumbai airport."

"I know. I know." Rocky said in a nonchalant tone.

"The fourth haul happened yesterday." Vicky added. "They nabbed our Nigerian pigeon. Rocky-da, I'm nervous. They're getting fucking good at it."

Ganjoo continued to guzzle down his peanuts. He mumbled. "That load was under dried fish and beef in the false bottom of the luggage, but they still found it. Can you believe it?" He looked in suspicion at the peanut that slipped away from his mouth.

"That's exactly why I'm starting the Thailand operation. Our buddy Tidarat has an oversupply. He needs to get rid of it." Rocky smiled. "And the beauty is that the security on the Thailand route is negligible. The government isn't suspicious yet."

"You are the man," declared Vicky, his eyes wide in admiration.

"I've paid off the customs officers. Our cargo boxes and the pigeons and their luggage won't be scrutinized. The pigeons can walk through the airport, in and out. "

"But what about that special pigeon in Phuket? How long are you going to keep her?" asked Ganjoo. He had found some time away from his peanuts as he stood at a mirror with a comb placing, parting and pasting, with masterful precision and passion, his ten strands of hair into a very specific profile over his bald head.

"Kriya was an unsuspecting pigeon. She didn't know she was couriering. Poor girl, she was doing it for love," Rocky said.

The saree clad lady tensed up. The sun was about to set in the twilight hours. Dark clouds gathered portent in the skies.

Ganjoo scowled. He didn't seem impressed with the explanation.

"Airport security detects by body language." Rocky continued. "A pigeon tenses up when he's aware of the drugs. Kriya was never detected because she never knew."

"But how long can we keep her." Ganjoo persisted. "*Bhai* wants us to finish her off. And we know *you* want to get into her pants."

"*Madarchod.*" Rocky coughed on his *chillum* puff. "I know I'm obsessed with her. She's such a fine piece of ass. But I don't want to force myself on her. I want to get into her pants with her consent. That's why I've kept her alive."

Ganjoo shook his head in disapproval. "You can always find another fine piece of ass. And when has consent ever stopped you? Are you getting a little soft?"

"*Bhonsadi-ke,* I know what I'm doing. I've given her an ultimatum. If she doesn't concede, she's dead by Boxing Day."

The saree-clad lady shuddered. Dark clouds thundered above her head.

"What's Boxing Day?" asked Vicky.

Rocky smirked. "On Boxing Day, everyone wears boxing gloves and plays boxing-boxing with each other, like our *dandiya*[73]."

"They do that? That's amazing. Dancing to *dandiya* songs with boxing gloves instead of the dancing sticks. *Dholee taro dhol baje, dhol baje, dhol baje dhol kee dham dham baje dhol.*" Vicky began playing an imaginary drum and dancing to its beat.

Rocky stared at him in disbelief. "Shut the fuck up, *Chutiye.* Boxing Day comes right after Christmas Day when gifts are boxed up for the servants."

"I'm sure it will be Kriya's last day. I know she'll say no to you," Ganjoo said.

"That *kutiya* will then get boxed and gifted to God." Vicky continued to play his drum. "*Dholee taro dhol baje, dhol baje, dhol baje dhol kee dham dham baje dhol.*"

The saree clad lady felt raindrops prick her arms. She wobbled and her head bumped against the window, making a loud noise. The three guys stood up, alarmed, and rushed to the window. She tried to move away, but stumbled in her saree.

"Go find out who she is and what she knows," Rocky shouted to Vicky. Lightning ripped into the Arabian Sea and thunder followed with deafening intensity.

---

73 Dandiya Raas is a traditional folk dance, with sticks in hands, to the beat of drums and songs.

The saree clad lady took off through the narrow lanes. Vicky ran behind her in hot pursuit. The huts on either side were pitiful structures made from scraps of plastic and cardboard. As she bumped into the huts she was afraid they'd collapse and fall down.

The dark and threatening sky above finally ruptured and cracked wide open. Rain poured down, making her saree stick to her body and climb up her legs. She couldn't run. She tripped over a stray pipe and fell down. She pulled off her saree and cast it aside. It was far easier to move in her top and tights. She looked back.

Vicky came running with his phone in hand; it was on speaker. He stopped. An evil grin ran across his face. "Rocky-da, it's that *kutiya*, Shakti."

Shakti dragged herself along the ground, inching backward while staring into Vicky's dark eyes. She could clearly hear the voice from the other end of the phone. "Finish her off. And join us in *Bhai*'s den in thirty minutes. He's waiting."

Shakti sprang to her feet and shot off again. She ran through puddles of fast-flowing water. In her fear, all the smells that had bothered her earlier now disappeared. She couldn't smell the gutters, or the reeking garbage beneath the tiny bridges, or the putrid waste in every nook and corner. She couldn't smell the stench from the cesspool of human and animal excretions and the discarded remnants of butchered chicken and goats.

The only smell that seeped through her nose was Kriya-di's cooking aroma. The only thought that reverberated in her mind was *Kriya-di is alive. I have to find her and rescue her. Kriya-di is alive! Kriya-di is alive!*

She came to an area where rows of clothing hung on long twines. There was nowhere else to go. She held her hands up by her head and ran through, brushing the clothing aside with each hand. She felt like *JR* fighting against the British. She recalled *JR*'s haunting image, riding on her horse with the reins held in her teeth and a sword in each hand as she rode into battle for one last time.

Shakti ran hard and fast. She ran until she came to a small alley. She turned right and scampered down the narrow pathway but it turned out to be a dead-end. She paused as footsteps approached the alley. She was trapped. She stood frozen.

She couldn't see much, but heard the footsteps come closer, slowing down as they approached, then stopping. She discerned a dark shadow at the opening of the alley. It was Vicky. He turned to look towards the back of the alley as he rubbed his neck.

Shakti stayed as motionless as she could, hidden under the shield of darkness. Every sound seemed more ominous. She closed her eyes and held her breath. *Please, don't let him find me.* The silence seemed to stretch on and on and then the footsteps continued once again. She heard them diminish as they went further away. She opened her eyes and let out her breath. She waited, and then took a slow step forward.

Out of nowhere, Vicky appeared at the top of the alley, with a glistening switchblade in his hand. "Shakti, Shakti, Shakti... We told you to mind your own business. Now you leave me no choice. You've walked into our den. Only death awaits you here."

She saw his face in the light reflected from the switchblade. There was no stammer in his speech. It was obscene to hear those terrifying words coming from the mouth of this innocent-looking boy. "Vicky, please. You can't..."

He slapped her hard across the face. "I can't do it because I'm a young boy? Did I surprise you? That's because I'm a brilliant actor. Guess how old I am?"

She didn't answer.

"I'm thirty-four years old...K...K...K...*Kutiya*." He said with practiced emphasis.

She was stunned. He wasn't really a boy. He had fooled them.

"Do you know why I look like a young boy? When I was growing up I never had enough to eat. I lived on people's leftovers and the garbage that I stole from trash cans at night." He held the switchblade to her throat.

"Vicky, I...I've never done anything to hurt you. I -" She felt the sharp serrations pressing more deeply into her throat. Stray dogs barked nearby.

He smiled. "Nothing personal. It's purely business. We've millions of rupees riding on this and we can't let you ruin it. K...K...K...*Kutiya*."

She felt as though a curtain had come down in front of her eyes. She saw everything through a gray and black haze. A part of her was outside, looking down in exasperation at what was happening.

"I had a wonderful party worked out for us but the boss is in a hurry, so we'll have to improvise, won't we?

She could feel the point of the knife digging into her neck. He moved the knife and slit open the front of her dress. *No Vicky. Please.*

"Pretty. Very pretty. But I have to go to *Bhai*'s den so we won't have time, will we? Too bad for you; I'm a great lover."

She stood suffocated, barely able to breathe.

He reached into his jacket pocket and pulled out a pint bottle that read *Big Boss Cashew Feni.* It held a pale liquid.

"Have you ever had feni? We'll drink to your accident, huh?"

He moved the knife away to open the bottle. Shakti was tempted to flee.

"Go ahead," Vicky said in a soft whisper, "Try it. Please."

Shakti bit her cracked lips. *I have to find a way out.* "Look I…I'll pay you. I'll…"

"Save your breath." He took a deep swallow from the bottle and handed it to her.

"No, I don't…"

"Drink it."

She held the bottle and took a small sip. *Oh my God. What was that?* The stink of that feni was worse than the Dharavi stench. She spit it out.

He laughed and took another deep swallow. "Want to try once more?"

She shook her head. The feni had a fierce smell and a taste that burned her mouth.

"Aaah…this *randi* has a bite." He quivered.

She watched him put the feni to his lips again. He might get drunk and fall asleep.

"I drink a quart at a time," Vicky boasted. He turned away for an instant and laid the empty bottle down on the ground.

In that moment, Shakti made a break for it. She slipped by him, her heart pounding. She ran for her life. She ran for Kriya-di's life. She reached the opening of the alley and was about to turn right when she felt a hand grab her hair and pull her back.

"*Kutiya.*" He was incredibly fast and strong.

She sought inspiration from *JR.* She kicked at him, aiming for his groin, but he dodged her knee. She flailed at his arms with her fingernails but he didn't flinch.

He yanked her hair back and pulled her face close to his. "Feisty *kutiya,* huh? Look what you did now." He raised his arm to reveal three, evenly spaced scratches, livid, bloody, and deep, running from the inside of his wrist to the elbow.

Shakti felt the switchblade dig deeper and pierce the skin between her shoulder blades. The barking of the stray dogs grew closer and crazier.

"Move." He dragged her, forcing her farther into the alley and against the wall. "You believe in happy endings, don't you? You're a fool. There are no happy endings."

Her chest heaved in fear. Twilight deepened. The cloudy sky turned a deep purple, the color of an old bruise, then faded to black.

Vicky ran his hands across her breasts, caressing them. He leaned forward and kissed them. "It's too bad we don't have more time. You'll never know what you missed." His bony body pressed into her.

The lightning increased its intensity. It had moved inland from the Arabian Sea and now struck closer to where they stood. In one such lightning flash she saw his face; she saw cold-blooded evil and death. The thunder grew louder and more frequent. It was as if someone had set a chain of deafening fire-crackers.

Shakti held the pendant around her neck. She pursed her lips and mustered all her faith in God. *Ring rang raksh raksh Goraksh.* All about her a wall of sulfurous smoke formed, stinging to the eye and noxious to the lungs.

Vicky grabbed her by the neck and kissed her on the lips. His breath reeked of the feni. *Uggh.* Clouds began to thunder an incessant, loud, and scary drum roll. He raised his hand up, ready to strike. The switchblade stared at her. Cold, glistening, and heartless.

"*Khuda Hafiz*[74], K…K…K…*Kutiya.*"

---

74 Khuda Hafiz: (Urdu) Goodbye, May God be your Guardian

"The most powerful hallucinogen on this planet is called love. Highly addictive!
You will see and hear things that do not exist!"
- Paulo Coelho, Brazilian lyricist and novelist

CHAPTER 12

"Hello, Harry? It's Sally...I'm in trouble."

Harry couldn't believe his ears. Was it really her? They hadn't spoken in a long time. "*G'day,* Sally. Such a surprise! Where have you been?" He was watching ESPN Sports on a lazy Friday evening at Shiva's San Francisco apartment.

The 49ers were on track to finish the 2004 season at the bottom of the Division for the first time since 1979, with a franchise worst record, but he was celebrating with a round of beers anyway. Their software had been put through a tough evaluation by an important potential customer, code name *Forbidden Fruit,* and had passed with flying colors, exceeding all the technical benchmark expectations. Now it was onto sales negotiation and contract closure.

Harry's India team was up and running and had played a key role in the evaluation. Shiva had come up with a solution to their office problems; it was a simple one: Get rid of the office and allow the team to work from home. No office anymore, hence no office issues. No power sabotages, no employee beatings. Their Mumbai employees worked incognito on their laptops from the security of their own houses.

"Listen Harry, I can't talk very long. I need your help. I've been kidnapped."

Harry wasn't sure if that was Australian slang for something. Kidnapped? What would that translate to? Aussies had the funniest and most irreverent words and phrases. "Sally, I don't get it. Are you making fun of me?"

"No, Harry. I'm not *poking borak at*[75] you. I'm serious. I've been kidnapped. I really need your help."

---

75 Poking borak at: Teasing

"What?! Why?! Who?!"

"Don't know these *blokes*, haven't seen them before. I don't..."

"Tell me where you are."

"I'm in Phi Phi Don in Thailand. They've locked me in this tiny room."

"Phi Phi Don?"

"I can see the Andaman Sea from this grimy warehouse on the hill."

"Grimy warehouse?"

"Yes, with wooden walls, black tile, murky windows, and dented aluminum. Harry, please help me. Someone's coming!"

"Sally, don't worry. I'll make –"

The phone went dead. Harry sank deeply into the couch. He felt the lard and color on his face abducted away, all at once. "Sally's been kidnapped in Thailand."

"You two were close to each other in college, right? Like wonton and soup," Hong asked in his unique way.

"We were tight like two peas in a pod but I haven't seen her in ages. I was so looking forward to meeting up with her in Mumbai."

Harry remembered her face. Sally wasn't beautiful by the classical definition, yet men seldom realized it once they had been captured by her charm, as he had been. She always meant what she said and she always said what she meant to. She smiled when she spoke, exaggerating her dimples. She poured honey from her eyes, and batted her curved, black eyelashes like a cute little hummingbird. All men were captivated.

Shiva said, "They were an unusual duo. One Yankee and the other Aussie. They didn't always swim with the tide."

"But why swim? I was always afloat when I was by her side." Harry smiled as dormant thoughts awakened. Such wonderful memories. Why had things turned out the way they did? "I visited her during the Aussie summer several years ago. Things got pretty serious between us on our road trip. But then something happened..."

"No one has impacted you as much as Sally," Shiva knew. He'd seen what Harry had gone through in that phase of his life.

Harry turned silent. He guzzled his beer. He was certain that Sally wasn't a bad person at heart. "I know, but she's in trouble right now and I need to help her." He took another gulp of his beer and plunged into a nostalgic trance. He swirled the beer, making waves inside the bottle. He recounted their story as he stared off into his memories...

"Waves. Wind. The whisper of waltzing azure Aussie waters. I can still feel them all, even today. I can still taste the tingle of the salt on my lips from the ocean mist. I can still hear the lilting sound of Sally's voice. I can still smell her sweet scent as she held me against the rhythm of her bosom. Her fingers played with my hair, weaving elaborate, everlasting memories.

We started in Sally's hometown of Melbourne; such a vibrant hub of style, sport, culture, wine tasting, and dining. I soaked in the culture. We discovered cafes, bars, and boutiques in lanes sprawling in secret off of the ordered streets. I danced with her till dawn. We wandered the parks and boulevards at night. There was no time for sleep in that city. Believe me; I had the time of my life in Melbourne.

I was amazed by the Aussie happy-go-lucky approach to life, and their funny, irreverent phrases. Their penchant for rhyming slang could perhaps be traced back to their origins when, during the 18th and 19th centuries, the British government transported large numbers of convicts to the various Australian penal colonies.

One day, Sally and I drove up the Great Ocean Drive along Victoria's dramatic coastline to see the Twelve Apostles[76]. She parked her car across the road and we were attacked by an incessant bunch of bush flies. I tried to flap them away from my face.

'Mate, this little bush fly is the great creator of the Aussie salute,' Sally had said.

'Aussie salute?' I asked her.

'It's what you're doing right now; waving your hand in front of your face.'

I laughed and kept flapping both my hands to drive the flies away. We went through a tunnel under the road. The bush flies followed us, undeterred and reinforced.

We walked on the boardwalk around the top of the cliffs and stood at a vista point. I was captivated. The world's tallest limestone stacks rose up in rugged splendor. The camera of my eyes captured the view, saving it for eternity in the photo album of my brain. The bush flies didn't bother me anymore.

The Apostles were gouged away from the limestone cliffs over thousands of years. Now they stood alone in the sea, away from the mainland. I fell in love with their solitude.

---

76 The Twelve Apostles is a collection of limestone stacks off the shore of the Port Campbell National Park, by the Great Ocean Road in Victoria, Australia.

'Beautiful isn't it?' Sally ruffled my hair as she settled in next to me by the perch.

I loved it when she did that. She was sure I wouldn't take offense. People didn't often ruffle my hair. And Sally was 'knee high to a grasshopper' – that's how she described herself; another crazy Aussie slang that meant 'someone short'.

It was amazing... I asked her if she went there often, and she replied,

'No, it's been a while. My manager brought me here the last time.'

I asked her, 'Is he Aussie or American?'

'Why?' she had answered me back, with a direct, frowning stare.

I was simply making conversation, trying to keep her near me as our arms rested on the perch, touching each other. The sudden wariness that bristled in the single word of her question surprised me. 'It's no big deal,' I said, smiling. 'I'm curious, that's all.'

She told me, 'He's Italian. We were training together as a group for the marathon. I came out to this spot and lost the sense of time and space. It helped me to put things in perspective. Sometimes you break your heart in the right way, if you know what I mean.'

I wasn't sure. But when she paused, expecting a reply, I nodded as if I understood.

'You learn something totally new when you break it that way,' she had continued, 'and you become free; something that only you can know or feel in that way.'

I had tried to piece together what she meant, but was distracted by the honey that poured from her eyes. And I knew, after that night, I'd never have that feeling anywhere but in Melbourne. I knew. I couldn't explain it, I just knew. I was at home, warm and safe.

'Yes, this place feels so spiritually healing,' I remember saying to her, as I looked at the Apostles in the distance and what lay beyond. 'It's amazing how the rocks were able to break free and remain standing in spite of all the pounding.'

'Mate, I really like you,' she had told me in a slow, low voice. She gazed at me through her soft, unpainted lashes. She ran her fingers through my unruly facial hair. *Face fungus* – that's what she called it.

I had felt myself flush, not from embarrassment, but from hope. Did she mean 'I love you?' I asked her, 'You do?' making the question sound more casual than it was.

'Yes. You're a good listener. It's so hard not to like someone who listens. Being listened to – really listened to – is the second best thing in the world,' she had said.

Of course I had to ask, 'What's the first best thing?'

'Everybody knows that,' she answered. 'The best thing in the world is freedom.'

'Oh is it?' I had asked, laughing, 'What about sex?'

She responded, 'Sex is only biology. Sex is only a rush. It's all over in a flash.'

'What about love?' I asked, 'Many people say it is the best thing in the world.'

She said, 'They're wrong. Love is contrary to freedom. That's why we fear love.'

'But the freedom to do what?' I remember asking, putting a little laugh into the last word.

She had answered, 'I don't know... Maybe simply the freedom to say no. If you've got that much freedom, you really don't need any more.'

Back in Melbourne, we went out with Sally's coworkers one night. After some gambling at Crown Casino, we got to the Yarra River waterfront. Something fiery and zesty and something aquatic and pungent floated on the gentle breeze, and told us that both a rich Indian Maha fish curry and English fish-n-chips were being cooked at the same time in two kitchens.

We chose the Indian restaurant. Sally asked for extra spicy food. I told her I liked spicy too. I don't know why I said such a stupid thing. I was trying to impress her. My taste buds were rudely popped awake from slumber and held hostage in a towering inferno. My skin turned fire-engine red. My eyes shed more water than a fire hose. And my head kept ringing a disaster alarm. My stomach contorted and rumbled like a python swallowing a fire truck. I tried to wash it all down with the chilled VB beer.

Sally drank *gee and tee* - Aussie for gin and tonic. She was a different person with her Aussie friends, smiling and giggling with practiced but passionless coquetry. Flirting was a habit with her. She flashed that dimpled smile of hers at her friends, the waiters, random strangers – at everyone. Many people criticized her; some of them were cruel to her for her flirtations. I don't agree with any of them.

Sally flirted with the world because it was the only real freedom she knew. It was her way of making sure that people – men – were nice to her. It wasn't a deep feeling; she didn't think much, and it didn't bother me. No real harm in it. And what the hell, she was a beautiful girl and she had a million dollar smile.

One coworker had a few too many to drink and said to me, 'Don't you have someone waiting for you back in America, or someone you should go to?'

'No,' I had told him, as I dabbed the sweat beads off my face with the napkin.

He had gone on, pointing towards Sally, 'How come you like our *Sheila*[77]?'

'Don't pay any attention to him,' Sally had interjected. 'He's *all piss and wind*[78].' She then turned towards him and winked at him. She gave him her 1000 watt smile. 'Mate,' she told him, 'you're *all froth and no beer*[79]. Stop being such a *dingaling*[80].'

When Sally went to the restroom, the drunk guy mouthed damaging things about her. I don't remember his exact words, but I do remember he called her *Yank bait*[81].

I was hopping mad. I said to him, 'You're such an ignoramus. Sally's not like that at all. You don't know her one bit, you moron. She's no saint but she has a heart and compassion and…and…you go fuck yourself.'"

Hong and Shiva listened intently to Harry's story.

He continued, "We put that episode behind us and made our way, on our romantic escapade, to the adventurous city of Cairns in the far north of Queensland. It was an enchantment. It made me gasp in delight. But here's where the wheels and everything else in our romantic ride came apart.

With the Coral Sea, the islands, and the reef at our doorstep, we could swim, snorkel, dive, and sail at will. We hopped between the pristine, palm-fringed islands and then explored the rainbow-colored coral islands below the sea.

The Great Barrier Reef was awe inspiring, a living masterpiece; it's so big you can see it from outer space. We dove together under the ocean to see the bright colors of the flora and the fauna; a smorgasbord of hidden worlds for our eyes to feast on. A myriad of fish swam towards us in the crystal clear water. Turtles, moray eels, bat fish, and clownfish among the multi-hued sea anemones. We were wonderstruck by the majesty of this underwater garden that had been nurtured over millions of years.

---

77 Sheila: A colloquial term for a girl or woman in Australia and New Zealand.

78 All piss and wind(Aussie slang): All talk and no action; without substance

79 All froth and no beer(Aussie slang): Full of himself

80 Dingaling(Aussie slang): Dick, prick, penis, stupid/silly person

81 Yank bait: Promiscuous Aussie women who tried to attract the affection of American soldiers in WWII

On the fatal next day, we rode the thrilling Kuranda scenic railway that snaked its way up the Macalister Range through the planet's oldest surviving tropical rainforest. We cut through sweeping views of waterfalls and then hopped onto an amphibian ride along the mangrove lined forests, amidst crocodiles, koala bears, and all kinds of kangaroos.

We mingled with the Aboriginals in the historic Kuranda Village. They taught us the *Didgeridoo*[82], a strange instrument that's played using circular breathing to create a continuous sound. Sally did pretty well and sustained a long drone with multiple harmonic resonances. At that moment, I didn't know how her pulsating vibrations were to ripple through my life and leave their permanent reverberations behind. I can still feel them like it happened yesterday, and the hair on my arms stand up in attention.

On our way down we boarded the Kuranda Skyrail cableway. Gliding barely meters above the rainforest canopy in a gondola cabin, we could see, hear, smell, and become one with nature. Sally and I...all by ourselves... We soaked in panoramic views of Cairns' tropical beaches and the glittering waters of the Coral Sea. It was as if the sky, the earth, and the sea were all meeting in one place...rejoicing in celebration.

We passed the Red Peak mid-station - the highest station above sea level and the one with the steepest slope. My heart was beating fast. I got down on one knee.

'Harry?' she had whispered, as surprising shadows from the passing trees streaked across her face.

I answered, 'Shhh...not yet.' I remember putting my index finger to her lips. I was as *nervous as a mother kangaroo in a room full of pickpockets.* 'You and I are great together. Our combo is greater than a la carte. I know you and I can create a delicious life as one. Now that it's tested and tried, shouldn't we sanctify our mélange?'

She had sat stunned in silence. She tried to gulp down a big lump that was forming in her throat; I could see it.

I went on anyway...'Sally, I know Melbourne is so different from San Francisco. You are accustomed to specific things, a distinct way of life. If that's what you require, I'll figure out how to make it happen. I'll find a way. But I know I can make you happy anywhere. Just give me a try.'

Her immediate response was, 'Are you saying you'll pack your bags and move to Melbourne for my sake?'

---

82 Didgeridoo: One of the oldest musical instruments to date that, according to western musicological classification, falls into the category of aerophone. A natural wooden trumpet.

I told her I'd move anywhere, if it meant so much to her, but I didn't want to go back to the U.S. alone. Our little summer jaunt wasn't enough. I wanted more. I asked her what she wanted.

She had whispered, 'Nothing. A good friend of mine once said that the real trick in life is to want nothing and to succeed at getting it.' Then she asked me, 'What do you want from me?'

I told her, 'Everything that's on life's menu.' I pressed her hand to my lips and kissed her fingers. I gazed straight into her eyes. 'Appetizers, main courses, and desserts; Love, sulking, and making-up; Cussing, cajoling, and canoodling; House, children, vacations; I want everything.' Then I said, 'Marry me, Sally.'

Sunlight tiptoed down the Macalister Range and tread across the valley, reaching the edge where our inn stood on the beach and then swam into the Coral Sea beyond.

I was too lazy to budge. The wine from the previous night was still having its effect. I fought the morning light. By the time I half opened my eyes the world outside the window was in sunny flames. The leaves on the sea almond trees shone fire red and orange. Hmmm…I was lying on the side of the bed where Sally should've been sleeping.

I was clueless. I thought she had gone downstairs for a cup of coffee. Then I heard on my phone the farewell voice mail she had left me - a miserable Sally waiting to fly out of Cairns airport. I knew my life was finished, all ashes and dust.

I put my palms on the edge of the bed and tried to heave myself up. My hands collapsed. My heaviness settled back on the mattress, crushed by a staggering agony. Fear filled my gut like a meal I couldn't digest. I opened my mouth to cry out, but I couldn't take in enough air for that.

I was upset. I didn't understand. She should've given me a reason. I decided not to communicate with her. And yet, when I heard her farewell message again, I wanted to see her and talk to her. It was February, still summer in the southern hemisphere – sunshine, warmth, and optimism. But I felt a cold, blizzard ridden, dark winter in my soul.

I was angry. I was seething. She could've at least said a proper good-bye. She owed me that much. Maybe I wouldn't have let her go. Maybe I would've argued. I tried to write to her how things could be different, how we could still be friends. I then wrote another email, a litany of blame, but I was too timorous to post it.

Losing Sally was like amputating an appendage – feeling the ache at the place where it used to be; in this case, my heart. I never knew love could hurt this bad, the worst ache I ever felt. I never knew it would feel like a heart attack. I swear, I never cried so much. I gazed into a foggy emptiness while my heart clearly couldn't let go of her.

The recognition that I might not see her again created a big hollow in my belly. I gave up meat for a month and lost twenty pounds in my grief. My pulse slowed down and my breathing grew shallow. I preferred to lock myself in, the window curtains drawn all the way down while I quivered in the darkness, not letting a single ray of light sneak in and disturb me from my cocoon of misery.

But I had to keep going. I had to persevere. I chose to switch from a hot to cold shower. I wanted to prove I had flexibility – a willingness to move on. I fumbled with the shampoo bottle and the soap. I let the water build up in the tub when I showered. I did push-ups and squats in the water. That was my way of regaining my strength.

I kept a wine bottle on the shelf by the bathtub. I would empty the whole bottle as I rested drunk in the tub water for hours and sank further down into my melancholy. Cold, foul, sad murky waters and the wailing whisper of loneliness. I would let the cold waves in the bathtub wash over me. My tears would blend with the waves and go down the drain. Silent. Meek. Abandoned."

As he finished his love story in Shiva's San Francisco apartment, Harry was still swirling his beer bottle. He stared at the beer waves. He took a sip. The beer tasted flat, corrosive. He put it down. He'd pulled a single strand and his entire Sally story had tumbled out. He felt Shiva's comforting hand on his shoulder. Shiva had helped him through the tough years that followed, to crawl back out of his depression.

"I have to go to Thailand and save Sally." Tears ran down Harry's cheeks. "You should come with me, Shiva. You're familiar with that part of the world." Cold wind blew in from across the Bay Bridge and through the window.

"We have the most important customer deal coming up." Hong reminded him about *Forbidden Fruit.* "The most important one in our company's entire history."

Harry lit up a cigarette and sucked it dry to ashes. "Yes I know, but this is a life-or-death situation. I have to help her."

"We've spent months on this evaluation," Hong said. "The upcoming meeting with their CEO is to close the deal. And we know that our competition has come back in and made him a sweet offer. It's now or never for us."

"I understand the business criticality." Harry placed his bottle, with care, in the precise circle of moisture it had left on the table in front of him.

"Sally enrolled in graduate school but then she lost interest," Shiva began in a measured tone. "When you proposed, she struggled with how to merge the roads before you two. She cared and then she didn't care. Sally hasn't seen you in ages. Does she expect you to simply cast aside whatever you're doing and rush across the world?"

"We're so close to a multi-million dollar deal," Hong added. "They'll switch all design groups to our software. We have to grab this opportunity with both hands."

"Guys, you're thinking with your rational minds, but my heart is involved here."

"You don't even know if she loves you. Her feelings for you were all mixed up, like parmesan cheese in noodle soup. And she left you at the altar, stranded." Hong bit his nails, oblivious to his culinary mix-ups.

"Oh please. Love is more than some formal arrangement," Harry said with tremendous difficulty, gasping to control his breath. "Love is sharing the happy moments and the miserable ones, and that means being at the beck and call when there's even the slightest threat to your beloved."

"Truth be told, I'm worried about you, my friend." Shiva's chin quivered. "I remember how bad you were hurt the last time. It took you so long to get over her and to get back your spirit and strength. I can't bear to see you like that again."

"True love means loving even her perfect imperfections, sheltering her weakness, defending her until she's secure again. I know in her heart she loves me, even if she didn't bring those words to her lips. Shiva, if you care about me so much, come with me."

"We can't throw our company's future to the wind," Shiva said. "Let's finish this important CEO meeting at least and then we can leave right after."

"That might be too late." Harry felt even more certain. He stubbed out a cigarette.

"But Harry, we've worked too hard for this and we have a responsibility to the shareholders, employees and their families. We can't –"

"Shiva, I know you're a tough guy. You've fought tough challenges. Getting fired wasn't easy. Starting a new company and getting customers was even harder," Harry had found his voice. He fished out another cigarette and lit it up. "But we hung in there. We fought tooth and nail against everything thrown at us, and we came out stronger."

Shiva stared at him, bewildered. "You've smoked too much. Take it easy now."

Harry took a deep puff. "Oh, come on." He began to cough. He attempted to clear his throat but the cough became a fit and blood rushed to his face.

"You okay, Harry? Let's talk about this tomorrow with clear minds."

Harry doused the cough with beer. "I know you've become ironclad. You've armored yourself to fight all the heavy artillery in our business." He examined the emptiness of the bottle and then set it down with tenderness, as if it was about to explode. His mouth twisted into a bitter grimace. "Now that iron armor has grown to swathe your heart. You let Shakti go. But I can't let Sally go. She needs me right now."

Shiva had run out of words. He looked stunned.

"I've decided to go." Harry got to his feet and stood tall, hovering over Shiva. "I urge you to come. I urge you to do the right thing. Let that armor around your heart melt and do what your soul says. Are you with me or not?"

Shiva sat slumped all alone in his apartment. He felt confusion grow inside him and a vast sense of helplessness. Harry's agitated words reverberated in his ears. Shiva was filled with a strange, unfamiliar anxiety that he couldn't understand. He felt he had failed his best friend. The muscles of his face and neck tightened up.

He stepped into the bathroom, turned on the tap, and splashed water on his face as cold as he could make it. When he looked up again, he caught sight of himself in the mirror. He couldn't help it – his fist rose up and smashed the mirror into shards. It was a dumb move and all it got him was broken glass and bruised knuckles.

The kicker was, although he didn't know it, his crazy night had only begun.

A restlessness that Shiva couldn't fight, forced him out of his apartment. He wandered lost on the aimless streets. He was starving and drunk. The shots of Patron he had gulped down earlier were now acting on his system. He found himself in his car, drifting in thought. Why doesn't Harry get it? We've put our heart and soul into this. It has been our dream, our life. While other serial entrepreneurs hit home run after home run, we've been at this single company. It isn't merely a company; it's our labor of love. And after ten years, finally we're getting a shot at our moment in the sun.

And Sally had only caused Harry pain. Nothing but terrible pain...

The *Forbidden Fruit* contract would be a massive win, opening the door to other marquee customers. It was Shiva's chance to prove himself to the world, to prove that he could be a victor; a *número uno*, not an *also ran*. It was his chance to prove himself to Pa and to make him proud. It was his chance to prove to himself that he had it in him.

It was a stormy night. He felt pounded by his inclement thoughts. He knew it wasn't the best idea to drive in his drunken state, but maybe a reckless plunge into the wilderness of the night might lead him out of his confusion. He found himself driving across the Bay Bridge. In his stupor, he saw a sign for I-580 W towards Point Richmond. He swerved towards the exit amidst angry honks.

His car drifted away from the road. He had underestimated the level of his inebriation and its debilitating effect on his senses. He caught his eyelids drooping. He slapped himself hard and scrambled to the middle lane, but time and again he woke up from the sound of his tires against the serrated shoulder of the highway. He couldn't keep his eyes open. He vaguely sensed other drivers flashing their high beams, honking, and even shouting obscenities as his car drifted in and out of their lanes.

He was inundated with memories of their fun times. Cornell classes, jokes played on teachers, the Friday night parties, and the lazy lounging. He remembered how they pulled all-nighters to get projects done and how Harry kept everyone energized with his funny stories. He remembered their adventures together at Alltech and now at their own start-up. How they'd survived near demises in the corporate game of life.

He remembered how they had grown close over the years as friends and brothers. It was the kind of closeness that needed no words to communicate. Sometimes, with no more than a look of an eye or an expression on a face, one would understand what the other had on his mind. And sometimes they would begin to laugh for no real reason, leaving outsiders befuddled.

Shiva convulsed as his car was about to crash against the central divider, but he managed to swerve back onto the highway. At first this seemed like the shock he needed to save him from his predicament, but after being at the edge of life's cliff several times, it took its toll. His arms and legs trembled from the effort and a chill filled his body. At times the entire highway disintegrated in front of him, flowing into some unknown place.

He didn't know whether to turn back or keep going. He measured his resolve, searching deep for the primal awareness that comes when one is so close to precipitous death. He watched the blinding lights of oncoming cars and felt his life energy dissipate. He realized he was in one of those classic drunk driving situations that you hear about in TV news. Some fool gets drunk and is stupid enough to get behind the steering wheel and damages property and ends up behind bars, or worse, fatally crashes his car and breaks his neck or hurts someone else. It happened all the time. Was it his turn?

Waves of unfamiliar emotions swept over him as dark shadows passed him by. The highway seemed to speak to him, plead with him, and call out to him. "Come," it said, in a devil's voice made up of a thousand snakes hissing together. "Here's a simple end to your ache. Join us. Run off the highway. It'll all be over in a moment. I'll take care of everything." And strange enough, that plea sounded appealing to a part of him, the part that was scared; the part that wanted his awful dilemma to pass.

Shiva sensed the sands of life in his hourglass gush down to nothingness. The din of his clamoring thoughts became unbearable. *Should I hear my rational mind or should I listen to my emotional heart?* He rolled the window down so that the cold air could knock some sobriety into him but it only chilled his blood. His spine felt like a frozen column of ice. A ball of snow formed in his chest.

He switched on his hazard blinkers and slowed down the car, veering to the freeway shoulder. He stopped and took a deep breath which brought much needed oxygen to his deprived body. That simple step brought a sudden surge of clarity to his panicked brain. He took a few more breaths. That brought back the life force that he had felt slipping away. It got him back in touch with his instinctive inner sense.

He looked up. A distance marker stood right in front of him. His car headlights shone on it, showing that Sebastopol was 45 miles away. *Sebastopol!*

Shiva remembered the day that Harry had made him drive up to Sebastopol in the chill of an early morning. Harry was so excited, he chattered non-stop. "Shiva, you've got to meet Gurunath. He's a true master and a yogi from India. He has healed and transformed millions of people all over the world."

But Shiva had grown cynical of sadhus and saints. He had heard and read so many stories in India of charlatans and con-artists that preyed on weak minds. "We'll see. Every mind must make its own rational choice between truth and falsehood."

As they drove up though, Shiva felt good to be out in nature, amidst hills, twisting along Sonoma County. They passed San Rafael, Petaluma, and Santa Rosa, and arrived into Sebastopol with its small town charm. It was once an apple growing region but wine grapes seemed predominant now, and nearly all the land was covered in vineyards. Harry informed him that the world famous horticulturist, Luther Burbank, had gardens in this fertile region and the city hosted a famous annual Apple Blossom Festival.

When they arrived at the park congregation, they spotted Gurunath on a settee in the center, amidst ranks of devotees dressed in pure white. Shiva and Harry settled into the back row. The peak of Mt. St. Helena in the background on the horizon adorned the crown of Gurunath's head.

Gurunath spoke in his rumbling Queen's English, "For thousands of years people have tried to prove God; they've failed. For thousands of years people have tried to disprove God and they've also failed. God is not a subject of intellectual speculation or exposition or philosophy or idle words. God is of your own personal experience."

Shiva listened to Gurunath's magnetic voice and realized that he wasn't skeptical anymore, although he had every reason to be. When he'd come, he had a stomach full of cynicism, a spirit that was flagging, and courage that was being tested. The pressures at his workplace were getting to him and making him anxious, but within a few minutes here he was calmed.

Gurunath continued, "I am not teaching from books or charts. I'm teaching from my personal experience. Allow your mind to get the hell out of the brain box. Put it out. Look, you're in your mind night and day...let go of the mind. Man lives in a bedlam of miseries created by his own thoughts, his own attitudes, and his own judgments. Shift your awareness, your consciousness, and your thoughts, from head to heart."

Shiva looked at him totally absorbed, straining his eyes and concentrating. A light emanated from him; a glowing sense of lucidity came from his transmission of wisdom. Shiva felt his presence, his great consciousness, and the peace it brought. Shiva sat up like an ardent youngster, soaking in everything. He felt comforted, healed, and revitalized.

"Today I'll teach you the source of where you came from. In the beginning was the word, the word was with God, and God was the word – *Om*, the sacred sound of creation, preservation, and dissolution. In the Christian world it's called *Amen*. In the Islamic world, *Amin*. It's the birthing hum of creation. When the great deep, the great primordial source, gives birth to the Universe, the birthing of billions of stars, galaxies, and nebulae makes the sound *Om*. We're all floating in the soup of the vibration of *Om*."

Here was a man who, with his indescribable power, split through the shield of Shiva's distrust. Shiva wondered if he was being weak-minded. Was he a hypnotized fool yearning for solace? Was he a floundering man in search of a crutch? He wasn't sure, but he had found peace sitting in the presence of Gurunath. It wasn't only him who reaped the tranquility, but also all of the people in the park around him and millions of others all over the world who responded to Gurunath, his call, his teachings. He had that effect.

"Behold ye man, you're not a corruptible body but a divine soul. And there is a pathway to express the divinity and that pathway is Yoga - the most scientific and divine way to get to God essence. I'm not talking about the popular physical postures but the veritable union of the individual soul with the Universal consciousness. Just like there's fire in the tinder; you rub the tinder and the fire manifests. There's oil in the seed; you squeeze the seed and the oil manifests. There's butter in the milk; you churn the milk and butter manifests. So also there's God in man; you breathe the man and God manifests."

Shiva and Harry stood in the line of devotees waiting to meet Gurunath. They were being led one by one to get his blessings. Shiva saw the devotees emerge from their personal moments with Gurunath joyous and transformed.

Shiva approached when it was his turn, knelt in front, and touched his feet in respect. Gurunath's face was lustrous with the sun shining on him. His hair was a striking silvery gold halo and his eyes an intense, penetrating radiance. He put his right hand on Shiva's head and said, "Don't think if you can, just know that you can. Clear your mind and settle in the heart. Trust your heart."

A car honked. Shiva jolted back to the present. He looked up again at the distance marker with Sebastopol at 45 miles away. It seemed so much closer to him than that.

It was a miracle. He had survived the freeway, his inebriation, and his turmoil. He felt like a cat with nine lives that night. He felt a divine intervention, a sense of destiny not shaped by his own deeds and desires. Right then a voice spoke distinctly and clearly: "*Trust your heart.*" He felt it had come from deep within him but scoffed at the idea; his mind wouldn't concede. "*Trust your heart,*" said the voice again, enduring and confident. It had the tone of certainty that knew its way.

Shiva felt the death of a part of himself. He was dead to his old, limited vision of things. He saw how myopic he'd been. The blindfold was removed and he saw the truth. Old boundaries of the Self were transcended. He was reborn into a new consciousness of connections. He saw who he was inside and how he fit into the cosmos. He felt within him a divine ability to soar above the normal confines of life.

"*Trust your heart.*" That is the only certainty that connects people to each other and to the entirety of humanity.

Harry stood alone at the departure gate at San Francisco International airport. He was on his way to Phuket, Thailand. A group of passengers squatted on the freshly mopped and sterilized floors of the waiting area. Some dozed off in their chairs while others stared into empty space as they held onto their passports and boarding passes.

The airport personnel made an announcement: *Now boarding first class, business class, and elite level members...*

The little kids in the waiting area excitedly ran around the chairs and other passengers. Their parents were frazzled, but nothing they said made any difference to the kids. The parents were elated when the airport personnel made the announcement: *Now boarding families with small children...*

Harry looked around. Did he catch a glimpse of Shiva? No, it was someone else. Would he show up? Would he value their friendship over business?

Airport personnel began general boarding from the rear of the aircraft. Harry didn't board even when his row was called out. He chose to wait. He was sure Shiva wouldn't disappoint him. Little by little, the crowds dwindled down and grew sparse.

Last call for passengers to...

Everyone else was now on the plane. Not a single soul remained in the waiting area. He gathered up his things and labored down the jet-bridge to the airplane.

He stepped onto the plane and was greeted by an effervescent flight attendant. He contrived a smile. He slid into his aisle seat and clasped his hands on top of his stomach. He gazed in despair at the empty seats across the aisle. The flight was ready to take off.

I can't believe it. Still no sign of Shiva.

"In the midst of life's journey I found myself in a dark wood,
for the right path was lost."

- Dante, Inferno

CHAPTER 13

The flight from Mumbai began its descent into Phuket, Thailand. Seat belt signs were on and all passengers securely seated. Even the flight attendants took their positions. Shakti surveyed the passengers. The plane shook hard; it was a bumpy descent. Shakti closed her eyes and recollected her ordeal in the slums of Dharavi.

Vicky had her cornered in the alley.

Shakti held on to the pendant around her neck. She pursed her lips and mustered all her faith in God. *Ring rang raksh raksh Goraksh.* All about her a wall of sulfurous smoke formed, stinging to the eyes and noxious to the lungs.

Vicky grabbed her by the neck and kissed her on the lips. His breath reeked of the feni. *Uggh.* Clouds began to thunder an incessant, loud, and scary drum roll. He raised his hand up, ready to strike. The switchblade stared at her; cold, glistening, and heartless.

"*Khuda Hafiz*[83], K…K…K…*Kutiya.*"

Swish. Something flew by fast and pierced the wooden wall by her left ear. Vicky was interrupted. He turned to glance at it. *A small blue dart.* It was a bolt from the blue.

Vicky turned around. Another blue dart flew by them, this time to her right, and also stuck in the wall. Lightning flashed. At the opening of the alley she saw a silhouette of someone seated on a small wooden platform with wheels, his legs folded beneath him. He held a slingshot in the thick, wrapped fingers of his massive hands.

Abdul!

---

83 Khuda Hafiz: (Urdu) Goodbye, May God be your Guardian

Vicky let out an angry growl. He lurched towards Abdul with his switch-blade. Abdul reached down to his platform and grabbed another dart. She knew he had only three darts. Two of them already wasted. This was the last one, their last chance.

Vicky was now only a few steps away from Abdul when he pulled back the slingshot band and let the dart fly. Time paused. Breath paused. But Vicky continued to bulldoze ahead. She looked to her left and then right on the wooden wall. Where did the last dart go; their last chance for survival? It looked like it had missed its mark.

Without warning, Vicky faltered in his stride and stumbled. He was hit. His raised hand slumped. The switchblade slipped from his fingers. He collapsed to the ground, lifeless.

"Naam Abdul hain mera...sab pe nazar rakhta hoon."[84]

Shakti opened her eyes. The plane shook hard again in its bumpy descent into Phuket. The wheels touched the ground, rocking all passengers back and forth. The plane screeched as the pilot yanked the brakes and began the slow crawl to the gate.

After her escape from Dharavi, she had tracked down Rocky's flight schedule. She tried to get a flight assignment to Phuket, but it wasn't easy. Trans Pacific had received several complaints about her. She was making simple mistakes on her flights; she was preoccupied, distracted. Passengers had complained. Other flight attendants had complained. It had become a pressure cooker situation. She knew if she made one more mistake she'd be grounded. She couldn't let that happen; she still needed to find Kriya-di.

Shakti clasped the Om pendant around her neck. It was ragged, rustic, and handmade, but held inside it was the power of Sanju's love. It was like a telepathic wiring that connected them together, with an automatic signal to him whenever she got into trouble. He was watching over her from the heavens, protecting her at every step.

Don't worry sis, you are not alone.

The pendant held Sanju's indomitable spirit and his penchant for life. It was a connector from his heart to hers - an invisible thread, but with greater tensile strength than even steel. Sometimes she felt that it tugged at her physically, trying to tell her something, and pulling her back when she ventured too far out into danger.

---

84   "Naam Abdul hain mera...sab pe nazar rakhta hoon" = "My name is Abdul...I keep an eye on everyone"

"What would force you to commit suicide?" asked Rocky in a grave, hushed tone. He'd caught up with her even as she rushed off, after all the passengers alighted.

"Take my life myself? I don't know. I don't believe I would," Shakti said. *Just lead me to Kriya-di. Her life is all I care for right now.*

She continued to walk at a brisk pace, clutching hard at her passport and ticket. She felt a tug from her pendant. She heard a warning, deep within – the one that tells you when something worse than one can imagine is set to pounce.

Rocky ambled alongside her with heavy steps. "What if you had terminal cancer, a malignant tumor that could never be eliminated? What if you knew you were going to die, bit by bit, in unbearable agony?"

She didn't reply. Fate plays it duty to warn us so we hear, but do we ever listen?

"What if you were hiding something from the bad guy and he knew you knew and he was going to torture you to find how much you knew and then kill you anyway?"

She stared at him without slowing down in her stride.

"What if you had a cyanide pill? Would you make use of it?"

"I don't know. I don't know." Her pulse was now beating at a frantic pace.

He stepped up in front of her, making her stop. He lunged forward towards her. She had no time to react as he reached out for her neck and yanked her Om pendant off.

"I know how much you're attached to this ragged thing. Come and get it at the Xmas party tomorrow night." He spoke in a low, solemn tone. "Let's celebrate together."

She was dumbfounded. Her face turned cold, and except for the quivering of her lips, she couldn't move.

He yanked her passport from her fingers. "Let's make sure you don't leave the country. I'll hold this for you at the *Down Under Club* on Patong Beach."

She floundered. The courage that had sprouted earlier against Inspector Gore and Vicky deserted her. She wanted to disappear. She wanted to flee and hide.

Rocky reached into his pocket. He thrust a small transparent packet into her hand with a colored pill inside. "It's a cyanide pill...in case you want to use it."

After Rocky walked away Shakti sat frozen in her chair at the Phuket airport café. Her deepest anxieties became aroused. Fear gripped her and fastened her down with heavy chains of morbid dread. She felt emptied of all courage, suddenly sapped of willpower like a toppled pail of water.

What was she doing in Phuket? She knew the scoundrels she was dealing with were way above her league. She was a mere flight attendant, trained for service and first aid. How could she swim with these dangerous sharks in the deep of their own hunting waters? These kidnapping, drug dealing murderers... The rising tide of her dilemma rose past her chin and seemed all set to drown her.

She couldn't feel her face. Her legs seemed to have fallen asleep and her arms refused to budge. The blinks of her eyes became sluggish, sorrowful sweeps. She felt the pulse in her neck slow down to a crawl. Her breath trickled out, barely.

She had lost Sanju's pendant. Could she succeed in her rescue attempt without his force, his protection? Should she simply take her bags and jump on a return flight to Mumbai? She'd be so much safer in the security of her house. She'd be far away from these scoundrels, the suffering, and the cyanide pill.

She stared at the pill in her palm. Bristles of fright stood up on her arms. Kriya-di was doomed and so was she. The horrors of drugs and death looming over Mumbai were inevitable. Mumbai was doomed. *Should I simply take the pill and end the torment?*

Shakti unstuck herself from the chair. She put the small transparent packet with the cyanide pill into her pocket. She lifted her bags with an unusual decisiveness and walked towards the door with a purpose.

She shouted for a taxi. One cab screeched and pulled over.

I'm Kriya-di's only hope. How can I ever forget she's the reason I'm alive? She's the reason I'm breathing and standing on my own feet today. When everything was dark and hopeless and life was a dead-end, she was the one who showed me the ray of light and hope. She gave me her helping hand to survive. She gave me my second life.

It was her moment of Apotheosis – the transformation. Tasting death moved her center from the ego to the Self, to the more godlike part of her. She delved deep inside to find her buried courage and spirit. She was ready to accept more responsibility than merely looking out for herself. She had to save Kriya-di.

If I don't find her it will be an everlasting loss. If I don't find her my entire life will be meaningless. I'll die inside. Kriya-di is the breath that fuels my body. If that breath is extinguished, I'll die of cold and hunger.

Shakti's willpower grew stronger, forged in fire and quenched in blood. Broken and remade, hammered and folded, hardened and sharpened and focused to a point, like the saber that *JR* carried.

JR was cheated twice by the British. First, when they annexed her city Jhansi upon the death of her husband; second, when they accused her of scheming in the mutiny and massacre in Jhansi. But she didn't balk. She transformed herself from a housewife to a leader of the Indian Rebellion, avowing the famous *Meri Jhansi Nahin Doongi*[85].

Shakti muttered to herself, *Meri Kriya-di Nahin Doongi*[86]. *I don't know what condition she is in. But I'll save her and bring her back. I vow that I will not rest until I find her and rescue her...or die trying.*

"Where, Madam?" the taxi-driver asked.

"Phuket Town," Shakti answered.

"400 baht." The red and yellow taxis in Phuket were supposed to use their meters, but this driver seemed reluctant.

"That's okay." She didn't have the energy to haggle over price. She knew that Phuket Town was about thirty kilometers to the south of the airport. 400 baht seemed reasonable. Phuket, about the size of Singapore, was the biggest island in Thailand, located in the Andaman Sea to the south. A large mountain range ran through the west of the island from the north to the south, running for 440 kilometers.

Shakti didn't realize she'd gotten into a dangerous roller coaster. The taxi ride through the mountains was horrendous. The driver drove at breakneck speed; he crossed lanes and overtook autos in the face of on-coming vehicles. He meandered between trucks and cars with inches to spare, even while going up a blind slope. The rickety condition of his taxi didn't help much either. She clutched at her seat belt and the back of the front seat as she anticipated a terrible crash any minute.

"What does Phuket mean?" Shakti asked the driver, trying to slow him down.

---

85 Meri Jhansi Nahin Doongi: I shall not part with my Jhansi
86 Meri Kriya-di Nahin Doongi: I shall not part with my Kriya-di

"It come from *Bukit*, which mean hill. If you look from mainland Thailand, Phuket Island look like hill."

The taxi swerved as he turned dangerously at a bend. Her heart popped into her throat. She looked out of the window, thinking about the mountainous effort in front of her. She took a deep breath of fresh air; she needed it for her treacherous climb ahead.

The taxi jerked and screeched to a halt. She looked ahead. The front bumper was a few inches from a man crossing the road. The driver yelled out curses, his animated head threatening from the window. The walking man cursed back in equal vigor. She was stunned. *I can't believe my luck. I'm going to die in a car accident today.*

A few miles up, the taxi stopped at the traffic light. When it turned green, all cars started to move, but hers didn't budge. She looked at her driver. *Oh my God.* He was keeled over the steering wheel, snoring.

"Driver!" She woke him up with a shriek.

"Sorry madam. I drive taxi nonstop. No sleep for 16 hours."

She realized the reason for his erratic driving. Poor guy hadn't rested enough. She needed to keep him engaged in conversation to make sure he stayed awake. "So, you have family in Phuket?"

"Yes, wife and two kids – boy and girl. Sad, my boy into drugs. He drop out of school and get caught stealing money. Bad time for family. He almost die with overdose. I work hard and drive long to help him live and fight drug habit."

"I'm so sorry to hear that. I hope he recovers fully." Shakti was moved by his story. The terrible things that a drug habit could do to young kids... You think it won't happen to your child, but by the time you realize the truth, it's too late. Then it becomes a quicksand that's hard to escape, sucking everyone in the family down into misery.

"In Phuket we now bring up whole generation of druggies. My boy was good kid, smart at school. But then all went wrong. These *samseng*[87] drug dealers destroy our kids, our city, and our future." The taxi-driver shifted in his seat. "Madam, you from India?"

"Yes, I am. Is that so easy to guess?"

"No, I guess from tongue."

She understood that he meant accent.

"You know India and Thailand joined for hundreds of years. India big influence on Thai culture. Many Thai words come from Sanskrit."

---

87 Samseng: baddies, bad guys

"Really? I didn't know that. I knew that Buddhism, the major religion of Thailand, originated in India."

"Yes. Also Indian story of *Ramayana* famous in Thailand. We call it *Ramakien.* Thai people are Indians of South East Asia. There is so much Indian-ness in Thai people. We are both people of Shakti – the female Goddess."

"Wow. You know what? My name is Shakti."

"That's why you look like Goddess, madam," said the driver with a straight face. "Every person has Shakti energy hidden in them. They simply need to discover it."

She blushed.

"Like India, every Thai woman is dancer. Every Thai man is singer. Like India, food is music inside body and music is food inside heart."

"You should've been a poet, not a taxi driver."

"Every Thai man is poet. And every Thai girl is princess."

Forest, rubber, pineapple, and palm oil plantations zoomed past them. She soaked in the fertile hilly expanse filled with mangrove forests, fishing villages, and small communities. The coast lay on either side of the hill. Phuket's west coast was filled with sandy beaches, while the east coast was mostly muddy. Tourists thronged the west coast.

As they sped down Highway 402, her eyes were drawn to an impressive monument that seemed like two women warriors. "What's that?"

"Madam, that's Two Heroines Monument."

"Two Heroines?"

"Yes. In honor of Kunying Jan and Mook. They fight the Burmese army. Kunying was Governor wife. Mook was Kunying sister. When Governor die people have no leader. Burmese army attack Phuket. All people scared. They not know what to do."

She looked with keenness at the memorial.

"Burmese army circle us for one month. But two heroines not afraid. They gather forces. They dress women as male soldiers. They make enemy think we've big army and soldiers. After one month Burmese army tired. They go back and leave us alone."

Shakti gazed in awe at the two heroines who had organized Phuket's defense and driven away the Burmese invasion. They were the two *JR's* of Phuket. She could feel their strength and fortitude permeating the atmosphere. In their faces she saw the images of Kriya-di and herself.

She knew she had to imbibe their heroine spirit to fight the battle against Rocky. She couldn't let his nefarious plans for Mumbai succeed. She couldn't let Mumbai's kids and families sink into the quicksand of heroin. *Heroine against Heroin.*

They entered Phuket Town and she realized it was a melting pot of Buddhists, Thai-Chinese, Muslims, and sea gypsies. She learnt from the driver that the town had a significant number of Muslims - descendants of the island's original sea dwelling people. She saw a number of *burkha* clad women walking on the streets.

The famous Sarasin Bridge vaulted across the blackness of the Andaman Sea. Filled end to end with slow moving car headlights, the bridge stretched along in suspended shadows. At its midpoint, where Phuket Island met mainland Thailand, two men stood at the barricade. It seemed like a theater setting, waiting for the hours of darkness to settle in and the curtains to rise on the show. The two men gazed out to the black sea, priming for the macabre plot they planned to enact.

"*Sa wat dee khrap*, Tidarat. It's nice of you to see me on such short notice," Rocky said. He took a deep breath. He loved the air out there.

"*Sa baai dee.* Any time for you," Tidarat replied.

Rocky lit up a cigarette and puffed out a toxic, white smoke that meandered around with disrespect for the pristine, black innocence of the Andaman Sea. "*Bhai* has sent his regards. He's very happy with your support and he's invited you to Mumbai for a New Year's celebration at his house."

"I'm honored. But I have a prior commitment."

"*Bhai* won't be too happy," Rocky said, but he meant, *Bhai* will be crazy pissed, you *madarchod.* He blew out a circular cloud into the air and then shot out an arrow of smoke through the center, right through the heart.

"I'll see if I can move around a few things. That's always possible." Beads of fret formed on Tidarat's forehead.

"Good. Very good. I'll inform *Bhai.* By the way, you'll be happy to hear that your first shipment sold like hot *samosas*[88] in Mumbai. Didn't I tell you we're going to have some fun doing business together?"

"That's great. We should celebrate." Tidarat put out a forced smile.

"See, I have a dream for Mumbai. I want to make drugs a party symbol in the city, a symbol of good times. I want the youth clamoring for more. But we have a challenge right now. We need more stuff."

"More stuff?"

---

88   A samosa is a fried or baked pastry with a savory filling. Typically, it is pyramid in shape.

"Yes. A whole lot more stuff."

"Are you asking me to supply you from my other factories?"

"Yes partner, the demand is too high and I want to capture the entire Mumbai market. I need to operate your other two plants."

"But you had promised." Beads of sweat trickled down Tidarat's cheeks and neck.

"You know how it is. Promises are like babies - easy to make and hard to deliver." Rocky rolled his neck. The bones creaked, making a menacing sound.

Tidarat stared at the black, distant Andaman Sea in disbelief. "So you want to take over all three of my manufacturing plants?"

"Yes partner, only for the time being. Once the demand and supply balances out, I'll give them back. That's my promise. And this one I will keep." Rocky smirked. *There are two types of people in this world: fuckers and suckers.*

He could sense Tidarat boiling from within; his face had turned all red. But Rocky still had the pictures and he knew Tidarat was helpless. Tidarat's arms were tied and so were his legs and mouth; he was a puppet, moving and acting at Rocky's whim.

"Ok. Only for a month though." Tidarat spoke in a hoarse voice.

"I need them for a year." There was no way Rocky would ever let go of the factories. Not in a year. Not ever.

Tidarat's expression hardened. "Okay, for one year only and no more. By the way, how long are you planning to keep that air hostess?"

"Don't worry; she'll decide her own fate soon." Rocky knew he couldn't show his face at *Bhai*'s New Year's party if he hadn't resolved the Kriya issue, but he didn't want to kill her. He hoped that she would make the right choice and their love would triumph.

"The guard tells me that your people aren't treating her well."

"Two days, Tidarat. We won't have to worry about the girl in two days."

The suspended shadows of the Sarasin Bridge as it vaulted across the blackness of the sea exuded a foreboding that something big, dark and sinister was about to run riot.

"Go to Put Jaw temple. The Goddess of Mercy will answer all your prayers." The earnest taxi driver had noticed Shakti's sadness and wanted to help her. Put Jaw, built more than 200 years ago, was the oldest Chinese Taoist temple in Phuket Town.

Shakti walked through the town, passing by fine mansions and shops - well preserved remnants of the 19th century tin boom era. Old Phuket Town displayed a Sino-Portuguese architectural style with a strong Mediterranean character. Shops presented a very narrow face onto the street, but stretched back a long way. Many had old wooden doors with Chinese fretwork carvings.

"Madam, we can stitch a dress for you in 24 hours. Very fast. Come inside," shouted a tailor from the door of his shop.

"Lovely suits and dresses. Perfect fitting, madam," shouted another tailor as he lured her towards his shop. She peeked into the store. It was too shabby for her liking.

The street block brimmed with ravenous hordes of touting tailors. But she was forewarned. The tailors were notorious for their cheap workmanship. Suits and dresses were merely glued together and would fall apart the first time they visited a dry cleaner.

Shakti walked straight ahead. She was amazed to see the large *songthaews*[89] and quirky little *tuk-tuks*. Phuket's *songthaews* somehow seemed larger than those in other areas of Thailand. They connected Phuket Town to the major beaches around the island and were the cheapest mode of transport for travel from town to town.

She passed the Ranong bus terminus and spotted the entrance to the Put Jaw temple. The fine carvings on the teak doors were striking. The main hall held statues of the Goddess of Mercy and her attendants. Inside the temple, Shakti heard the priest talking to a Frenchman. The priest handed him two canisters, each containing what looked like numerous special bamboo chopsticks. She went closer for a look.

"Are you trailing me, *Mademoiselle*?" the Frenchman asked with a smile.

"I was curious."

"*Oui*. It's simple. One canister diagnoses illness. The other canister tells your fortune. Do you want to try?"

"Some other time, but I do want to try the mango halves. Where are they?" She remembered the taxi driver's advice: If you have a question that bothers you, any question, go ask the mango blocks. You will get a 100% right answer.

"*Oui*. Up there, *Mademoiselle*. Near the altar..."

---

89 Songthaews: Two- or three-bench pick-up trucks

She spotted the famous mango blocks - red bamboo root blocks, shaped like the halves of a mango. She had only one question on her mind; will she find Kriya-di? She held the mango halves close to her chest and mumbled a little prayer. She then threw them in the air and made certain that her eyes were closed tight.

I know Kriya-di is safe. I'll make a pact with you, God. When I open my eyes, the mango halves won't have the same side up; they can't. I know I'll find Kriya-di.

She refused to look even when the mango halves landed with a thud. *What if...*

"You can open now. The Goddess won't alter her answer," the Frenchman joked.

She opened her eyes. *YES! Oui. Oui. Oui.*

One mango half had its face down and the other half had its face up.

YES. I will find Kriya-di. Thank You Goddess of Mercy!

Shakti stepped out of the temple, her eyes lit up and radiant like pearls. Outside, specialist shops gleamed with souvenir cultured pearls and ornaments. Streets throbbed with tourists dressed in summer wear; sarongs and floppies. Shoppers thronged the street malls with endless stalls to get local stuff at cheap prices. It reminded her of Mumbai's Fashion Street. Some high-end boutiques sold traditional handicrafts and antiques.

The gust brought along a stream of food aromas. She saw a stall selling deep fried pineapple and banana dumplings with an array of toppings: milk, chocolate, and honey. So many sweets and savories, the tourists were spoilt for choice. She spotted some brave visitors gulping quail eggs. She could sense their cholesterol shooting up to the roof.

The streets buzzed with noise, color, and energy. But amidst the sea of bobbing tourist heads she noticed an anomaly; a short, bald, pudgy middle-aged man stood out like a wolf in a flock of sheep. *Déjà vu.* He was very dark. He had a large black scar that ran across from the top of his right eye, over his crooked nose and rough cheeks, and all the way down left to his stubbly chin. What was Ganjoo doing there?

Shakti turned towards him. He avoided her stare and pretended to check out the quail eggs. She bolted away, but ran into a group of drunken men, zigzagging and stumbling along their way. "Excuse me," she said as she brushed by one of them.

"You silly girl, watch your step," the drunk said without even looking at her and without missing a beat. "You can't run in a straight line at this hour."

She sidestepped the drunk and ran. But Ganjoo was good. He had nailed the art of trailing people to a T. He stalked exactly the right number of steps behind her, weaving in and out of the stalls with professional ease. She ran faster, dodging the street peddlers.

A boy kept shouting, "Fresh meat cut into tiny pieces!" with a monotonous brain-stifling regularity. Winding her way down the series of food stalls, she came to a junction. The street block on the right brimmed with those ravenous hordes of touting tailors, trying again to lure her from the street corner.

"Lovely suits and dresses for you in 24 hours. Perfect fitting. Come inside."

She turned onto the street and hurried into a shop. A salesman walked towards her to help. She asked, "Do you have a ready-made *burkha*?"

"You're in luck, madam. We have precisely the right size for you."

Shakti draped the *burkha*. It was oversized but that didn't matter. She pulled down the veil to cover her face and peered out to see Ganjoo staring up and down the street, trying to locate her. She mustered her courage and stepped out, passing right by him. A scary ogre atop a night-light pillar cast a blinding spotlight on her. Her heart pounded and her lungs pumped hard, but Ganjoo continued looking up and down the street. Groups of *burkha* clad ladies walked all around.

She stopped by the lighted pillar with the ogre on top and feigned looking through her handbag. She dug around inside as she watched out of the corner of her eye through her veil. She was invisible to him. He stepped into a tailoring shop and came out frustrated. His phone rang. She observed and listened.

"Yes, boss. No, I lost her. She's on the tailor street but I can't find her." Long pause. Ganjoo's pudgy face shrunk while he was chided. The long tirade finally ended. "Sorry, boss. Ok. I'll see you there in thirty minutes."

Ganjoo walked back onto the main street as Shakti trailed him. She had learned from him the art of following. She stepped into his skin and blended in with the surroundings. She stayed precisely the right number of steps behind. She weaved in and out of the stalls. *The hunted was now seeking out the hunter.*

The road ahead curved in a hairpin turn and when she spilled out onto the pavement there was no sign of Ganjoo. Had he gone straight? Turned left? She couldn't lose him now. Her head spun around frantically in all directions while seconds ticked away, when seconds mattered most.

Finally she spotted his shiny head climb into a *songthaew*. She was relieved. She ran and got in. The *songthaew* meandered through the town loading on more passengers. She looked out of the dusty window. Phuket Town was so different from the all-out assault on the senses of other places in Thailand. Some people characterized it as slow and boring. She felt it had a distinct Asian flavor, and was an acquired taste. It was a true depiction of Thai culture - fun, slightly corny, and no one taking anything too seriously.

The *songthaew* proceeded across the hills, and crawled into Patong through Bangla Road. Her eyes took in the flashy neon lights and big, bold, seedy colors. The contrast between Phuket Town and Patong was like heaven and hell. Patong Beach was the party capital of Asia with a world famous nightlife. It was a hodgepodge of hotels, world class restaurants, neon signs, nightclubs, and tourist attractions.

It was a hedonist's paradise. Countless entertainment centers and bars clustered around Bangla Road. She saw massage parlors in the therapeutic category and also of the erotic type. She guessed the wellness seekers went to the less alcohol and drug infested venues. She spotted ads of expert masseuses practicing atop bamboo mats on beach sands. She was intrigued by signs that said, *Happy ending massage available.*

The *songthaew* stopped and passengers alighted. She was a few steps behind Ganjoo as he walked into a theater that said, *Simon Cabaret Show.* It was like a movie house with Kenny G saxophone music, plush seats, and dimmed lights. She spotted Ganjoo and Rocky in the middle row. There were still a few empty seats behind them.

As Shakti settled into her seat, a bass voice announced the show and the theater went dark. The curtain rose to live performers, glistening in sequins and shimmering with feathers. The girls were beautiful, slender, and fair with perfect figures.

The show presented an entire range of musical theatre from cultures around the world - from Thailand to Egypt to Latin America to China. There were themed displays of classical dance and song in Thai, English, Japanese, and Korean. It was a theatrical extravaganza. Stunning costumes, bright lights, excellent sound, and expensive sets. And possibly, a theater operations director ready to have a nervous breakdown.

Ganjoo whispered to Rocky, "Look at that graceful ballerina in the corner, tiptoeing and extending one slender leg behind her, like a dog at a fire hydrant."

"I'm sure these *bhenchods* take hormones that make them look so fucking girly," Rocky said, staring at the tall, slim girls with great body proportions.

It wasn't until after a few songs that Shakti was struck with a big realization; *Oh my God... The pretty girls on stage are really boys!* She couldn't tell the difference and could think of several ladies who'd die to have figures like the lady boys on stage.

"Years of training, hormones, and surgeries," Ganjoo said. "I read it somewhere."

"Look at the high heels, the fucking smiles, the fucking make-up and costumes. I don't ever want to look or walk like them," Rocky snarled.

Shakti appreciated the clever choreography. The performers were born in male bodies but were living life as beautiful women, expressing their talent through cabaret.

"Boss, what they need is a handsome man like you on the show."

"Handsome? When two people have sex it's a twosome. When it's three people it's a threesome. I don't like the word handsome; it's no fucking compliment."

Ganjoo shook his head side to side.

"I'm headed to Phi Phi tomorrow at noon," Rocky said. "You stay in Phuket and keep an eye on Kriya."

"But Zeenat can do that. And we have Chanarong. Can't I come with you?"

"No. Zeenat has to go to Mumbai. And I don't want any trouble. That Shakti may cause some nuisance."

On stage a Tina Turner impersonator made everyone laugh. Then "Diana Ross" jerked her head back and almost lost her wig to audience guffaws. Shakti didn't smile; she was lapping up every word she heard from Rocky and Ganjoo.

"I now have full control of all of Tidarat's factories. It's time to unleash hell in Mumbai." Rocky shrugged and rolled his neck.

"When will you be back from Phi Phi?" asked Ganjoo.

"I need those *madarchod* plant workers to get their act straight. They've got to produce twice the output. I should be back by night."

"Oh, good. You can't miss the Christmas night celebrations at *Down Under.*"

"No fucking way. Tomorrow night it's time to get drunk, get wasted, and fuck some real Thai pussy. No fake lady boy stuff. You got the brown sugar, right?"

"The best," Ganjoo replied in vigor.

‿

"*Sa wat dee khrap*, Chanarong," Ganjoo said to the guard.

The guard grunted and handed over the keys. He said, "The girl is sleeping."

Shakti crouched behind a dumpster. She had followed Ganjoo back to Phuket Town and to the apartment where Kriya-di was held hostage. She had only one day left to rescue Kriya-di. If she failed she wouldn't forgive herself for the rest of her life.

Ganjoo unlocked the apartment door and turned on the lights. Shakti wasn't sure how long she'd have to wait but he stepped out soon and handed the keys back to the guard. He mumbled through the food in his mouth, "Keep a close watch and don't fall asleep. I'll be back in a little while."

She waited. It was late at night. Her eyelids were heavy. She forced them open. An hour passed and she saw the guard get sluggish with weariness. His heavy arms, held across the chest, heaved up and down slowly as he receded into a swimming drowsiness.

She ventured out and closed in on him; he seemed fast asleep. She saw the keys peer out of his pocket. She picked a small twig and tried to yank them out. He shook all of a sudden and made a guttural noise. She froze. He changed sides but was still fast asleep. Her heart beat faster. She tried again with the twig and pulled the keys out. She waited for a few seconds. He didn't budge. She sped to the door and unlocked it. She chose not to turn the lights on.

Out of nowhere, a silhouette rushed towards her from across the dark room. After a few shaky steps, the shadow twitched into a more effective feline stride. Shakti's hands assumed a defensive stance as she took a step backward.

Shakti saw the crazy eyes. The dark figure wanted to fight her, perhaps even kill her. The figure came within a whisker, shouting out, "You dirty, rotten scoundrels!"

"Kriya-di? It's me...It's Shakti." Kriya-di stopped. The expression on her face changed as she reigned in her anger. Her frenzied expression collapsed into a pitiable misery. She gazed at Shakti with soft black eyes that teetered on the verge of a breakdown. Slowly the stutter of a smile flickered across her face as if animated by an electric pulse.

Shakti hugged Kriya-di's frail body. The knot in her stomach twisted tighter, wrung with mixed emotions of anxiety and happiness. Her fingers went cold and numb. The sheer incredulity of finding Kriya-di, and reuniting with her, paralyzed Shakti where she stood. Her chin quivered. She screamed in joy, but no sound came from her throat.

The joy on Kriya-di's face was everything to her; the entire world. A pulsating beckoning of harmonious chants wafted through the air from a nearby Buddhist monastery. *Buddham saranam gacchami...dhammam saranam gacchami*[90]. Vibrations of divine love touched their hearts, and sisterly love streamed down from their eyes, summoned by the incantation. Shakti was content, unafraid, and almost happy.

The lights turned on. Ganjoo stood at the door, brandishing a gun and a scorn. Shakti recoiled from the stench of his flabby flesh. The thick scar that ran down his face gave a lopsided and unsettling twist to his smile. The scarred half of his face didn't move at all which made the other half look all the more menacing and intimidating.

"Now I feel like a fucking *bhenchod*...fucking up this sister reunion."

---

90 Buddham saranam gacchami... dhammam saranam gacchami: To the Buddha for refuge I go... To the Laws of Nature for refuge I go

"No one wants to die. And yet death is the destination we all share.
No one has ever escaped it."

- Steve Jobs, Apple founder and CEO

CHAPTER 14

Another plane began its descent into Phuket, Thailand. This one came from San Francisco. Harry looked out of the plane window as the aircraft followed its approach path over the bay and its graphic limestone karsts, isolated green islets, and multihued fishing boats. The bay appeared like a gripping kaleidoscope of sharp colors and contours.

Passengers alighted and walked through the jet-bridge with their luggage. Harry trundled out of the plane with his large carry-on bag. He felt ragged and tired. His hair was a mess and he had an overgrowth of stubble. He hadn't caught a wink of sleep. He kept thinking of Sally. How was she doing? Was she safe?

And right behind him, Shiva walked out with his light backpack.

Several hours ago at the San Francisco airport, the personnel had made the last and final announcement before takeoff.

Last call for the flight to…

Harry looked at the vacant plane door. It was about to shut. He hung his head down, sighing. Then Shiva scurried through the door, panting and breathless.

Harry jumped out of his seat, almost bumping into the overhead compartment. He gave Shiva a big bear hug. A part of him always knew that Shiva would never desert him in his ordeal. A part of him never doubted that his friend would come through.

"What about the 'Forbidden Fruit' meeting?" Harry asked.

"I've talked to Hong. He knows how to handle it."

"Isn't the customer expecting *you*?"

"I told them I have a critical family emergency. The CEO understands."

"But Shiva, it's a make or break time for our company. Only you can pull it off."

"Hong can do it. I trust him."

"Multi-million dollars are at stake. Hong is good, but he hasn't done it before."

"Look Harry, you're far more important to me. And your friendship is far more precious. I'll take the risk of losing a customer."

Now at Phuket airport, Harry was glad Shiva was with him. They had done some good work together and achieved reasonable success. And when they had failed, he knew that they had always tried hard. He trusted Shiva's instincts. He felt much more confident now. *I know I can rescue Sally from whatever trouble she is in.*

Harry paused and pulled out a map. "So, where are we going?"

"Well, look here, the Phi Phi Islands are a group of six islands off the Phuket coast. We get to Phuket Town first. Then tomorrow, we take a ferry to Phi Phi."

"What sort of a name is that? Phi Phi?"

"It comes from a legend dating back to the prehistoric period. An ancient sword was unearthed prior to its founding and that's what the name stands for."

"A sword huh?" Harry searched for a sword in the contours.

"Yeah, but when I look at the map, Phi Phi doesn't look like any sword to me. In fact, the two largest islands look like guns."

"Are you trying to scare me?" He wondered why it had to be fighting weapons.

"No, really, take a closer look. Phi Phi Don and Phi Phi Lee look like Colt Walkers pointing towards the mainland. The four other islands look like tiny bullets."

"Is that what you think is waiting for us?" He was averse to violence.

"I don't know. We're crossing the Rubicon. There's no turning back now."

"Yes, the die is cast. We're beyond the point of no return." He said it with confidence but felt trepidation in his heart. They'd taken a decisive, irrevocable stride in spite of the warnings from their rational minds and the incessant admonitions from Hong.

Outside their hotel lobby in Phuket Town, a bunch of lady boys surrounded Harry. They jostled each other and shoved their business cards into his hands. They were all imprinted with corny lines: *No ifs, all Butts, Bond Boys,* and *Be my Thai Master.*

"You're such a lady-magnet." Shiva winked at him.

Harry remembered Hong's words: *Stay alert. The lady boys are notorious for pickpocketing.* Harry said to them, "I've no money." They didn't believe him but stepped aside begrudgingly, clamoring in Thai. One winked at him and gestured to call him.

Harry's phone buzzed. It was a text from Hong: *Hope u guyz reached ok.* He dialed Hong's number. "Hey, we got into Phuket Town, all safe and sound."

"Great. Be careful. Do you guys need anything from me?"

"Of course we need you. We need you to be our eyes and ears. Tell us what we should expect on the Phi Phi Islands."

"Ok. Here you go." Hong rattled off all the details of his online research while Harry listened in rapt attention. The Phi Phi islands lay 50 kilometers to the south-east of Phuket and were part of a National Park, famous for corals and marine life. The largest of the group, Phi Phi Don, the one that Sally had mentioned, was 28 square kilometers in area and filled with limestone mountains, cliffs, caves, and long, white sandy beaches.

"I don't think we'll go to the beaches," Harry said. He remembered the time he'd spent with Sally in Australia. The beaches. The limestone stacks of the Twelve Apostles.

"Speaking of beaches, remember the Leonardo Di Caprio movie, *The Beach*?" Hong added. "Well, that movie was filmed on Phi Phi Lee."

"Really?"

"The movie got criticized for environmental damage. Areas were bulldozed and palm trees planted to make it look like the book it was based on. The filmmakers fought the accusations; one thing they couldn't deny was that the film led to a surge in tourism."

"But we aren't going to Phi Phi Lee. Sally is somewhere on Phi Phi Don."

"That's right. Phi Phi Don is the only populated island of that group. Here's something crude…Phi Phi is in fact pronounced 'pee pee' as in 'peeing.'"

"Yikes…"

"It means, *The Fiery Isle.*"

"Hey, thanks for all the info. I'm not sure if our cell phones will work tomorrow, so, good night…and wish us luck."

"Go break a leg and find Sally. Call me as soon as you get back to Phuket."

"Yeah, we will. And I wish you a Merry Christmas in advance."

"Merry Christmas to you too. Hey, can you try one thing tonight for me?"

"Listen Hong, we don't have the time or the inclination to visit a massage parlor or a cabaret show or any other dirty thing you're thinking of."

"No, no, no. Not that. Can you try the bird's nest soup for me?"

"What? Bird's nest soup? How the heck do you eat or drink a bird's nest?"

"It's an Asian delicacy. Male cave swifts build these nests from their saliva during the breeding season. They are shaped like shallow cups and stuck to the cave wall."

"Tell me you're joking. Saliva? Is this your way of torturing us simply because we ignored your advice and came here?"

"You won't believe it, but the nests are among the most expensive animal products consumed by humans."

"Most expensive? Like how much?"

"The last time I was in Hong Kong, a bowl of bird's nest soup was about a hundred U.S. dollars. It could be higher now."

"How long will it take to get to Phi Phi Don?" Shiva asked at the ferry terminal. He'd gotten up at dawn; jet lag and the excitement of their adventure wouldn't let him sleep. He woke Harry up and they were at the pier by 8am.

"Next ferry leaves at 8:30am and you reach Phi Phi Don at 10am."

Shiva was surprised by the sheer number of tourists. Families with kids. Trekkers. Honeymooners. Groups of single men and women. All excited about their vacations. The top deck was open and a flag fluttered in the wind. He sat along the front edge, gazing at the crystal clear, sublime waters and the gentle waves. Some folks hung their legs across the railing, enjoying the fresh sea breeze that tickled their feet and soles.

Soon the distant island silhouettes appeared closer and larger. "Wow. The rocks are magnificent. I'm amazed every time," an Israeli man sitting next to him exclaimed.

Large limestone rocks jutted out of the tropical turquoise waters. Captivating, out-of-this-world limestone creations and steep cliffs rose into the sky. Shiva felt it was the perfect inspiration for the setting of a futuristic sci-fi movie with alien avatars. No wonder it had earned the title of being one of the most incredible islands on the planet.

"Phi Phi is a world-class destination for rock climbing," continued the Israeli man. "There are over 600 rock climbing routes in this area. I come here every December."

Shiva quietly soaked in the ethereal sight. It was a perfect day with a bright sun and a few fleecy clouds in the welcoming skies. The air was filled with a pleasant aroma from the inviting sea. The island didn't look like a sword. It didn't look like a gun. It was beautiful. Maybe it was like Mata Hari[91]; unsuspicious in appearance, but the cause of many innocent deaths. Maybe the island was a silent, beautiful killer. It lured you into a spellbinding stupor, and then death snuck up on you with surreptitious cunning.

The ferry reached ashore on Phi Phi Don and docked at the large, deep-water pier on Tonsai bay. The Israeli tourist told him that most of the development and civilization was situated in and around Tonsai village, located on a low, sandy isthmus that joined the two hilly spurs that made up the rest of the island. They walked to the village, where shops sold beach gear and souvenirs. Harry asked about a grimy warehouse on the hill, but the shopkeepers were busy. Either they didn't know or they didn't care.

"I'm hungry," pleaded a tired Harry.

"Okay. Let's eat something before we continue our search." For such a small place, Shiva was surprised that the island boasted such a large number of restaurants; French fare, local Thai cuisine, and simple, quick, burger joints. Harry complained that there were no golden arches of McDonald's, his favorite.

They walked in the beating sun. The Papaya Restaurant, opposite Reggae bar, and next to Tiger bar, looked interesting. It was run by the friendly Mr. Nod. It looked plain, but was crowded and served authentic Thai food; hot and spicy, as it should be. The staff allowed them to express the spiciness in percentile terms with 100% being "Thai spicy".

"It's hot here." Harry dabbed the sweat beads off his forehead.

Mr. Nod heard him and walked over. "Phi Phi has two seasons - hot or wet. The hot season is now, from November to April, and the wet one is from May to October. You should try our ice beer," he said, as he dropped ice cubes into his own chilled beer.

Harry's shocked face shouted "*Sacrilege!*" but he soon got into a conversation with Mr. Nod, who nodded a little more than anyone else. Perhaps his name came from that. He was fairly big around the middle, but had bony hands and a scrawny neck.

"Phi Phi isn't too far from Phuket, but it seems light years away," Mr. Nod said as he nodded. "Many people from all over the world decided it's

---

91 Mata Hari: The famous Dutch exotic dancer, courtesan who was a spy for Germany during World War I.

the most ideal place to live and work, making it a hub for entrepreneurs. Folks left their previous lives behind and started fresh in a place where traffic lights don't affect the quality of their day."

Phi Phi was a nice little hideaway from the stresses of city life, a perfect place for rejuvenation. Visitors thronged its beaches to kayak, scuba-dive, and snorkel. The entire island was without motorized transport. *No motorized transport!* This was an unthinkable concept to most city folks. Shiva wished there were many more places like this.

When Harry asked Mr. Nod if he knew about the grimy warehouse on the hill, he nodded. Shiva wasn't sure if he was simply nodding or if he really knew where it was.

"It's up on the north side of the island near Laem Tong Cape," said Mr. Nod, nodding his head in accelerated confidence. "There's a Gypsy village up there where sea gypsies came from Malaysia a long time ago."

"We've been asking but no one knew. I had begun to doubt if it really exists."

"Of course it does. In a remote part of the island, accessible only by long-tail."

"Long-tail?"

"Traditional Thai wooden boat fitted with motors and propellers. Don't worry. I can set one up for you." Mr. Nod continued his animated head bobbing.

"Great. That would be so much help. Thanks a million, Mr. Nod."

"Remember, there are two drop-off points for the long-tail. The first one has a gentle winding climb but it takes longer. The second one is shorter but it's a treacherous climb through the rocks. Avoid the second one. Last month, two tourists died on it."

Mr. Nod's nodding was so vigorous that Shiva felt his head would come off and roll down to the floor. Then all of a sudden, his nodding came to a standstill. With a voice hushed and distant, he said, "Be careful. It's a dangerous place."

Mr. Nod's man took them to the pier where a procession of long-tail boats was lined up. Adorned with garlands of flowers on the bow, the striking vessels blended in with nature. Shiva noticed a lot of variation – different sizes, colors, and styles. Some had evolved from traditional watercrafts while others had a more modern, improvised look. The sole defining trait was the secondhand car or truck engine used to drive them.

They climbed aboard a boat that was a lightweight canoe hull, about 20 meters long. Its engine was mounted on an inboard turret like pole which rotated 180 degrees. The propeller was mounted directly on the driveshaft, extended by several meters of metal rod, giving the long-tail boat its name and distinct appearance.

The driver used his hands, legs and entire body as he toyed with the long-tail and the propeller. He moved the propeller in and out of the water, shifting it to the right and left. He straddled the long-tail, his body in all kinds of weird contortions.

"Maybe someone could start a new workout craze back in San Francisco - the Long-tail Fitness Regime," Harry said with a chuckle.

Further out into the Andaman Sea, they saw larger boats with more than one 'tail' manned by several operators, piloting, contorting, and working out the "Long-tail Fitness Regime" in tandem. The boat took them along a curving bay past Monkey Beach, where dozens of primates roamed the shore as if it was their private property.

"Be careful. Keep your hands inside," the boat driver instructed in a stern voice.

"Why? The monkeys look gentle," Harry asked, his arms flapping.

"If you don't give food, monkeys get angry. Last week tourists tease monkeys. Crazy people. Monkeys attack and bite them. Bad. Very bad."

Harry retracted his hands and folded them into safety.

Soon they arrived at the first drop-off point. Laem Tong Cape was remoteness personified. Mr. Nod had said, "It's one of the best getaways on the island. No noisy crowds. No discos or loud music at night." It was nestled among coconut orchards and a pristine, secluded beach. A handful of the elite snorkeled in the clear, shallow waters leading up to the reef where the depth seemed to drop off in a dramatic fashion.

The walk from the beach and up the hill wasn't too hard, but it was a scorching day. The view was unique. Two white sandy beaches curved away from each other against the backdrop of the imperial limestone rocks and the majestic Andaman Sea.

"You know what, Shiva? I'll rescue Sally and bring her back to America. I'll take good care of her and keep her safe and satisfy all her fantasies."

Shiva paused, looked back and smiled. He knew how much Sally meant to Harry.

"We'll grow old together, with silver streaks in our hair, and watch our merged Yankssie kids rule the northern Yankee and the southern Aussie hemispheres."

Shiva patted his shoulder. Harry was drenched; his soaked shirt stuck to his back and chest, and his cheeks glistened red. They had carried water bottles to keep hydrated. The water was chilled when they started; it was lukewarm now.

"I hate this heat. I wish I had a portable fan." Harry pulled out a kerchief and tied it around his head. "I bet its ten degrees cooler at the beach below." He gazed at the sandy strip nestled in the coconut orchards. He tried his cellphone. No signal.

They passed a small Gypsy village. They were losing hope, and their progress was slowed down by the draining heat.

Slowly, the warehouse crept into their view. It was a decrepit structure that looked unsympathetic and unapologetic. Grimy, wooden walls, black tile, murky windows, deserted underbrush, and dented aluminum. It had a surgical frostiness and aloofness. It seemed like a convoluted structure, an intermediate space, a doorway built to reach some final place that was never built.

It had the look of a place where bloodstains had recently been scrubbed away. Should they go in? Shiva felt a door would open and they'd be called in. Then ghastly things would happen before they were set free...*if* they were set free. They hid at a distance, behind dirty piles of debris and a wild writhe of hedges and plants.

He studied the warehouse for any signs of activity. A big guard stood at the front door with a tall gun, towering over everything else around him.

"Well, we can't simply sit here getting kidney stones," Harry whispered. "I know Sally's in there. I can sense it."

"There must be another way inside. It's too big a place to have only one entrance," Shiva said. No way could they go past the guard. They had to go around him.

Shiva detected a narrow, hidden path that veered along the side towards the rear. It was filthy. They tiptoed over rank, scum-covered pools of dark, putrid, sludge. The side walls of the warehouse were wooden and patched together with nails. The walls were swarming with a wormy tangle of creepers, weeds, and thick, black patches of oil.

Harry spotted a wooden door at the rear, concealed from view. He pushed at it with caution. It was unlocked and swung inward with a rusty creak of complaint. They stepped inside and the door swung shut. Darkness engulfed them. They paused while their eyes adjusted to the dimness.

The warehouse had a small room at the rear and four big rooms leading to the front. A wide corridor connected all the rooms, looking out to the cliffs and the Andaman Sea beyond. Shiva moved slowly forward and Harry followed. A stink oozed out from the rear where the restrooms stood. Several boxed and stacked up crates of oil lined the corridor. At the front end, an armed guard lounged on a chair.

"Let's get out of this place," Harry whispered. "Too many armed people here and I don't see Sally. Let's sneak out through the back-door."

Shiva glared at him. They had come all this way to find Sally; they weren't turning back so soon. He scrutinized the area for any clues that would lead to her.

The first big room held about fifteen young kids engaged in a meticulous activity, busy working at their tables, processing and packaging a white powdery substance. One boy whistled a melody, at once very intricate and simple. It seemed to flow out of him as though he were a flute. It had the edge to hang in there amidst all that insensitive, frosty air, piercing through all the clatter in the warehouse.

The armed guard at the front let out a lazy yawn. He scratched his ear and then his back. He yawned again, groggy after a big lunch. He stood up, unwinding at a snail's pace, and began to crawl towards the rear of the warehouse - right towards them.

They tiptoed backwards, trying to get away without drawing attention. They turned into a nook and waited. They couldn't hear the guard's steps. Harry snuck his head out of the nook to confirm. Perhaps he had walked back into one of the rooms.

"Hands up. Keep them where I can see," the guard ordered.

Shiva and Harry stepped out of the nook with hands held up.

"Walk straight down towards the rear. Any mischief and I'll shoot you dead."

Harry stepped out in an awkward manner, tripping over his own feet. He balanced himself and followed Shiva to the small room in the rear.

"See, I told you we shouldn't have come," Harry whispered.

"You are the one who insisted, and then convinced me to come on this adventure: 'I urge you to do the right thing. Let that ironclad armor melt. Do what your soul says.'"

"Well, you should've talked me out of it."

"Shut the fuck up," the guard ordered.

Another guard came in. "Who are these idiots? How did they get in here?"

"I don't know. We'll find out."

"Hey, the boss is here. He can grill these jokers."

The door swung open wide and a man walked in with an air of un-challenged authority. He was towering, and noticeably erect. He had long black tresses that rolled down over his ears to his jaw and neck, and the rough stubble of a bristly goatee. His eyes lit up when he saw Shiva.

"Look who we have here... Mr. Shiva himself. What an unexpected honor!"

Shiva was taken aback. How did this man know him? He tried search-ing his memory bank, trying to remember where he'd seen this face before. There was something very familiar about the man's face, but he couldn't place it.

The boss man's grin widened. He realized Shiva couldn't remember. He ordered his men, "Show them some of our hospitality."

Shiva and Harry were dragged to the middle of the room. Their hands were tied behind their backs with crude, hemp rope. Shoes, phones, and wallets were removed and thrown aside. Coils and coils of rope were wound around their shoulders and arms, locking them up. Their bodies were then hauled up to hang at chest height from a hook, face down, with the hook lodged through the coils of rope.

Harry was sweating bullets. Shiva could picture a cinema reel playing in Harry's mind. This wasn't anticipated. Harry had expected a different movie...riding in on his white stallion, a knight in shining armor, swooping down and rescuing Sally from distress. Now Harry looked petrified. He was appalled by what was unfolding in the warehouse.

"Sir, we're sorry," Harry said. "We shouldn't have intruded on your property. A terrible mistake. We're so sorry. Please let us go and you'll never see us again."

"But you've seen this place now. You're a danger."

"I promise we won't tell anybody. Please let us go. We'll be off of this island on a helicopter and then out of this country. We won't cause any more trouble."

The boss man stared with disdain. "Men, he wants a helicopter."

Shiva and Harry were spun round and round. The hook hung their bound bodies from the coiled ropes. They whirled and spun until they lost all orientation. Soon their heads hung almost level with their dangling feet. Then the beatings began. The men hit their spinning bodies with cane sticks as hard and as often as they could. The stinging blows struck with piercing pain through the ropes; on their arms, back, legs, and feet.

Harry screamed his lungs out. Shiva could feel the scream rising up inside him but he clenched his jaw and gave pain no sound of his own. He wouldn't let them hear him scream. He wouldn't let them hear him beg. *Silence is the tortured man's revenge.*

The whirling stopped suddenly, but the respite was momentary. They were now spun in the opposite direction and the beatings continued.

Questions ran amuck in Shiva's head. Who were these people? Why were they meting out such third degree treatment? How did they know him? Had this boss man mistaken him for someone else? Would someone come to help?

When the beating stopped at last, the boss man ordered them to be unhooked. They fell to the floor in a heap and the men removed the coiled ropes. The boss man stood menacingly over them with his fists on his hips. He kicked Shiva several times and let out a series of expletives. He ordered the men to lift Shiva and stand him up so they could be face to face.

Shiva couldn't feel their hands on his deadened skin. The boss man said something vicious to his face, but his ears were still ringing too loudly for him to hear. There was a fog in front of his eyes. A taste, thick and bitter, grew at the back of his mouth. He struggled to swallow it and then he knew, he remembered. As Harry would remind him, it was the rage; the anger of the Hulk. Shiva struggled to swallow it down.

The boss man spat in his face. He screamed out, and the words came through loud and clear this time; "You fucker. You're a dead man."

Somewhere inside Shiva, a drum began to beat. It might've been his heart. He felt his whole body tense and clench as if it was a fist. He tried to raise his hands to hit back, but he struggled to even nudge them.

"I still remember that day in the boxing ring, the ring that I owned. I was the king of the jungle until..." the boss man began...

Shiva stared at him in disbelief.

"...that episode," he continued, "It's etched in my head like an undying malignant tumor that can never be removed. It gets bigger and more toxic every passing moment."

A bright and clear flash exploded in Shiva's mind. The same face, a few more cold years added. The same style, but more crude and vicious than before. The same anger, but even more evil than before. Yes, it was Raktim, the big bully from high school.

"You aren't that smart; it took you so long." He rolled his neck. "I don't know what got into you that day. You were possessed. I remember it like it was yesterday." He began to recount...

I yelled at you, "Hey *madarchod*, you have to win in five rounds!"

The boxing arena went mute. Pin drop silence.

You looked at me, "But Raktim, you had said three rounds."

"Now I say five rounds, let's go," and I brought up my gloved fists.

"No way, Raktim," Coach said from the sideline. His head tilted sideways and shook. His eyebrows rose in defiance. "You can't trick the boy out of his win."

"Who the fuck asked you anything, old man?" I lowered my chin to look down at him. I felt my blood pressure rise with a roiling heat in my belly.

He snorted out, "I'm not afraid of you. The boy beat you within the rules and without a doubt. I can't let you steal that away from him."

I turned to face you head-on. "Put your gloves up, Coach's new blue-eyed boy. Let's get on with the fight. You and me."

You raised your fists, but he shouted, "You take off your gloves, Shiva. You aren't fighting another round. Come on down, right now."

"Yeah, go and hide behind the Coach's back, you sissy boy!"

"Coach, I will fight him and win," you said with your fighting gloves primed and your head bobbing for action.

I was gaining control of the situation again. I flashed a grin at the Coach.

"NO," he declared with an inevitability that hissed through his pinched mouth, clenched jaw, and narrowed eyes. "Shiva beat you, big guy. He beat you right in front of our eyes and right out in the open. It was beautiful. What is it, big guy? You can't take it that this new boy beat you fair and square in your own ring?"

I told him, "Coach, get back into your office before I pummel you."

He said, "Don't bully me. Does big guy have to pick on his old Coach the day another boy became the better boxer? The day when big guy had to eat shit?"

The entire crowd cheered him. They broke into a frenzied run towards the ring, shouting out your name. Squealing. Whooping. Hollering. The stupid people danced and embraced each other. Some climbed up into the ring and hoisted you on their shoulders and paraded you around like the new prince of the house.

My muscles trembled as I sank to the ground. I hated it. I hated it with all my might. That day changed my life forever. And I hated school thereafter. I had to live with all the whispers behind my back.

Shiva stood shell-shocked. A part of him felt sympathy for Raktim. Such repressed feelings over so many years. Raktim had let the hurt fester in the darkness of his unconscious. He had kept his emotions and hatred hidden for so long, feeding them and growing them into this monstrosity.

"Listen, Raktim. That was a long time ago. You need to forgive and forget. Even our Coach loved you; he told me so many times."

"Really?"

"Yeah, Coach loved your boxing. He told me, 'I've never seen a guy work so hard as Raktim. You have to hand it to him. He might not be the most affable kid in the world, but I know he has something in him. When he's boxing in the ring, I simply stop right in the middle of whatever I'm doing and watch him flow. It's like poetry in motion.'"

"He said that? Why didn't he say it to me?"

"You know how he was. But he really liked you. You should let bygones be bygones. Hatred can be a dangerous thing."

"Well, we're different people, you and I," Raktim said, staring out at the distant Andaman Sea. "You don't understand. You can't understand."

"I understand that hate kills you, Raktim, if you can't let it go."

"No, Shiva," he said with emphasis. His eyes gleamed. A strange expression was affixed to his swarthy face.

Shiva had seen the expression before. Harry wore it when he talked about Sally and about destiny and fate. It was the sort of expression some men assume when they talk about the experience of God.

"My hate is what saved me," Raktim said with a feverish zeal. "Hate is a very resilient thing. Hate is a survivor. I had to hide my hate for a long time. People couldn't handle it. They were spooked by it. So I sent my hate outside myself, flying in all directions. I transported drugs, shot men, cut their throats, and my hate survived out there. It got stronger and it moved outside Mumbai and even outside India."

In another time, another place, another life, Raktim would've read God's words aloud, from the Gita, the Bible, or the Koran, moving all those who heard him to tears.

"Then one day, I saw you again in Mumbai. I could feel the hate creep back into me. It's here now, inside me, where it belongs. I'm glad. I need it. It's stronger than I am. My hate is my hero." He held a fanatic gaze far out into the horizon. The sky darkened as a dirty, grey tide of clouds crossed the mountains and tumbled on towards the deserted beach. "Remember the taxi driver on your way to the airport? He was my man. The SEEPZ power disruptions. The goon who beat up your engineers. All were my men."

Shiva felt unsettled. He knew if he unlocked his knees and let his legs relax, they'd crumple and fold beneath him.

"And the MLA? He was all set to help you... that bastard. But one email from me and he was silly putty in my hands."

"Everyone has forgotten about the boxing episode. Why dig out dead, cremated corpses?" said Shiva, wary of Raktim's song of hate.

"But I haven't. And that's what counts. The only way I'll forget is by destroying everything you care for – your company, your girlfriend, your life. Once you're a forgotten *madarchod*, then I'll forget it."

A freezing wind blew and Shiva shuddered, unsteadied. "My girlfriend?"

"Surprise, surprise! I have your girlfriend here with me, and I'm gonna do things to her that you can't possibly imagine."

"What?" Shiva gasped out what really wasn't a question. He doubled over as if from a blow to the stomach. If he had had food in him he would've been sick, but he experienced a retching of his soul instead. How could Raktim know about Shakti?

A couple of men dragged in a girl and threw her at Raktim's feet. Her face was covered with a brown canvas bag and her hands coiled in rope.

"I saw you sipping Capiroshka's at Aurus and laughing out loud. My blood boiled, furious for revenge. I couldn't help myself. I took a picture of you two love-birds."

"Oh, that was you in the navy blue blazer?" Shiva groaned. He had almost grabbed Raktim outside Aurus, but he got away in the taxi.

"Imagine my surprise when I saw her again in Phuket, walking all by herself at the night mall. Don't worry; we've taken good care of her, haven't we, darling?" A hard silence. The sort of silence that drives itself into one's memory deeper than the sharpest sound. He removed the bag from her head.

"Sally!" Harry screamed.

Sally spit the gag from her mouth, "Harry, you found me."

Raktim was stunned. He had lost his elation for the big planned moment of revenge. This was a man who was in the habit of getting what he wanted. For the first time, his superior affect seemed to crack right down the middle. He stood crestfallen.

Shiva seized the opening. "Let these two go, they are innocent bystanders. You have an axe to grind with me. What have they done to deserve this?"

"Well, life's a dick. Sometimes it gets hard for no reason," Rocky smirked.

"I want you to know that I love you..." Sally said, in an earnest voice.

Harry smiled in understanding. "I never stopped loving you."

"Now enough of this melodrama," Raktim interjected, his eyes moving faster.

"I'm so sorry for leaving you like that," she continued, "I panicked."

He grabbed her by the hair and yanked hard. "I said enough, you midget."

"Ouch! *Ya fuckin' wanker!*" she screamed.

He glared with piercing, bloodshot eyes. "Who are you calling a *fuckin' wanker*, you white cunt." He pulled out his Smith & Wesson revolver and pointed it at her. "Better be afraid of me. Be very afraid."

"I'm afraid only of God. I love him and fear only him." Her voice was now thin and sharp as a whip.

"Right now, I *am* God. I've got the power. I can take your life anytime I want."

"You are no God, you two-bit poser." The whip was in her voice again, every word a stinging stroke.

Bang, bang, bang, bang, bang, bang. "Die bitch! Now who's God?" Raktim laughed the most deluded laugh. His cohorts echoed along in morbid fear.

"Beware the wrath of the Almighty," she gasped, glaring with venom at him from the corners of her closing eyes. She took her last breath as she slumped to the floor.

"SALLLYYYY!!! Noooo!!!" Harry cried. He looked around, confused, as if pieces of his heart had splintered all over. He was angry and he was afraid; a strange kind of fear – the kind of arctic dread that only the loss of love can cause.

Raktim walked over to Harry, wielding his reloaded revolver. He studied Harry's face, reading him as he held the gun to his temple. "Do you want to join her? I can help. I love blood... how it flows. I love its overpowering smell."

Shiva and Harry stared at the madman.

"The only good thing my parents did was to name me Raktim. RAKTIM. Blood Red. Spilling your blood will make my own blood tingle. Spilling your blood will -"

The door opened and a guard ran in. "Boss, there's an emergency in Phuket. It needs your urgent attention."

"*Chutiye.* Don't interrupt me. I was beginning to have some fun."

"It's about Ganjoo and your pigeon. You need to leave now to catch the ferry..."

"Keep an eye on these jokers." He began to walk away when he turned suddenly towards Shiva. "This isn't over. I'll be back for you."

That's one thing we agree about, Raktim, Shiva thought. *It definitely isn't over yet. You and I have one final round to go. Only one of us will be the last man standing.*

Raktim's laughter as he walked away from them was loud and cruel. It didn't fool Shiva though. He felt that the laughter was weak and false. He'd heard it before from his Alltech ex-Boss. He knew it well. *Cruelty is a type of cowardice. Cruel laughter is the way cowards cry when they're not alone. And causing pain is how they grieve.*

Harry rushed towards Sally; she remained motionless. He reached out and touched her face, his hands beginning to shake. Shiva wished he could do more for his friend, but Harry's hand kept trembling; it started at his elbow, a pain drawn from within, and went straight to his palm. He clenched his fist and waited for the trembling to pass. The shaking stopped but then it came back again.

Harry began to compress her chest with his shaking hand and tried to blow air in her mouth. But life had deserted her. The small tension of will that kept her body taut had collapsed. Her face, though, was tranquil and unblemished, even amidst the thickening pool of blood. Her eyes and mouth were closed as if in a still sleep; she seemed at peace. She was able to meet Harry and confess her love for him, but she was so serene in her death that poor Harry's heart refused to believe she was gone.

Harry held her head in his lap and relived their memories in the outline of her face. He cradled her in his arms and against his chest. When Shiva touched his shoulder, he came to the moment as if from a nightmare. His eyes cleared and he looked around as if seeing everything for the first time. He gaped at Shiva, eyes popping from their sockets with fear - the desolate terror of a man who knows fate has abandoned him.

Shiva couldn't figure out what to do. No one knew they were on this forsaken island. No one except Hong. If he didn't hear back from them, Hong would guess something was wrong. In time he'd know. They had to get a message out to him, but how? And would he be able to do anything? And even if he did, would it be before they die? This island was like a black hole. No light, no news, escaped from here. Even if they vanished from the face of the earth, no one would know.

Thoughts buzzed and swarmed in Shiva's spiraling head. His mind drifted in fevered visions. He thought of Pa, Ma, his cousins and relatives, his friends and colleagues. He thought of Harry who sat in a sad heap next to him. He wished he could tell Harry how much his honest and generous friendship meant to him.

But his thoughts always found their way back to Shakti. He was thinking of her when the guards nudged him. When they gave him water that seemed like the nectar of life to his dry, parched throat, his dreaming mind saw beatific visions of Shakti.

He moved his head to look at the ceiling and he saw a pair of eyes peering through the air duct vent; a pair of eyes that shone with a glimmer of hope.

"Jo dar gaya so mar gaya." (One who is scared, is as good as dead.)
- Shiva's Boxing Coach

CHAPTER 15

The guards moved Sally's body out and vacated the room, leaving Shiva to console Harry. But Shiva himself felt melancholy. He looked up at the vent, searching, but he didn't see the pair of eyes again. Maybe he'd imagined them. Maybe the helicopter twirling and the beating had caused him to hallucinate.

Shiva's breath came in short puffs. Sally was gone and it was their turn next. He put up a brave front and put his hand around Harry's shoulder, shoring him up.

An unexpected small noise came from the air duct vent and the cover was pulled off. Shiva gaped in surprise at the face that peered through the gap. He rubbed his eyes to make sure he wasn't dreaming. Shakti's face shone through like an angel. He glanced at Harry whose eyes confirmed that the beatific vision was indeed a reality. She flew down from the vent like an angelic knight in shining wings.

"What are you doing here?" Shakti asked as she hugged him. He held the same question in his mind. She whispered, "We can all escape through the duct. But we have to move fast before the guards show up."

He knew she was right; they didn't have much of a choice. Staying back in the room was tantamount to certain death. In the short span of the eclipse created by the guards' absence, they were invisible and they had to make their move, and the escape plan had to succeed. If it failed, the guards were quite capable of shooting them to death.

"Get up Harry. This is our chance. We've to give it a try." He reached out and shook Harry, helping him back onto his feet. They had a tiny window of opportunity, but Harry was an emotional and physical tangle. He seemed disconsolate; his tears rolled down in a sad trickle, and he was lost in a distant, inconsolable world.

Standing on Shiva's shoulder, Shakti climbed up first into the air duct. Shiva then hoisted Harry up with help from her and a trembling chair. Harry was heavy and uncoordinated; he almost slipped down.

"Excuse me. A little bit of help would be useful, if it's not too much trouble," Harry said. He was cramped in a precarious way and Shiva gave him a haul, somehow managing to push him through.

As he went up last, Shiva kicked off the chair and put the vent-cover back in its place. Their escape route needed to be concealed from the guards for as long as possible.

"Follow me," Shakti said, as she stretched out on her stomach and crawled at a fast pace. She had navigated the route before. Shiva and Harry followed her, slower and slowest. The duct stretched out in a grid pattern. It was pitch black inside except for the vent light that trickled in at regular intervals. The duct was all covered in white dust.

Shiva knew they didn't have long to make their escape. His guess was about ten minutes, maybe less, before the guards found them missing. In that time they had to get through the duct, sneak through the wild shrubbery to the front gate, trek down the hill to the beach, and then sail in the long-tail boat to freedom. The clock was ticking.

To make matters worse, their progress in the duct had to be slow and cautious. If they moved too fast, it would attract attention from the men below. The empty room and their escape route were bound to be found out any minute. They could be hunted down in the duct or on the hill or the beach…if they even make it that far.

It was a tough crawl. The beatings had bruised Shiva's body, making it sore. He could hear Harry's labored breathing. At one bend Harry got stuck. He couldn't move forward or backward. He contorted his body and tucked in his chest and stomach, but it was hopeless. Blood rushed to his face from all the strain. He seemed stuck for good.

Shiva wriggled back like a worm. It was dark and Harry's body blocked all the light. Shiva scrambled around, trying to get a better view and some leverage. "Harry, move your neck aside." As soon as Harry did that, light came through and Shiva saw what had trapped him. It was Harry's leather belt – a thick, Texan belt with a big, longhorn buckle.

Harry undid his belt and yanked it away from his waist. Then, he squeezed through the bend like a smooth, slippery walrus. They were right above an assembly area. The boys below had begun to stare towards the ceiling. Shiva held his breath. The boys looked down again, laughed and continued with their work. One boy whistled a tune.

They continued crawling. It seemed they were getting closer to the exit and that they'd soon be out of the warehouse, until Harry began to clear his throat. He coughed. It was explosive. The sound echoed like a gunshot in Shiva's ears.

"Harry, quiet!" Shiva said in a low voice.

"It's the dust," he whispered, and coughed again. Dust blew around in white swirls. "I couldn't help it. I couldn't." Down below, an armed guard walked slower.

"Shhhh... Be quiet." Shiva's heart thumped in his chest.

"Anyway, it doesn't matter. We're far away. He can't hear us."

The guard stopped. He walked towards the vent, trying to detect the noise.

"Of course, he can hear us."

"Well, how should I know?" Harry coughed again.

Shiva waited in the silence that followed, his ears still ringing with the diminishing echoes of Harry's coughing. His heart, like a trapped bird, hurled itself against the cage of his chest. The guard stood there for what seemed like an eternity and then moved away. *Phew*. They were still undetected.

At last they came to an opening at the rear of the warehouse. Shakti pushed the vent door and it fell out with a clang. Shiva hoped no one else heard the sound; they were so close to escape. They slid out and put the vent door back.

The armed guards at the front were looking in every direction but theirs. If one guard had turned their way, it would've been game over. Shakti crawled like a cat on all fours. Shiva and Harry followed suit and all of them snuck behind a big rock. No one had spotted them yet. No one had come out running. No one had screamed they were missing.

Shiva hunkered down next to Shakti. He was so glad to see her again. She spun around, brushing him on his wrist with her slender fingers. Her head drew closer and her eyes met his. Her sandy brown eyes sparkled with courage and other mysteries. She smiled, but a transparent wrinkle creased her forehead. She was brave and fragile and lovely all in the same instant.

She blinked and turned to look at the sea below as if considering their options. Behind them were the cliffs laden with sharp rocky edges and dark crevices. Her long, loose shirt clung to the outline of her figure in the strong breeze. He still felt her fingers on his skin well after they were gone, maybe even more deeply now.

His mind raced with the breeze. *Shakti, I'm so glad to see you again. You're the angel of my life. I think of you wherever I am. You accompany me in my heart to meetings, to business dinners, and to customer visits. You join arguments you haven't even heard. I imagine you next to me in places you've never been to. You permeate each and every aspect of my life. And I'm so glad you are here now, next to me, for real.*

She caught his long gaze. "What is it, Shiva?"

He paused, weighing his thoughts. "Your dress is all messed up and dirty," he said, shying away on the outside while dying to say so much more on the inside.

Shiva swiveled towards Harry, who was lost in thought, staring at the sheer cliffs below. He kept leaning out dangerously close to the edge as if thinking how easy it would be to keep bending over, tipping until his weight carried him down. His eyes were blanched white and wide open as if imagining himself fall, belly flapping in the wind, feet rotating, and then a crack of the skull, a quick crack, and then, silence.

"It's a certain fall to death," Harry said out loud. "We'll never get through these rocks. Let's go back into the warehouse and pretend this never happened."

"We can't go back," Shakti said. "If we go back, we're as good as dead."

"Well, what the heck are we gonna do?" Harry demanded, shouting with everything but his voice. Sweat dripped from his face. He rubbed his palms and began talking to himself.

"Get a grip on yourself, Harry," Shiva said. "I think there are two possibilities..."

"Tell us."

"First option: We climb around the warehouse. Somehow we avoid the gaze of the guards. It'll get us back onto the smooth hill, further down from the front gate."

"That's it?"

"That's the first plan."

"But...they'll see us," Shakti said. "Either the guards or the young kids in the warehouse will see us."

"Yeah, there's a strong chance of that."

"And they'll start shooting at us." Harry said.

"Yeah." The thought had screamed through Shiva's mind as well.

"They'll shoot us," Harry repeated.

"You said that already," Shiva sighed.

"Well, curse me," Harry said. "I think it bears repeating. It's a helluva salient point to a helluva dangerous plan, don't you think?"

"I figure that two of us may get through, maybe, and one of us may get shot."

They considered the odds in silence.

"I hate the plan," Harry said.

"So do I," Shakti agreed. Her eyebrows gathered. "What's the second plan?"

"The second plan is, we trek down through these rocks and cliffs. No guards or guns to worry about. We go to the other beach and take the long-tail from there," Shiva said, while Mr. Nod's words rang in his mind: *The second route is shorter but it's treacherous. Avoid the second one. Last month two tourists died on that path.*

Shiva tried to sound confident and strong, but there are some tales that the body simply doesn't believe and his words came out as a squeak. The second escape plan was the kind that people call heroic if it succeeds, and insane if it fails.

They had a difficult choice to make. They were up against trigger-happy men with evil intentions on the one hand, and the precarious nature of the treacherous cliffs on the other. They didn't have much time to decide.

"Do any of you smoke?" Shakti asked. She had an idea.

"I do, but..." Harry said, with a puzzled expression that suggested it wasn't the time or the place.

"Do you have a lighter...or matches?" she persisted.

Harry searched his pockets, found a matchbox, and handed it over. She lit up a few matches and flung them towards the oil covered pools of black liquid.

"Shiva, do you smoke?" she asked.

"No, I don't. I can't stand smoke."

She smiled. She was glad he didn't. He was so much like her.

The stagnant pools burst into flames that spread to the thick, black patches of oil on the wooden walls. The fire spread fast, burning the oil and igniting the wood. The warehouse would be engulfed in a blaze soon. She knew the workers had sufficient time to escape, but the warehouse was certain to be reduced to ashes.

The smoke filled Shakti's lungs and the place reeked with a burning stench. Harry coughed, and his eyes watered in the cloud of smoke, but for the first time, she felt no nausea. For the first time, she didn't hate that disgusting odor; she didn't cough.

She had to destroy the warehouse. She had to stop the onslaught of Rocky's drug carnage. She had to save those innocent Mumbai children and their unsuspecting families.

She looked back one last time. She felt satisfied with the fire's progress. Then they began the treacherous trek down the cliffs.

Shakti reflected on the unimaginable series of events. She had really mastered the knack of getting caught between a rock and a hard place… time and time again. She had followed Rocky to this God-forsaken warehouse to get back her passport and pendant. And now she was engineering an escape with Shiva and Harry. Unbelievable.

Shakti thought of the previous night when Ganjoo had trapped them.

The lights turned on. Ganjoo stood at the door brandishing a gun and a scorn. Shakti recoiled from the stench of his flabby flesh. The scarred half of his face didn't smile at all which made the other half look more menacing and intimidating.

"Now I feel like a fucking *bhenchod*…fucking up this sister reunion."

Shakti and Kriya-di cowered down against the wall. Scared and trapped again.

"Boss, I've got them," Ganjoo called Rocky. "If they try any funny business I'll crush them like peanuts." He made an ominous gesture, pointing his index and middle fingers in a V at his eyes, and then pointing the V menacingly at them.

Almost an hour passed. Shakti and Kriya-di sat against the wall, sharing their ordeals over the past few months. Shakti's eyes moistened and her heart filled with disgust and anger as she heard about Kriya-di's torment.

"Can I have something to drink? I'm parched," Shakti asked, as she wiped her eyes. A plan took form in her mind.

"You better stop gossiping. That's what's drying your throat."

"Please. I'm really thirsty. Do you have any juice?"

Ganjoo checked the refrigerator with reluctance. "There's orange juice."

"Yes, that'll be great. Thanks so much."

He got her the juice and shoved it in her face, as if to say it was the last time she could ask for anything. His hands were as soft as old leather. He walked back and stood at a mirror with a comb, parting and pasting, with masterful precision and passion. His ten strands of hair were styled into a very specific profile over his bald head.

"Yikes…this tastes bad," Shakti interrupted.

"What's bad?" He gawked at her with contempt.

"The juice. Taste it yourself and see." She made a contorted face.

He dragged himself over. He smelled as foul and scented as rotting flowers on a grave. He grabbed the glass and sipped. "It tastes fine to me." He gulped down the entire glass. "Now you don't get any. Simply stay quiet and don't bother me anymore."

A few minutes passed by and he shuffled in his chair. He appeared uncomfortable. He put his hand to his chest as it heaved up and down. "I can't breathe." He flailed his arms, making gestures as if he was suffocating.

Shakti looked at him from afar - a look of knowing anticipation.

"What did you give to me, *kutiya*?" He stumbled out of the chair. He walked towards them in giddy, unsure steps. "I'll kill you." He reached for his gun and held it up. His face and body changed into an unusual cherry red and pink color. He stumbled his way across and loomed over them, his index finger at the trigger of the gun.

Shakti was glad Rocky had handed her the cyanide pill; it had come handy. But she wasn't sure how long it took for the poison to take its full effect. If it took any longer, Ganjoo wasn't the only one dying this night.

His body shook as if he was having a heart attack. The seizure lasted for a few seconds and then he collapsed. He lay immobile at their feet, but they didn't dare to move. She pushed his knee with her foot to make sure he wouldn't wake up all of a sudden.

They picked up Kriya-di's stuff from the room and snuck out. The guard was snoring outside in spite of the commotion inside. They ran by him and the barking street dogs. They ran by the dimly lit Buddhist monastery and its emancipating chants. *Buddham saranam gacchami… dhammam saranam gacchami*[92]. They ran until they came to the unshackled Andaman Sea and its liberated waves.

Shakti had left Kriya-di under trusted care, in a safe place. She waited for Rocky at noon at the Phuket ferry terminal and then followed him to this God-forsaken warehouse to get back her passport and pendant.

And now she was engineering an escape down this treacherous path.

---

92 Buddham saranam gacchami… dhammam saranam gacchami: To the Buddha for refuge I go… To the Laws of Nature for refuge I go

Legend had it that *JR* made her escape with her son tied to her back as she rode through enemy lines. The British surrounded Jhansi for ten days, bombarding it with artillery. How she managed to get away was unclear; laxity by the soldiers who left their post to loot? Deception by another woman, who misled the troops and was captured? Absolute daring on *JR*'s part, pretending to lead a part of British cavalry? No one knew.

Shakti soon realized that the walls of the bare, mountainous rock weren't what they first seemed. They came in waves of cliffs, ravines, and tiered crevices. Ledges of barren earth wound through the rocky slopes. In places, the ledges were so jagged and narrow that she had to fret over every footstep with careful, trembling consideration.

The sun went under the sea and the skies were stricken with bold dashes of blood red. Down below the surging sea crashed its angry waves on the black rocks.

Soon a full moon appeared in the darkening sky, but the slippery path led them through narrow passes between tall rocks, drowning them in gloom. Mysterious eyes stared out of the eternal darkness and the shifting shadows made the stones seem to stir. The night came alive with eerie shrieks of distant birds and the not so distant winds. Vast black gulfs of air howled through the deserted crevices making her wonder about what lay hidden in the darkness, and making cold sweat trickle down her back.

They inched their way along the blind clefts, pressed hard against the stone, shuffling and stumbling into one another. In the black walled corridors she couldn't see her own hand even when held to her face. Harry slowed down the trek for everyone; he breathed hard and took frequent rest breaks. He seemed so unsure of his steps that she was scared he might slip and fall.

She gazed at Shiva's silhouette against the moonlight that escaped through the rocks. So much had happened since the last time they'd met at the Mumbai airport. She was glad to be with him, in spite of their current circumstance. She stepped closer to him. Outside, the breeze was getting cooler, but it mingled with his warmth by her side. His breathing was calm and even. His teeth flashed white beneath a comforting smile. She smiled back at him, cheeks pulled in, trying to make her face look slimmer.

The path beneath her feet was no wider than the length of her arm. On her right was the smooth rock face of a sheer wall. On her left was a steep drop onto the rubble of broken boulders. She felt an irritating cramp developing in her left hip. The cramp soon became a piercing knot of pain. The more she tried to ignore it, the more agonizing it felt.

Attempting to relieve the stress on her hip, she stretched her left leg. She reached with her right hand into a crevice for support and shifted all her weight onto her right leg. Her hand grasped at a slippery cup-like object, breaking it by accident. There was an eerie sound, and out of nowhere, a couple of cave swifts fluttered out from the crevice. Their nest had broken. The birds flew dangerously close to her face - their narrow wings beating fast and their sharp beaks bristling with irritation.

Shock stole her breath as she lost the earth below her feet. She plunged. Instincts sent her limbs flailing and she stopped with a wrenching snap as her right hand held onto a twig. She dangled in free space over a black abyss. Inch by inch she felt the downward creep, the slipping creak of the stem as she slid further. She could hear shouts above.

She grasped the rocks by her left fingertips and began to drag herself back up to the ledge. She choked a scream as she slipped backwards. The right hand and the twig held again and she dangled over the gap, her situation even more desperate. The panic that lived beneath her skin rose through to the surface as she gasped in fatigue.

She looked up towards the sky. She thought of her Aai. The light from the full moon touched her face. She felt the energy of the moon seep into her skin, through her bones and blood, and into her heart. Her mind went blank - almost in a state of thoughtlessness. She felt her spine tingle and come alive with a transforming force.

She spotted a twig above her to the left. Working with an intuition that starts as fear and turns into adrenaline, she swung herself to the left and up. As she did, the twig in her right hand broke. She was suspended in thin air. Terror ballooned in her heart. The fingers of her left hand managed to seize and hold onto the twig. Barely...

She felt strong hands reach out, grab both her arms, and pull her back onto the ledge. Shiva's hands tightened on her arms as he moved her away from the edge with a gentle pressure. "Shakti, don't you dare do that again."

"Yes, I'm fine." She gazed at him, eyes filled with gratitude. She felt the fabric of his shirt against her, the rough cut of the collar, and the scraping of the buttons against her head. She felt comfort under his reassuring, angular jaw.

They pushed on and hiked for what seemed like an eternity, hugging the cold stone of the canyon silo and the blackness with nothing but faith and the will to survive. They kept going even as the rocks blocked all visibility and made it tough to predict height and distance.

"Eureka!" Shakti ran as a sandy expanse appeared out of nowhere. The warm feel of the soft grains and the moonlight reflecting off its surface ushered in hope. She looked up to the top of the cliffs; the warehouse had burned down to ashes and smoke.

Shiva checked with the ferryman and was told to wait for the next long-tail boat. He sat on the sands alongside Shakti, watching the mysterious coast, both exhausted from the trek. The sky looked so close, like you could reach out and touch the moon. The seas were calm, with very few waves, and the water shone like liquid crystal in the moonlight. The night stars sparkled brighter, sprinkling their enchanting light on the white sandy beach. Then, something magical happened.

Wave after wave of sea turtles emerged from the waters, waddling up the beach to their baby turtles in the safety of their homes. They had dug deep, circular holes and filled them with clutches of soft-shelled eggs. The shy hatchlings were now emerging and waiting for their lumbering parents. Thousands of sea turtles crawled ashore from the ocean and clambered to precise spots on the dunes. It was a breathtaking procession.

One tiny turtle baby lost its way and rubbed the side of Shakti's foot, trying to get a better glimpse of her moonlit face. It was a wonderful little guy, genuinely curious and utterly adorable, but missing a flipper. She gently picked up the baby turtle, sweet-talking and mollycoddling him, and then placed him back in the safety of his circular home.

Shiva recognized an expression on Shakti's face that he hadn't seen before - one of barely suppressed excitement. Anticipation suffused her breathing.

The sea turtles had a miraculous effect on them. Their eyes met and held. Hers twinkled in the light from the night sky and her hair stirred in the wind. She moistened her fine, pink lips and they parted to reveal the tip of her tongue. Tides of the breeze rippled through the loose silk of her shirt, revealing and concealing her perfect breasts.

He put an arm around her, caressing her silk shirt; it was so smooth it seemed to run through his fingers like water. Her eyes lingered, watching him with interest. He was still trying to read her when she drew closer and kissed his cheek. It was an impulsive kiss, short and friendly, but he let himself believe it was more. His heart beat to a joyous parade. Thousands of little turtles of emotions ran through the sands of his body, waiting and begging to be set free. He forced them to stay inside, in the safety of home.

The long-tail boat finally arrived. Too soon, though, for Shiva's liking, since he had to separate from Shakti. He stood up stiffly to his feet, every joint in his body aching.

The driver asked, "You know who burn the mountain house?" but no one spoke. He blinked at them, blank-faced, with fear in his mismatched eyes. "Bad sign. Run away from island. Run away fast. Bad man will hunt and kill you."

Shiva helped Harry onto the boat and sat by his grieving friend with an arm around him. Harry was lost in a wilderness of sorrowful shame. *You've got to hold it together, my dear friend. You've got to come out of this. It's not your fault.*

Harry had made it his mission to rescue Sally. But she was dead – killed in front of his eyes, and he was still alive. Worse, he wasn't even wounded. Harry was reacting as if his own life, the mere fact of his existence, was an act of treachery. He had failed Sally.

Shakti sat at the end, giving them the privacy to reconcile and recover from Sally's loss. The long-tail motor purred aloud and she seemed adrift in her own thoughts.

"I'm sorry about Sally," Shiva's voice broke out soft, steady, and cautious. "You gave it all you had. I wish it was different and she was here with us."

Harry didn't speak. The grief, the beating and exhaustion, had all taken such a toll on him that he looked ill. The color still hadn't returned to his face. His cheeks slumped and dark bags drooped in sadness beneath his eyes, all hope lost.

"When people are beaten down it's dead easy to give up," Shiva continued. "It's dead easy to think of dying. To keep on living is the hard part."

Harry's face was filled with a deep, fearsome anguish that made him slow to react, as if his heart had slowed down its beat. Anguish furrowed his forehead as he tried to re-establish himself in a new frame of reference in time and space.

Shiva gazed at the night sky with its blanket of distant twinkling stars. "Harry, the Universe indeed is so much larger than you and me. And it works in such mysterious ways that we can't comprehend or even imagine. When we stare at the array of stars in the Milky Way, we realize how tiny we are and how little we know."

Harry tried to move but his limbs were limp, as if on strike. They refused to move even an inch, incapacitated by his loss and the long crawl through the rocks. He tried to say something but the sound refused to come out. His voice had abandoned him.

"I know Sally's relaxing up there in her laid-back Aussie style," Shiva reassured him. "This starry view reminds me so much of *Makar Sankranti*[93]. Mumbai skies filled with thousands of kites during both day and at night. Colorful offerings to the Gods."

He looked up towards the sky. Beacons of light filled the goblet of the night sky to the brim. And the chalice overflowed down onto the unperturbed reflection in the Andaman Sea. They were surrounded by luminous signs of hope.

"The fun part wasn't flying the kites; it wasn't how high or far they went. It was the kite fights. Excitement up in the skies, raising our heartbeats until one string was cut, and a kite drifted away. The winning kite strutted through the skies, its head held high."

Harry showed a little glint in his eyes. Life was crawling back in.

"Harry, I was never really a good kite flyer but I was a great kite runner. You know what that is, right?"

"One who chases down the drifting kite?" Harry nodded and whispered, his voice finally stumbling out in a mumble. He groped for more words but they didn't come.

"You got it. Other kite runners ran like madmen, as if their life depended on it. Some held long twigs. If the kite drifted left they ran left. If it drifted right they ran right. But a kite has a mind of its own and it's fickle. I didn't run after it. I assessed its height, the structures around, and the wind. I went and stood someplace where no one else was."

"But what if the wind changed?"

"I adjusted my compass reference and found another secluded spot. I waited patiently. Invariably the kite drifted towards me. I could see the dozens of frantic kite runners chasing behind it, exhausted from all the running. The gentle kite would come in and settle in my outstretched fingers. It was magical."

"Hmmm…"

"Of course there were other kites as well, the ones that didn't come to me. We weren't meant to be together, at least not in this lifetime."

---

93 Makar Sankranti is the transition of the Sun into Capricorn. This day in January begins a six-month period when the Sun appears to travel north. The deeper metaphor is a reminder to all to keep going higher and higher towards the Light and never to the darkness.

"No madam, we don't run ferries to Phuket pier on Christmas night. We can't help you. Tonsai bay is shut." Five different ferrymen said the same thing to Shakti. "You stay back in Phi Phi and celebrate Jesus Christ's birthday tonight. Big party here."

"No, I can't. I'll give you extra money." She persisted. She knew the warehouse armed guards would be looking for them. It wasn't safe to stay on the island much longer.

"Mr. Nod," Harry said. "He might be able to help us."

"Take me to him," she pleaded.

They walked along the bay to Tonsai village. Jazz, blues, and Christmassy music emanated from the hotels. The romantics lounged on patios with their loved ones, sipping cocktails and drowning in one another's eyes. The *Eagles* played *Please Come Home for Christmas… If not for Christmas by New Year's night.*

Further down, folks frolicked with bright but empty looks in their eyes; Shakti smelled weed in the air. The beach was full of Scandinavian party goers and service staff on extended holidays from home. Several beautiful, tanned blondes walked around.

Harry located his friend, Mr. Nod. "We need your help. We need a speed boat."

"I saw the fire in the warehouse up on the hill." Mr. Nod's stern, cold eyes scrutinized them over his ice filled beer jug. "Did you have anything to do with it?"

"Ummm… Mr. Nod… See what happened was –"

"Did you or did you not?"

"Mr. Nod, we didn't intend to but –"

"Answer my question, goddammit."

"I set the warehouse on fire. They had nothing to do with it." Shakti interjected.

Mr. Nod's stern face changed its demeanor. "I was worried about the illicit activities up there. I'm glad you burnt it down. Good riddance." He nodded his head in earnest. "Thanks on behalf of the entire island."

She was taken aback. "You're welcome, Mr. Nod. So, can you help?"

"Everyone is gearing up for the Xmas party. But don't worry. Give me an hour. Go eat and relax on the beach," said Mr. Nod, nodding his head in accelerated confidence.

"Thank you. I really appreciate it." She gave him a respectful bow.

"Dinner's on me. I'll get you our best dishes and Mojitos," Mr. Nod said, along with his animated head bobbing. Soon many dishes with savory aromas ended up on their table, increasing the clamor of Shakti's growling stomach. "You like spicy, right? *Nam phrik kung siap* is a mixture of dried chili, smoked shrimps, and fresh vegetables."

"Great food," she said, and looked at Harry, but he had put only a nominal amount on his plate. He was playing with his food, tossing it around with a fork. He brought a bite close to his mouth and then lowered it back to the plate.

"You'll love this." Mr. Nod held a gleam in his eye. "Bird's nest soup. Very healthy. Rich in calcium, iron, potassium, and magnesium."

Harry looked at the soup but didn't try it. He seemed to have lost his appetite.

"My grandma says it improves digestion, voice, asthma, libido, focus, and also the immune system." Mr. Nod's nodding was vigorous.

"Well, we could sure use the stronger immunity," Shakti said, as she recollected the cliffs and how she had survived the fall from the bird's nest.

Shakti was by herself, gazing out to the sea and lost in her thoughts. A shooting star passed through the skies with a bright afterglow. She closed her eyes and wished.

"A penny for your thoughts?" Shiva asked, as he sat next to her on the sands.

She turned towards him. The sound of his voice and the sight of his face pulled the air from her lungs and set her heart pounding. "The speedboat," she said as she strained against her feelings, determined not to let him know the effect he had on her.

It was a clear night. Calm, warm light from the moon tried to placate the turbulent sea. A milky band of stars emerged drenched and quivering from the ocean waves and rose into the mysterious skies above.

"I have to get to Patong Beach tonight to meet Rocky," she continued.

"Why? What do you mean? We escaped from his men only a short time ago."

"It's a long story, Shiva." She looked up at the night sky. It was as if the constellations themselves were outlines of an immense Rubik's cube that revolved and realigned to reach the single moment that fate had reserved for her. Too much that she didn't understand. Too much that she wouldn't allow herself to ask or be asked. She felt anxiety and anticipation about the web of connections and concealments.

"We've got quite some time. Tell me. I want to know. I'm all ears."

She flinched, or perhaps it was a shivery response to the wind from the sea. She clasped her arms across her chest and turned away to watch a lone, distant figure on the beach. She looked back at Shiva and saw the earnest-ness in his eyes. And so she let go.

She told him about her entire ordeal, from the disappearance of Kriya-di to the near-death Dharavi encounter, to the reunion with Kriya-di in Phuket. She revealed how she had escaped from Ganjoo and how she had followed Rocky to Phi Phi.

"Shakti, I didn't know. You've really been through hell. I'm glad you found Kriya-di, rescued her and us, and now all is well." He reached out to touch her forearm. His strong, gentle fingers felt warm against her cool skin. "But I don't get it. Why go to Patong Beach? You can join Kriya-di in Phuket Town and fly straight to Mumbai."

She hugged her knees, her bare feet buried in the sand. "I have some unfinished business." She turned to the sea and exhaled a slow sigh. She had already shared so much and he had listened with patience. He didn't push her to tell more. She was glad he didn't. They sat in silence, feeling the breeze, warm and cool alternating with each other.

He sat close to her, but not touching. In the dark, humid night, the moisture beads on his arm were like many glistening stars and his skin was like a span of the night sky. She pressed her lips against the sky and touched the stars.

Shiva leaned over to pick up a spiral shell and let the sand drain out of it. He looked across at Shakti. She was still silent. Poor girl, tough girl... Her eyes held a pain; a pain whose source only she knew. A pain she wasn't willing to share. A pain that her brave face tried to hide, but her eyes gave away. He pressed the shell with his fingers, the serrations digging into his skin. Then, he threw it into the waves.

A spectacular fire show got underway on the beach. Masterful young men skillfully juggled with fire, barefoot. They launched into the air burn-ing sticks, balls of fire, and jump rope, all inflamed in danger. The au-dience screamed and clapped, enjoying the fiery display. Meanwhile, the waiters served their famous Thai "buckets of joy" - a mix of your choice of drinks – whisky, vodka, soda, in a small bucket with lots of straws.

"I feel sorry for Harry," Shakti said. "He's very kind and good-hearted. I pray to God that he recovers soon. You've been friends for a long time, haven't you?"

"Yes, forever. Like you and Kriya." Shiva recounted his memories, and she listened good-naturedly. After the moon moved some through the stars, he paused.

The beachside was getting crowded, but Shakti had found a clear space. Nearby, a large group of young tourists looked stoned. Relentless techno music thumped from the rumbling throat of a monster stereo system. The wild tourists sipped Thai "buckets of joy" and swayed and swung, all in high spirits, all in a happy place far, far away.

"So, what are the *women* like in America?" she asked out of the blue. Her lips clamped around the question. She gently slapped him on the shoulders as he laughed. "I mean it. Tell me what they are like." She made a perfect pout of her perfect mouth. She had asked with such sincerity that his heart began to beat hard against his chest.

"Well, they're beautiful; a lot of beautiful women in the U.S. They like to talk and they like to party. They're pretty wild. They're direct. And they're fiercely independent."

"Fiercely independent?" Her gaze narrowed in the acuteness of her curiosity.

"Yes, fiercely independent. They're what *they* want to be, not what other cultures think women should be." He laughed but she didn't laugh with him.

"Hmmm..."

"American women refuse to be stereotyped and pushed into the background. They won't be left behind to follow and obey."

"I think America is cool," she said. "I'd love to go there."

He put his arm around her. When she turned to face his smile, he couldn't help but dive into the sandy brown of her eyes. "I'd love to take you there."

I'd love to hear the sound of your voice as we lounge in the lawns of Yerba Buena Gardens. I'd love to feel your dark brown hair as it tumbles down the light of your face at the Exploratorium. I love how you toss your hair when you're happy. I love the twitch of your nose when you're nervous. I love the way you move, the way you arrange your limbs when you crawl, sit, or walk. I love the way your face looks when I look at you. I love you.

She clasped her hand in his and watched him in silence, almost matching her breathing to his. Her eyes moved across his features as if searching for an anchor. He turned to the horizon, trying to distract attention from his sharp nose, while basking her in the beguiling embrace of his soft, warm smile. She rested her head against his chest.

Gentle waves caressed the shore and a mild wind rocked gently, moving them to a double rhythm. The misty spray of the water and the feathery swish of the wind became a balmy blanket of comfort that bundled them together in secure warmth. They held each other in tenderness, cradled in love and worship.

The outdoor stereo from the beachside restaurant went quiet. The clamor of the dance music gave way to slow classics. *When I'm by Your Side* from the Broadway classic *Side Show* played on the speakers. Shakti sang along with the words, "*Happy to be your companion…*"

She stood up and began to dance and sway with a surprising elegance. Shiva watched her in admiration, mesmerized, and clapped along. She filled his heart with happiness. He felt as grand as the canyon with her by his side. He forgot all his worries. He forgot about San Francisco, *Forbidden Fruit,* and the meeting with the CEO.

She paused, turned her steps towards him, and reached out to grasp his wrists with both her hands. "Come on. Let's dance."

"Do what? Here?" He protested and tried to fight her off.

"Dance to the song. It's such a perfect moment." She began to drag him.

He stopped. He surrendered. "You bet we can." It was one of those things you don't think about and analyze. You simply go with the moment, the urge and the flow.

The moon was full and smiled at them, beaming bright and wide. It cast a luminous glow over the beach, the waters, and the two of them.

Shakti held her soft, magical fingers around his neck. He saw the moon reflect in her shining eyes. They swayed and swayed and swayed. Time totally went away, leaving them alone. And they danced away by the light of the moon.

"Speedboat is ready. Come on over!" Mr. Nod screamed at the top of his lungs.

Shakti thanked him; he'd been a great help. But as she got aboard the speedboat, she noticed a couple of men on the beach pointing towards them. Something wasn't right. The clamor in their voices rose. Oh my God! The guards from the warehouse!

"Shiva, Harry, come on. Get in fast. Driver, please start the speedboat!" Shakti yelled as the first gunshot whizzed by them. It plopped in the water next to the boat. "These guys don't give up, do they? I thought we'd lost them on the cliffs."

The driver started the engine and the boat jumped off the water. The guards shouted abuse as they opened an indiscriminate spray of spiteful bullets.

"Keep your heads down," the driver warned as he thrust the boat in motion, but the handle swerved and hit his arm. He lost balance but still managed to stay on board. He zigzagged through the sea, creating a misty spray and fogging the guards' view. He crisscrossed between the jutting limestone rocks, perilously close to the precipitous edges.

Soon they were out of sight and out of shooting distance. They lost sight of the guards and Shakti sighed in relief. The waters got quieter.

Shiva's phone rang. He put on the speaker and turned it towards Harry.

"Where were you? I've been calling the entire day. I was worried sick."

"Hong, our cell wasn't working." Shiva gave him a short version of the encounter with Rocky, Sally's demise, and their unbelievable escape.

"I'm sorry to hear about Sally but I'm glad you two are safe."

"How are the preparations for your big meeting?"

"I had a pre-meeting with sales and some tricky questions came up. I'm nervous. Hey…why don't you hop on the next flight? You can still make it to the CEO meeting."

"Hong, you'll be fine. I need to help someone here. We'll be back soon."

"What the hell are you doing?" Hong exclaimed in an unusual burst of emotion. "You're not James Bond. This Rocky is into hardcore stuff, hard drugs and hard weapons. Not our cup of tea. We're soft guys who write software. You get out of there. NOW!"

"Your voice is breaking up…I can't hear you…battery is dying…sorry, gotta go."

A few minutes of silence passed them by. The driver rested his injured arm while Shiva drove the speedboat. As it flew through the waves, Shakti's mind raced to Patong Beach, unsure of what awaited her.

"That's Promthep Cape, southernmost point of Phuket." The driver pointed.

"Looks dangerous," Shiva said. The Cape fell into the sea in precipitous cliffs.

"Very popular," the driver said, "also called Brahma's Cape after the God of purity. Great sunset view from up there. Nice temple and wood elephants. You should go."

"No disrespect to Brahma, but we're done with cliffs and rocks." Shiva rubbed his palms and grimaced.

Shakti nodded at him. Their hands and feet were all scraped, bruised, and aching.

"Don't go to Patong Beach." Shiva's eyes and mouth narrowed in worry.

"What?" Shakti laughed. She was surprised.

"Don't go to Patong Beach to meet Rocky."

"Why not?"

"I don't want you to."

"What's that supposed to mean?"

"Exactly what I said. I don't want you to go."

"Okay." She looked at his eyes. "So, *why* don't you want me to go?"

"You've got what you came looking for. You have Kriya in a safe place. There's no reason to put yourself in grave danger again. You don't have to go."

"No Shiva. I have no choice. Rocky has my passport and my pendant."

"In that case, I'm coming with you."

"No, you're *not*. I've to do this myself." Shakti's stubbornness began to rouse itself. "Don't worry. I'll go and claim my things from Rocky and be off."

"And you expect me to –"

"You should hop onto the next available flight to San Francisco. You can still make it to the big meeting. Your company needs you."

He held his hand up in surrender. "I'll only keep an eye." He spoke in a soft tone, trying to win her agreement. "I'll stay hidden and at a distance, invisible. I'll do anything you want me to."

"No, you won't do any of that." A part of her wanted him to come, but the other part was worried for him.

"But, why?"

"Rocky hates you with all his might. I can't put your life at risk." *Every person I've loved has died or disappeared. Aai. Sanju. Baba. Kriya-di. I love you, Shiva. I care for you. I'll never forgive myself if anything happens to you.*

"This is more than your quest for Kriya, isn't it?"

"Yes, it is. It's more than that. It's a quest to find myself and who I am within." She had to fight this battle alone. She didn't know how, but she had to.

"I can help you find yourself."

"You said you'll do anything I want. I want you to go back to America." *And don't worry about me. I always come out unscathed as if protected by a divine force.*

"How can I?"

"I won't talk to you if you come to Patong." She tottered back, her palm raised and her bruised fingers as stiff and unyielding as stone.

"Now, now... What's that supposed to mean?"

"Exactly what I said." She saw the worship in his face. She saw he was in love with her eyes, but he didn't read them. When one is in love, drunk in a hallucinogenic bliss, we somehow miss what a lover really says.

"Is that some sort of warning? Is that an ultimatum?" He asked softly but with a precipitous glare like the sheer cliff of Brahma's Cape.

"You can call it what you like," she said, her teeth clenched. "It's a fact. If you come to Patong, I won't talk to you. It's my battle and I have to fight it alone."

"You're being childish, Shakti. It's too dangerous for you alone."

"I mean it."

Shiva gazed up at the horizon. The charcoal gray sky summoned the jet black sea, and at the line where they separated, emerged the coast of Phuket.

He hadn't spoken to Shakti after that dialogue; he didn't want to argue. Their speedboat reached the shore at Phuket pier and the driver docked and dropped anchor. Shiva woke up Harry from his deep slumber and lugged him over to the shore. He looked up at the pier, shielding his eyes from the bright lamp to seek out Shakti.

But Shakti was gone. There was nothing but traceless, empty, wind-swept sheets of sand. There was nothing but lonely layers of white foam left behind by the deserting waves, then the fickle foam fizzled into oblivion.

"The most dangerous weapon is the heart of the warrior."

- Zen and martial art wisdom

CHAPTER 16

03:55 am. December 26, 2004
Patong Beach, Thailand

"*B**hai*, don't worry," Rocky said into his cellphone. He stood outside the *Down Under Club* on Patong Beach. "Yes, we lost one warehouse, but I've got the other two."

He was irked by the relentless pulsations assaulting him from the pubs, flashy neon signs, and go-go bars on Bangla Road. But the crazy strobe lights inside his head were even more intense and shrill. Fuck. How he hated his agonizing migraines.

"I know you can't have anything go wrong. It won't happen again. Believe me, I've got things under control." Rocky felt his anger rise.

But *Bhai* seemed angrier.

"No *Bhai*. You don't have to come here. I've got five big shipments going out tomorrow. *Inshallah,* trust me. All is well."

Long silence...

"Why did I choose to ship on Boxing Day? Because everyone will be in a festive mood and the security dogs will all be napping."

He could smell the prostitutes soliciting on the side streets of Bangla Road. Their cheap, fucking perfumes were nauseating. He felt his sinus membrane about to rupture. Everything felt repulsive. He looked away to gaze at the two mile stretch of the serene beach and to breathe in the fresh marine breeze, but it was useless.

"Yes, I won't let emotions cramp my style. I'll kill anyone standing in my way."

Fuck. I'm single-handedly running the Thai operations. I'm doing a better job than even Bhai ever could. One small hiccup and he's all upset. One small diarrhea blast and he's ready to check in for colon surgery.

Rocky said none of those things. When the call was finished, he gazed at the Andaman Sea as it simmered in the shadow of the night. *Bhai* was so far up his ass that he couldn't even breathe. A goon approached him with an inane problem. Rocky slapped him hard and the man sank into the sand. "No excuses. I don't want any fucking excuses."

Rocky stared at the disintegrating image of the moon. "How come that *kutiya* Shakti hasn't shown up yet? Looks like she got cold fucking feet." He broke into a thunderous guffaw when he turned and saw Shakti walk towards him. This was his chance to set things right again. The goon at his feet shuddered.

Shakti glanced up as a shroud of smog shifted and the moonlight silhouetted Rocky. He stood tall and motionless, backlit by the moon, his shadow looming over her. She thought the sea spray splashing up behind him gave him the appearance of a grotesque, carved stone gargoyle, with sunken, wolf like eyes.

Gazing straight up at him, she was riveted by his sinister stare. She moved closer, knowing in her heart that she was stepping into the wolf's lair, alone and defenseless. His demeanor could have scared and paralyzed anyone, but she wasn't afraid anymore.

"Merry Christmas, Shakti. I thought you weren't coming."

His long, black hair lashed in the wind all across his hard, unforgiving face. But she felt there was something more, something that conjured up pure evil. His eyes... Yes, his eyes had a psychotic gaze, as if he was hypnotized by the devil himself to do his work.

"Let's go grab a drink. What will you have?"

"I'm not thirsty. You go ahead." A tingling sensation began in the bottom of her heel. It didn't bode well.

He led her into the *Down Under Club*. A party was in full swing. Tweaked-out boys, and twice as many girls, stomped to the music. He ordered drinks. "Look, isn't that an awesome beach view?" While her head was turned, unbeknownst to Shakti, he quickly slipped something into her cocktail. "Cheers to a long life."

"Rocky, I'm really fine. Can you simply give me my passport and pendant?"

"You killed Vicky. Poisoned Ganjoo. Burned down my warehouse. Messed with my plans for Mumbai. Now you want more from me?"

"Rocky, the cup you seek to fill has no bottom. When will you stop?"

"And above all, you took my precious Kriya away. Tell me where she is."

"You don't go anywhere near Kriya-di. If you touch her again, I'll …" The tingling sensation in her heel was now a burning rage.

"I can't live without her. Here, have them." He pulled out the passport and put it on the counter. He dropped the pendant into her cocktail glass and smirked. "Drink this up and you can have the stoneware at the bottom."

"No. That's God. You can't drop him into alcohol." She strained to steady herself.

"Who's going to stop me? Your God? Where is he? Chained to this ragged thing? Resting in some temple, church, or mosque?"

Her hands were sweating. She wiped them on her windbreaker.

"Drink it." As he looked at her, his pale eyes seemed to strip the clothes away from her, leaving her naked before him.

She picked up the glass and moved it to her lips. "What if I don't?"

"I'll do things to you that you can never imagine." He picked the cherry toothpick from his drink and bit off the cherry. He reached up and drew with the tip of the toothpick softly down the exposed skin of her neck all the way to her chest.

"I'm not afraid." She stopped his hand and pushed away the toothpick.

"You better be afraid. Here's some news for you. I can take your life anytime I want. I am God." He spoke with a blood-red mouth.

"You're no God. You better beware the wrath of the Almighty." She glared at him. The spirit of Sally, Kriya-di, and *JR* blazed through her eyes.

Dawn stirred up a fire in the eastern sky. Shiva stood alone and determined on the sands of Patong Beach. His mind had told him not to come, but his heart knew better. Wind driven clouds streamed across the faraway horizon, scarlet-hued with the burning kisses of the promise of a sunrise.

He gazed with gravity at the red rising ball of fire, seeking strength and courage. He felt the sun's warm energy seep through his skin, his bones and blood, and into his heart. His spine tingled and came alive with an intense rush of a dynamic, transforming force. He felt like the Greek legend Prometheus who took the sacred fire from the Gods. White light exploded in his brain and his mind went blank. He felt his heart burn with the vigor of a fusion reactor core, in the same way the sun burns its heart out.

Shiva walked into the *Down Under Club,* and even amidst all the crowds and commotion, his eyes met with Shakti's. She held an untouched cocktail glass. His eyes communicated to her loud and clear. *You mean more to me than any business meeting. We're in this together whether you like it or not. We've got to look out for each other.*

Rocky stared at them, surprised. He looked from Shiva's face to Shakti's and back to Shiva's, astonished by their visual conversation. An evil glint shone in his grinning eyes. He twisted his lips, exposing his stained teeth as if to say, "Oh, so this is your real girlfriend. What a sweet coincidence! Now you can watch her die."

All of a sudden the earth shook. Shiva, Shakti, Rocky, and all the people in the *Down Under Club* staggered and stumbled. It was an earthquake.

The shocks subsided and the fight began without a word. Six or seven goons ran in swinging, gesticulating at Shiva, in a frenzy to lay a punch. He stood his ground, covering his head with fists held to his temples, employing Muhammad Ali's *rope-a-dope.* His elbows protected his body. Street fighting was no different from his formal training. Rule number one: *Always size up your opponent before you make the first move.*

The ferocity of their initial assault subsided. The underlings had nothing on him. He struck out left and right, connecting with every punch. The goons flew off him like swatted flies. One came closer; Shiva threw a textbook cross that splattered his nose. Blood smeared the sands. The other goons backed off, suddenly unsure of themselves. He charged at them, shouting at the top of his lungs like a wild jungle animal. They turned and ran. Rule number two: *Act crazier than your enemy to pummel in the dagger of fear.*

He noticed Shakti secure her passport in her jacket. She dumped the cocktail onto the floor, wiped her pendant with paper napkins, and put it around her neck. When a goon tried to attack her, she grabbed a liquor bottle from the bar and smashed it on his head.

Shiva failed to see Rocky slither behind him with all the slyness that evil brings with it. Rocky punched him in his lower back with a bone rattling force that took him by surprise and sent pain shrieking through his spine. He steadied his feet, not wanting to lose his psychological edge, and turned towards Rocky without missing a beat.

Rocky's eyes bulged with bewilderment and fear; it was the last thing he had expected. Shiva lashed out a flying front kick. Rocky hadn't expected that either. The ball of Shiva's foot struck him in the chest. Rocky took several faltering steps backward. Rule number three: *Never lose your ground unless you're setting up a counter-attack.*

Shiva followed him with a flurry of jabs and overhand rights. Rocky put his head down and tried to cover his face. Shiva punched him in the stomach. *This one's for Sally... And this one's for troubling Shakti.* Rocky was a bigger man and at least as strong physically, but he was no fighter. He buckled and fell to his knees.

"Fire! Fire!" People screamed and ran out from the club. Fire had broken out inside. Some ran towards the beach while others towards Bangla Road.

"Water! Water!" People scampered, looking for water to douse the flames. Shiva was surprised to see Harry amongst them. *That's my bud...he came to help me.*

Shiva looked towards Bangla Road and spotted Shakti.

Rocky lay fallen on the sands. "Come on, finish me, and go scurry after her," he incited. There was nothing but loathing in his eyes, nothing but the vilest contempt. "You might even have some time to fondle a breast or two along Bangla Road, in passing."

A part of Shiva told him to finish off the scumbag. Show no mercy. He felt blood rush away from his face and hands. The veins in his arms and neck bulged out like cables, turning a furious blue and green. His jaw clenched, his knuckles tightened, but another part told him to make the right choice. Shiva said, "Every soul deserves a second chance."

"My wet nurse said the same thing," Rocky's voice echoed above the ruckus on the beach. "Never believe anything you hear at a woman's tit."

In his younger days, Shiva would've seethed with rage. Now, he was a changed man. Forgiveness was the key to overcome hate, the only cure to the cesspool festering inside Rocky. Shiva felt a sense of empathy swamp him and morph his rage into mercy. He dropped his hands and said, "Leave her alone." Then he walked away from Rocky.

"WATER! WATER!" This time, the shouts came from behind Shiva. They were louder. More frantic. More hysterical. He looked back and saw waves of tourists, locals, and party folks running toward him. Fear gushed in their faces as they ran away from the shore. The waters of the Andaman Sea had receded back an alarming distance. Something was wrong. Something big was coming.

Shiva rushed towards Shakti, screaming out from afar, "Shakti! Run! Run faster!"

The end, when it comes, is always too soon. Shakti's skin tightened up on her face, drawn back by the tension in her neck. That tension, in turn, was pulled taut by her stinging shoulders and bruised arms.

She heard an explosion behind her. She didn't know what to make of it. Was it a sewer line breaking? Or maybe a terrorist attack? She heard more distant explosions to the north along the beach, sounding like canon fire. She didn't realize the explosions were, in reality, coming from the initial large tsunami wave that slapped into concrete buildings, and were reaching successive points farther along the beach.

The first rumbles of the water she heard were far away. But then the rumbles got closer. *Here it comes.* The words chattered through her mind as if someone else spoke to her, as if someone else was preparing her for the end.

She saw others running hard, screaming and panting in distress. It was a stampede. She tried to run faster but her legs seemed wooden and numb. People passed her by. She saw her legs move, step after step, but she couldn't feel them.

She glanced back. A swell of floodwater was headed her way. A roiling mass with debris threatening at its leading edge. A big fifteen-foot wave travelling at great speed. It had such tremendous, smashing force, it brought down everything in its way. The coastal buildings and hotels crumbled like fake mud houses.

It took a gigantic effort of Shakti's will to send her legs an SOS message and command them to greater speed. At last she stumbled into a faster sprint. She ran, expecting the water to hit her back at any moment. Her heart churned in her chest. She heard a man go down less than fifty meters behind her, screaming at the top of his lungs.

Here it comes. The voice spoke again, this time, with a groundswell of certainty.

"Shakti, get to the top of the building!" Shiva's scream pierced through the thunderous rumble of the gushing water.

She raced up the vacant stairs at the side of the structure. Her breathing came in gasping, grunting little puffs of air. She got to higher ground barely in time, as the big wave passed by. A meandering gush of water followed her up the stairs, coming perilously close to sweeping her away.

She climbed onto the terrace and was shocked to witness the entire stretch of Bangla Road flooded. Everyone and everything was at the mercy of the rushing water. Shops were all washed away. Even the *tuk-tuks* and *songthaews* floated about like paper boats, slamming into each other and into the walls of the buildings.

People drifted, flailing their arms for help. No one was spared – from rich businessmen and tourists, to local laborers and lady boys, from local women, to those in expensive, designer dresses. Patong - *the forest filled with banana leaves* - was now transfigured into an aquatic forest filled with the leavings of steel, debris, and people.

Where was Shiva? She couldn't see him anywhere. The scene reminded her of the Latur earthquake and terrified her. She didn't want to lose any more loved ones.

She finally spotted him on the terrace of another building about twenty meters away. She was so relieved. *Thank you, God.* He ran towards her, jumping across the packed buildings. She took a few steps towards him, extending her arms to settle herself in the safety of his embrace.

But then, from the corner of her eye, she caught a tall, dark silhouette with a gun aimed at Shiva. She shrieked and flung herself at Shiva, bringing him down with the sound of the gunshot. They rolled and got behind a water tank. Another gunshot. She noticed blood. Blood on Shiva's clothes and on the floor. He was hit.

"It merely grazed me. No big deal," he said. A gash on his left arm spouted blood. The tear was deep, but not deep enough to expose the bone. His shirt was soaked in blood. He pulled it off, tore a large shred of cloth, rolled it into a bandage, and pressed it against the wound to slow down the blood flow.

She tore another long shred and wrapped it tightly around the first. She took what remained of his shirt and wiped off the blood from his body; his shoulders, chest, and abdomen. He was smiling at her, that mischievous grin of his. She made an angry face, but her concern seeped through her anger. She pinched him hard on his good right arm.

"Ouch…that hurt more than the bullet wound! What was that for?"

"I told you to not come to Patong."

"Shakti, I had to. I wouldn't be able to live with myself if I didn't."

"I told you. Rocky wants you dead, and I can't see that happen."

"But I'm alive, thanks to you, again. If the bullet had hit me a few inches to the right it would have gone through my heart."

"Don't talk to me now." She kissed his arm.

A gunshot from much closer quarters whizzed by the water tank and hit the wall. The shooter was approaching fast; he knew their hiding spot.

"Come with me." Shiva held out her hand. They moved in stealth and slipped over the terrace wall onto the parapet awning at the side of the building. They perched precariously on the tight four foot by two foot space.

She peered down and her heart jumped into her throat. They were at the top of a three-storey building; it was a steep fall below. And the metallic *songthaew* that was stuck into the wall beneath would ensure instant bleeding and death.

Shiva waited with an intense stillness on the parapet. He heard footsteps approach and pause at the water tank to examine the fresh blood. Rocky bellowed, "You should have finished me off at the beach! Now you can't escape my hate and your fate!"

While Rocky had his attention on the blood, Shiva moved with a vigorous alacrity and sense of purpose. He leaped into the air over the terrace wall, breaking his fall with a side-roll on the hard surface. He sprung onto his feet in one smooth continuous motion. Before Rocky realized what was happening, Shiva was in his face.

Rule number four: *Always keep something in the reserve.*

The last of Shiva's energy exploded in a thrust, knocking the gun out of Rocky's hand and driving a powerful kick into his groin. Rocky yelped out a scream, pressed his legs together, and crouched down. Shiva swung around to punch him in the face four or five times; on the nose, the cheeks, and the hinge of his jaw. He felt Rocky's nose break and his strength ooze from him, along with his blood.

Rocky rolled over on his side, curled up with his knees to his chest. He collapsed into a ball, his arms and knees covering his face as he begged for his life. *One who is scared, is as good as dead.*

Shiva heard a scream. Was that Shakti? He took a step back and looked behind. He didn't see Rocky sneak out a knife from his shoe. The scream for help came again. It sounded like a little boy. Shiva didn't notice Rocky get back onto his feet. By the time he saw some movement from the corner of his eye, it was too late.

Rocky was up in the air and the knife in his hands was descending in a malicious arc. It sped towards Shiva's neck with an alarming certainty. He had no time to react. Everything froze. Deathly silence as time stopped. It was all over for him.

"Two types of people in this world: Fuckers and -" Sharp words from Rocky stabbed Shiva's eardrums.

Bang! Bang! Rocky's knife was inches from Shiva's neck when suddenly Rocky jerked back and came crashing down to the floor. He gasped for air, and then in a flash, life deserted him.

"Suckers... And no one ever knows when they morph from one to the other."

Shiva tripped and stumbled to the floor from his momentum. He looked back to where the words had come from. Shakti stood there like a warrior princess, holding Rocky's Smith & Wesson revolver in a double-handed grip. She had a pale, tearstained face and quivering lips, but absolutely steady hands.

Shakti had never in her life pulled a trigger. Final rule, number five of fighting: *The most dangerous weapon is the heart of the warrior. The battle is won or lost in the heart.* She had won the battle. The power of love had overcome Rocky's love of power.

Shakti was relieved. She felt her heart swell inside. *Take that you monster! You can't snatch Kriya-di away from me again. You can't victimize any more people. You can't inflict terror and death over my Mumbai's innocent. Take that!*

She kissed Sanju's pendant and his words echoed in her ears, "Nobody messes with my little sister." Her eyes met with Shiva's and she took a step towards him, when she heard the little boy scream again. She looked across to the terrace wall, then to Shiva, and then back to the wall. She walked towards the wall and bent over it to peer below.

The tsunami waters had risen and swept along a Thai boy of about seven. Fortunately he had grabbed a lamp post and the concrete structure at its base took the brunt of the force of the water. But it wasn't clear how long it would stand. The boy had climbed up to the top of the lamp post and was holding onto it for dear life as it swayed and shook like a flimsy plant in strong winds.

She stretched across and offered her hand while holding onto a TV antenna with the other. "Here, grab my hand. Let go of the lamp post. You'll be fine."

But the Thai boy was too scared. He couldn't get himself to let go. She extended further and the antenna bowed with a groan. A sudden surge of water surprised the boy. The pressure became too great, ungluing him from the post. His face turned white as all courage was swept away.

Shakti's outstretched hand somehow managed to get a hold of him and swing him up onto the terrace. As he landed to safety the antenna gave way, and Shakti plunged towards the gushing water.

A horrible, blood-freezing scream came from somewhere close. She realized it was her own. She plummeted into a soundless world where she could feel the chill of death against her skin, the choking struggle for breath, the shock of deafening silence.

She felt her head bob to the surface and she gasped for air. A smell exploded into her semi-consciousness. It was the scent of her own death; the damp, rancid stench of rotting food and animal remnants; an appalling, unworldly smell... And then she was again plunged into the deep, dreadful darkness. Her body was swept away by unrelenting currents. The depth seemed forever. There was no light, no air, and no hope.

It seemed to Shakti as though she'd been falling for years.

Swim, a voice mumbled in the dark waters, but she didn't know how.

The surface was so far above her she could barely make it out through the dark whirlpools that spun around her. But she could feel how fast she was falling, and she knew what was waiting for her down there. A cold nothingness. She wanted to weep.

No weeping. Swim. The voice was low and deep.

She looked around to see where it was coming from. A golden baby turtle was spiraling down with her. It was missing a flipper but was still flapping around her.

"Are you really a turtle?" Shakti asked.

Are you really falling? the turtle inquired as it fluttered about her head.

"What are you doing to me," she asked the turtle, tearfully.

Teaching you how to swim.

"I can't."

You're swimming right now.

"I'm falling!"

LOOK UP!

She looked up and saw the sky rushing towards her. She could see everything so clearly that for a moment she forgot to be afraid. She saw the Latur earthquake, Aai, Sanju, Baba, the big tsunami, and her Kriya-di.

Now you know why you must live, the turtle whispered.

She looked at the turtle and the turtle looked back. It had three eyes and the third eye was full of a terrible knowledge.

"Can a girl be brave if she's afraid?" She heard her own voice, small and far away. Death reached for her.

That is the only time a girl can be brave.

Shakti spread her arms and flapped her legs. Unseen fins cut through the water current and pulled her upward. The darkness receded below her and the sea opened up to the light. "I'm swimming!" she cried out in delight.

I've noticed, said the three-eyed turtle. It began to flap in her face, slowing her, and blinding her. She faltered as its flipper poked at her and she felt a sudden throbbing pain in the middle of her forehead between her eyes.

"What are you doing?" she screamed.

The golden baby turtle opened its mouth, swirling around her. And then, as if a veil had been ripped away, she saw that the turtle was really a man, a tall man with a striking face and deep, warm olive skin, and she was sure she knew him from somewhere.

Shiva picked himself up and rushed to the terrace wall. Everything had happened in the blink of an eye. He stared hard at the flowing water, trying to spot Shakti but she had disappeared under. He hoped he would see something, anything, but he saw nothing.

Shiva assured the little boy, "You are safe now." He told him to stay put and that someone would come to take him to a shelter.

The gushing water raced ahead. Shiva began to run alongside. A restlessness that he couldn't fight propelled him forward. The dense concrete structures were packed together and he crossed them, jumping over the rooftops using anything and everything that helped him continue his motion.

He came to an abrupt stop at a wide chasm between two hotels; the structure in the middle had collapsed. It was humanly impossible to jump across. A Toyota pickup truck was lodged hopelessly in the gap, tilted at an angle. He descended onto the railing of a balcony and climbed onto the top of the truck. He tried to balance himself but the truck was greasy with sand and oil and his foot slipped, plunging him below.

Somehow he grabbed onto a swinging door. An agonizing pain shot through his wounded left arm. He knew he couldn't hold on for too long. He glanced below to the metallic debris; it was certain death. *I can't die. No. Not yet. I've got to save Shakti.* Using his last ounce of strength, he swung back onto the pickup and then jumped onto the roof of the building. Without a respite, he broke into a run, gawping for signs of Shakti.

Her angelic face flashed in his mind. It drove his restlessness to a frenzy and he choked with love and longing. All the affection he felt for her collected and combined in his heart, swelling it with love.

At last he spotted her bobbing head. He drew in a deep breath, plunged himself into the water, and swam through the floating debris like a man possessed.

He reached out to grab her, his chest heaving with the passion that still ran amuck in him. But Shakti remained listless. Her eyes were shut and her languid limbs flailed with the waters. He hauled her body out onto a newly formed concrete bank. He lifted her in his arms and propped her up. Her face was as blue as the evening sky on the darkest day of winter. Too much water had found its way into her lungs.

He pressed at her heart, willing it to beat. He breathed into her lungs, willing them inhale. He kept at it. In desperation. In hope. Incessant. Pressing her heart. Breathing into her lungs. But she remained lifeless. No pulse. No heartbeat. No breath.

His thoughts floated back to their serendipitous meeting at the Mumbai airport. The song of her voice, her sandy brown eyes, her flowing hair, and her lilting fragrance ran on a loop in his mind. Shakti couldn't vanish so soon from his life. There was so much to be said and heard, so much to be shared and given. Their love had barely begun to flourish. How could it end so mercilessly? How could it go unfulfilled?

Without a warning she stuttered, deep inside her chest. She coughed out the life-sucking water from her lungs. Her breath began to flow again. She coughed some more. Her breathing was slow. But color returned to her face as spring sunshine drove away the blue winter darkness. Her brown hair glistened with tiny rainbows in the water drops.

Shakti opened her eyes, expecting to see the golden baby turtle. She eased into the warmth of Shiva's embrace instead. He had dragged her limp body in his strong arms back up the whole length of a long dark well. She felt like she'd been through a narrow, long birth canal. She felt resurrected and reborn in a bright new world.

She felt as if she knew Shiva from some past life. His face... His smile... It was a good smile, a handsome smile, a smile that knew they were meant to be together. She'd known he would come for her. She'd known he would find her and save her. She knew he completed her. She didn't know how she knew, but she knew.

An age of longing passed from her eyes to his. An age of passion passed from his eyes into hers. All the emotions, all the latent unexpressed feelings, streamed from eye to eye. No word was spoken. No word needed to be spoken.

The air was warm. A faint coastal breeze stirred the humid morning. Shakti pressed herself up against Shiva and kissed him on the cheek. Well, mainly on the cheek; the edge of her mouth touched the edge of his, bristles grazing her own upper lip. And then it wasn't merely a kiss on the cheek. His hands encircled her body in tenderness.

Both pairs of lips moved with a volition of their own, like two rivers coming together. Their lips made thoughts somehow, without words - the type of thoughts that feelings have, the type of thoughts that ardor stirs. Their lips met like waves that crest and merge, like the whirl of storming seas, and like the force of a tsunami.

Shakti felt the force of goodness in Shiva. His goodness came from his intensity. It was hard to resist. It was hard not to succumb to its power.

She surrendered and submerged. She felt that she was falling - in joy and abandon. She was falling at last, into a love that blossomed lotus-layered within her. And together they did fall; they fell the length of her brown hair onto the warm sand below.

The wailing moan that accompanied their kiss was with the hope that yearning and ecstasy wrings from lovers, as it floods their souls with bliss.

When their lips parted, the sky seemed filled with the most beautiful rainbow. A captivating opus of colors. A great chromatic symphony. The colors seeped into their hearts, and the rainbow within intertwined their souls.

"Help me! Somebody help me!" a drowning voice screamed.

Shiva knew that voice. He glanced back and saw a panic-stricken Harry holding onto a small wooden plank, trying to stay afloat.

Harry spotted Shiva and shouted a scared, out of his wits plea, "Shiva, help me!" His head plunged under the water as the ruthless current dragged him away.

Shiva pulled away but his hands still held onto Shakti, held her tight. His gaze and his breath told her he didn't want to leave, but he knew it was the right thing to do. And he knew that she knew it too.

"Harry can't swim. I've got to go help him." Shiva's eyes, his face, and his heart said something else, but Harry was fighting for his life.

Shiva cast a forlorn glance at Shakti and then he plunged into the water. He knew that when he returned he might not find her there again. He knew that this might be his last chance at true love. He knew for sure that he had left behind a part of his heart, or perhaps all of it.

Epilogue

December 29, 2004
Phuket, Thailand
3 days after the Tsunami...

For three days and three nights Harry and Shiva worked hand in hand with Thai ambulance crews and volunteers. They helped tend to the wounded and patch up their lacerations. They helped evacuate the dead and the injured from various sectors of Phuket.

Several of the injured sought urgent attention. A young Thai woman had a broken right arm, and multiple lesions contaminated with sand. Harry rigged up a splint for her from a broken piece of furniture. A German man had severe left shoulder bruises, abrasions, and thick tar adhering to his skin. Shiva used bottled water to clean and cut up sheets as make-do bandages to dress the man's wounds.

Hundreds of people streamed to the shoreline areas to volunteer their help. Harry felt a very odd thing happen. Unlike the usual isolation among the various tourists and locals, most people now wanted to talk to each other. The volunteers carrying out the relief efforts exchanged a knowing nod as they passed each other. Though there was sadness and death all around, life went on, driven by human spirit, hope, and love.

Their taxi cab was now heading to Phuket airport. Harry had expected the road to be congested. He was surprised it had only a little flood debris - so different from the previous night when defunct buses and boats had blocked the streets. Dangerous 220 volt electrical wires and poles had lain strewn all around. Tsunami rumors in the middle of the night had produced panic and stampedes from the beach to higher ground.

Harry noticed a billboard sign for the Big Buddha project. A glorious Buddha statue in white Burmese marble was planned, but the construction was stuck due to wrangling over money and building rights. He hoped the local people's dream would be fulfilled, to have the Buddha to look over them and protect them from future disasters.

The thought and memory of Sally flooded his mind with sorrow. A wave of melancholy crested through his body and tears welled up looking for an outlet. He remembered one of Buddha's favorite phrases: *We are what we think. All that we are arises with our thoughts. With our thoughts, we make the world.*

Harry had always believed that fate was something unchangeable, fixed for everyone at birth and as constant as the circuit of stars. The Buddha nudged him with a gentle tug of realization. Harry now became aware that life is stranger and more beautiful than that. He understood what the enlightened one meant.

Every human thought and will has the power to transform one's fate.

An innate peace now manifested in his heightened perception. His melancholy melted away. He accepted the truth that no matter what sort of situation you found yourself in, no matter how good or bad your luck, you could change your entire life with a single thought, a single act of love or courage.

He realized that Sally lived on in his memory. Her energy, her spirit, and her courage to stand up for her beliefs, lived on with a conviction of immortality. He knew her strength would help him mend the scars of his heart. He knew he was only bent but not broken. And he knew he would learn to love again.

The taxi cab pulled into Phuket airport. Shiva expected the terminal to be crammed. For some strange reason it wasn't. The ticket agent told him that ten additional flights were added for the mass exodus. Shiva spotted an Italian Air Force C-141 and a Thai cargo plane on the tarmac. Other than that, the only evidence of anything unusual was the occasional tourist with bruises or lacerations.

Shiva looked at Harry, who gave him a sympathetic, realized smile. It was time to move on, for this is what we do. Put one foot in front of the other and keep moving. Pick up the broken pieces of our hearts and put on a cheer to forget the grief. Set in motion our valiant spirits into the horizon of a new day. Follow the path of selfless action.

Passengers huddled around the TV monitors, trying to lap up every bit of new information that trickled in. Shiva was surprised by the magnitude of the disaster. He had thought the tsunami that hit Thailand was localized. He was shocked to learn that it had impacted 14 countries, inundated coastal communities with waves up to 30 meters high, and killed over 200,000 people.

The BBC newscaster on TV shed more light:

The Boxing Day tsunami in the Indian Ocean was triggered by an undersea mega-thrust earthquake with an epicenter off the west coast of Indonesia.

With a magnitude of 9.1 to 9.3 on the Richter scale, it was the third largest earthquake ever recorded on a seismograph and of the longest duration ever observed - ten minutes. Indonesia was the hardest hit, followed by Sri Lanka, India, and Thailand. It caused the entire planet to vibrate as much as 1 centimeter and triggered other earthquakes as far away as Alaska.

The tsunami caused extensive damage to Thailand's west coast, killing 5,300 people nationwide. Some 250 were reported dead in Phuket, including foreign tourists. Patong was one of the worst affected areas.

A lesson was learnt the hard way. Thousands of lives would have been saved if there was a warning system of tsunami-detection buoys around the Indian Ocean. Life was gradually returning to normal, but it would take significant time and a strenuous recovery program to rebuild the nations, the people, and the morale.

Shiva walked to the payphone and dialed Hong.

"Hey Shiva, I'm so glad to hear your voice." Hong couldn't contain his excitement and relief. "Is Harry okay too?"

"We're both fine. Sorry we couldn't connect with you. It was frenetic out here."

"I've been watching all the news on TV and the internet. This was a big one. It's a miracle you two survived. I feel so reassured. Where are you right now?"

"Phuket airport, waiting for our flight. Everything's on time."

"Good. I'll come pick you up at SFO. I wanted to give you a tiny bit of news."

"Yes, what is it?"

"By the way, I figured out who Salman Khan is."

"What!?"

"He's simply a regular human being like you and me, trying to realize what being human is. He's made mistakes, grappled with life's ups and downs. But he's got a heart, he cares, and he gives to the needy. He's a deeper human being than what he shows."

"That's your news?"

"No. Listen up. We closed a 20 million dollar, three year deal, much higher than expected. Signed, sealed, and delivered. We're in serious business!"

Hong's news was great, but Shiva's heart didn't leap; it still ached. He had gone back so many times to the spot where he'd left Shakti, but it was all flooded and wrecked. He asked around about her but no one seemed to know. He hoped she was safe.

Shiva looked at the horizon through the terminal window. He saw Shakti's sandy brown eyes; he felt sad that he couldn't immerse and lose himself in them. He heard her voice; he felt sad that he couldn't understand what she said. He held her hands; he felt sad that he couldn't feel the warmth of her skin.

He felt a numbing void in his chest where his heart was. He knew he should be building a life with her, creating memorable moments with her, and composing a musical symphony with her. It dawned on him: *In life, nothing truly valuable happens from ambition; it arises rather from love and devotion.*

Harry nodded as if reading his mind. "She's a lovely girl and you're an awesome guy. You two are more alike than people think. You both can't stand injustice. You both have a musical rhythm that flows. You have a sense of humor and you both love to laugh. You'll be a great couple. And I think you'll get her, I know you will. Like that gentle kite that comes and settles onto your outstretched fingers. I've seen the way she looks at you even when you're not looking."

Shiva closed his eyes. Shakti promptly appeared on his mind's cinematic screen. His mental movie reel rolled and he spoke to her with messianic belief:

"I've only one thing to say to you, Shakti. And I'll never say it to anyone else. In this chaotic cosmos such conviction comes only once, like the Big Bang, and never again.

The sole purpose of my sojourn on earth is our love. Without you, I am nothing. You, my love, are both my prayer and my liberation. Every breath I breathe, I breathe it for you. And I know we shall come together, no matter how many rebirths it takes..."

Shakti dragged her feet towards the airplane. She stopped and glanced back. Did someone call out her name? She surveyed all around the terminal. She sensed a vision of Shiva running through the crowds and jumping over the bags towards her. She waited.

Kriya-di nudged her from her wheelchair. Shakti turned around in dismay and stood half-heartedly in the boarding line to take on a new journey. She got a newspaper from the flight attendant as she settled into her seat next to Kriya-di.

Shakti grimaced at the newspaper photos of Phi Phi Don; the entire island was devastated. The tsunami had hit the island from both the bays to meet in the middle of the sandy isthmus at Tonsai. More than two-thirds of the buildings were destroyed and thousands were reported dead or missing. The island was being evacuated and the Thai government declared it closed in the interim.

Further down in the news was a short blurb on the suicide of a certain Tidarat Thongchai – a rich businessman with properties and belongings worth millions. His innocent façade was exposed when he was revealed as the ruthless kingpin of the Thai drug industry. The police had photos of his involvement in a series of tourist deaths. All his warehouses and properties were destroyed by angry waves. His family survived but they were left with nothing.

The plane rose into a dark fog. Shakti took a deep breath and looked through the window, feeling as uncertain as the outside. In so many ways this day should have been a relief. Kriya-di was safe and rescued. Rocky and his nefarious plans were destroyed. Mumbai and her innocent children were out of harm's way. Events had happened that Shakti didn't think possible. So, why this unease? Was it because Shiva wasn't with her?

Kriya-di sat up and gazed at her. "How you've changed and grown up. I'm so proud of you." She rested her head on Shakti's shoulder with the peace of someone who knew she was in good hands. A circle of life had closed and a new one was about to begin. Kriya-di put one of her earphones into Shakti's ear. Their favorite song, Starship's *Good Heart* was playing.

Shakti leaned back in her seat, letting the song wash over her and seep into her body, mind, and soul. She looked outside again. Bright sunlight sparkled as the ascending plane topped the dark fog and showed a clear sky, the bluest blue sky, and soft clouds below, like an angel's playing field. The music swelled inside her, increasing its pace and sloshing around sweet sensations.

Inside her, something released - a flooding in, an expansion as if she were a sail filling with wind. She put her palm on the earphone, pressing it in, making the music even louder in her ear, trying to crowd out all thought. She felt a sublime current flow and light up every fiber of her body, filling her with bliss and opening a door to an unknown place.

'Yada Yada Hi Dharmasya, Glanirva Bhavathi Bharatha,

Abhyuthanam Adharmaysya, Tadatmanam Srijami Aham'.

Shakti remembered the couplet from the Bhagavad Gita[94] - *Whenever righteousness falls and unrighteousness grows, there's a cry for a redeeming savior - the bearer of the shining blade, whose valor will annihilate satanic influences and liberate the land. And Divine Energy reveals Her presence. The Supreme, though unborn and undying, manifests in elements of nature and in human form and spirit to overthrow the dark forces of malevolence, immorality, greed and lust.*

She clasped the Om of Sanju's pendant tightly, and then it dawned on her; the invisible spirit had always been within her. The courage was always within her. She realized that within her was the Elixir of life - the essence and the soul that helps defeat negative forces of evil and death. She always had the inner lioness, the inner *JR*...to roar and fight against the likes of Rocky.

Kriya-di's soft black eyes narrowed as she smiled and said out aloud to her, the words resonating in Shakti's heart, "My little sister, wipe off your tears and put on that lovely smile. Whatever happens, happens for the best!"

---

94 Bhagavad Gita: *The Song of the Lord*, the Sanskrit scripture from the ancient epic Mahabharata.

APPENDIX

Harry's Numerology for Birthdates[95]

Personality: *Based on (birthday) e.g. 18th -> 1+8 = 9 -> Mars (from table below)*
Life-purpose: *Based on (birthday + month + year) e.g. 03 Sep, 1942 ->*

3 + 9 + (1+9+4+2) = 16 = (1+6) = 7

(3 + 9 + 7)

= 19 = (1+9) = 10 = (1+0) = 1 -> Sun (from table below)

1: **Sun:** Ego, soul, inspiration, fire, gold, stiff, loner, self, father, entrepreneur, beginning of an era

ORIGINATE/PIONEER - Ruled by the Sun which shows entrepreneur abilities. Sun originates light/energy by burning himself. The Sun starts something new. And that is why on the 1st day or year you start something new. Beginning of an era that sets the tone and foundation for the future.

2: **Moon:** Sentimental, people contact/leadership, water, silver, mother, moody, nurturing, spreading

SPREAD/POPULIST - Ruled by the Moon which carries and transfers what was originated by the Sun, even after it sets. Passing good information around, networking, sales. Date of 2 spreads what was started on the 1st day. The seeds of change planted during 1 now start to grow in 2.

3: **Jupiter:** Optimism, individual achievers, thought leaders, unpopular, learned, blossoming

ACHIEVEMENT - Ruled by Jupiter: This is the date when the idea started on 1 brings great achievement and result. This is the date which is chosen by individual achievers. So on the 3rd day, year or month, the idea brings in the maximum results. Efforts begin to show fruit.

4: **Uranus:** Weird, absent-minded genius, change, electricity, electronics

CHANGE - Ruled by the absent minded weird planet of Uranus, known to be 50 years ahead of its time. The idea started in 1 is changed/tweaked in 4, to keep what is good, delete what is unnecessary and change what needs further polish. Date of change agents.

95 Source: http://www.astromnc.com/, http://www.numerology.com, http://www.numerologyguide.com

5: **Mercury:** Expression, cartoons, humor, short writing, share market, drama, freedom

EXPRESSION/TRADING – Ruled by Mercury. Incremental benefits. Connection with others. Date of traders, the folks that make things better and get some profit in between. Obviously, when you have changed something on the 4th day, you will have incremental gains on the 5th day.

6: **Venus:** Well mannered, harmony, balance, lucky, artistic, all-rounder

BEAUTY: Ruled by Venus, the planet of beauty. The idea which has spread, achieved, changed to give incremental benefits, will now be made more attractive. Rough edges will be smoothened out. A feel good, artistic approach will be brought in.

7: **Neptune:** Spiritual, big, fast, body language, secret message decoder, visible and invisible.

INNOVATION: Ruled by Neptune which represents the state between the known and the unknown. This date chiefly represents innovation, wild imagination, something beyond articulation. This date/year is certain to innovate and think out of the box.

8: **Saturn:** Conservative, slow, steady, lawful, serious, control, depression, elderly, philosopher.

AUDIT: Ruled by Saturn. Hard scrutiny, conservatism that either stops the idea completely or makes a lot of changes to get rid of unwanted excesses. Brings stress, tension and hardships. An important part of life cycle making you do the changes that are necessary for survival. A blessing in disguise.

9: **Mars:** Aggression, rebel, arrogance, sports, charity, commitment to cause, energy, end of an era

SPEED: Ruled by Mars. Aggression that takes forward the completely scrutinized, honed, lithe form coming out of the audit of 8, with great speed. The date of charity, rooting and fighting for the poor/weaker guy. Marks the beginning of the ending of an era.

ACKNOWLEDGMENTS

This novel would not have been possible without the encouragement, support, and infinite patience of my wife, Bansi. I thank my daughter, Riya and my son, Ranvir, for their continued love and admiration. I thank them for helping me learn to live life to its fullest and in the present moment, and to dream without fear.

I thank my parents for their loving efforts in raising a caring family, and my brothers for their genuine backing. They taught me the foundational values that have stayed with me all these years. I thank my father-in-law, who we miss dearly, for his youthful heart and his gift to make everyone laugh. Their confidence in me and inspiration throughout my life has meant more than I can express.

I appreciate the invaluable contribution from my early readers: Nitasha, JK, Priya, Anjali, Jesal, Sid, Lily, Manjiv, Bill and Joan, who provided me many great suggestions. Their constructive feedback and attention to detail played a big hand in transforming this novel into a compelling read.

Above all, I thank the Divine presence for rousing me towards higher aspirations, and for bestowing upon me the courage to conceive and complete what has been a challenging yet fulfilling accomplishment of my life.

About the Author:

Rahul Deokar was raised in Mumbai, India, before he moved to USA for his higher studies a couple of decades ago. He has attended Iowa State University, New York University, and Santa Clara University for his MS computer engineering and MBA. He has experienced a roller coaster technology start-up journey, being eventually acquired by a leading software company, and now works as a high-tech executive in Silicon Valley, California. In his debut novel, he takes you on a thrilling romantic adventure where East meets West, technology talks to tradition, and hope dances with despair. He currently lives in the San Francisco Bay Area with his loving Wife 1.0 and two adorable kids.

More information at:
www.rahuldeokar.com
www.facebook.com/QuestForKriya
http://google.com/+RahulDeokar-QuestForKriya
https://twitter.com/QuestForKriya

www.ingramcontent.com/pod-product-compliance
Lightning Source LLC
Chambersburg PA
CBHW050357260626

47156CB00003B/773